Tex and the
Gangs of Suburbia

by

Stuart R. West

Tex and the Gangs of Suburbia

Cover Art by *Lea Schizas*

The Wild Rose Press, Inc.
PO Box 708
Adams Basin, NY 14410-0708
Visit us at www.thewildrosepress.com

Publishing History
First Edition, 2022
Trade Paperback ISBN 978-1-5092-4523-9
Digital ISBN 978-1-5092-4524-6

Published in the United States of America

Another buzzing sound, this time akin to bacon sizzling on the stove. Then the low, rumbling, guttural laughter started. In the corner of the room, two narrow orbs of green light materialized out of the blackness. I recognized the spectral eyes immediately. *Bob Bellman.*

Swinging the flashlight toward the doorway, the green eyes snapped shut as soon as I turned the light on. Nothing there. I swept the beam around the room, seeing only distorted shadows lurking within every nook, corner, and table. I ran for the windows and bumped into a table. I dashed the light behind me again, directly into the grotesque visage of Bellman. He grinned at me savagely, his mouth opening impossibly wide. A pale, green hue bathed his entire body. He swung his log-like arms up at me, thus dispelling movie myths that ghosts move slowly to be more creepily effective.

I fell back onto one of the lab tables, dropping my flashlight. The light spun around on the floor, illuminating the room like a strobe light at a wild rave. I continued my momentum and completed a clumsy backward somersault to the floor, positioning the table between myself and Bellman. He reached across the table, his letter jacket crawling back on his arms. I jumped to my feet, struggling to keep my grip on the bobblehead while keeping my eyes focused on Bellman. He emitted a loud, long shriek from someplace very dark within him.

Praise for Tex and the Gangs of Suburbia

"The plot explores bullies, friendships, paranormal, witchcraft, suspense, and just a touch of romance. Strong, well-written characters. Mickey is another favourite. The mystery had me guessing, right up to the end, and well, I was wrong."

~ Heather Greenis, Author

"One of the most hilarious, roll over laughing books I've read in a long time, but with a real message behind it. The reveal was heartbreaking, teaching a lesson I hope no teen has to learn."

~ Suzanne de Montigny, Author

Dedication

Tex And The Gangs Of Suburbia goes out to Patricia McQueen for being a great mother-in-law and lending her expert English teaching eyes in editing. And, as always, to my supportive wife, Cydney, and wondrous daughter, Sarah.

Chapter One

"Come on, Tex," said Ian. "Just chill out."

"Easy for you to say." I kicked the skateboard up and sat on the skate park curb. The park was crowded today, as the unusually warm April day brought spring-seekers out in droves. My board's wheels continued to spin, taking on a life of their own. Kinda like my life. Rolling out of control as if by magic.

Magic. Did I mention I'm a witch? I know, right? I never wanted to be a witch, nor would I say it'd ever been high on my list of future vocational choices. Typically, I didn't have any say in the matter. Through the modern miracle of genetics, I inherited my witch-hood from my mother. It's not all bad. Last year, during my sophomore year at Clearwell High School, witchcraft helped save my friends' lives.

Little did I know that as my junior year slowly crept to an end, witchcraft would once again play an important part in people's lives. Or lack thereof. It was the year I loved and lost. And the year I found myself caught in the middle of a gang war.

"Oh, boy, here we go." Ian rolled his eyes. "You're *not* gonna go on about Olivia again, are you?"

Yes, that's *exactly* what I wanted to do. "No." I stretched out my legs and picked at the torn striping of my black high-tops. The pentagram on my skateboard gleamed in the afternoon sunlight. Olivia'd painted it

1

there. "It's just…why would she break up with me?"

Ian snorted. "Come on, Tex, she's a *chick*. Nobody understands girls…or what they're thinking."

"But…it's *Olivia*. She's different." Olivia Furman is truly different. Exciting, wild, smart, extremely self-reliant—she's one of a kind. And she's beautiful and happened to be my first serious girlfriend (not counting little Sherrie Strom in fourth grade who I actually held hands with by the jungle gym).

Ian sat, plopping his skateboard between us. "Yeah, whatever. You can't wallow around in self-pity the rest of your life."

"I'd hardly consider two days the rest of my life, Ian." The hammer came smashing down on me only two days ago, although it feels like I've been through an eternity of pain. And I'm beginning to sound like a teenage vampire romance novel. *Not* cool.

"I brought you to the skate park to get your mind off Olivia." I looked around to see if any of the other skaters snuck glances at my lovelorn and broken-hearted sad-sack state. "Now, shake it off. There're other girls out there."

"Yeah. But they're not Olivia." I felt I'd never again find another perfect girlfriend. And, to be honest, the sheer, terrifying notion of starting to date again filled me with more fear than a locker room full of bullies.

"Jesus, Tex!" Ian jumped to his feet and hopped on his board. "Let's roll."

Taking love advice from Ian Stapleton probably didn't rule as one of my better decisions, and, believe me, there's a lot of competition when it comes to my bad decisions. I've known Ian since grade school.

Against the odds of fleeting teenage friendships, we've maintained our relationship through the years. I guess you'd call Ian a pseudo-goth. His fingernails are painted black, his hair dyed to match, and occasionally, he'd wear eyeliner. Incredibly high-strung, he insists upon being different to the point where it gets him in trouble. If Ian were to ever start a protest, he'd possibly find himself the only member in the Fight Mainstream Sensibilities Club. Nothing upset Ian more than people who follow cliques, dress in trendy clothing, and gossip over the newest hot topic or bland boy singer. It's never come up, but I've wanted to point out to him he's sorta following a trend himself—that of the sullen and brooding goth kid. But it's easier to let him be. An agitated, confrontational Ian is an unpleasant Ian. Let him ride, fast and easy, just like his skateboard.

Ian raced off, effortlessly rolling up and down the skate ramp walls. I threw down my board and followed him, skating recklessly, trying to stay ahead of my despair. After about fifteen minutes, I noticed we'd attracted an audience.

Ian pulled up beside me, his face paler than usual. "Tex," he whispered, "we've got to get out of here. *Now*." He snuck glimpses at the two kids watching us.

"What's wrong?"

"*Crap*! Here they come. Do *not* tell them what school you're from…or your name."

"Yo, kid, nice moves," said the taller boy. He wore a long red bandanna tied around his head. His Tripp pants, fully decked out with chains, jangled as he walked. Red-dyed shoelaces, matching his bandanna, held his battered sneakers together.

"Um…thanks." Edgy as he rocked back and forth

on his heels, Ian looked ready to rabbit.

"Where you go to school?" The tall kid squinted his blue eyes.

"Ah...Red Valley." Ian nodded in agreement.

"Cool...cool..." He broke into a wide grin. "What's your name?"

"Bob...Bellman." An unexpected breeze crawled down the back of my neck, raising goose bumps. The first name that popped into my mind, Bob Bellman, was the terrifying school bully who had been murdered last year and never far from my thoughts. Or nightmares.

"I'm B-Rryce." He held his fist out to be bumped. "This here's Coo-Coo." Coo-Coo stepped forward and swung his hand up. I held my fist out for another bump. Coo-Coo ignored me, reached into his pocket, and plucked out a cigarette. Much shorter than B-Ryce, Coo-Coo's teeth appeared crooked as a road map. Absurdly turned sideways, a red ball cap sat atop his greasy blond hair. He lit the cigarette and blew a cloud of smoke into my face.

I coughed and said, "Are you coo-coo for smoko-puffs?" Ian nudged me. Coo-Coo stepped closer and narrowed his eyes, the cigarette dangerously close to my face.

"Yo, you crackin' wise on me, bitch?" He reached out to grab my collar, but since I wore a tight T-shirt, his fingers fumbled down the front of my chest.

"Um, no, I'm not crackin' wise." Ian inhaled loudly while the two boys stared at me in silence. Suddenly, B-Ryce laughed.

"Yo, let up, G." He slapped Coo-Coo on the back. "He's a'ight." His laughter rose, leaving Coo-Coo to sulk like a dog kicked away from the sofa. Finally,

Coo-Coo backed off a few steps, muttering.

"Me and my boy are from Ridge Creek High," said B-Ryce. "We got no beef with Red Valley."

"That's good." Okay, it wasn't much of a response, but I had nothing.

"Where'd you homies learn to skate like that?" he asked.

Ian stared at his feet, wishing to be anywhere but here. I, on the other hand, wished Ian would say something to help me out of this awkward situation. But he maintained his nervous radio silence.

"Our friend...Josh," I said. "He taught us everything we know...before he..." I trailed off. The memory of our late friend still hurt, and I didn't feel right talking about him with these clowns.

"What happened to him?" B-Ryce narrowed his eyes again.

"He...died last year." Ian poked me in the ribs hard enough I imagined I'd bruise later.

"Yeah? How'd he die?"

"Car accident." Total lie. But these guys hadn't earned the right to hear of Josh's sad tale.

"That's too bad, yo, too bad." B-Ryce shook his head and made a sucking sound through his teeth. "We lost a homie, too." He shot a look at Coo-Coo, who nodded dutifully.

"Hey, sorry to hear that." As an afterthought, I added, "yo." They stared blankly at me as I failed miserably in my quest for coolness. "Um, we've gotta go." I looked to Ian for corroboration. He'd already dropped his skateboard, one foot perched on top.

"'S cool,'s cool," said B-Ryce. "Yo, maybe we'll catch you 'round here again." I bumped his fist again, experiencing more fist-bumping than I'd participated in over the last two years combined, since Olivia'd forbidden us to do it. She called it a behavior best suited for Neanderthals.

"Yeah, catch you later," I called back. A fire lit under his ass, Ian already had a good head start on me.

Once out of the park, I hollered at Ian to stop. "Okay, what was that all about?"

"Tex, don't you know who that was?" Ian's eyes grew wide with disbelief, maybe even fear.

"Yeah…B-Ryce and Coo-Coo."

Ian chuckled. "Yeah, *cool* names. Maybe you can be *Tea-Ex* and I'll be *Supah Jiggy E-N*." Laughing, we sat down on the street curb. A rickety lawnmower from down the street threatened to drown us out. "*Seriously*. Those guys are dangerous."

"Really? Well, maybe Coo-Coo."

"They're the Young Bloods!" Ian sucked in air as if suffering from an asthma attack. He stared at me, waiting for his shocking revelation to sink in. I shrugged and tossed my hands in the air. All blood pretty much looked the same to me.

"They're a *gang*, Tex. They call themselves the Young Bloods, and they pretty much terrify the student body at Ridge Creek."

"A 'gang'?"

"Yeah, they beat kids up…and shoot and stab people and all kinds of scary, crazy crap!" Ian thrashed his hands about, looking over his shoulder for lurking eavesdroppers.

"'Shoot and stab people'?" I found it all a little hard to believe.

"Mostly, they're out looking for the Modern

Gangstas," said Ian.

"Wait…*what*?"

"The Modern Gangstas. That's Clearwell High's gang."

"*We* have a gang?"

"Shit, yeah! You haven't heard of 'em?" Ian rolled his skateboard back and forth with his foot.

"No…I guess I haven't. Who's in the Modern Gangstas?"

"I'm not sure. They keep a low profile. But they're *real*."

"Oh, come on, Ian. How do you know this…*gang* crap is real?" It all sounded way too cray. I mean, it's one thing to be terrorized by school bullies, but now a mysterious, shadowy gang is overrunning Clearwell High?

"People talk." Ian lowered his voice. "Haven't you seen the tagging?"

"Yeah, I guess I have." I *had* seen 'Modern Gangstas' painted several times on the walls surrounding the skate park. Also a tag in the school bathroom. I just figured the artists liked a band or were just…I dunno, "arting." "So, these two gangs just run around…and beat each other up?"

"Yeah."

"Why?"

"Beats me. Maybe you should ask your new friend Coo-Coo." He grinned and adopted a pseudo-gangsta stance, his hands tucked into his armpits.

"But…these are suburban kids. What do *they* have to war over?"

"Maybe it's their financial portfolios."

"They're going to shoot it out over their stock

options?" We joked about the suburban gangs of Kansas all the way home. Little did I realize how deadly serious the situation would become.

****

I walked past the Battle Bucket in the driveway and up the sidewalk. Overgrown and unkempt, our lawn practically begged me to give it a haircut. I hate mowing, particularly since I'm allergic to grass and about a hundred other things born of nature. But since my dad's in a wheelchair, it's my responsibility. I wondered about the possibility of a spell to prohibit grass growth, then quickly discarded the notion. It'd tick a personal gain box, one of the great no-nos of witchcraft—for the good guys, anyway.

Several cats camped out on the front stoop as I carefully sidestepped them. Even before I became aware of my witchiness, cats have plagued me with their constant presence. Mickey—my witch mentor—told me they're my familiars. I still don't quite get that. They may be familiar with me, but I sure don't want to be as well acquainted with them. Allergies and all, natch. I sneezed three times, sending them scampering like a reverse Pied Piper.

"Dad, I'm home."

"Hi, Tex," he called out. "We're in the kitchen." *Great, his girlfriend's with him.* Ruth Crandall's a nice woman, but the last thing I want to deal with right now is a giddily happy couple.

In the kitchen, Ruth stuffed a forkful of food into my dad's mouth, both of them giggling. I fought the urge to make a gagging sound. "Hi, Dad. Ruth."

"Hey, son." Dad wiped his mouth with a napkin. "How was school?"

"Fine." I attempted to scoot by them quickly but felt trapped by the mandates of social niceties. "Nothing new."

"How's Olivia, Tex?" Ruth tilted her head, smiled.

Dad cleared his throat. "Ah…Tex and Olivia broke up." He placed his hand on top of hers. "Hey," he continued, abruptly shifting into phony-happy mode, "there's lasagna in the oven. It turned out really good."

"I'm not hungry. Maybe later." I slouched off to the TV room. Behind me, whispered voices drifted out of the kitchen, no doubt discussing my heartbroken state.

Dad and Ruth began seeing each other at the same time Olivia and I first hooked up. At our annual Christmas gathering last year, Dad sprang her on me like an unexpected jack-in-the-box. At first, it took me aback that Dad wanted to date again. I thought it sort of disrespectful to my late mother's memory. But I quickly realized how selfish my thoughts sounded. Even old people need romance, I guess. It'd been over two years since Mom'd died. So, that Christmas, two relationships had blossomed in the McKenna household, flowering in unexpected ways.

We'd even arranged several double dates with disastrous results. Try as they might, Olivia and Ruth never found common ground. Worse, Olivia relished shocking Ruth with her brashness. One evening, it fell on our turn to pick the flick for movie night. With a great big, sloppy grin, Olivia whipped out a zombie movie. By the conclusion of the film, Ruth had turned as pale as one of the walking dead herself.

Dad and Ruth's relationship developed slowly and, I suspect remained somewhat chaste. At least I thought so. Fine, I absolutely hoped so. I really, *really* didn't want to know any of those sorts of details. Still, I'd never seen anything more than brief kisses pass between them. Even on those rare occasions, Ruth appeared embarrassed at her own brazen, shocking PDA. Olivia retaliated by launching into a full feeding-frenzy on my face. Ruth always blushed, while Dad would more often than not attempt to cover a smile.

Yet, Dad and Ruth made it work. And it did my heart wonders to see Dad happy again. The first two years after my mother's death, I'd seen the pain etched on his face, his wrinkles somehow deeper, his thoughts more cloaked. He and I'd tried to maintain our relationship while under an oppressive umbrella of grief and sadness. Time helped to fold away the umbrella. For the first time in years, laughter rang frequently through the house.

And right now, I wanted nothing of their happiness. Instead, I chose to dwell on my misfortunes in the romance arena. Why can't the world have a little respect for me and see how damned *important* this is? I flopped onto the sofa, releasing a big whoosh from the cushions. With an angsty sigh, I picked up the TV remote.

Quickly flipping through the channels, I chanced upon a romantic movie, a doting couple in a toothpaste commercial, and dogs in love. Not today, thank you very much. Even an elderly couple found their romance vastly improved by the man's use of hemorrhoid cream, for God's sake. Old people with hemorrhoids were in love! Where are the entertainment options for the romantically impaired?

"*Gah!*" I tossed the remote onto the table.

My cell phone rang. I scrambled through my pocket, hoping against hope that Olivia had seen the light fantastic, begging to take me back. Sure enough, "Olivia's home" scrawled across my phone's face. Celestial trumpets! A marching band—heavy on the tubas—blared out a triumphant fight ballad! Half-naked angels flit about and sang, "Hallelujah!"

But why didn't she call from her cell phone?

"Hello?" The trembling tenor of my voice sounded like I belonged in the high-pitched triumphant angels' chorus.

"Hi, Tex, it's Mrs. Furman." An awkward silence passed between us. "Olivia's mother."

"Oh, yeah." I gulped, *way* too loudly. "Yeah, I know who you are, Mrs. Furman." *Smooth, Tex, smooth as butter.*

"Well, ah… Look, Tex, I hope I'm not bothering you by calling…"

"No…no."

"I know I may be overstepping my boundaries here, but I'm very sorry to hear about you and Olivia."

"Thanks." *What fresh hell is this?*

"I really had grown…quite attached to you, Tex. I thought of you like my own son. And I think you were good for Olivia."

It surprised me how her sentiment affected me. Then again, I'd nearly burst into tears over a hemorrhoid commercial earlier, so anything goes in the weepy department.

"If you'd be open to a little bit of advice?" she asked.

"Sure."

"Leave her alone for now. Give her some time.

11

Make her miss you. Whatever you do, *don't* befriend her. If you do that… she won't have a chance to miss you."

Too late for that. We'd already agreed to preserve our friendship, as painful a choice as I've ever made. But she'd become such an integral part of my life; any part of Olivia surely would be better than none.

"Okay…"

"If it makes you feel any better," she continued, "I don't think there's another boy. She'll come around. Just give her time. But stay away from her for now."

"I'll try. Sounds like good advice." Okay, this phone call can end now.

"Please don't ever let Olivia know I called you, okay? I don't think she'd…ah…approve of my interference." Understatement.

"Okay."

"Just heed my advice, Tex," she repeated.

"Thanks, Mrs. Furman." She hung up, leaving me in a state of shock. It's not every day you get a call from your ex-girlfriend's mother, attempting to conspire with you to win back her daughter.

Maybe she's right. If I stay away from Olivia for a while—not allow her the comfort of my friendship—then surely she'll come back to me. Bonus! I felt illuminated, inspired. Stronger than all X-Men combined. Like a Phoenix rising, a whole new Tex rose from the fires stoked and stirred by Mrs. Furman's call. No more wallowing around in shameless self-pity and despair. Definitely, most certainly beyond time to move on.

Thirty minutes later, I called Olivia.

"Tex?" she answered.

"Hi…" I suck at putting on a strong front. "Have you…changed your mind? About us, I mean?"

"Tex…" She sighed. "I'm sorry. I don't want to hurt you. But nothing's changed."

"But…I still don't *understand*."

"It's like I told you two days ago…"

"Is there another guy?" Even though the sudden sense of betrayal would be extremely painful, at least I could wrap my head around a solid reason for the break-up.

"What? *No!* Look…I still care about you…and there's no 'other guy.'" Amusement affected her voice, whereas I felt far less than amused. My whole world had crashed down around me.

"I guess I'll see you tomorrow." I hung up before I burst into tears.

I stretched back onto the sofa and relived our conversation from two days ago. What an endless, futile, and self-punishing pastime I'd developed. I played it over and over again in my mind, concocting different scenarios, thinking of cooler things I could've said. Yet it always ended with the same, inevitable, tragic results.

During the last month or so of our relationship, I'd sensed Olivia growing more distant. She didn't show interest in the things we'd enjoyed as a couple before and had become colder, more aloof. In certain ways, I guess I knew we'd stagnated as a couple. We'd spent nearly a year and a half kissing in every variation possible, avoiding the looming issue of sex. A couple times, we talked about it and realized neither one of us felt ready to take that alluring, yet frightening, deep dive into the unknown. Finally, once I thought myself ready, she slipped away in the opposite direction.

Two days ago, at lunch, she grabbed my arm and told me we needed to talk. Dreaded words no guy wants to hear, *never* a good sign, particularly when females announce it.

She met me in my trust-worthy Battle Bucket—the only thing loyal to me over the years, even though it, too, had been lately threatening to quit on me—and slid into the passenger seat.

"Tex…" She looked down at her folded hands. "I think we need to break up…" Her gaze locked onto mine as my mouth fell open with horror. "At least for the time being," she added quickly.

"What are you *talking* about?" Flabbergasted, I waited for the nightmare to end.

"It's just…I don't know. Over the last month, I haven't been *happy*. Maybe 'happy' isn't the right word. I think I'm just scared…maybe…" She offered me a hint of a smile.

"*Scared*? Scared of *what*?" My hands gripped the steering wheel as if I'd lost control of a speeding car careening down an ice-covered highway with no brakes.

She thrust her clenched fists in the air, shaking them with frustration. "I don't want to be one of *those* couples."

"What couples?"

"You know. The girl who ends up marrying her first boyfriend from high school. And always wondering if there might be something else out there. And then getting pregnant. And divorced in two years. And then on welfare." Tears welled up in her eyes, although she snorted upon realizing how ridiculous her argument sounded.

"'Welfare'? Where did *that* come from?" I nearly joined her with a chuckle. Olivia's one of the very few people who I can consistently count on to find amusement in even the most awful circumstances. Even though it felt like the biggest fight of my life ever.

"Oh, Tex." She placed her hand on top of mine, her bracelets jangling together like a drum riff in a bad movie. "You *know* what I'm talking about…"

"No. No, I don't…not really."

"I still care about you. I…might even still…*love* you…"

"Then why *do* this?"

"I…I just need to take care of myself for a while." Her hand still on top of mine weighed as heavy as my heart. Out of anger, I felt like jerking mine from underneath hers but fought the impulse. "I just want to be single…for a while…"

I sat there, stunned, staring out the windshield at another young couple, gleefully holding hands and swinging them like a human jump rope. I wanted to raise my fists to the heavens and shout, "*No, no, no,*" repeatedly. But defiantly, I fought the one cliché I wouldn't fall victim to. Probably the only one. Baby steps.

"I'm sorry, Tex. I don't want to hurt you. I think it's best this way…" She looked at me, moisture glistening her beautiful eyes. "Who's to say we won't get back together again at some point?" But I sensed she threw her addendum out there more for my benefit than hers. She probably thought false hope is better than no hope. Of course, I'd take it, undoubtedly hang on it.

"When?"

"What?"

"When will we get back together?"

She held her dark red painted fingernails against her lips, stifling a laugh. "Tex…"

I took in a deep breath and closed my eyes. "You know I love you."

"I know…"

I leaned over and kissed her gently. The ever-familiar smell of sweet flowers intermixed with vanilla overwhelmed me, particularly since I realized I wouldn't be able to enjoy her scent again. She kissed me back and held it for a wonderful, yet brief moment, before she turned her head away.

"I would…really like it…if we could remain friends."

"Okay." But I didn't know if I'd be able to.

"Cool."

I nodded. 'Cool' isn't exactly how I'd describe this encounter. Far worse than uncool. It embodied the Antichrist of uncool, a world-shattering, uber-destroying apocalypse of uncool.

And just like that, no more than a dying wisp of smoke in the ginormous fireplace of love, my great romance ended. Not with a whimper, not with a bang, but with a softened mallet blow to the head. Her words effectively consoled herself but not me.

I mustered all the strength I could to get off the sofa. I peeked into the kitchen to see Dad still dallying with Ruth. Shaking my head at the unfair fates that guide romance and love, I announced my bedtime departure.

"Tex?" Dad looked at his watch. "It's only a little after seven. Are you all right?" A frown stretched across his face, the creases in his forehead mimicking his mouth.

"Yeah. I'm just tired."

"Let me know if I can do anything for you." He rolled his chair toward me and placed his hand on my forearm.

"Okay, Dad. Goodnight, Ruth."

"Goodnight, Tex." Ruth placed a few fingers over her lower lip and stared at me with huge, sad eyes, a living Precious Moments statuette.

I trudged up the stairs and fell into bed, fully clothed. I kicked off my high-tops with a bit of a struggle, sending one flying across the room into the wall with a *clump*. As it slid to the floor, I felt an instant kinship with my hastily, harshly discarded shoe.

Outside my window, trees bloomed in full force. Green leaves waved gently in the spring breeze, taunting me with their carefree friskiness. Usually, this is the time of year when the promise of the upcoming summer break fills me with hope and excitement about the future. But now, I could only think how unfair it is my romance with Olivia had only survived through *one* summer and *two* cold, brittle winters. We would be deprived of being springtime lovers again, holding hands and walking through the renewal and greening of the earth...and all the rest of that crap the media feeds you daily, forcing the lonely to realize how hollow and empty our lives truly are.

Maybe I need to take matters into my own hands. By whatever means necessary. *Witchcraft* means. I know it goes against everything I've been taught, but I'm desperate, and these are desperate times. I formulated a plan to win back Olivia.

Yet, as it turned out, the fates had other plans in store for me. If only witchcraft gave me the power of foresight. Dark forces, from both the spiritual and physical planes, were currently aligning to drag me into their affairs. Shadows loomed over Clearwell, targeting me like an angry, but one-track minded hunter, sent to remind me just how vulnerable and mortal I am. Once again, murder would come tap-tap-tapping at my door. And I would become the unwitting agent for unknown forces. Most bizarre, however, would be the unexpected help I'd receive from this world and beyond.

Chapter Two

I followed Ian through the cafeteria line, pushing his tray on the rollers with my own. Ian'd never asked me to do this, and we never spoke about it. But ever since Bob Bellman ran him over last year, Ian still couldn't close his left hand completely. As I felt partially responsible for the incident, I didn't mind helping him out.

"Tex," he said under his breath, "something's going on. I heard the cops were questioning everybody." Ian grabbed a plastic burger, held it up for inspection, and dropped it onto his tray.

"Gross. How can you eat those all the time?"

Ian cackled. "Nothing beats mystery meat."

I grabbed a salad, hard to fake. "So…what do you think's going on?"

"I dunno. But it's something *big*. I've heard rumors…" The scary lunch lady never took her heavily mascaraed eyes off our trays as she rang up the meals. Carefully, Ian balanced his tray with his good hand as we headed for our usual table. I saw Olivia sitting there and braved myself. The cafeteria felt like my emotional battlefield, and I came down on the General Custer side of things. Olivia, my erstwhile opponent, had slain me with heart-piercing arrows, while I ran out of ammunition of love.

Ian sat next to Olivia, and I grabbed a chair across

from him. "Hey, O," said Ian. Several days ago, Ian said that as a sign of male solidarity, he'd blow Olivia off, but I talked him out of it. I told him Olivia and I'd decided to remain friends, so he grudgingly gave in.

"Hey, guys," she said.

"Hey." I directed my full attention toward the salad as if I were spelunking for rare artifacts.

"Why are the cops here?" Olivia swiveled her head back and forth between me and Ian.

"Don't know."

"Hey." Brandon Townsend, resident bad boy and the newest inductee into our band of misfits and unwanted toys, stood behind Olivia. Without even attempting to hide my feelings, I rolled my eyes. I'd designated Brandon the bane of my existence. I didn't care what Olivia or Mrs. Furman told me; I couldn't help but think the reason for my crushed romance stood before me.

Ripped jeans barely clung to his slim hips. His extremely tight death metal band T-shirt may as well have been painted onto his six-packed torso. He brushed back long, brown hair with one hand as if zephyr winds and glorious bugles announced his triumphant arrival. Ignoring the rest of us, his chiseled jaw aimed toward Olivia.

Man, did I hate him.

"Anyone sitting here?" He pointed at the chair next to Olivia.

Olivia slid the chair out. She smiled at him, batting long eyelashes. "You are, Brandon. Park it."

Brandon swiveled the chair around and straddled it backward, depositing his tray in front of him in one smooth motion. Just tossing another log onto my fiery hatred.

Olivia had adopted Brandon and brought him into our group. She'd met him in her math class and went on at great lengths about his coolness factor for weeks before we met him. Immediately, I disliked him, for no real reason other than the effect he had on many of the girls at Clearwell. When he walked down the hallways, girls would stop, stare, giggle, and point as he slouched by them. The ultimate anti-Tex, his very slick existence irked me. Petty, I know. I really tried to get over it, particularly since my new mantra didn't allow for anyone to be turned away, but his ludicrously easy-peasy smoothness offended my awkward sensibilities.

Honestly, we knew next to nothing about him, other than he'd transferred from a school somewhere in Missouri and rode a motorcycle, which Olivia found fascinating. He never treated anyone badly and seemed friendly enough, but I always thought he'd fit in better elsewhere. Somewhere, like say, I don't know…100 miles from Clearwell. Maybe the way Olivia fawned over him just dredged up the ol' green-eyed monster in me.

"What's going on?" he asked, finally acknowledging the rest of us.

"Not much." Olivia grinned, leaning her shoulder slightly in toward him. "The cops are here today, though."

"Yeah," he said. "Don't know how true it is, but I heard James Badger was killed last night."

I put my fork down into the bed of wilting lettuce. "Who's James Badger?" I didn't recognize the name, but the thought of another murder at Clearwell High filled me with a sudden chill. The second unexpected chill I'd experienced in two days.

Brandon shrugged his shoulders, his hair bobbing up and down like that of a male model. "Second-year freshman. I didn't really know him. Some grade school kids found his body over at Elmleaf...on the playground. He was shot."

"Wow." Ian glanced at me in what I suppose he considered a surreptitious manner.

"Did you know him, Ian?"

"No. I just knew who he was. Kinda bad news is what I heard."

Olivia said, "So help me, God, we *better* not have another serial killer here." Turning to me, her eyes narrowed.

"Don't look at me," I said. "I don't know anything about this."

Olivia pressed her lips into a tight, thin line. "Just stay out of it, Tex. Don't get wrapped up in something that doesn't concern you." At least she still cared enough to worry about me.

"Wait. What am I missing?" Brandon still hadn't eaten his food but found it fascinating to roll a meatball back and forth with his fork. Probably how he keeps in such effortless, physical shape. *Dick.*

Olivia placed her hand on his shoulder. The same way she'd touched me many times in the past. "I'll fill you in later." I wondered if this implied they'd meet somewhere after school...or if she meant during math class.

"Okay." Brandon shrugged and went back to playing meatball soccer.

"So," I said, "why was James 'bad news?'"

"I dunno," said Ian, "I heard he was a bully...and

kinda scary."

Everyone fell silent, pondering the all-too-familiar world of murdered bullies before Brandon broke the ice. "I actually heard James was cool."

I studied Brandon's movements. Could he possibly know something about this? Or is it just wishful thinking on my part? If he's involved in the Badger kid's death, that would be one sure way to even the playing field with Olivia. And I totally suck-suckity-sucked for thinking such a thing.

"Why would anyone want to shoot him?" I asked. Ian gave a swift kick to my leg. I yelped. "Sorry! Thought I saw a caterpillar in my lettuce..." Not an uncommon sighting in our lovely cafeteria's meals, after all.

Olivia stretched her arms across the table, tucked her head down, and chuckled quietly. I offered a tepid smile.

Daniel Cross raced toward the table, a welcome distraction from my embarrassment. "*Guys*! Hey, did you hear?"

"Yeah, Dan, we heard," said Ian. "James Badger was shot and murdered." He sighed and pointed to the chair at the end of the table.

Out of breath, Daniel scurried toward the chair and sat down. He pushed his glasses up toward the bridge of his nose and squinted. His shoulders caved, as if disappointed someone beat him to the punch in delivering shocking news.

****

I'd met Daniel Cross in my psychology class at the beginning of the semester. The only reason I chose psychology as an elective is because Mr. Jensen taught it, one of the very few teachers at Clearwell I respected. Not only as a fair-minded teacher, but last year he'd also proven to be someone I could trust when he aided in the capture of our resident serial-killer janitor. Long story, that.

On the first day of class, I ambled in, a little late as usual, and found an open seat in the back of the room. I squeezed my tall frame into the chair and noticed a small kid next to me.

"Hey." I extended my hand. "I'm Tex. Tex McKenna."

He accepted my hand, shaking it rapidly. "I know who you are. That was pretty cool what you did last year...I mean for Josh and everything."

"Yeah, well..." I scrunched down further in my chair. Good or bad, I tried to avoid all attention. And I really didn't feel all that heroic or worthy since so many people had been killed despite my best efforts.

"I'm Daniel Cross." He continued pumping my hand.

"Um..." I inclined my head toward our hands.

"Oh! Sorry." Finally releasing his grip, he swept his mop of hair over to one side of his head. The part in his hair stood out so obviously, he could've been parting the Red Sea, a hairstyle straight out of the 60s Kennedy era. What parent would let their kid sport that hairstyle nowadays? "I'm just a sophomore, but I'm taking honors classes."

"That's cool," I said.

"And I have a genius I.Q."

"Now, that's *really* cool. You mentioned my friend, Josh. Did you know him?"

"Yeah. We hung a little bit before...well, you

know..."

"Yeah...I know."

Daniel wanted to continue our talk, but five minutes in, Mr. Jensen appeared agitated, so I told him to chill. Throughout class, Daniel scribbled in his notebook fervently. Figuring him to be a Shakespeare of mad note-taking skills, his endless—nearly frantic—writing became a distraction. *Scritch, scritch, scratch...* At the end of class, I snuck a glimpse at his book. Five anime-styled drawings of a vulpine character, with a human female body, in various poses and states of dress, lay across two pages.

"Hey, that's pretty good," I said. "Is that your character? Or is that from some manga?"

"No, I created her." Daniel beamed. I got the feeling he didn't receive too much adulation. "I call her 'Foxy La-La'. I love her..." He looked down as if ashamed of his declaration. Even though a professed love for his own drawing did seem kinda weird, if he'd been a friend of Josh's, that was more than good enough for me.

At first, Olivia and Ian turned their noses up at Daniel, finding him to be too much of a geek. I reminded them we leave no man behind, and they agreed. With reservations. Amongst Daniel's many talents, we soon discovered him to be an unparalleled computer whiz. If we had any problems with programs, software, or hardware, Daniel found a way to fix it. He had a real aptitude for teaching, too. With seemingly unlimited patience, he instructed us fully and carefully. And if we ever needed information on practically anything, he fit the go-to guy mode. Repeatedly, he'd proven to be a valuable addition to our group. Although

Olivia never came completely around to him and his quirks, she at least grew to accept him. Ian became genuinely fond of Danny, hanging out with him while Olivia and I did our thing.

Out of desperation, Olivia actually tried to give Daniel a half-hearted makeover. Unfortunately, Danny fit the stereotype of a typical computer geek, helping no one but the bullies around him. More often than not, his hair hung in greasy clumps, and the unfortunate hairstyle made it even worse. He wore glasses way too big for his small, pimply face. Clothing choices were likewise challenged—ill-fitting khakis and dress slacks mismatched with checkered, short-sleeve oxford shirts. I suspected he didn't own a pair of jeans. If he did, we never saw them. Once she told him she'd pay for the excursion, Olivia finally talked him into going to a hair salon. He departed with a better hairstyle, but Olivia threw her arms up in defeat when he refused to do anything about his clothing or glasses.

"It's who I am," he proclaimed proudly. And, by God, if I didn't take pride in him then, too.

One fall evening, Daniel had invited the three of us over to his house for dinner.

"I just want to warn you guys," he said. "My parents are kinda...*weird*."

Taking this information into consideration, Olivia, Ian, and I prepared ourselves for the family from hell. When we arrived, Daniel's super-smiley and preternaturally happy mother met us at the door, appearing as if she'd just stepped out of a fifties movie. Wrapped up in a long white dress, a necklace of pearls, and an old-fashioned apron tied around her waist, I understood where Daniel's Kennedy-era hairstyle came from.

"You must be Daniel's friends." She smiled so hard that her eyes nearly closed. "Come in, come in." Ian chuckled while I jabbed him in the ribs with my elbow.

"Have a seat." She pointed toward the dining room table, eloquently adorned with a white, frilly tablecloth and a bowl of obviously plastic fruit. "Daniel will be down in a minute." She passed her hand over the table, game-show model style, and scooted off to the kitchen.

"Danny's right," whispered Ian. "His mom *is* weird."

"I think she's sweet," Olivia said with a giggle.

Still wearing his ludicrous school clothes, Daniel bounded down the stairs and sat at the table with us. He squirmed like a little kid forced to wear his Sunday's best.

"Thanks for coming, guys." More fidgety than usual, he couldn't meet our eyes for very long.

Daniel's mother floated into the room on the clouds of Camelot, humming The Beach Boys, light on her feet. "We're having meatloaf, kids. Daniel's favorite."

"Mom!"

"Bob," called out Mrs. Cross. "Bob, dinner time!" We heard a grunt, a rattle of newspaper. Ian appeared excited what unexpected horror show would soon materialize from the den.

A small bespectacled man, with one of the worst comb-overs I'd ever witnessed, bounced into the room and grinned broadly. His three-piece suit looked like an antique. A pipe dangling from his mouth would've sealed the deal sweetly. His excitement at seeing us nearly palpable, I half-expected him to honk our noses and juggle. "Hello, kids. I'm Mr. Cross." Sunshine and goodwill filled Daniel's entire family like a turkey stuffed with kisses and puppies. Or maybe the Cross family single-handedly kept the Clearwell caffeine industry booming.

"I'm sure the little missus has told you we're having meatloaf." He assumed the seat at the head of the table. "It's Daniel's favorite."

Ian snorted, while Olivia twisted her mouth to the side, trying not to join in. Quickly, I ran interference. "I'll bet it's very good, Mr. Cross." Clearly, I'd crossed over into an old-fashioned family situation comedy.

"You bet your boots it is, kiddo," said Mr. Cross. I bit my lip and looked down at my empty plate. I didn't know if Daniel's assessment of his parents being 'weird' could be considered accurate, but I certainly didn't expect to travel through time.

The front door flew open with a *whack*. A tall boy wearing a jean jacket slowly swayed in, heaving his shoulders over-exaggeratedly from left to right. I recognized him immediately as Ken Cross, a surly senior whom I knew by reputation only. Someone to stay far away from. I'd never put two and two together before, and didn't realize Danny had an older brother, let alone this lug. Of course, it didn't help that Danny had never mentioned him.

"Ken, would you like to join Daniel and his friends for supper?" sang out Mrs. Cross.

Ken swaggered up to the table and surveyed us as if we were goods to be purchased—or stolen—at the pawnshop. Without saying a word, he pushed his long hair across his forehead, shook his head in disgust, and stomped up the stairs. Well, the entire family didn't float on sunshine after all. Frankly, I felt great relief he wouldn't break bread with us.

"You'll have to excuse Ken, kids." Mr. Cross leaned into the table. "He's a bit tired." He patted my hand, nearly making me jump, and offered everyone at the table a knowing wink.

Several times throughout dinner, Mr. or Mrs. Cross brought up Danny's many academic achievements and bragged about his genius status. I couldn't help but feel sorry for Danny, as he remained fairly quiet.

After the almost never-ending dinner came to a halt—but not before apple pie à la mode!—the four of us made a beeline to Daniel's room. We passed what I assumed to be Ken's room, death metal blasting out from behind the closed door. I wondered how Daniel's parents fit death metal into their rose-colored world-view.

When we entered Daniel's room, awe transfixed me. Sketches and paintings of his artistic creation Foxy La-La covered the walls. Literally hundreds of gigantic anime eyes stared down at us, evoking a paranoid, claustrophobic feeling. How in the world could he *sleep* in there? In the center of the room, a long table sat, weighed down with three computers and masses of wires pouring out the back of them. Dr. Frankenstein's lab if he'd created his monster in the age of the Internet.

No doubt about it, Daniel Cross was a true bona-fide geek, but he was *our* geek.

****

So, that day in the cafeteria, when it seemed very important for Daniel to be the first to deliver the news of James Badger's murder, I felt the need to toss him a reassuring bone.

"What else have you heard, Danny? About Badger?" If anyone knew anything, it would be Daniel. If he didn't know, then he could soon find out information cybernetically.

"Not much, really." Once again in his pedagogical element, he put on a serious, all-knowing face. "I know he was a second-year freshman...not very bright, really." He flashed a brief smile. "Oh! I heard something else, maybe. But I haven't been able to verify it—"

"What?"

"He may've been in a gang here..."

I raised my eyes at Ian, who looked like he wanted to crawl under the table. Brandon lifted his head from his idle food play and stared at Daniel solemnly.

****

"Ian, hold up." As soon as the bell rang, Ian bounced from the cafeteria table like an over-caffeinated kangaroo. Or he simply didn't want to talk about James Badger any longer.

He turned around in the crowded hallway. "Ian, what else do you know about James Badger's death?" I lowered my voice and added, "Was he part of the Modern Gangstas?"

Ian swept his gaze around the hallway. Grabbing my arm, he dragged me to his locker. He swung the locker door open and made me hunch down into his makeshift cone of silence.

"Look, I don't know much more than what Daniel said, but I'm thinking that's right—"

"*What's* right?"

"James Badger was in the Modern Gangstas." Ian

quickly scanned the hallway again as if on a covert spy operation. "I think he may have even been the leader."

"What makes you think so?" I felt foolish hunkering down behind Ian's locker door, but it seemed like the only way he'd talk. Other students giggled and smirked while they passed us. I even heard that lovely ol' acorn, *fags*, whispered our way.

"I *don't* know. Not for sure. I've just heard rumors."

"What else do you know about Badger?"

"Just that he had a girlfriend—Rebecca Hogan—and they were crazy! She's actually a sophomore. She didn't get held back like Badger did. And they always made a big deal about being engaged. Then they'd break up...then they'd get engaged again. She's got a loud mouth, but I didn't really know either one of them. I just knew who they were. You couldn't miss hearing them."

I sighed. Even wayward gangsta second-year freshmen had blossoming romances.

"Ian...do you think our new pals, B-Ryce and Coo-Coo, did this?" I suppose that's what connected me, intrigued me almost. Not that I wanted to get involved in intra-school gang shoot-ups, but I wondered if Ian and I were privy to knowledge the cops may be missing.

Ian slammed his locker door. "Yeah, that's *exactly* what I think happened, Tex. And I don't want to talk about it anymore." Ian brushed past me and torpedoed down the hallway. I couldn't understand what terrified him so much about this. Miles of comfort shielding separated us from anything gang related.

When I turned around to head to class, the looming

presence of Arville Hastings—resident fascist vice-principal, friend of football and enemy of anyone who dares to be unpopular—blocked my departure. On top of his rectangular head rested a briar patch of black hair. His hawk-like nose jutted out nearly as far as his lantern jaw, sniffing out those who wouldn't conform. I'd always assumed a mad scientist cobbled him somewhere deep in southern Texas, utilizing assorted parts of a mad bull and a rabid Doberman pinscher. His beady-eyed gaze locked onto me, burning a hole through my soul.

"Ah…excuse me, Mr. Hastings." I attempted to sidestep him, while he hopped over to block me again. Apparently, he signed on as my dancing partner for the Texas two-step. Yee-*ha*! "I've got to get to class." Once more, he impeded my path to education.

"Now, hold on a second there, Richard," he drawled. As always, he stubbornly refused to call me Tex, the childhood nickname my friends call me. I never corrected him. We'd had our fair share of encounters last year. I tried to stay off his radar this year, but it looked like once he located you, you're a constant huge blip.

"What were you and your little friend there discussin'?" He pointed down the hallway where Ian'd just fled.

"You know, classes…homework." I smiled the best I could. Soooo dumb.

"That's weird. I could've sworn I heard you mention James Badger." Apparently, Commandant Hastings had been eavesdropping. How in the world we didn't notice this big, hulking bulldog lurking nearby astonished me.

"Badger...hmmmm...James Badger..." I looked up toward the dull neon lights as if trying to find sudden divine inspiration. "I don't know. Wait! Oh, some of the kids were talking about how something happened to him last night...or something..." I trailed off.

"You don't know what happened." It sounded more like a disbelieving statement than a question. He leaned down closer to me. I stood at five feet eleven inches but Hastings had at least five inches of height on me. Garlic intermixed with nicotine rolled off his breath.

"I mean, I've heard rumors. But I don't know anything. I didn't even know James Badger..."

"Look, Richard, I still don't know how, but you and your friends were knee-deep in that...mess...last year." I quickly noted that three murders constituted an inconvenient "mess" for Vice Principal Hastings. "And I'm wondering what your involvement is with the Badger boy..." He hovered over me, a detective sweating me for a confession. Suddenly, the bell rang, jolting me into action.

"Mr. Hastings, I *swear* I don't know anything. I've *really* got to get to class—"

"I don't care if you do *need* to get to class, Richard." So much for the arbiters of higher education. "What do you *know*?"

"Nothing. Honestly!"

Hastings straightened up and sniffed. "I'll be watching you, boy." He pointed his two stubby fingers at his eyes and then at me. "I'm watching..." I slid underneath his arm, which had been resting above me on the lockers.

As I made a mad dash to class, I slowly felt the uncomfortable yet familiar sensation of a noose tightening around my neck. And here I am, all but swinging in the wind, perilously perched on my tiptoes, waiting for the trap door to swing open beneath me.

Rushing into the classroom, I nearly bowled Mr. Jensen over. Not an easy task.

"You're late, Tex." He turned back toward the chalkboard where he erased something from the previous class. "Where've you been?" My fellow students tittered, some leaning forward, anticipating an exciting confrontation.

"Sorry, Mr. Jensen. Mr. Hastings stopped me in the hallway and wanted to talk to me about…I dunno…something, I guess, or whatever."

He pushed his glasses up, sighed, and then nodded. "Take your seat."

I looked at Daniel, fidgeting in his seat.

"Tex, what did Hastings want?"

Mr. Jensen dashed off an irritated glance in our direction. "Later," I whispered.

"Okay, class," said Mr. Jensen. "Before we were so rudely interrupted…" He turned around to glance at me, with an accusatory eyebrow lifted. "We were discussing the unfortunate circumstances surrounding James Badger. Would anyone like to contribute anything?"

The class remained silent. Quite a subdued reception compared to the New Orleans-styled she-bang for the demise of several football players last year. Either no one really knew Badger, or he didn't matter very much to anyone. Indifferent restlessness and a few yawns were the new order of the day.

"Well, then, this is psychology, so I'll start,"

continued Mr. Jensen. "For those who don't know, James Badger—a freshman here at Clearwell—was found shot dead this morning on a grade school playground." He stopped erasing and faced the class to address us. Pacing back and forth, the linoleum beneath his feet squeaked from his punishing weight. "Personally, I didn't know this student. But any time someone dies, it's a tragedy." He stopped in front of several students in the front row, ensuring their attention.

"And any time a weapon is used?" He shook his head slowly. "It's damned *ridiculous*, that's what it is." His voice rose in anger. "You guys are students...*kids*. There shouldn't be a place in your world for *guns*, for death. What in the *world* could possibly have been so important...for someone to take another person's life?" He turned and slammed his large fist down onto his desk, prompting a few students to jerk awake.

A cheerleader in the front row raised her hand. "Mr. Jensen?"

"Yes, Theresa?"

"Did he kill himself?"

Mr. Jensen looked out the window before responding. "Honestly, Theresa, I don't have an answer for that. I'm not included in the law's findings. But from what I understand, it's not likely." He flashed a quick smile at Theresa. "But thanks for your pertinent question."

Theresa beamed as if she received a gold star. Daniel grinned and rolled his eyes.

Mr. Jensen blew air out from his pursed lips not unlike a whale through his blowhole. "Look, guys. No matter if James Badger was murdered or committed suicide, I want you all to realize…just how precious your lives are. There are *no* second chances. *Think* before you act. This isn't like…calling someone a name and being able to issue an apology later. Just *think*, people. Damnit, just think…" Springs ground loudly as Mr. Jensen nearly collapsed into his chair. He looked down at his desk and folded his hands. An unnatural stillness claimed the students. Several of them glanced about nervously, while others dove into their textbooks, hoping to avoid the uncomfortable situation by losing themselves in their familiar daily grind.

Finally, Mr. Jensen said, "Okay. Chapter Ten…"

****

I made my way through the parking lot toward the Bucket when I heard someone shouting at me. *"Tex. Tex, wait up, damnit."*

Olivia raced toward me, struggling with the backpack over her shoulder, her black flats slapping against the pavement. I waited for her to catch up.

"Tex, *what* is going on?"

"What do you mean?"

"Oh, don't give me that." She tossed her backpack to the ground. "I saw those looks you and Ian gave each other at lunch when we were talking about James Badger."

"Olivia, I don't know what you're talking about—"

"Bullshit!" She wrinkled her nose and frowned. "Are you mixed up in this? Do you know something about Badger's death?"

"Olivia, I honestly know as much as you do."

"And why don't I believe you?"

"I'm *not* involved in this. I don't know anything—

"

Olivia kicked her backpack. "I *still* don't believe you. Look, just because we're broken up, doesn't mean I don't still care about you. Don't do anything stupid. Just…be careful."

"Okay."

She turned to leave, stopped, and called out, "And if you ever need my help…you know you can count on me, right?"

I smiled, naively optimistic that her iceberg attitude toward me had begun melting. "I know." Still fighting her behemoth backpack, she stalked off toward her car.

I opened my car door and slid in. Suddenly, the passenger door flew open, giving me a jolt. Too reminiscent of last year when a surprise visitor attacked me in the same parking lot. Detective Ryan Cowlings scooted in next to me.

"Hello, Tex," he said. "It's been a long time."

"Hey, Detective Cowlings." He grabbed my hand firmly and shook it. Last year, Detective Cowlings turned out to be a sharp, perceptive cop, perhaps too much so. He suspected there was more to me than I let on. However, I had learned to trust him. He proved a kindred spirit, having to fight hard on the force as possibly the only gay cop in Clearwell, Kansas.

"I thought this might be a good place to have a chat without the…ah…interference from your vice-principal." He smoothed out a crease in his pants leg.

"Too late. Hastings already gave me a grilling."

Cowlings shook his head. "Yes, he was adamant about calling you into his office, but I settled him down." He reached into his jacket pocket and pulled out his ever-present notebook and flipped it open. I noticed cartoon puppies prancing around playfully on the cover of this edition.

"Oh, you like puppies?"

Cowlings just stared at me, perplexed, then shook his head.

"Never mind," I mumbled.

Undeterred, Cowlings slipped right back into detective mode. "Tex, do you know why I'm here?" He slapped his thigh with his notebook, disturbing the puppies at play.

"Something to do with James Badger's death, I guess?"

"Correct. Last year, you proved to be—well, let's just say—*intuitive* regarding the murders that occurred here." He raised his eyebrows, peering at me through his small rectangular-framed glasses. "I wanted to check with you, see if you might know something."

Carefully, I weighed my words before speaking. "I really, *really* don't know anything, Detective. I didn't even know this kid." I wondered how much—if any—I should mention to him about the Young Bloods and the Modern Gangstas, but what did I know, other than rumors and Ian's hyperbole?

"Tex, please understand me. I don't suspect you're involved in the boy's death. I'm coming to you to see what you've *heard*. I know your fellow students are talking."

"All I know is James Badger was a two-year freshman—not the sharpest kid around." Cowlings smiled and nodded in agreement. "He had a girlfriend—her name's Rebecca Hogan. I don't know her either. I guess they had a kinda crazy on-again, off-again romance. Apparently, they were engaged several times."

"Yep, she was supposed to be my next stop, but she wasn't here today." He stopped writing and stared at me. "Fine, cards on the table...what are you *not* telling me?"

"Okay. I've heard rumors he was in a...gang. The Modern Gangstas."

Cowlings lifted one eyebrow and attacked his notebook. "A gang. What can you tell me about this gang?"

"They hang out at skate parks from what I hear. There's a rumor they're into guns."

Cowlings shot me an urgent look. "Who's in this gang?" He held his pen poised, ready to write down a list that wouldn't be forthcoming.

"*That* I couldn't tell you." Cowlings offered a doubting smirk. "No, really. I've no idea who's in the gang. This is all new info to me, too." An uncomfortable silence filled the Bucket's interior. "Um, Detective? How did Badger die, anyway? I mean I've heard stories..."

"I really shouldn't give you this information ...but it'll be all over the news tonight, anyway. He was shot three times in the chest."

"So. I guess we can rule out suicide?"

"Yes, Tex, *we* can rule it out. The gun wasn't found at the scene of the crime. Some unfortunate grade-schoolers found his body on their playground."

"I'll bet that was a recess to remember..." Cowlings snapped his head toward me. "Sorry, sorry. Detective...um, one other thing. I've heard there's a rival gang at Ridge Creek High. The Young Bloods. Apparently, they hated one another."

Cowlings studied me as he would a curious specimen ripe for dissecting. "I've actually heard things about the Modern Gangstas, but the Young Bloods are new to me…"

"You might want to talk to two kids at Ridge Creek—B-Ryce and Coo-Coo."

Cowlings threw his hands up, banging them into the car's torn lining. "You've *got* to be kidding me."

I laughed. "I *know*, right? But those are the only names I know." When I saw Cowlings not joining me in my merriment, I stopped laughing and cleared my throat.

"And, how do you know…B-Ryce and Coo-Coo, Tex?"

"I…just met them at the skate park the other day. I'm not even sure they're in a gang."

"The Clearwell Park?" I nodded. "And you don't have any last names?"

"Nope. Now you know everything I know."

"And once again, Tex, you seem to know…quite a lot." He deftly removed a business card from his jacket pocket and handed it to me. "If you hear anything else, please don't hesitate to call me. And do *not* throw the card away this time. They don't grow on trees."

"Yes, they do," I said.

"What?"

"Well, technically…the cards are made from trees…" Why can't I learn when to shut up?

"You're *not* going to lecture me about political correctness, Tex," he said, smiling. "I've put great expenditure into these cards to have them printed on recyclable paper."

"Okay…okay…" I waved my hands in surrender.

"By the way, how are you and Olivia getting along?" I straightened up in my seat. I didn't even realize Cowlings knew we were a couple.

"Um…we're not. We…broke up."

"Hm. That's not what it looked like to me just now." Like Santa Claus, Detective Cowlings knows all and sees all. "Her body language was not that of a disinterested party."

"Really? You think?" Okay, I'll gladly take the small beacon of hope…even if it came from an old cop.

Cowlings laughed. "Hang in there." He punched me lightly in the shoulder, before jiggling the car door handle, which hadn't worked as long as I've had the Bucket. "Um…Tex?"

"Yeah?"

"Would you let me out of your car?"

"Oh, yeah. Right." I scurried around, anxious to get rid of him. When I opened the door, he stepped out and smoothed out his pants legs.

"Tex, there is one last thing." He stood in front of me, commanding my full attention. "I don't even know if it's relevant, but I thought you might want to know."

Suddenly, I had a bad feeling. "What's that?"

"James Badger…was Bob Bellman's cousin."

"Huh."

Chapter Three

As I drove across town, I felt like I just got whacked upside the head with a massive clout of déjà vu. Once again, there'd been another student murder, Hastings busied himself trying to pin anything he could on me, and here comes Detective Cowlings sniffing around. There's also the troubling fact that Bob Bellman's name popped up several times. It seemed his specter still wanted to haunt me for a while, just for grins, even though I thought I'd finished with him. *Twice.* I also couldn't shake the feeling the murder connected to me in ways I hadn't even thought of yet.

I parked the Bucket in front of Mickey Goldfarb's house and got out. Cotton willow seeds flew gently on the breeze, like some bizarre spring snowfall. Mickey's garden thrived in full bloom; myriad colors taunting the neighbors' failed attempts at raising flowers this early in the spring. I've never seen Mickey do any gardening, prompting me to wonder if her garden hadn't been a little witchcraft-enhanced.

Mickey Goldfarb's my witch-mentor, something I inherited from my late mother. She comes across like your typical "you kids get outta my yard" cranky, blue-rinse old lady, but her appearance is deceiving. Mickey's sharp, with a true understanding and command of witchcraft. I visit her every three weeks or so for training and education; but this is an unscheduled meeting. And, man, does she hate when I don't schedule.

I knocked and waited a seeming eternity for her to answer.

"Who is it?" she barked from behind the door.

"It's Tex, Mickey."

She pulled open the door, tightening the chain lock with a clank. Eyes peered out from behind her floating spectacles, ensuring I told the truth regarding my identity. She slammed the door shut again. The usual clawing and scrabbling with the chain ensued as I waited. A whiz with witchcraft, Mickey still hadn't mastered the chain lock.

"Hey, kid."

"Hey, Mickey. Sorry I didn't call, but I brought fried chicken." I held the red and white plastic bag up for inspection, her favored form of payment for services rendered. Since I dropped by unannounced, I knew I'd better be fully armed.

"Come in, come in." She shooed her cats upstairs, our usual tradition as the cat hair bothered me. "How are you?"

"I'm okay. How're you?"

"Can't complain." She whipped around to glare up at me. "What do you want?"

"Well…I was hoping we could have…an impromptu session." I chose my words carefully; no sense in letting her know what I *really* wanted.

"Okay, sit down at the table." She scurried into her small kitchen and grabbed two paper plates and napkins from the pantry. She plopped them onto the table and sat down across from me.

"Do you like my tablecloth? It's new. I thought I'd

treat myself."

"Yeah…it's, um, red and white. It matches the chicken bucket." I held up the bag to show her my clever color coordination abilities.

She snickered. "Tex, you're something else."

"Yeah. Hey, sorry I didn't get mashed potatoes this time, but I don't have a job, and I'm kinda' broke right now. " She reached into the bag and snagged a chicken thigh.

"I'd be happy if you took your limited funds and got a haircut." She set the piece of chicken down onto the plate and chortled, which inevitably turned into a coughing spasm.

"Yeah, well, I'll think about it." I pulled out a chicken leg and bit into it half-heartedly.

"So, I heard on the TV there was another murder at your school."

I sighed. "Yep."

"Did you know the boy?"

"No…no, I didn't."

"Well, you ain't gonna become "Encyclopedia Brown" and try to investigate it, now, are you?"

I had no idea who she referred to but assumed it to be a detective on one of her soap operas. "Not if I can help it, Mickey. Hey, that's something I wanted to ask you. My witchcraft powers…do they attract trouble?"

"What do you mean?"

"It just seems like every time there's—I dunno—a murder or something, I find myself drawn into the middle of it." I tossed my napkin over the chicken leg remains, any semblance of hunger long gone.

Mickey tucked her upper lip into her lower lip, the wrinkles looking like a tightly drawn string around a bag of marbles. As if in pain, she shut her eyes before opening them again. She leaned in closer. "Sometimes, there's an alignment of mystical powers at play. When there are things going on that aren't natural in the physical plane, sometimes it affects the spiritual plane. Since you got pretty damn strong witchcraft powers, that might make you a catalyst for events."

"I don't get it."

She let out a long raspberry. I figured it'd be beyond rude to wipe the wet "friendly fire" from my face. "Okay, kid. Murder's not natural, right?"

"I hope not."

"So, when it happens, it's unnatural...right?"

"Yeah...I guess so."

"Unnatural events on the physical plane affect the spiritual plane," she said slowly, as if speaking to a toddler. "And if there's a strong, supernaturally gifted catalyst—that would be you, Tex—connected to the events, sometimes it—you—would act like a lightning rod for the planes to connect...drawing you into the middle of things." Her eyes widened even further. Sunlight danced off her glasses. Excitement built in her eyes as if recounting a ghost story around a campfire.

"So...I really am a trouble magnet." It's sorta what I suspected, but it still sucked hearing it.

Mickey cackled, just killing her today. "Yeah, I guess you could say that."

"Well, *crap*." Mickey stood up quickly, crossed around the table, and thwacked me on the backside of my head.

"Ow! *Damn* it."

"You watch your mouth, kiddo." *Thwack.*

"*Jesus.*"

Smack. "And don't you blaspheme!"

I covered the back of my head with my hands, anticipating another attack. "Okay, sorry." I've honestly heard Mickey use much worse language, but...her kitchen, her laws.

"Anyway, before you got all potty-mouthed, I was gonna explain that it's all just part of the rules," she said.

Some rules. Nobody ever consults me about the rules, even though I'm playing the game of witchcraft and hardly by choice. Frankly, I'd like a major time-out from this game.

"Now. Let's go outside for a bit." Mickey held the front door open before I got up from my chair. On the porch, she plopped into her favored, flower-patterned porch swing. She lit a cigarette and blew a chimney's worth of smoke into the air. Smoke intermingled with floating cotton willows, looking like an after-effect of an apocalyptic acid rain.

I sat next to her. "Mickey, have you considered an electric cigarette?"

She looked shocked. "What the hell are you talking about, Tex? You can't plug in a cigarette."

"Never mind." I thought it best to avoid the unfathomable realm of electronics with Mickey. Last year, I tried to give her a DVR. She rejected it, unable to figure out what it was.

"The very idea." She shook her head. "I don't know where you come up with this stuff, Tex. Honestly, electric cigarettes. Heh."

"Um...yeah. I guess I just let my imagination take over sometimes." We'd had enough fun at my expense, so I quickly changed the subject. "Hey, Mickey? What can you teach me about love spells?" I tossed it out there as nonchalantly as I could.

She whipped her head toward me, the earlier smile melting into a grimace. "Why do you want to know?"

"No real reason." I lied. "I just think…maybe I should probably know everything that you can teach me. If I'm going to be a responsible witch…" I smiled, hoping my twitching lower lip wouldn't give me away.

She continued glowering at me. "Are you still courting that Olivia girl?"

"Oh, yeah. Everything's great. Just great." I crossed my ankles and stretched back into the porch swing, relaxed man about town.

Mickey swished her mouth back and forth as if gargling. "Listen, kid. What's the *first* rule about witchcraft?"

"Ah. Never use it for personal gain?"

"That's right." She stubbed her cigarette out into her over-flowing ashtray. "You're not thinking about *using* a love spell, are you?"

"No, of course not."

"Bad things could come of it…" Utilizing a six-point move, she swiveled her small body halfway in the swing to face me.

I couldn't meet her eyes. "I understand. But do they actually work? Or are they, you know…a myth?"

"You're a *witch,* and you're asking me if love spells are a myth? After everything you've seen and experienced over the past year, you're gonna ask me a dumb question like *that*?" She gave me a condescending stare. Okay. Better that than suspicion.

"Yeah, I guess that is kind of a dumb question."

"Okay, I'll tell you one of the easiest love spells I

know…and one of the most potent. But don't get any damn fool ideas in your head. And don't *use* it." She poked her surprisingly strong finger into my chest for emphasis. "Got that?"

"Yeah, sure, of course I get it."

After a moment's silence, she began to rattle off the spell. "Take a cloth—any piece of cloth will be fine." She shut her eyes, dredging up the ingredients from her mind's filing cabinet. "And this has to be done between the hours of midnight and one a.m. on a full moon. Next, take two teaspoons of sugar and pour it into the cloth—"

"Sugar?"

"Yes, sugar. Love is supposed to be something sweet, after all."

"Got it."

"Tie the cloth with a colored ribbon." She placed her finger underneath her chin and looked up. "Pink or blue ribbon works best. Then take either a photograph of the desired person, or a hair, place it in front of the tied cloth and say the person's name five times. Finish by saying 'You Shall Love Me.' Finally, you pour a little bit of the sugar into the desired person's food." She slapped her hands down on her thighs, signifying this particular lesson had come to a close. She swung her legs beneath her, building up muscle power to jettison off the swing. Arms akimbo, she stood in front of me.

"You got all that, kid?"

"I believe so." I averted my gaze.

"And you won't try it, right?" She wore an odd grin, something I'd never witnessed in the many faces of Mickey.

"Right." With locomotive-like speed, she snaked her arm behind my head and whacked me again.

"What was *that* for?" I rubbed my head, the victim of many a blow today.

"Just in case you're thinkin' of using it."

"You know me better than that, Mickey."

And, of course, as soon as our session ended, I drove home, hunted down the love spell ingredients, and waited excitedly for the midnight hour.

****

I chose lunchtime to launch my dastardly, desperately lovelorn plan. While my plan couldn't be considered *good* witchcraft by any means (as much as I tried to fudge the truth and smear the edges and adorn rose-colored glasses), it would be perpetrated in the name of love, and therefore, could be justified. After all, nothing's purer than love, right? Not like I would ask for wealth, or harm to come to someone, or stacks and stacks of cash, right?

Following Ian down the lunch line again, I reached for a plate of the rubbery green gelatin and waited for Ian's inevitable response. But he just stared at me.

"*What?*"

"You never eat that green crap," he snickered. "You always say it'd make good tires, and you make fun of Olivia for eating it."

Exactly. Olivia couldn't resist it, all part of the most important plan of the century. "Just wanted to try something different, I guess." Ian shrugged his shoulders. "Ian, I forgot something. You go on ahead, and I'll be there in a minute."

I went to the condiment section and fished the tied cloth out of my pocket. A quick glimpse around ensured I had no onlookers. I untied the makeshift bag and sprinkled a pinch of sugar over the dessert. The sugar stood out like dandruff on a black suit. Like a surgeon at the top of his game, I sliced the square in half and put the top half over the lower, making a nice gelatinous love spell sandwich.

Olivia, Ian, and Daniel sat at our usual table. Boldly, I sat directly across from Olivia. I flashed an award-winning smile.

"Hey, guys." Of course, I'd never be able to approximate the casual cool of Brandon Townsend, he of even the poetically symmetrical name, but determination always won the day.

"Hey, Tex." While absent-mindedly fidgeting with the long lock of hair hanging over her eye, Olivia scrutinized the contents of my tray. "What's up?"

The guys took this awkward confrontation in with silent, casual interest.

"Not much. Danny, hey, you ready for the psych test?"

"Sure am. Studied all night."

I wished I had. Love spell preparation and, you know, the usual witchcraft business at hand didn't come easy, very time-consuming. "Cool," I replied. I ate as much of the spaghetti I could tolerate and then pushed my tray forward, exhaling loudly. "Woooo, I think I got too much food today." Once the words came out, I realized they sounded preposterously staged, but I hoped my thespian skills would carry my performance. "Hey, O', I don't think I can eat this. You want it?" I edged the gelatin toward her, the serpent tempting Eve with the very bad apple.

Ian held up his hands in frustration. Olivia eyed the

gelatin with suspicion and then looked at me. "Why did you even *get* this? You've never liked it."

"I dunno. Guess I thought I'd give it another try. My dad says taste buds change over the years." Okay, a lame response at best, but drastic times calls for drastic measures. I scrabbled madly to keep aloft on this ledge of intrigue.

"Whatever." Slowly, Olivia cast her hand out toward the green mass, hooked it, then reeled it in.

Brandon slouched up like a lazy, intrusive salesman. "Hey." Once again, he shook back his hair as if it were an annoyance. Maybe he should get a haircut. Gah! Now, I'm turning into Mickey. At least he didn't sit backward in his chair this time. Who *does* that, anyway? He sidled up next to Olivia.

"What's going on?" It killed me when I saw her eyes brighten at the sight of Brandon. Not for much longer, though.

"Not much." Brandon began wolfing down his food, too cool to use the plastic utensils. Olivia appeared fascinated by how he slowly dropped French fries into his mouth, one at a time, not stopping to chew until his mouth was packed.

I asked, "Has anyone heard anything else about James Badger?" Ian nearly choked on his daily plastic-burger. Olivia frowned. Daniel's eyes widened. And Brandon stopped chewing, remnants of fries dangling from his mouth. Silence. If nothing else, I had a talent for clearing the room.

"Um, according to the news last night, it was definitely a murder," I said quietly. Of course, I hadn't really watched the news; too many romantic commercials. I just aped what Cowlings told me would be reported.

"That's just…crazy." Brandon resumed chewing. "Hey, Tex, my bike's in the shop. You think you could give me a ride home after school?" Olivia's eyes practically bled disappointment he hadn't asked her. I really didn't want to give him a ride, but better me, than Olivia.

"Uh…sure. Wait. Ian and I were gonna check out that other skate park—the Warton one—about ten miles from here?"

Ian nodded, still maintaining his silence.

"Cool…cool," said Brandon. "Mind if I hang? My board's in my locker."

"Yeah, okay, whatever. Where do you live?"

He pointed at Ian. "Not far from Ian."

"Okay." The people I had to put up with to get my love life back online. "Just meet at my car after school."

"Cool, cool." Suddenly, he turned toward Olivia. "Hey. You gonna eat that?" He tossed a thumb at the gelatin. Olivia shook her head, and said, "It's all yours."

As I watched Brandon grotesquely suck the green goo off the plate, my stomach rose. Bile gathered at the back of my throat. My face grew cold and clammy. This *can't* be good. What if the spell strengthens their oh-so-obvious infatuation with one another? What if I inadvertently just sealed their future relationship? Could this be the dangerous results of love spells Mickey warned me about?

I pushed back my chair and excused myself with a mumbled, "I'm not feelin' so good." I tossed my trash in the canister and threw the dishes onto the lunch-window ledge, the terrifying dishwashing lady none too happy about my rude abruptness. As I vacantly shoved my way through the students, I glanced over my shoulder.

Brandon and Olivia held their heads inclined slightly toward one another. Olivia's unmistakable high-pitched guffaw shot out through the cafeteria and ricocheted back toward me; a direct shot to the heart. Feeling like I needed to get rid of my hastily devoured spaghetti, I stumbled my way toward the closest bathroom.

Once there, I raced toward the farthest stall, nearly slipping on the wet tiled floor. Mercifully, no one else occupied the john. For some reason, whenever anyone hurled, students found it newsworthy. At least on school days when there's not a murder.

Leaning over the toilet, I awaited the acidic avalanche of awfulness. Sweat slid down off my forehead. When it became apparent my stomach held onto its glorious faux-noodles, I sat on the toilet seat. Chin cupped in shaking hands, I studied the stall door graffiti. Besides good time announcements, love proclamations, and anatomically incorrect drawings, a Modern Gangstas's tag dominated the back of the stall door. Drawn in the usual bulbous, outlined cartoonish style taggers preferred, the artist had been at his masterpiece for a while. Wrapped within the words, a crude drawing of a skull held a gun between gritted teeth. Behind the skull, two small wings looked prepared to take flight. Could this be a supernatural circumstance where everything aligned for a reason? Blame it on synchronicity? Or flat-out paranoia, my old friend?

At the sink, I splashed cold water on my face. The

door pushed open and Johnny Malinowski walked in. Another large football goon followed, still ridiculously wearing his letter jacket, even though football season had long ended, not to mention the temperature had tipped at 80 outside.

The school's second-biggest bully, only overshadowed by the late Bob Bellman (which I guess made Malinowski the biggest bully now), Johnny Malinowski reveled in his fearful status. Absolutely swam in it. Hooray for social-climbing status. At the end of last year, I truly thought Malinowski and I'd called an uneven truce of sorts, particularly due to my unwillingness to be bullied any longer. However, it slowly became apparent he ached to jump back into his old bullying ways, as the name-calling fired up again. Guess you can't tame a wild animal.

"Look what we have here," sneered Malinowski. Like a snake, he slithered up next to me. His extremely narrow eyes, alarmingly far apart, coupled with his small mouth, gave him the visage of a crazed, ravenous rat. "Fags should go to the girl's bathroom." He smiled, exposing what looked like tiny, sharp teeth. Arms folded and grinning, his Cro-Magnon pal leaned by the door, thoroughly enjoying the show.

I stared straight into the mirror, splashing water on my face. Trying not to look into the visage of the devil. "Malinowski…" I sighed. "I *really* don't have time for this. I've got to get to class."

"What? Is it your time of the month? Oh, maybe you have to get to feminine hygiene class." His pal giggled in a surprisingly high-pitched falsetto, the sound echoing overhead and resembling the stabby theme from *Psycho*.

I glanced at him before looking back into the mirror. "I guess you haven't realized there hasn't been feminine hygiene classes since—what?—the fifties? And shouldn't you be getting to 'The Complete Idiot's Guide to Bullying' class?"

The smile slipped off Malinowski's face, a melting wax figure. "Shut your goddamn *mouth!*" He shoved me, hard, into the mirror, where I caught an up-close and personal distorted, funhouse close-up of my face.

Suddenly, the weak neon lights fluttered with a low, buzzing sound, a horde of dying flies. They flashed on and off several times, illuminating us in lightning strokes. Finally, they stayed on, but at a much lower wattage, as if most of the bulbs had burned out. An eerie, green pallor from nowhere cast over us. Malinowski shifted his attention between the bulbs and his dumbstruck ox of a friend.

Something creaked behind me. Afraid to turn around, I looked into the mirror. The stall door of the toilet I'd been in slowly swung open. Time stood still as the door, now silent, continued to open at a slower than snail's pace. Two nearly fluorescent green circles appeared in stark contrast to the pale green light flooding the bathroom. Unusually sallow and white cheekbones slowly emerged from the shadows, forming a parody of a face. The figure grinned, exposing rotted teeth. I stared at the unmistakable reflection of Bob Bellman. He looked the same as when I'd summoned him last year from the spiritual plane. Yet something seemed different. Last year, a mixture of swirling, phantasmagorical mists and bones comprised his being; now, he appeared to be more *corporeal*. His full body appeared in the open stall door. Near delirium, I realized he wore his letter jacket, although torn, dirt-encrusted, and filthy. As if he'd clawed his way out of the grave and maybe he had.

Again, bile rose in my throat. I shut my eyes and opened them, hoping this illusion brought on by my sudden nausea would vanish. No such luck. He stood motionless, leering his idiotic, crazed smile that, ironically, even when alive, made him look somewhat like a corpse. My stomach flipped over, the floodgates giving way. I turned toward Malinowski, still with his nose pointed toward the flickering lights, and threw up on the front of his shirt.

The thug at the door screamed with hysterical laughter, apparently triggering the fluorescent lights to completely snap on again.

"You...*dick*!" Stunned, Malinowski looked down on the dripping present I bestowed. I glanced back into the mirror to see the stall door shut once again. "You *hurled on me*!"

I debated looking under the stall door for Bellman's feet and decided... Nope. I brushed by the dripping Malinowski. His buffoon allowed me safe passage, as apparently, his hilarity mattered more than a good pummeling. Outside the bathroom, I stopped by the water fountain. Taking a long drink, I splashed my face again and dashed to psychology class.

Just what in hell—or whatever realm—was going on?

****

After explaining to Mr. Jensen that sudden illness caused my tardiness, he hopped back a couple of steps, then finally let me off with a warning. "One more time, Tex," he said, "and you're going to see Hastings." His patience clearly tried, I couldn't help but think he let me off the hook because I'd accrued some back stock of goodwill with him. I must've been visibly shaken as Daniel kept pestering me what had happened. After my third attempt at trying to quiet Daniel, Mr. Jensen slammed his hands down on his desk and gave both of us long, cold stares. That finally shut Daniel up. When the bell rang, I left him in a cloud of dust, not caring to relive the nightmare in the bathroom.

I couldn't exactly explain it anyway. I hoped to blame it on a mild hallucination brought on by queasiness. Sort of like a drug flashback, I guess. But, knowing my life, it's probably not the case. I needed to talk to Mickey about it, but on the other hand, I kinda wanted to put that visit off for as long as possible. No telling how she'd react upon learning I'd botched a verboten love spell. Wonder if I could snatch one of the football helmets from the gym?

The rest of the day, I couldn't pay attention during my classes. The lectures just zoomed over my head, total nonsense. I sorely wanted out of there and relished the idea of skating with Ian—and, yes, even Brandon—and just leave the haunted halls of Clearwell High behind. I contemplated telling Ian—maybe, even Olivia—about Bellman's apparition, but ultimately decided against it. At least until I had more concrete information and could rule out my powers glitching or whatever. If it continued, I'd tell them. They, too, had been terrorized by him in the past and had a right to know.

When I got to the Bucket, Ian looked impatient, idly spinning the wheels of his skateboard with his hand.

"Sucks Brandon's gotta go with us," I grumbled. "I really couldn't get out of it."

"He's not so bad." Not exactly the most social of our little group, Ian surprised me. "Give him a chance."

"Oh, whatever…"

"And, hey, will you knock off talking about the Badger kid, already?"

"Ian, what exactly is your damage regarding that topic?"

Flustered, he sighed. "Look, we *don't* want to get wrapped up in this gang crap." He peered around the parking lot. "Besides…we don't know who's even in the gang. It could be anyone."

"I get it. But honestly? I'm not even sure if there are gangs. Maybe it's just overblown hype." Once I put it out there, I immediately doubted my own words.

"Just cool your shit. Okay?"

"Okay."

"Hey, guys." Brandon sauntered up behind us lackadaisically, the only way he knew how to walk. I imagined Brandon put my class lateness record to shame. *Outstanding Chronic Tardiness* stamped across every school file on him.

"'Sup," said Ian.

"Ready?" I asked. He nodded, and the three of us jumped into the Bucket.

After a long bout of silence, Brandon asked, "Tell me, again, why we're going to Warton Park instead of Clearwell?"

I looked at Ian, who immediately shot me a warning look. "Um, there're just a couple of guys we're trying to avoid," I said. "You know…just a couple of annoying douches." Ian relaxed, apparently finding my answer satisfactory.

"'S cool, cool," said Brandon.

I gritted my teeth. Everything about Brandon bugged me. Incapable of forming entire sentences half the time, it seemed miraculous he'd made it this far in school. Briefly, I questioned my open friend policy again. But I resigned myself to it. Whatever. I created our newfound policy, mostly as a sort of tribute to Josh, and I didn't plan on reneging on my word.

As soon as we arrived at the park, we immediately hit the ramp. A much smaller, more run-down park than Clearwell, it suited our needs just fine. Ian and I skated while Brandon sat down on the edge of the ramp, soaking in his surroundings. I pulled my best Ollies and other moves Josh had taught us. It didn't take a brain surgeon to realize I tried to one-up Brandon at every chance; to show I could achieve *something* better than him. In my over-zealous need for male dominance, I wildly miscalculated a few times, kept wiping out, and skinned my knee like a flayed rabbit.

From afar, a couple of girls took an interest in us. They gathered their gargantuan soft drinks and sat on the ledge, checking out our skating prowess. I nudged Ian and nodded toward them. He leered back at me. Of course, we both knew we wouldn't do anything about it. But it felt *good*.

One foot upon his skateboard, Brandon stood in the middle of the ramp. He grabbed his shirt and pulled it off, tying it loosely around his neck. Unnaturally tanned—whereas I perpetually fluctuated between onion white and beet red—he appeared not to have a worry (*a thought*?) in his perfectly coiffed head as the girls looked on in swooniness. For the pleasure of the world, he exposed not only a muscular six-pack, but I *swear* there may've been some extra ribs surgically implanted at one time. Unintentionally, he posed, shaking out his perfect mane of hair, gazing up into the sunlight, oblivious to the entire world. He even sweated perfectly, wearing a glowing, oil-like sheen across his chest.

After witnessing this display of Roman godliness, I slipped my T-shirt back on over my thin-as-a-rail body. Cursed with the ability to produce lakes underneath my armpits, obvious stains blemished my shirt. When the two girls giggled and sighed at Brandon, I deflated like a balloon; a weak, 96-pound, ineffective balloon. To make matters worse, Brandon skated just as well as Josh. And unlike me and Ian, he never struggled, using jet-propelled calves. Man, did he *suck*.

"Damnit." I went up to the opposite ledge of the ramp and sat down, nursing my skinned knee.

Ian rolled up and sat beside me. "What's wrong?"

I pointed at Brandon at the far end of the ramp. "Him."

Ian chuckled. "Whatever…are you jealous?"

I opened my mouth but couldn't think of a thing to say in my defense.

"Is it because of him and Olivia?"

Despite the harsh sunlight, I glared at Ian as best I could. "What? Are they a couple now?" My heart raced to my throat, and this sudden, new terror slammed home harder than the ghostly visions of Bob Bellman.

"No, no, *chill*. At least, I don't think they hooked up. But they sure flirt a lot…"

"Yeah, I've noticed. He's just so…damned…*perfect*." Venom dripped from my words. "And he sucks." I looked toward Brandon, hoping he hadn't heard me.

"Don't worry about it."

I knew these words supposedly granted comfort to me somehow, but really, they offered absolutely *no* constructive criticism or methods of how to cope with my searing, agonizing, nothing-more-important pain.

"What*ever*." This is why I'm king of the snappy comebacks.

After thirty minutes longer of Greek skating gods staring regally and nobly up into the sunlight, complete with fawning fans, I'd had enough. "Brandon, we've gotta go. I need to pick up my dad from work." Actually, while true, I still had a good hour before I needed to do so.

Brandon looked around, slumbering deeply in his sleepy demeanor. "Okay…cool."

"Yeah, everything's *cool* with you," I said quietly, much to Ian's amusement.

Ian asked to be dropped off first, because he had a lot of cramming to do for a test tomorrow. I considered telling him I knew what he could cram, as I didn't really want to spend any more quality time with Brandon than necessary, but gave in.

"Okay, Brandon," I said, "where do you live?"

"Couple blocks from here." He pointed westward. I gunned the Bucket, a little too harshly, and pulled into the street.

"Tex?" Brandon looked out the window at the suburban houses zipping by.

"Yeah?"

"Do you have a problem with me?" I kept my eyes on the road but felt his accursed huge, puppy-dog brown eyes piercing my soul.

"No…no. We're cool." Probably not the best way to handle it, but maybe—perhaps—I truly didn't give him a fair chance. I quickly discarded that notion and hoped to turn this quickly derailing train wreck of a conversation back on track. "I don't really know anything about you, that's all."

"What do you want to know?" His unblinking stare creeped me out.

"Where'd you come from?"

"I transferred from a small dunghole in Missouri—Kaplin, Missouri. Kaplin High, home of the 'Fighting Kangaroos'…" He smiled his lazy grin.

"What do 'Fighting Kangaroos' have to do with Kaplin, Missouri?"

"I spent most of my waking hours wondering that same thing."

I laughed until I realized he didn't have a sense of humor.

"Anyway, my parents split up, and I moved in with my mom. My dad bought me a motorcycle, and that was the last time I saw him." He looked out the window again. I wondered if he turned away to hide tears, but realized his robotic programming didn't include emotion.

"Man, that sucks. I know what it's like to lose a parent."

"Your folks split up?"

"No. My mom passed away nearly three years ago."

"Oh…sorry."

"It's okay. I'm used to telling people about it now." I suddenly realized the truth in my own words. Any mention of my mother used to bring on a torrential downpour of tears, but I now knew that sometime, somehow, I'd grown stronger and better equipped to handle my painful—and loving—memories of my mother.

"Anyway…" Back to his tale of woe since the banalities of my life story apparently bored him stiff. "My mom lost her job. She was a factory worker in Kaplin. She got laid off. Through a cousin, she got hired onto another factory job in Kansas City. We're barely scraping by…"

Oh, boy, I really didn't want to start feeling sorry for this guy. "Ah…that's rough."

"'S okay," he said. *"Oh, turn here."* The unexpected rise in his otherwise monotone voice jolted me, prompting me to prematurely turn into a curb.

"Crap."

"Sorry," said Brandon. I backed the car up slightly and proceeded down the street Brandon'd indicated. "Here's my house."

I pulled up and kept the engine running. Brandon apparently didn't understand his cue to get out. Suddenly, he leaned across the car, his face hovering uncomfortably close to mine. When he put his arm behind my head and attempted to pull me toward him, I finally—shockingly—realized the deal.

"Whoa! What are you *doing?"* I shoved him back.

Sheepishly, he looked at me. "Man. Guess I misread the signs."

"I'm *not* gay."

"Neither am I…" he said. "I'm bi… Aren't you?"

"No. Why does everyone *think* that about me?" I threw my hands up in the air.

Brandon laughed. "'S cool… 's cool." Why does everyone keep trying to convince me that topsy-turvy craziness is *cool*, when it's definitely anything *but* cool? "I guess you just sort of give off that…vibe."

"My…vibe?"

"Yeah. I just sorta thought you went both ways. My bad."

"You do realize Olivia and I just broke up, right?"

"No, I hadn't heard that," he replied calmly. The fact Olivia'd thought this not important enough to tell Brandon made my heart sink. "Look, sorry about that. I hope we can be cool with one another."

I swallowed hard. "Yeah…I'll be fine." Awkwardly, I avoided eye contact, afraid I'd turn to stone. "I have nothing against people of different orientations. It's just that I'm not that way." So totally inadequate at dealing with this unexpected scenario, I longed for spectral bathroom apparitions—*anything* but this.

Brandon chuckled. Apparently, nothing ever shook his watertight sense of calm. Or sleepiness, maybe. "Don't worry about it, Tex. Everything's cool."

"Um, does Olivia know about…" I trailed off.

Brandon stared ahead as if pondering this tough question. "Don't think so. It's never come up."

"Huh."

"Anyway, gotta go." He struggled with the door handle. I rolled my eyes and got out of the car, nearly tripping on my own feet. I glanced around, hoping people wouldn't see me opening the car door for Brandon as if we were on a date. My attitude shamed me a bit.

"Yeah, sorry, that inner door handle never has

worked." I opened it, and Brandon jumped out, skateboard in hand.

"Okay, see ya." As he strolled through his yard, his shirt fell to the ground behind him. I watched as he bent to pick it up.

On the back of his right shoulder nestled a small tattoo, a skull with a gun between the teeth. And two inked wings threatened to fly Brandon's Adonis-like body back to Heaven, from whence the gods had surely delivered him to screw with my life.

Chapter Four

Well, today sucked. Since lunch, everything hammered me with such alarming ferocity I couldn't catch my breath or mentally attend my annoying classes, needy for my attention.

So, not only is Brandon Townsend bi-sexual, but apparently he's a member of the Modern Gangstas. If the Gangstas are as much a menace as Ian indicated, that puts us all in danger. Particularly Olivia, if she's falling for this guy. Do I warn her? Or is it too early? If I tell her my suspicions now, it might end up pushing her farther away. And really, all I have to go on at this point is a briefly glimpsed tattoo. No, I'd better wait until I have absolute evidence. Besides, I didn't want to proclaim Brandon as a criminal unfairly. That's a feeling I'm all too familiar with, what with Hastings and his unjust investigations into me. There's also the unsettling realization I now understand Brandon a bit better and feel a bit of empathy regarding his circumstances. But what to do next?

An awful thought wormed into my brain like an unshakeable commercial jingle. The love spell. Brandon ate the tainted gelatin. Did this prompt his sudden, passionate interest in me? He'd shown no such attention before. Then again, he is rather somnolent regarding pretty much everything, sleepwalking through life as he does.

Could Brandon be such a self-centered, arrogant tool who assumes everyone—regardless of gender or sexual preference—is helpless in denying his charm? Surely, even he's not that vain.

No, unfortunately, it looks like Mickey's right once again. I should never have attempted a love potion as it'd gone mind-blowingly awry. I had no one to blame for Brandon's advances but myself. He ingested the spell. It backfired on me, and now I have a male pursuer. Good God. I need to find a way to retract the spell. Of course, it'd be best if I could do it without Mickey's knowledge. Otherwise, I might as well wear protective headgear on my next visit.

Lost in thought, I almost nailed the car in front of me. I slammed on the brakes. The Bucket screeched to a halt, inches from the other car's back bumper. I waved an embarrassed apology and carefully reentered the world of cognizant driving.

And what's up with Bob Bellman's apparition? I nearly prayed—not really sure to who or what—that it was going to be a one-time deal. Maybe the last time I called upon him, I never fully banished him to the dark regions of Hell. Could someone or something else have conjured him to come after me? Or, maybe—and possibly most troublesome—I'm stark-raving nuts. I had to at least consider it. Then again, Detective Cowlings said Bellman was James Badger's cousin. Could Badger's murder have been enough to dredge Bellman out of Hell? Either way, if it happens again, I'll have to bring Mickey in on it.

On the bright side, I threw up on Johnny Malinowski today. The look on his horrified face while my spaghetti lunch dripped off his shirt? *Priceless.*

Sure, there might be repercussions I'll have to face later, but that's the least of my worries. My half-glass full approach, thank you very much, I'll take it.

As I pulled into Dad's bank lot and parked, I only vaguely remembered the drive there. Something must've been guiding me. Maybe God—or whatever—was my copilot? Or *something* like that.

I offered my usual waves to Dad's co-workers. Already halfway across the room to greet me, Dad eagerly rolled toward me. It seems he's become faster, more energetic, since Ruth entered his life.

"Hey, son."

"Hi, Dad." I held the door open as he rolled outside, a nice respite from the cold, climate-controlled capitalism he toiled in nine hours a day. We got into the Bucket in record time.

"How was your day?" His hands folded in his lap while the legs of his pants hitched high up on his ankles.

"Not bad." But I really wanted to tell him a gangsta tried to kiss me, I puked on a bully, I further screwed up my lack of a love life, and a ghost visited me.

"Good, good." Making a big production out of it, he turned in the car seat to face me, his go-to move when our talks turn serious. "Say, Tex, Bill told me a boy from your school was found murdered yesterday."

Ah, the all-knowing Bill Pearson. A retired cop, he's now the security guard at the bank. I think the bank keeps him around because when things turn dull, Bill could always be counted on to regale the employees with stories of who was murdering whom in the fair city of Clearwell, Kansas. Obviously still in contact with his old cop buddies, Bill had a wide-open ear to intake gossip and a big mouth to spew it out.

"Yep." I sighed. "Another school year...another murder."

"Tex..." Dad fought a smile, even though I knew he thought this kind of uncaring flippancy shouldn't go unpunished.

"Sorry." I wiped the grin off my face. I had to find humor somewhere today, even if it's straight from the gallows. "I didn't know the Badger kid, if that's what you wanna know."

Dad stared at me. I wish I could invoke Ian's newfound, though delusional, talent of invisibility. "Well, it's a shame, nonetheless. Bill says he was involved in a gang."

"Dad, I don't know anything about any school gangs. I've heard rumors...but it hasn't affected me in any way, okay?" I gave him a comforting smile. "Don't worry, all right?"

"Well..." He shut his eyes and furrowed his brow—his usual look of deep concentration, although to me it looks like he's constipated. "Please, *please* don't get involved in this. Promise me, Tex."

"Sure." Maybe it's already too late.

"Anyway..." He didn't follow up. I was relieved this signified an ending to the topic of Clearwell High gangs and murder.

Quickly, I lobbed the interrogation back at him. "How was your day?"

"Fine. Did you talk to Olivia today?" Annnnnd, here we go. Every day the same question. I believe he thinks our break-up's a silly little teenage spat that will blow over in a few days. While I wish it were true, it's beginning to feel like a done deal. I know Dad wants me to be happy—he's seen how depressed I've been over the past several days—but his incessant questioning about Olivia doesn't help.

"Dad, I'd rather not talk about it. Okay?"

"All right. Just know I'm here for you."

"I know."

"If you ever need to talk…"

"Okay, got it."

Clearly, Dad saw my agitation, but he couldn't ever sit in silence without delivering a final word of father knows best. "Ruth also said if you ever need to talk—"

"Okay, *Dad*."

"You know…if you ever need any motherly advice—"

"She's *not* my *mother*." My words tore through Dad like shrapnel from a land mine. The fallout from my outburst permeated the car so oppressively that the words might as well have taken on physical form.

"Dad…look, I'm sorry I snapped at you. I actually like Ruth. I think she's good for you. I'm happy for both of you. But, *please*…quit trying to force her on me." He nodded. "If I *do* need to talk to her, I promise I'll take her up on her invitation, okay?" I added, hoping to put some salve on the emotional gash I opened.

"I'm just trying to help."

"I know."

"I love you, Tex, you know that."

"I know. Love you, too."

We finished the ride home in silence.

****

Perched on his porch like a vulture, Mr. Cavanaugh

sought out new neighborhood prey to pick apart. Generally, a harmless enough pest, but I'd still rather not deal with his nonstop nosiness right now.

"Hi, Mr. Cavanaugh." I waved.

"Richard. Jerry." He stood and leaned over the railing.

"Hi, Ted," said Dad. "Nice day, isn't it?" I unloaded the wheelchair as fast as I could to escape today's grand inquisition.

"Sure is. Say, Richard, I haven't seen your little…'friend' around lately. Is everything fine between you two kids?" He smiled unctuously, like Alice's Cheshire cat.

"She's fine."

"I'd sure hate to see you kids part ways."

"I'm sure you would," I said, *sotto voce*.

"What's that?" he called as I scooted Dad's chair up the sidewalk.

"Gotta go." I shooed away the ever-present welcoming committee of cats and ushered Dad inside.

We quickly prepared dinner—warmed-up chili—and ate in front of the TV, mostly in silence. Shortly after we cleaned up, I excused myself and bolted for my room.

Guilt gnawed at me over my plan to try and win back Olivia's love by forces beyond her control. In retrospect, I knew all along it was the wrong thing to do, but I regarded it as a "love conquers all" scenario, my trump card. While not quite ready to confess, I felt I should check in with her, if for no other reason than to assuage my guilt.

But, mostly, I worried that my idiotic attempt at a love spell had backfired and somehow made the stunning Brandon Townsend even more desirable in her eyes. I nearly had an anxiety attack realizing just how out of control this love spell could become. Did I create a romance-chasing monster in Brandon—someone who'd chase after anyone who stumbled within the vicinity of the accursed, doctored green slime?

"Hey." Olivia answered upon the first ring, her phone never far.

"Hi, O'. Just wanted to see how you're doing."

"I'm okay."

"Um… Is there anything new?"

"I just saw you at lunch." She laughed. "What the hell could be new?" Part of me wished she'd show more anguish over our break-up, rather than be the carefree, fun-loving girl I'd fallen for. "How are *you* doing? You ran out of lunch like a bat outta Hell."

"Yeah, um, I felt kind of sick."

"Are you okay now?"

"Guess so. I threw up on Johnny Malinowski in the bathroom."

Her loud, raucous whoop of laughter prompted me to pull the phone away. "You're *kidding* me."

"No, I really did."

"How'd he take it?"

"Wet." For one glorious moment, I felt like we were a couple again. After the laughter died down, I pursued my line of questioning. "Um, Olivia? What's up with you and Brandon?"

She sniffed. "What do you mean?"

"How do you…ah…feel about Brandon?"

"Tex, you're *not* going to turn stalky-jealous on me, are you?" *Soooooo* avoiding the question.

"I hope I won't turn 'stalky-jealous.'" I fought a

monster lump in my throat. "Is there any reason for me to go into stealthy stalk mode?"

The following long, uncomfortable silence felt worse than a judge declaring guilty, guilty, guilty. "Okay. How do I *feel* about Brandon? Well...he's *hawt*. But, if you're asking me if I'm dating him? No...I'm not. Does *that* make you feel better?" Her voice rose in irritation, so I felt it best to back off.

"Okay, okay. Sorry I asked. Anyway, I gotta go. Night, O'."

"Night."

I didn't feel necessarily comforted by our conversation, but I did trust her not to lie to me. While her declaration of Brandon's hotness proved upsetting, it appears the spell hasn't affected her in any other manner. Not yet, at least. I hope. Either way, I have to find a way to break the spell.

****

After racing through the school door, I immediately headed toward Ian's locker. Allison Brubaker stood next to Ian, cradling her books in front of her, while Ian fished through his mess of a locker.

Another new friend, I inducted Allison from my art class last semester. When I'd first entered the slovenly pit of the art classroom, I surveyed the lay of the land. Eight large, tall, rectangular tables sat around the room like king-sized coffins. Paint, carvings, and graffiti decorated the weathered wooden tops, giving the impression of random pieces of modern art themselves. Four high stools surrounded each table. All the tables were fully occupied except for the one in back, where a lone student sat, her large elbows resting on the table-top, her chin anchored between her palms. Even while sitting on a stool, she towered over everyone else in the classroom. Her long brown hair appeared mousey, with a rather child-like braid resting across the top of her head. Her huge, red-framed glasses pretty much overwhelmed her narrow eyes. She wore clothing best described as matronly—a red sweater tightly adorning her body, with a fully buttoned-up white collar jutting out crookedly around her neck. Clothing doesn't faze me. Other than maybe Olivia, none of the people I hang out with could be considered fashion icons.

I made my way through the maze of tables and hopped up onto the stool next to her. "Hi, I'm Tex," I said, offering my hand.

"Oh." She jolted her head up and looked at my hand questioningly before accepting it. She shook it briefly and pulled her hand back, as if afraid of being bitten by a rabid dog. "I'm Allison." I leaned closer to hear her feather of a voice over the roar of the other students.

"I don't remember seeing you before, Allison. Are you a new student?"

"No." Her gaze flit down to her hands, now tucked into her lap. "I'm a junior, like you. We've had a couple of classes together before."

Okay, yay me. Way to be the type of self-involved jackass I've ranted and railed against in the past. "Oh, that's right," I said, attempting an impossible rebound. "Now I remember. You were in my Sociology class last year…" I tossed out a guess and quickly realized I'd opened my big mouth and crammed my foot right into it.

"No, it was algebra last semester." She smiled wanly, and I got the unsettling feeling she hadn't experienced a social interaction in a while. If I didn't think it'd give her a heart attack, I would've offered her a reassuring hug.

"That's right. Anyway, it's nice to finally meet you, Allison. I mean…again."

She stared at me passively before a small grin broke through the melting ice. "Nice to meet you, too, Tex. Will you sit with me again tomorrow?" As my heart shattered into a thousand pieces, I vowed right then and there that she'd become our new best friend, no matter what it took.

And it definitely took a lot of effort. Every day I'd sit with Allison, attempting small talk while we'd tackle our daily art assignments, ranging from pottery to drawings of still life. For weeks, she limited her responses to short sentences, delivered in variable tones, from inaudible to hushed whispers. Every time she'd speak, she covered her mouth with her fingertips as if to capture an escaping wisp of bad breath. But every day, she'd open up a little bit more, finally feeling comfortable enough to laugh with me. I still knew next to nothing about this girl. And I wondered what in the hell had happened to make her such a shy, sad person.

Even though I'm ashamed to say it took me about two weeks, I finally realized she shared our lunch period. One day I saw her sitting at the end of a table by herself, three boys at the opposite end, ignoring her. I approached her.

"Hi, Allison."

"Oh, hi, Tex." She covered her mouth while she chewed.

"Why don't you join us?" I hitched my thumb in

the direction of our table.

"Um...I don't know."

"Come on." She needed prompting, so I grabbed her tray. "Ready?"

"Okay." Eyes locked on her feet, she followed me back to the table.

I introduced her to Olivia, Ian, and Daniel. She remained quiet, although my friends attempted to include her in the conversation. Later, they asked me what was up with her. I told them it'd be a slow introductory process for her before she felt comfortable enough to open up. The next day, I noticed her sitting by herself again, so I repeated the process. After that, I asked her every day in art if she'd join us. She nodded, wrinkled up her eyes, and offered me her sad, small smile.

About a month into art class, the teacher—Mr. Browning, a sort of hairy, ex-hippie, prone to flights of stopping his lectures to daydream and stare out the window—called the students, one by one, to stand on top of the front table to pose as live subjects. Allison grew increasingly uncomfortable as the procedure snaked its way to our table.

"Allison?" called Mr. Browning. "It's your turn to pose." Some of the students tittered. I shot an angry glance at anyone I caught doing so. Allison shook her head firmly back and forth but said nothing.

I leaned over and whispered, "Allison, it'll be all right. Just look at me. I'm here for you."

Her eyes moistened. Hesitantly, she walked toward the table. Mr. Browning placed a folding chair on top for her to sit on. She looked around desperately, and I knew the impending struggle to mount the table mortified her. I ran toward her, grabbed another folding chair from against the wall, and placed it next to the table. "Here you go. Everyone needs a helping hand sometimes." I glared at several of the louder students, hoping to silence their laughter. Allison stepped onto the chair and then up to the table. I held my breath, hoping my fellow classmates would have the decency not to ridicule her Herculean efforts.

Back in my seat, I scrawled across the paper madly. One thing that art class taught me is I lacked any artistic abilities. Allison had proven to be quite good, while I remained stuck in borderline grade school at best. But I strove to make Allison's portrait as nice as I could, since I knew some of the other kids would be harsh in their renderings. I scribbled, erased, drew and re-drew, halfway imagining what Allison might look like with one of Olivia's makeovers. Even though not entirely truthful, I subtracted a lot of weight as well.

When the bell rang, Allison slid off the table, appearing horrified, yet relieved. She glimpsed at my drawing and smiled, possibly the widest grin I'd seen from her.

"I think I captured you," I said. "Except my art kind of sucks."

"That's me?"

"Yep. Sorry, but my lame art skills couldn't do you justice." I held the drawing up as if studying it. "But I don't know if the canvass could truly hold your ravishing beauty." I knew I laid it on thick, but by God, she deserved it.

She giggled. "Thank you, Tex."

"For what?"

"For being my friend."

After another month, Allison handed us small handmade invitations to her birthday party. We all accepted gracefully, even though Ian groused about it later. When the four of us showed up at her home, a small, hunched-over old woman answered the door.

"Oh, you must be Allison's friends from church," she said, a wide smile threatening to swallow her head.

"Um, I'm Olivia. This is Tex, Ian, and Daniel." Olivia smiled back at the old woman, thankfully ignoring her mistaken identity assumption. Like human dominoes, we tumbled into the small, musty-smelling house. An abundance of clutter and dust lined the shelves along the walls. Olivia turned toward me and wrinkled her nose. I took her hand and squeezed it sharply.

"I'm Allison's grandmother. Allison and her little brother live with me." Something I didn't know about Allison; in fact, after two months of art and lunch, I *still* knew next to nothing about her.

Allison bounded down the stairwell, making quite an entrance, wearing what looked like a rented blue prom dress. Even though she was spilling out from edges, she looked nice and had her hair and makeup done. Professionally so, by my untrained eye.

"Hi, guys," she said. "Come on in."

We ate cake, drank punch, and joked around for nearly two hours before I realized we were to be her only guests. I suggested she open her presents. She seemed truly touched by our rather meager offerings.

Throughout the party, an obnoxious younger boy had taken to lurking in the stairwell, giggling non-stop when he wasn't throwing things into the cramped living room where we were gathered. Since both Allison and her grandmother chose to ignore him, we followed suit. I later found out this rodent was Andrew, Allison's younger brother, even though formal introductions were never made.

Once the gifts were opened, amusing stories from our past were shared. Allison's story came last and proved by far the most memorable.

"All my life, my brother made fun of me," she said, nodding her head in his direction. When we looked toward him, he scampered back upstairs like a frightened dog. "We used to plow back on my parents' farm..." I wanted to ask what happened to her parents, but decided against it. "And he used to hit my ankles with the hoe, over and over again." She giggled. "Now, when I walk downstairs, my ankles always crack." She stuck her legs into the air and wiggled them for effect, but I heard no cracking. Then she burst into full-bellied laughter.

I sat in silent shock. Her idea of a comical anecdote from her past seemed tantamount to abuse in my mind. I looked around and caught the horror in my friends' eyes. But as an uncomfortably, captive audience, we had no other choice but to join in her laughter, while her grandmother sat, obliviously rocking in her chair.

After the party, we drove home, lingering on the quiet sadness of the entire affair.

"Okay," I said. "Now I'm beginning to understand Allison a little better." Olivia, Ian, and Daniel nodded, murmuring quiet affirmations. "Olivia, would you please give her one of your makeovers? Soon?"

"Oh, *hell* yeah."

"And everyone's going to be cool to her, right?" I looked in the rear-view mirror at Ian. "Right, *Ian*?"

"Yeah, sure, Jesus, Tex, of course."

From that moment on, we banded together over our common goal—turning Allison into an improvement project, even though it's a rather demeaning way of looking at a human being. But we all tackled our areas of expertise with gusto. I continued to work on her socialization skills; Olivia did a knockout job with her hair and directing her toward more flattering, modern clothing—she even gave her tips on boys—while Daniel and Allison bonded over art and anime. Ian—well, Ian was Ian—but he warmed up to her.

Warmed up a *lot*, which explains why she now stood by his locker. For a while, I suspected there might be a burgeoning romance, but they both were too timid to act upon it.

"Morning, Allison."

"Hi, Tex." Allison leaned in and hugged me, which is one of her new traits—constant, annoying hugs. She'd come a long way since I first met her. I wish she still shared our lunch period this semester. The thought of her regressing and sitting by herself filled me with compassion, but maybe she'd soldiered on through that part of her shyness and made new friends. I could only hope so.

"Hey, Ian, I won't be at lunch today." Frankly, I couldn't deal with facing Brandon right now. And my guilt over attempting to give Olivia a love spell. Okay, I'm a teenage boy. It's my right—it's expected of me—to make mistakes, damnit.

"What's going on?" he asked.

"I've got to do some research in the library." A true statement. Even though hilariously antiquated and limited regarding witchcraft, surely the school's books would offer something simple enough to help me negate the effectiveness of a love spell.

"Whatever. I'll give everyone your best." He smacked me in the shoulder—way too hard—obviously attempting machismo for Allison's sake. Well, good for them. Everyone in the world is in love right now except me. I even imagined Arville Hastings having an adoring wife waiting for him at home. Then I remembered even Hitler had a girlfriend. Gah! I need to get a life.

Chapter Five

As I crossed through the plastic white portal, part metal detector, part scanner, I noticed the library appeared typically as dead as a morgue. The very few students in attendance sat behind computers, no doubt checking out social media, while the metallic columns of books stood lonely and devoid of visitors. The cranky librarian—I've never met any other kind— didn't even look up from her work as I flew by her desk. I thought it pretty telling that books were becoming extinct where even librarians would rather bury their faces in a computer. But I've found that witchcraft information gathered on the Internet usually contradicts that on every other website. And Mickey warned me that half of these sites are kids making stuff up. So, time to go the traditional route.

A typically snooty and condescending book, *The Myths and Fictions of Witchcraft* had been given the local P.T.A.'s blessing. Every account of witchcraft detailed in the book followed with a knowing scholarly wink from the author by way of a snide comment, denying any veracity to the subject. Why even bother writing the book?

The only other book that might prove useful was *The Complete Encyclopedia of Witchcraft*. While not as sarcastically written as the other book, it had obviously been written some time back, with much incorrect information. However, it detailed a lengthy section on love spells, parts of it highlighted in yellow. Apparently, there had been at least one other lovelorn witch crossing through the halls of Clearwell High before me.

Standing in the lonely book aisle, I scanned the chapter for pertinent information. The row of books in front of me quickly slid back with a hollow thump. I bent down to look into the newly excavated hole. Two eyes glared back at me, unblinking, the irises unnaturally light blue. Within the middle of these blazingly blue eyes swam the tiniest pinpricks of pupils I've ever seen. In stark contrast, heavy black eyeliner surrounded the eyes. Obviously female, she wore raven-black lipstick on her tiny mouth and four round metal studs lined her small, pert nose. The face floated in the shadows of the bookshelves, ghostly pale white.

"Hi, Tex," she said, her voice little more than a whisper.

"Um...hi."

"Listen carefully to me. Soon, you're going to be in danger—in both the physical realm and the spiritual realm. Your witchcraft abilities may not be enough to save you. You're going to need help."

"Wait...what?"

"My name is Elspeth Chambers, and I'll be in touch soon."

The books quickly snapped back into place, startling me into stumbling backward. Still holding onto the witchcraft book, my thumb in the chapter on love spells, I hurried to the end of the book row. Fast as a startled deer, I caught a glimpse of her leaping—nearly skipping—through the metal detector and out of the library, expertly maneuvering her way on high heels. She wore her black hair pushed up into a towering faux-hawk, giving her the appearance of a punked-out rooster run amok. A loose black T-shirt flapped over a tight leather miniskirt as she raced down the hall, her leggings adorned with what looked like spider webs. I hurried after her, the librarian still too busy to look up at the commotion. As I ran through the portal, a high-pitched shrieking sound rang out. Crap. The witchcraft book I still had set off the alarm. Without stopping, I pushed open the door. Suddenly, my hand wrenched upward, the book dangling precariously over my head.

"Well, what do we have *here*?" growled Arville Hastings. He firmly squeezed my wrist, shaking it in the air.

Ignoring Hastings, I quickly looked around, hoping to glimpse the mystery girl again. Only a few students sauntered by, gawking, wondering what I'd done now.

"You stealing a book, Richard?" With a growing scowl and features downturned, he looked like a melting wax figure.

"No, it's not like that." I raised my voice to be heard over the competing scream of the library scanner. "There was this girl and—" And what? I couldn't tell Hastings a mysterious—and hot—girl just told me I'm in danger. And she knows I'm a witch. Could she have been another supernatural apparition?

"A girl."

"Um, yeah. I was just following this girl out of the library."

"Were you stalking this girl, Richard?"

I rolled my eyes. "No, I wasn't stalking her." I sighed, slumped, and resigned myself to whatever torture Hastings had in mind for me.

Hastings finally released my wrist and grabbed the book out of my hand, carefully opening the pages to where my thumb had been. "*The Complete Encyclopedia of Witchcraft?*" He flipped through the pages. "Love spells? I *knew* you were into some hinky crap since last year. You're coming with me." Hastings looked through the glass door, captured the librarian's attention, and drew his finger across his neck. The librarian nodded and turned off the alarm.

Hastings prodded me down the hallway toward his office, while I began to concoct a plausible explanation.

He shoved me down hard into the seat across from his desk and fell into his chair, releasing the whizzing air from his cushion. He stared at me in silence, while he folded his hands on top of his desk.

"What are you planning on doing with a book about love spells and witchcraft, Richard?" he finally asked.

"No, you don't understand, Mr. Hastings." I attempted a weak smile. "It's not like that. I was doing research for my creative writing class."

"Creative writing." He sneered as if it were an alien concept.

"Yeah. I'm writing a story about witches in Salem."

Hastings unfolded his hands, leaned over, and tapped the top of his look-alike bobblehead, a new addition since I'd last had the pleasure of being in his office. Surely, a student hadn't made it for him? No, more than likely, he ordered it himself, because what would be more wonderful to Hastings than to look at a miniature version of himself? The plastic head nodded and smiled at me as if to say, "We have you now, Tex. Your ass is *ours.*"

"You and I both know that's a bunch of…bullshit…" He lowered his voice as if afraid his curse might belie his rosy persona. "Don't we, Richard?"

"No, sir, it's the truth."

"Uh-huh." He nodded in unison with his bobble-head. "And, if you don't mind telling me, what do love spells have to do with the Salem witch trials?" He would've been a *great* Salem witch-hunter.

"Oh, I was just trying to add some…creativity."

"Who's your creative writing teacher?"

"Mrs. Swanson."

"You can bet I'll be talking to her."

"I would imagine so." Okay, I'm going to have to write a story about the Salem witch trials now.

"I'm gonna call your father, Richard. I think he'd better be made aware of what you're up to."

"Well, I'm not up to anything. But if you think you need to bother him at work, then…whatever…" I shrugged my shoulders. I knew Dad would have my back, but he'd be irritated. And this new ordeal would worry him as well.

After Hastings ordered the ever-frightening Mrs. Carbody to phone my father, I listened half-amusedly to the one-sided phone call. Hastings, staring at me the entire length of the conversation, tried to convince Dad of my satanic ways. From the gist of the talk, I realized Dad backed up my story about the creative writing class and finally calmed Hastings. Lecture time tonight, though. Yay.

"Well," said Hastings, slamming the phone down.

"Your father seems to think this is not a big deal, Richard." He leaned closer toward me. "I happen to think differently."

"Um...sorry?"

"Yes, you *will* be sorry. Okay, trying to steal a library book..." He smiled. "How does a detention next week sound to you?"

How do I answer this? "It sounds...fair? I guess? But I wasn't really trying to steal—"

He gave me a harsh, loaded look. "I've got my eyes on you."

"And I feel very secure in that notion." Uh-oh.

"Would you like two detentions?"

"No, sir. Ah...Mr. Hastings? Could you write me a late pass for Mr. Jensen's psych class?" Absolutely pushing it, sure, but I couldn't afford another unexcused tardy. I didn't want to grow old in detention.

Roughly, Hastings yanked open his top drawer, still keeping his vigilant glare glued on me. He took out a pad and scribbled across it, tore the page out, and tossed it at me. It fluttered through the air as I awkwardly tried to grab it.

"Thanks, Mr. Hastings."

He dismissed me with his favorite salute, the two fingers pointing from his eyes toward mine.

****

Once you're late, what could a little more lateness hurt?

I knocked on the door of the security office, and a voice called out, "Come in." Over last year's Christmas break, Clearwell High had finally installed security cameras throughout the school and in the parking lots. This innovation probably had something to do with the fact we'd had a serial killer running rampant through the halls last year and the ensuing uproar from worried parents. While it stoked me they finally did this, I wished it would've happened sooner, as it might've saved Josh's life. Regardless, it remained a welcome— and way overdue—addition to the high school experience.

No larger than a storage closet, the small office had been sloppily and hastily constructed to adjoin the main school office area. Behind the cramped desk, overflowing with computers and video screens, sat Alf Lampbert, Clearwell High's Head of Security.

Mr. Lampbert had been with Clearwell for many years, and his handlebar mustache—the kind on which cops and cowboys usually had a monopoly—had aged into a salt and pepper spray. Always friendly to the students when he walked his school beat, after being retired to the computer closet, he reportedly grew grumpier. Persistent rumors abounded that he'd shot himself in his foot, not once, but twice. How, why, and where that could've happened, I had no clue, but I long ago learned to pay no heed to rumors.

"Hi, Mr. Lampbert." I extended my hand. "I'm Richard McKenna."

"Oh, sure." He jumped out of his seat. "You're the boy who helped put Red away last year." He grabbed my hand and gave it a firm shake. "Never did like Red." A good sign for me.

"Yep, that was me, all right." Usually sick of my notoriety, for once I thought I could use it to my advantage.

"That was good police...good police," he said.

"Thank you, sir." From my limited knowledge of

police—television—if you treat them with respect, they'll return it in kind.

"Call me Alf, son." He squeezed behind his desk and sat down, placing his hands behind his neck. "What can I do you for?"

"Well, um, Alf...I'm writing a story for creative writing." His eyes widened expectantly. "And I wanted to get some information about your work here." I pointed toward the monitors.

"What can I tell you?" His lips curled into a sneer. "I'd much rather be out patrolling the school, instead of...sitting in front of these damn things all day."

"Yes, but you do such good...and thorough...work." I danced fast to stave off the disgruntled security cop I'd unleashed.

"Thanks, son. What would you like to know?"

"Well, for instance...about thirty minutes ago in the library, there was a minor incident. Would it be possible for me to look at the footage?"

Alf stared at me and kicked his feet up onto the desk's one barren spot. He broke into a throaty chuckle. "I'm sorry, Richard, but that goes against school policy. You'd need permission from Hastings or the principal."

My heart sank. "Could I ask you to look at that footage? And tell me what you see?" I tried to affect large, sad eyes, but I probably just looked foolish.

"Sorry. No can do. Would you like me to call Mr. Hastings and ask him?"

"Uh...*no*."

"Yep, our Mr. Hastings can be a real down-right handful, can't he?" Yeah, a handful of heinous hatred.

"You can say that again." Okay, I found mutual ground again.

"Look, Richard. What's this *really* all about?" I think I may've underestimated Alf and his good-ol'-boy, down-home, southern charm.

"Okay. There was this girl in the library thirty minutes ago. I just wanted to see if you know who she is."

Alf grinned warmly. "Well, now, why didn't you say this was about a girl?" He kicked his feet off his desk. I hoped he wouldn't accidentally put a bullet through either one of them again. "There's one thing that ol' Alf is, and that's a romantic at heart." Yes, indeed, romance flooded everyone's mind in the fledgling days of spring, as I once again remembered the arbitrary and fickle unfairness of the love gods.

Alf pushed buttons and dragged a mouse across a well-used pad. "Let's see what we can do for you."

"I really appreciate it, Alf." My wandering gaze fell on a photo of whom I presumed to be Alf's wife. "Your wife's very pretty."

"Ex-wife." Uh-oh. I thought I burned another bridge but his reassuring smile surprised me.

"But, um, if you don't mind my asking…why do you still keep her picture on your desk?"

"We started seeing one another again. Hope springs eternal, Richard." Perhaps Alf is actually Cupid, in human guise with a handlebar mustache, doling out wisdom about love. Weirder things have happened in the last two days. "You said thirty minutes ago?"

"Yeah, sounds about right."

"Okay, here we go." He turned the screen slightly toward me. I couldn't really see anything, so I sidled up behind him, nearly bumping my head into a dangerously low-hanging shelf. "Is that her?"

Definitely. This time, the view caught her front side as she agilely danced through the library, briefly glancing up into the security camera as if daring me to find her. She gave a quick, lopsided smile before bounding out of view. My heart leaped with joy, because if the camera captured her—and Alf saw her— that means she's not another apparition. At least, I *hope* that's what it means.

"Well, she's a mighty fine looker, Richard," said Alf. "But…"

"But what?"

"I doubt she's a student here." His mouth and 'stache drooped in sadness, as if he failed in cementing a love connection for me.

"How can you tell?"

"Well, her clothes wouldn't pass muster for school dress code, you know."

"You're right. Hey, can you find out where she went after she left the library?"

"Let's see." He fiddled with the mouse. "Outside the library… Ah…There's you and our friend, Mr. Hastings."

I grimaced. "Yeah, well, I chased the girl out of there without realizing I was still holding a library book."

Alf shook his head. "Okay. Wait." He switched the screen to the camera covering the exit of the girls' restroom, closest to the library. "Got her."

I watched as she gracefully leaped through the bathroom door. We watched for nearly five minutes, waiting for her to exit. A few more girls entered the bathroom, some left, but still no sign of her leaving. Alf sped the video up until we hit the current time.

"Richard...ah...it looks like she still may be in there. She's been in there an awful long time. I'm a bit worried."

"Yeah, that's weird." Fear clutched my stomach with a nauseating grip.

"Okay, here's what I can do. I'll have that ol' biddy, Mrs. Carbody, check the restroom out."

"Okay." Alf called Mrs. Carbody. He explained to her there was a strange-looking girl—possibly not a student—who'd been in the bathroom for nearly forty-five minutes. Soon, we watched Mrs. Carbody waddle into the bathroom. Several minutes later, she poked her head out, walked closer toward the camera, and splayed her hands, shaking her head. *Empty.*

I sighed. "Well, I guess I've lost my, um, dream girl, Alf." A chill pulsated up and down my spine.

"Sorry about that, buddy," he said. "There might've been a glitch in the camera. It could've gone out briefly while she left. It's happened before. Sure is weird, though."

"Yeah, it is."

"Well, let's just keep this our little secret, okay?" He offered his hand to me again. "About my letting you watch some of the tapes—although they're not really tapes—but you know what I mean..."

"Thanks for everything."

"No problem. Keep your chin up, Richard, you'll find her."

But I harbored doubt. And if I did find her, did I want to? Who—or *what*—is Elspeth Chambers?

****

With five minutes of class remaining, I opened the door and cautiously approached Mr. Jensen, who sat quietly at his desk. The rest of the class buried their heads in their psych textbooks.

"Sorry, Mr. Jensen," I whispered. I handed him my pass from Hastings. "I have a written excuse. Mr. Hastings wanted to talk to me."

Mr. Jensen grabbed the slip, looked at it, and tossed it onto his desk. He said nothing as I slunk to my desk like a whipped dog. Daniel eyeballed me, itching to ask what happened. Purposefully, I ignored him. I tore off a piece of notebook paper and wrote Elspeth Chambers's name on it.

When the bell rang, I asked Daniel if he had plans after school.

"Nothing but studies. What's up?"

I handed him the slip of paper. "Can you do some research for me? On this girl? Do you know her?"

"'Elspeth Chambers,'" he read. "No. I'd remember a name like that. Why? Who is she?"

"That's what I'm hoping you can help me find out."

"Okay. Can you give me a ride home?"

"Sure, no problem, Danny."

"Great." He looked tremendously grateful. "I'll text my mom to stay at home." Obviously ecstatic over my rescuing him from one day's worth of potential embarrassment from his mother, Daniel flew down the hall, texting, while bumping into students like a small, random pinball at odds with the taller, sturdier bumpers.

I'm coming for you, Elspeth Chambers.

****

Mrs. Cross knocked timidly on Daniel's door. "Daniel?" she called. "Would you and Tex like some cookies? They're your favorite, snickerdoodles."

"*God*, no, Mom." He rolled his eyes while I stifled the urge to laugh. Honestly, I found Mrs. Cross endearing in her absolute refusal to abandon the persona of the fifties perfect housewife she'd so carefully constructed. And I enjoyed the Cross household as a somewhat odd, yet warm haven from the harsh realities of modern life.

"Hey, Dan, I wouldn't mind some cookies," I said.

Daniel groaned. "Okay, Mom, we'll take 'em."

Mrs. Cross pushed the door open and brought in a plate, overflowing with cookies. "They're fresh out of the oven. I hope you boys enjoy them. Should I see if Ken would like to join you?"

"No! *God*. He's not home anyway. He never is."

"Oh, yes, of course." For a brief moment, Mrs. Cross frowned. The worried visage aged her quite a bit, making her momentarily appear as if she lived in the here and now. "I forget sometimes Ken has his activities and groups." She smiled again, suddenly vanquishing the demons of worry and sorrow. "No matter. You boys enjoy now."

"Thanks, Mrs. Cross."

"Thanks, Mom."

She closed the door behind her. As she toddled down the hall, I heard her humming brightly.

"Sorry about that."

"Hey, no worries. Your mom's nice."

"I guess..." For some reason, most of my friends think their parents are monstrous creatures put on earth to torture them. While the old folks have strange tics to their personalities, I generally find them to be likable people. And whenever I enter a household such as Daniel's—where the love showered on their child is so obvious—it sometimes makes me long for an alternate life where my mother'd never passed away.

"Hey, it's probably none of my business…but what activities and groups does your brother belong to, anyway?" Absolutely none of my concern, but the laughable notion of the sullen Ken Cross belonging to the stamp collecting club or whatever boggled my mind.

Daniel pursed his lips. "You know what, Tex? Not only do I not know, but I really don't care, either."

Well, that's the end of *this* topic. "Sorry."

"It's okay… Sorry if I was…cranky. It's just…we don't get along that well."

"I get it. Forget I asked." I couldn't help but wonder if Ken Cross didn't make his little brother's life a living hell. Not only is Daniel prime bully-bait at school, but he probably receives it at home as well. "Anyway…Elspeth Chambers," I said.

"Yeah. What's the deal here, Tex?" Daniel didn't know about my state of witchiness, and I really didn't want to drag him into my world, especially since it'd proven to be dangerous to my two friends who do know—Olivia and Ian. So I had to be careful what I told him.

"Okay, this girl showed up in the library today. And she was super freaky and hot. But she acted like she knew me and just said some sort of…weird things."

"'Weird?' 'Weird' like how?"

"I don't know. Just 'weird.' She said I was in danger. I'd just like to find out who she is and what she was going on about."

"Okay, let's see what I can do." Daniel shoved an entire cookie into his mouth, struggling to engulf it all.

He sat at his terminal and gracefully flew back and forth in front of three screens, typing rapidly, never looking up. A master artist at work, fully in command of his medium, Daniel acted like an entirely different guy. If only he could apply this seemingly effortless elegance to his social skills, he'd be truly formidable.

After thirty-five minutes, Daniel came up for air. "Cookie me," he ordered. As his dutiful co-pilot, I brought the plate toward him. He grabbed one and nibbled at it ferociously as if I'd just brought him life-sustaining food.

"Your Elspeth Chambers doesn't appear to exist on the Internet, Tex," he said. "I started with high school records at Clearwell." I raised my eyebrows. "Don't ask." He laughed, spitting out cookie crumbs. "But if she's a student there, she's not listed. Could be she's a new transfer, but I doubt it. My databases are kept up to date."

"Huh." Defeated, I sprawled out onto his immaculately made bed.

"I then checked the usual suspects," he continued. "All the social media sites. Still no sign. I ran exhaustive searches through the local news, then spread my web further across the country...*still* no sign of her. Next, I tried arrest records and the likes of that. Once again, don't ask." I'd never seen him filled with such confidence. He reminded me of Mickey and her absolute mastery over everything witchy. "Finally, I tried cell phone numbers." He frowned. "Now, my databases for these aren't nearly as complete as I would hope, but I came up blank. She plain and simply...does *not* exist on the web!"

"I know what I saw, Danny. And what I heard her

say."

"I know. I'm not doubting you. She's just not out there to be found, and it's really weird for a teenage girl to not have an Internet presence these days."

"Yeah, you're right."

"Could she have changed her name?"

I thought for a moment. "Well, Elspeth Chambers...does sort of sound like it came out of a ridiculous romance novel, doesn't it?"

Daniel laughed and reached for another cookie. "Yeah, it does."

"But for some odd reason, I think she was telling me the truth." I heard it in Elspeth's tone and felt the sincerity, the urgency, in her searing eyes.

"Sorry. I don't know what to tell you."

"Oh, hey, no need to be sorry. You did amazing work. I'm really astounded by what you can do."

Daniel immediately brightened up. "Well, thanks."

A profound sense of disappointment, mixed with impending fear, washed over me. I sighed and rolled over. "Daniel?"

"Yeah?"

"How do you get your bed to look so...neat and perfect?"

"Um, my mom makes it," he said quietly.

I bolted up and gave him a crazed look. "Dan, I need to have a talk with you..." We burst out laughing.

"Shut *up*."

A knock came at the door. "Boys?" asked Mrs. Cross. "Is everything all right in there?"

"Yes, *Mom*." We stopped laughing long enough to stare at each other, prompting another fit of uncontrollable giggling, which try as we might just couldn't be helped.

****

When I got home, I threw out my daily "hello" and "get the hell off my porch" to the neighborhood gaggle of cats. I made my way in, only barely escaping Mr. Cavanaugh in the process. He had to be at least part cat; he mystically sensed my comings and goings.

Still a few hours until Dad got off work, I went upstairs and pulled out my box containing the last two years' worth of high school yearbooks.

I knew it'd be a futile search, since Daniel had been more than thorough, but I had to try. Painstakingly, I pored through every page of every class, looking for both the first and last name of the mystery girl. The freshman pages wielded no entries for anyone named Elspeth, and the few Chambers listed bore no resemblance whatsoever. The sophomore sections proved just as much of a waste of time. Out of desperation, I flipped through the back pages where the various activities and clubs were listed. I studied each picture at great length, looking at the hazy photography until my eyes watered.

Then I stumbled across a listing for the art club. The photograph had been taken outside in front of one of the large elm trees in the courtyard. The usual suspects you'd expect to find in an art club—the pretentious hipsters, the ever-ubiquitous stoner Paul Jacobson (who seemed to get around, which always surprised me for such a slacker), and the ladder-climbing, socialite trophy wives of the future—all posed in front of the tree. In the background—nothing more than a blur—stood a figure staring straight into the camera. Her tall black faux-hawk pointed toward the sky like a dark beacon. She appeared to be clad in a black mini-skirt.

Quickly, I scrambled around in my desk for my magnifying glass. I slowly drew it across the portrait, paying careful attention to her eyes. The less than clear photograph didn't help, but as far as I could tell, her eyes looked blank. I ran over the names in the photo again and still came up empty, nothing even resembling the name Elspeth Chambers. In fact, this person didn't even list. I considered giving Paul Jacobsen a call regarding the art club membership, but I quickly discarded the idea because, in his generally stoned lifestyle, his reliability might be suspect.

As a last-ditch effort, I called Ian.

"What's up?"

"Hey, what's goin' on?"

"Not much. I'm thinkin' of beginning to get ready to prepare to think about blowin' off homework."

"Shoot for the stars, Ian. Shoot for the stars." After a little more give and take, I finally asked, "Do you know an Elspeth Chambers?"

So many crickets. "No, I don't," he finally said. "Who is she?"

"That's what I'm trying to find out." Past time to bring Ian up-to-date. If what this Elspeth told me is true, I may be in danger, and Ian may well be, too, through default. Like last year.

"Ian...yesterday, I saw Bob Bellman in the bathroom."

"What?" Ian's joviality vanished. "Tex...what are you talking about? That bastard's dead."

"I know. I think it was his ghost. At least, I *hope* that's all it was."

"What the *hell*?"

"Maybe he's a demon or something. I don't know. But I thought you needed to know." I filled Ian in on the entire encounter. At least my puke-worthy incident with Malinowski provoked a chuckle from him.

"This is just…crazy. Some crazy shit."

"I know, right? But there's more. Today, a weird punk girl visited me in the library. She gave me a warning I was in danger. Ian…she knows I'm a witch." I debated about asking the next question, but I had to. "You haven't told anyone, have you? About me?"

"Of course not. You *know* I wouldn't." I didn't blame Ian for being pissed at me. A fishing expedition, I sorely wanted a rational explanation regarding her impossible knowledge.

"Sorry, dude. I know you wouldn't. But it just doesn't make sense."

"Whatever. It's cool, I guess, but you know you can trust me."

"I do." I finished telling him about my visit from Elspeth Chambers.

"Tex…what *is* going on?"

"I'm not sure. But it can't be good."

"And you said this girl was hot?" Well, I didn't, but in retrospect, yes, yes she was hot, thank you very much.

"Yeah, pretty hot."

"You said her eyes were really, really, *really* pale blue?" The excitement rose in his voice, possibly due to the nature of Ian's overly imaginative sexual fantasies.

"Yeah, crazy blue. Why?"

"Well, last year, there was a girl in my algebra class. A freshman. Her name's Elizabeth Blackmer."

"Yeah?" I couldn't really see the relevance.

"Yeah. And her eyes were incredibly blue. She almost looks blind. It's freaky."

My heart banged, begging to be released from my ribcage. Elspeth Chambers. Elizabeth Blackmer. The names were near anagrams. Sort of.

"But, Tex," continued Ian, "this *can't* be your girl."

"Why?"

"Because, let me tell you something about her. She's the most stuck-up, preppy, spoiled, rich *bee-yotch* I've ever met. I tried to talk to her in class, and she turned her nose up and said something like 'I don't consort with low-lifes.'"

"Did she *really* say that, Ian? *Really*?"

"Well…probably not. But you know what I'm talking about." Actually, yes, I did. "Besides, she doesn't look anything like how you described her."

"What's she look like?"

"She has long, pretty, princess blonde hair, always perfectly brushed. She wears nothing but buttoned-down, designer sweaters and 'tasteful' skirts and pantsuits. She's a goddamn young Republican, Tex. No way she's your girl." He snorted. "No *way*."

"I need to meet her…just in case."

"You'll be sorry."

"Come on, I need to know.'

"Okay, whatever. She's actually in our lunch period. I'll point her out to you tomorrow."

****

I awoke around four a.m., sweating. Stripping off my soaking wet T-shirt, I threw it to the floor. I looked through the blinds at the clear night sky and half-formed memories of my nightmare came flooding back.

Trapped in a pit, crumbling, red-hot clay walls fell apart in my fingers as I tried to climb out. Hard, hot lashes struck out against my back, which left my entire body wracked with convulsions. I didn't dare turn around to look at my tormentor. But I knew it was Bob Bellman, Satan's newest preferred soldier, ripping into my back with his weapon. I recognized his familiar and frightening laughter. A hand reached over the pit, offering me help. I grasped it and she pulled me up easily. Once at the top, Elspeth Chambers's face thrust right into mine, her once beautiful blue eyes now fiery red. Her forked tongue lashed out at me and licked my face. In shock, I fell back into the hellish pit.

I stayed up the rest of the night, not knowing what to believe anymore. I felt extremely vulnerable and open to attack, particularly when my senses couldn't be trusted. I didn't know reality from fiction from a dream, who to trust, or where to turn. Could Elspeth Chambers be an ally, perhaps even of supernatural nature, like she'd indicated? Or an enemy? Was she even real? Or alive?

I'd find out at lunchtime.

Chapter Six

"Ian, where's Elizabeth Blackmer?" The ogre-sandwich-lady plopped a grilled cheese onto my tray, probably the safest edible bet today.

"Just chill. When I see her, I'll let you know."

"Fine, whatever. Hey, has Brandon said anything to you the past couple of days?" They call me "Mr. Subtlety." Well, okay, nobody does.

"What're you talking about?" Ian narrowed his eyes. "I mean, yeah, he's said stuff to me."

"Hmm."

"*Now* what's going on, Tex?" Much to the annoyance of the students behind us, Ian stopped the lunch line.

"Um, I'll tell you later. Let's just get outta here."

Ian pushed off toward our table with Olivia and Daniel already holding down the fort.

"Hey, guys. What's up?" Olivia looked awesome in her tattered jean jacket, fully adorned with retro band buttons. Maybe too awesome.

"Tex is keeping secrets again," said Ian.

Olivia glared at me. "*What?*" She dropped her fork in her meal and crossed her arms, the buttons clanking against one another. "*What* secrets, Tex?"

Daniel giggled and leaned in for the sure-to-be explosive confrontation.

"Nothing. I mean...we'll talk later, okay?" I

suppose I should tell Olivia about everything that's gone on in the past couple of days, since she, too, may be in danger, but I didn't relish the idea. Every conversation with her dredged up painful memories of what we once were.

Ian dug his elbow into my side. "There she is."

A girl with long, flowing blonde hair strolled by, shoulders held back perfectly, as if she'd just graduated from etiquette school. A drawing of a puppy had been stitched onto the side of her white sweater, perfectly preppy in its playfulness. Her immaculately ironed skinny jeans proudly displayed a straight-out-of-the-store, expensive dark blue. Her hair bounced behind her, every strand in perfect unison as if one giant living organism. *"That's* Elizabeth Blackmer?" I asked Ian. She looked like a living fashion doll, the antithesis of Elspeth Chambers.

Ian laughed. "Told ya."

Brandon slunk up to the table. "Hey."

I nodded and stood up, sandwich in hand. "Brandon," I mumbled, failing to meet his eyes. "Sorry, guys, but I gotta do something." Not the most gracious of exits, but then grace isn't my friend. Olivia tossed her hands in the air. Brandon grinned his usual inane smile.

I followed the bouncing blonde head until she sat at a table with three similar girls, all sharing the same elitist, prep school appearance and mannerisms. I didn't know any of them, but as they were all sophomores, not too unexpected. Whatever loins are, I tried to gird them and stepped up to the table.

"Ah…Elizabeth?" Part of me wanted to back out, but way too late.

She lifted her head, her brilliantly blue eyes swimming around tiny irises. Unbelievably, unmistakably, I found Elspeth. *Gotcha!*

With her head tilted inquisitively, she resembled the dog on her sweater. Until a small pouty frown formed. Her blonde eyebrows arched. "Yes?"

"Um, I'm Tex McKenna. You don't know me...well, I guess—"

"I know who you are," she fired back. The other girls stared aghast at me as if I were Quasimodo, coming to abduct their friend to the bell tower. "What. Do. You. *Want?*" She spat out every word with slow, deliberate rancor. The other girls tittered. I felt like the unwanted fox in the henhouse, not an entirely new sensation.

I leaned over to whisper in her ear. The other girls stopped laughing, and one even gasped. "Hi, Elspeth," I said quietly.

Her eyes widened, the twin laser beams burning a hole into my soul. Impotently, I waved my sandwich in front of me, tossing up a shield of melted cheese and soggy bread. Impossibly maintaining her perfect posture, she shot straight up.

"Not here," she whispered. "Meet me over by the condiments."

"Okay." I felt like I stepped into a bad spy film, meeting a femme fatale, although the cafeteria condiments rack hardly resembled a very exotic locale. I edged away and waited.

After a few minutes, she rushed up and stood beside me, her head down as if studying the merits of ketchup. "What do you know?" She still wouldn't look at me. I sighed and turned toward her.

"What do *you* know? I mean, *you*—or *Elspeth*, whatever—started this." I flopped my sandwich onto the countertop, abandoning all hope of chewing through the rubbery, cheesy blandness.

"You met Elspeth?"

"Yeah, I guess so."

Finally, she snapped her head toward me, her hair bouncing once before settling into a solid rock formation. "I'm *not* crazy, you know." She looked around to see if anyone saw her intermingling with a boy born not of her caste.

"I know you're not."

For a brief moment, she softened as if relieved someone believed her. "What did she say to you?"

"Look, I can't handle this cloak and dagger crap. Can we meet somewhere where we can, you know, actually talk?"

She drummed long tapered, pink fingernails on the metal countertop. "Okay. But it can't be here. *Not* at school."

"Okay. What*ever*."

"I can't tonight. I have Science Club." Of *course* you do. "Tomorrow at six, meet me at the Hasty Shop on 79th Street." She leaned her head in, her eyebrows raised. "You got that?"

"Yeah, I got it. But why do we have to meet so far away?"

She huffed, her mouth open in indignation. "Duh!" She continued to stare at me for another few seconds like I didn't understand the way the world works before dismissing me with a royal wave of the hand. With shoulders straightened for a grand exit, she shook her perfectly sculpted hair and brushed by me.

Well, *that* could've gone better. And I know nothing more than I did yesterday, except for some weird reason, the totally dreadful Elizabeth and the mysteriously, enchanting Elspeth are indeed, the same person.

I glanced back at our lunch table and saw Olivia and Brandon staring at me. Looking at my uneaten grilled cheese sandwich, I groaned and then tossed it in the trash. Rather than go back to the table, I decided to go to Mr. Jensen's class early for a change. Maybe make his year or whatever.

****

After school, I found Olivia waiting by the Battle Bucket. The air deflated out of me like a sad, abandoned balloon. I really didn't want another slap-down. "Hey."

"Tex, you said you'd explain later. *Explain.*" Arms crossed in her never-back-down warrior stance. Dark sunglasses hid her undoubtedly furious eyes.

"Olivia, a lot is going on right now, but I don't have any definite information. When I do, I'll let you know, but right now, I know next to nothing. Nothing for sure, anyway."

She glowered at me. "Is it... Is witchcraft involved?"

"Yeah. Maybe. I don't know." I felt trapped in one of those weird fever-dreams where you know you have to accomplish one particular undertaking, but other, newer formidable tasks keep popping up, stopping you from reaching your desired goal. Criminally botched love spells, teenage gangs, a mystery girl, the ghost of Bob Bellman, and oh yeah, another murder, overflowed my plate.

"Do you need my help?" She placed her hand on my arm.

"If I do, O', you'll be the first one to know." I smiled weakly, fighting the urge to grab her and kiss her. But I figured that move only works in rom-coms.

"Okay, just swear to me you will." On the defensive again, she yanked her hand away. "*Promise* me."

"I promise. And I'll be careful, okay?"

"Fine, whatever..." Clearly she didn't believe me.

"Um, there is one thing you should know. I saw Bob Bellman's ghost in the bathroom the other day."

"*What?*" She fell back against my car as if she'd just seen his ghost. I told her of my ethereal bathroom encounter.

"What fresh *hell* is this? What's it mean?"

"I don't know. But I've got reason to believe that I—and maybe you and Ian—could be in trouble. Now, I want *you* to promise me you'll be careful, all right?"

"I will."

"And if you should see anything...weird...let me know, okay?"

"Okay."

"I'm going to start getting some answers soon, I hope, then I'll let you know."

For a few awkward moments, we stood quietly, the light spring breeze softly touching me, both of us staring at nothing in particular. Finally, Olivia spoke. "Tex, I did see something really, *really* weird." She cast a slight, ironic smile.

"What's that?"

"Just what in *hell* do you think you're doing with Elizabeth Blackmer?"

"What do you mean?" I couldn't help smiling. If I didn't know better, Olivia'd just been stung by the evil green monster, jealousy. Welcome to my world.

"You *know* what I mean." She stomped a foot on the concrete. "Do you *know* what kinda *vile* chick she is?"

"Oh, I don't know. She doesn't seem that bad." Of course I lied, but I felt no shame in using every weapon in my arsenal.

"She's a stuck-up, snooty, arrogant, snobby, spoiled *bitch*." Some meandering students stopped to watch Olivia's fall-out. "Take a picture, *Goddamnit,* it'll last longer." They quickly hustled off. Olivia'd gathered a reputation of someone not to be messed with, otherwise, you may find yourself at the mercy of her toxic tongue. Something I realize I've missed.

"You *can't* tell me she's your type," she continued.

By far the best thing that's happened to me in days. "Olivia…ya' think?"

Olivia jut her fists at her side repeatedly, as if cranking herself down to a more tolerant level. Finally, she snorted. "Okay…okay. I guess you do get she's not your type. And I guess it's really not any of my business anymore…"

I didn't know what to say. I wanted to tell her yes, please make it your business, come back to me, and I'll never talk to another girl again. But for once, my inner censor hadn't blown a fuse. Silence seemed the better option.

"I just don't want to see you get hurt, Tex." Her voice cracked. "If you're thinking of rebounding with her? Well, It's a really, *really* sucky idea."

"I get that."

"Whatever. What were you doing with her?"

"It's hard to explain. She might know something. When I find out more, I'll let you know. Um, *if* she wants me to tell you." My last words appeared to stab Olivia like a knife wound to the heart. She sat on the car trunk, her shoulders sunken, her head down. She stared at her feet swaying a few inches off the ground. Did she realize she wouldn't be the only girl in my life? I could only hope. Alf, the love god of the security set, absolutely nailed it...love springs eternal.

"Okay, Tex." She hopped off my car and sparked a huge smile. "See you tomorrow." And she skittered across the parking lot to her car, her nonchalant manner suddenly and magically restored. *Damnit.*

****

Tonight, Ruth planned to pick up Dad and come for dinner. Just before they arrived, I popped the stuffed chicken breasts into the oven. After my last outburst with Dad, I thought I owed him and would try and deal with their silly, romantic nonsense for one night, even if it kills me.

"Hey, son, how're you doing?" All rainbows and unicorns, they giggled and clung all over each other like they'd downed a gallon of my love potion. I bit my lower lip and quickly turned back toward the oven.

"Hi, Tex," said Ruth. "Something sure smells good." That God-awful, sad smile thing she constantly did when speaking to me somehow molded her face into an even more obvious circle. Her eyebrows raised in concern, her forehead wrinkled. She clasped her hands together underneath her chin, as if praying. Choosing her words carefully, she delivered them deliberately, yet the underlying meaning rang out loud and clear: "Tex, you poor, poor, pitiful, lovelorn boy, you."

"Yeah, stuffed chicken breasts with crab and mushrooms." I grinned, but it felt more like anguish.

"Good deal, son. Anything new at school?"

"No, same old stuff."

Dad smiled at me, before his usual fatherly look of concern flooded it away. "Ah, have you talked to—" He stopped, as if refraining from saying Olivia's name might make his question easier to digest. Lifting his eyebrows expectantly, he waited for my answer.

I didn't play along. I looked at him as if I didn't understand whom he was talking about.

"You know...Olivia." He nearly whispered her name, apparently in fear of evoking The Unnameable One.

"Oh, oh, my." Ruth batted her huge eyes and shook her head.

"Dad, we're broken up. Dinner should be ready soon, can you guys set the table?" I flew out of the kitchen before they could respond.

I planned to hide out until dinner and try not to blow a head gasket.

****

We wrapped up dinner before eight o'clock. Every time the conversation circled back to me, I dodged and deflected expertly. I asked Ruth inane questions regarding her librarian position and how the Dewey Decimal System changed her life. I nodded blankly, like Hastings's bobblehead, not attending to her answers, nor remembering any of them. But the three of us made it through a potentially volatile dinner.

At eight, the doorbell rang. I didn't care if Bob

Bellman's ghost had taken up door-to-door haunting, I jumped at the chance to escape. Dad, on the other hand, looked like someone had just filled him up with gallons of dread. His rosy romantic red flushed away into a stark bone-white. I couldn't blame him. Last year, every time the doorbell rang, it signified Detective Cowlings calling or some other form of bad news.

"Why, I wonder who in the world that could be at this hour?" asked Ruth. I hardly considered eight as an ungodly hour, but Dad and Ruth exchanged looks like characters in a solemn, ponderous Swedish art film.

"I'll get it." I folded my napkin and put it on my plate. I thought how ridiculous it seemed that the sound of a doorbell could instill such unwarranted fear. As it turns out, I should've heeded the warning signs.

I pulled the door open and stared into the faces of the Young Bloods.

"*Yo*! Bob Bellman. Or should I say Richard McKenna?" B-Ryce's words dripped with melodramatic menace. "You're comin' wit' us, Holmes." Coo-Coo giggled hysterically as they dragged me out between them, leaving the door open.

"Tex?" Dad called out. "Is everything okay?"

They pulled me toward a hybrid, the engine running, one wheel up in the yard.

Then it rained cats. *Literally*.

Coo-Coo screamed. "Get this damn mofo' *bitch* offa' me!" Benny—Mr. Cavanaugh's cat —slowly slid down Coo-Coo's face, claws extended and drawing thin lines of blood. Coo-Coo successfully wrangled Benny to the ground when two more cats—my familiars, I guess—attacked B-Ryce. One cat hung onto B-Ryce's flailing arm as if from a tree limb in a wind storm, while the other clawed into his back. B-Ryce and Coo-Coo released their grasp on me, full attention on batting away the felines. For once, I wished Mr. Cavanaugh held his ever-steady neighborhood watch, but all lights were off in his home. A calico cat launched itself onto Coo-Coo's face, while I stumbled back, not sure what to do. Do I help the cats? Or these two idiots? I did nothing, partially out of being stunned by the sudden surrealism of it all.

"Tex? What's going on?" yelled Ruth, framed in the doorway. "Is there trouble?"

"Go back inside, Ruth! Everything's fine." Of course, things were anything *but* fine, since these two ludicrously-dressed boys tumbled around my front yard with cats hanging on them like ornaments. But I wanted Dad and Ruth to remain safe from whatever the fates had in store for me. Mercifully, Ruth vanished back inside.

"Get offa' me, you Goddamn *pussy!*" In spite of the danger, I laughed at Coo-Coo's ironic exclamation.

B-Ryce wrested his two cats away with a few well-aimed blows while Coo-Coo rolled around the yard, as if trying to put a fire out. Every time he'd roll on top of the Calico cat, it'd *rowr* loudly, yet still regain its top position. B-Ryce kicked the cat off Coo-Coo with a sickening thud, sending it scampering for shelter. Several other cats milled mere feet away from the battleground, their backs arched, hissing menacingly. B-Ryce pulled Coo-Coo up by his collar, and they raced toward me.

"God*damn*," shouted B-Ryce. They pushed toward the running car and shoved me into the back seat, flanking me on both sides. The tall driver, so tall he hunkered down beneath the ceiling, looked uncomfortable. He wore shoulder-length hair covered with a red bandanna, a doo-rag hanging down the back side, the Davey Crockett of gangstas. "Yo, what caused *that* shit?" asked B-Ryce.

Suddenly, Ruth barreled out the front door, wielding my dad's old baseball bat. "*Hey*! Hey!" Her kitchen apron wrapped around her, she ran toward us with fierce abandon, her squat figure belying her speed. "You let him *go,* you...*punks.*" A nightmarish vision straight outta *Cooks Gone Wild.* I feared for her life but marveled at her heretofore hidden, inner fighter. She banged into the car, while my captors stared at her in open-mouthed amazement.

Coo-Coo cackled, the blood still streaming down his face. "Is that *crazy* bee-yotch your old lady?" Resembling a car-wreck victim, Coo-Coo really shouldn't cast "crazy" accusations around.

Ruth slammed the bat against the car door, jolting the driver into action. He sped out, sending grass and gravel flying. I looked back and saw Ruth, standing in the middle of the road, waving the bat above her head.

"I've got your license plate number, you *punks! Don't* you harm him!"

"No, she's not my mother." Now that Dad and Ruth were safe, relief loosened my tensed up shoulders. Of course, I just had to survive now.

"Richard, say what-up to Diddy-Bang." B-Ryce nodded toward the driver.

"Yo," he said.

"Hey. What's this all about, B-Ryce? I thought we were...homies." I thought it best to communicate with them through their own language, as ridiculous as it sounds.

B-Ryce laughed, and Coo-Coo followed suit. "Yeah, I thought we was cool 'till I found out you been layin' down shizz on us, yadadamean?" No, I can barely understand you. I need a gangsta translator. "You said you was Bob Bellman. That ain't right. Why you lyin' to us, forizzle?"

"Okay...I *did* give you a phony name. I just...well...I didn't know you guys and was sorta scared, maybe?" I thought if I played up to their own self-sense of awesome danger, it might help matters. Or, you know, save my life?

"My man here, Diddy-Bang, checked out the pitcha of you on Coo-Coo's camera and said you looked fame," said B-Ryce. "So, he did some leekin' and saw you be Richard McKenna, who put away your school crazy-ass killer last year."

"Yeah, that's me. So, Diddy-Bang, are you these guys' archivist?" A stupid question, to be sure, but I needed to keep things friendly.

"Yo, *believe it*." Diddy-Bang let out a wild whoop and pounded the roof of the car, letting go of the steering wheel. We careened wildly down the street. "I *believes* everything gotta be torn down, G."

"Ah, no, I think you mean 'anarchist', which is...never mind." I slunk back against the seat. Coo-Coo gritted his teeth at me.

"So you was a'scared of us, cuz?" asked B-Ryce.

"Yeah, I guess so."

B-Ryce smiled, instilling fear apparently his hobby. "That's wack, that's wack, man." Okay, "wack" must be good? "And that was solid, what you did wit' that crazy-ass killah." He punched me hard in the shoulder.

"Um, thanks."

"So, lay the smack down on me, cuz. Did you call Five-O on us?" He glowered at me.

"Noooo, no, no, no. I wouldn't do that to you…homeboys." Again, I lied. It seemed a bad habit I'd formed lately, but hey, self-preservation and all. "Look, first of all, I don't even know *why* I'd call…Five-O…on you. As far as I know, you haven't done anything. Secondly, you guys seem pretty cool." My lower lip trembled, my voice quavered, and I hadn't sold the mother of all lies with much conviction.

The car sped around a corner, popped up and down off the curb, and forced me up against Coo-Coo. "Ow, damnit! Get offa' me, *bee-yotch*." He shoved me against B-Ryce, giving brotherly togetherness new meaning.

"Yo, step off, Coo-Coo." B-Ryce looked out the window. "Someone called Five-O on us. We gots some shaved cop breathin' down our backs. I wanna know who fingered us."

"B-Ryce…maybe it was someone at your school…maybe? Probably?"

B-Ryce contemplated this unfathomable notion. "Nah, they all knows better."

"Oh, yeah, sure, you're right, of course."

Except for Coo-Coo's incessant chuckling, they fell silent as the car sped frantically through the suburban streets. Soon, we flew up a highway on-ramp, heading toward downtown Kansas City. The factory lights lining the highways flashed by at rapid speed as Diddy-Bang recklessly swerved from lane to lane, laughing merrily at his terrifying lack of driving skills.

"You know what, G? I believe our boy, Richie. He tight, he tight," said B-Ryce. Clearly Coo-Coo didn't like his leader's assessment and scowled.

"But since you done us a bad by lying to us, you gots to do us a solid. Fo' payback. Anytime you mess wit da' Young Bloods, there gotta' be payback!"

"Dat's right...*bee-yotch*," said Coo-Coo, master of the eloquent retort.

We exited off the highway, dumping us directly into a poorly lit section of Kansas City I'd never seen before. As Diddy-Bang careened past dilapidated buildings and closed businesses, his speed increased. The further we traveled, the sparser the streetlights became. I sensed eyes peering out from every darkened alleyway and doorless entry.

"So here's what I'm 'spectin' outta' you, Richie," said B-Ryce. We tore around another corner, prompting another driver to lay on his horn. "You get word to those punk-ass bee-yotches at your school—the Modern Gangstas—that we didn't put no cap in their boy's ass."

"Um, but I thought you..." I trailed off, realizing a disagreement could very well end up with my ass capped. Something I wouldn't even consider going on my future bucket list.

"You sayin' I'm lyin', *bee-yotch*?" B-Ryce leaned his head in closer, the third time a male'd done this to me in three days. Maybe my love spell's taking over Clearwell, Kansas. "My *word* is my *solid*."

"No, no, no! I believe you. *Really*. But...I don't know the Modern Gangstas. I don't even know who's in their...gang."

"Don't matter none. As I said, you done us a bad. If you wants to get back on our good side, you do us this solid."

I didn't *want* to be on their good side or any of their sides, for that matter, but no sense debating the point now.

"You tell them beeyotches to chill. We didn't whack their boy. So you tell 'em, Richie. You tell 'em not to come retaliatin' on our asses."

"Okay…"

The town around us lay in shambles. Debris littered the streets, the sidewalks cracked and canted up like icebergs in a deathly dark ocean. One forlorn house stared at us sadly, shuttered windows drooping, its face slanted like that of a stroke victim.

"Stop the wheels, Diddy-Bang," ordered B-Ryce. Diddy-Bang slammed the brakes on, sending the three of us headfirst into the back of the front cushion. "*Damnit,* Diddy! Not like that!"

"Sorry, B."

"Now, get out." Coo-Coo jumped out his door and reached in to grab my arm.

"Here?" I looked around, uncertain if it'd be safer to stay with these idiots or take my chances outside.

"*Yeah,* here." Not wanting to incur the wrath of B-Ryce again, I slid across the seat. I may be lost, but at least I'm alive. I stepped out into the night air and took in a deep breath. "Now, are we chill, or what, Richie?"

"Yeah, B-Ryce," I said. "We're chill, so chill, so damn chilly I'm freezing."

"I be scopin' out." He offered me the annoyingly universal sign of pointing his fingers toward his eyes and then toward me. Could I have stumbled across Arville Hastings's long-lost love child?

The car sped out and jumped into the street, nearly

avoiding a head-on collision with a parked car. I looked at my alien surroundings. Decaying old homes stood dark and empty, glaring at me with their dead, closed eyes. I ran across the street to an abandoned gas station, making note of the cross-street signs. Immediately, I called Dad who would be scared half to death.

"Dad, it's me. I'm okay...but I think I'm going to need a ride."

"Thank *God*." Obviously fraught with nerves, his voice reached a higher pitch than usual. "Where are you? You're sure you're okay? Who *were* those boys?"

"Dad, Dad...I'll tell you about it when I get home."

"Okay, tell me where you are, and I'll arrange a ride."

I told him my location, cowered back into the shadows of the station, and waited for rescue.

****

About thirty minutes later, a Cadillac pulled slowly into the gas station parking lot. I didn't recognize the car, but when the man stepped out and called my name, I sprinted toward him.

"Detective Cowlings, what're you doing here?"

He surveyed the gas station and immediate surroundings. "Nice hangout, Tex."

"Well...it's not by choice, I can assure you." Without waiting for his invitation, I clambered into the car, welcoming the refuge. He joined me as I locked my door and shivered.

"When you were...abducted, your father called me immediately." He flipped open his notebook in preparation. "At least your father managed to keep hold of my business card from last year," he added. "Unlike some young man I know."

"Yeah, well, that's my dad. Always frugal."

"Anyway, I volunteered to pick you up." He yawned and shook his head. "You mind telling me what's going on here, Tex?"

"Okay..." I took in a deep breath and blew it out. "I have some information for you that I think you're gonna want to hear."

"I'm listening."

"B-Ryce and Coo-Coo grabbed me from my house."

Cowlings consulted his notebook, flipping through the pages furiously. "Bryce Johnson and...Harold Grindling from Ridge Creek High." He stared at me for corroboration.

"*Harold Grindling?* Coo-Coo's name is...*Harold?*" I laughed while Cowlings grinned. "No *wonder* he changed it."

"Okay, okay...did they hurt you? Would you like to press charges?"

"No, it wasn't anything like that. They didn't hurt me. And I don't want to bring charges against them. I *really* don't want anything else to do with them, but they said something..."

"Yes?"

"They want Clearwell's gang—the Modern Gangstas—to know they had nothing to do with James Badger's murder. They're afraid of retaliation."

Cowlings snapped his notebook shut. "Damnit." He sat in silence before turning on the ignition. Cautiously, he backed his car out into the street. "Do you believe them, Tex?"

I thought for a minute before answering. "Yeah, yeah, I think I do."

"Why?"

"Well, you talked with these guys, right?"

Cowlings drove down the street, checking his rearview mirror every few seconds. "That's right."

"Okay, so you know how...ludicrous they are. Don't you think if they had anything to do with Badger's murder, they'd be proudly shouting it from the rooftops, wanting to claim it as their own, to show how bad-ass they are? Plus, they seem to be pretty...well, dumb."

Cowlings nodded. "As much as it pains me to say so, I have to agree with you." He suddenly turned onto a busier cross street, once again sending me thumping into the door. "They were my only lead," he added quietly.

"Yeah, sorry, Detective." I couldn't help but feel guilty for the bad news I delivered. "They, um, also wanted to know if I contacted the police about them."

"What'd you tell them?"

"Well, I said 'no', because technically, I didn't." Once again I found loopholes to justify my behavior. Perhaps a career as a lawyer—or maybe a politician—wouldn't be such a bad idea.

"Okay, fine. Look, Tex...are you telling me everything?"

"Sure."

"What makes them think *you* can get word to the Modern Gangstas?"

"I don't know, really. I guess it's just because I go to the same school, maybe."

"And you're *sure* you don't know anyone in the Gangstas?"

"Positive." I averted my eyes to peer out the

window and saw with relief the homes lining the streets were at least now occupied.

"And, you're *not* going to try and contact them, correct?"

"No way. Look, Detective, I don't want to be involved in this at all. I had enough of the criminal element last year to last me a lifetime."

"Seems like I've heard this song and dance before. You stay out of this, you understand me?" He turned his attention from the traffic to me.

"Got it."

"And, for God's sake, keep my card. And *use* it if you should happen to hear anything. Or stumble across anything."

"Understood." I could practically feel my nose growing from all of my lies.

****

As soon as Cowlings walked me up the sidewalk, Ruth yanked open the front door. Dad strained to see from behind her.

"Are you all right?"

"I'm okay, Dad." I nodded toward Cowlings to verify my story, as he'd lend more credence to my assessment.

"He's fine, Mr. McKenna. It seems to be little more than a teenage prank pulled by some students from a competing school." Clearly, Cowlings remembered how worked up my dad gets from last year.

"It didn't look much like a prank," murmured Ruth, the warrior woman now retreating back into the sad-eyed matron.

"It's okay, Ruth." I offered her a smile.

"Tex, I swear, you're not in any kind of trouble again, are you?"

"No, Dad."

"Mr. McKenna, please don't hesitate to call me if you should need me again." Cowlings walked back toward the door to leave. He turned around, catching me in his gaze. "It's my job." He raised his eyebrows, attempting to sear his common sense into my soul.

"Thank you, Detective," said Dad.

"Yeah, thanks," I added.

"Good night." Cowlings pulled the door shut behind him.

Ruth let out a great sigh of relief, flapping her hands at her side. Still wearing the kitchen apron—her body armor—she finally untied it. "Well, now that everything's fine here…" She shot me a sharp, little frown. "I suppose I should be getting home. It's awfully late."

I cleared my throat. "Um, Ruth…" I hesitated, not really knowing what to say.

"Yes?" She smiled at me, her rainbow-arced eyebrows shining brightly over her sunny eyes once again.

I moved toward her and threw my arms around her.

"Oh!" Slowly, gently, she patted my back.

"Thank you," I said, struggling around the lump in my throat. "What you did was…unnecessary…but I really, *really* do appreciate it. I just wanted to let you know that." I broke our awkward embrace and stepped back. Dad beamed.

"It's okay, Tex," she said. "If I can do *anything* for you, I will." Her cheeks blushed a deep red. "Well…" She leaned over, placed one hand on the side of my dad's face, and kissed him on the cheek. "Good night."

"Night, Ruth."

"Night," I said. She strolled to the door, turned around, and delivered another final sad smile to both of us.

"Okay, Dad, I'd better get to bed, too."

"Son, you *are* telling me everything, right?"

"Yeah, of course."

Disbelief colored his face. "Fine. Goodnight, Tex." He lifted his arms, wheeled himself around, and rolled toward his bedroom.

"Got a little more homework to do," I called after him. "But it shouldn't take too long."

"Don't stay up too late." He stopped in front of his bedroom door. "And, son?"

"Yeah?"

"Thanks for what you did with Ruth. It meant a lot to me." He entered his bedroom.

"No problem," I said, under my breath.

Luckily, a full moon rode high in the night sky as midnight drew near—prerequisites for a house protection spell. I had started one of these last year, but because of circumstances beyond my control, I never completed it. It took more time—between digging holes in the yard, burning candles, reciting incantations and what-not—and it had to be repeated for seven nights. But obviously I needed it now more than ever.

After completing night number one of the spell, I quietly came back inside and opened the refrigerator. I grabbed the carton of milk, sniffed it, and poured a large amount into a saucer. Outside, I set it down onto the front stoop.

The cats slinked out of the shadows toward their

just reward for protecting me earlier. I noted with relief the calico cat B-Ryce had brutally kicked appeared to be fully functioning.

"Thanks, cats," I whispered. They stopped to look up at me, tails swinging in unison. "You guys earned this. I'll try and be nicer to you from now on." Several of the cats purred as if in response. I pointed toward the saucer. "Get it." They lapped up the milk as I stepped over them. Maybe I could put my "Pussy Posse" to better use. Great, now I was even beginning to think in gangsta.

I crawled upstairs to my bedroom, shed my clothes on the floor, then fell into bed. Of course, now, even though exhausted, I couldn't sleep.

This stupid so-called *gang war* has now suddenly become my war as well, through absolutely no fault of my own. *Gang War, Tex Style*. I needed to get the Bloods's message to the Modern Gangstas and the only way to accomplish this—if I could put my embarrassment behind me—is to approach Brandon.

But, what worried me more is the question, if the Young Bloods didn't kill James Badger, who did?

Chapter Seven

"Hey, Brandon, how's it going?" I sounded ridiculously chipper. Brandon slid into the chair next to Olivia, a canary-eating grin stretching over his impossibly white, perfect teeth. I hoped it wasn't a lecherous smile aimed at me. Maybe I suffered from a newfound hint of homophobia—biphobia? Gah! I suck.

"Hey." Brandon's heavy eyelids drooped. I wanted to buy him a cup of coffee.

"How ya' doin'?" I wanted to kill him with kindness. Instead, I slaughtered him with sunshine, like one of those vacant-eyed, sugary-sweet, door-to-door religion-pumpers who always visit too early on Saturday mornings.

Brandon stared blankly at Olivia then toward me. "I'm doin' all right. You?"

"Just great." Okay, I need to shut up now. "Thanks for asking." Note to self: never play poker.

Perplexed, Ian held his fork poised in front of his mouth during the entire interchange, spaghetti dangling off it. He gazed back and forth between us, as though afraid if he took a bite, he might miss out on a second of this sudden insanity. Daniel obliviously wolfed down his food.

Olivia guffawed. "Okay, *what* the hell? Is there some sort of new bromance going on here I should know about?"

Brandon joined in her laughter and leaned his shoulder into Olivia's. The two of them looked like two giddy school kids in love, finding common ground in my awkwardness. During that brief moment, I wanted to kill Brandon with something besides kindness.

"No, no. I'm just feeling good today." I tittered and felt the blood rush to my face. "That's all, just feelin' good. Nothing more to it, nothing at all. Feelin' *gooooood.*" I finally stopped and stared at my salad, seeking solace within the sad, dead greens.

"Jesus, Tex." Ian dropped his fork after finally depositing the perilously perched spaghetti into his mouth. His laughter turned into a coughing fit. While I hoped I wouldn't have to Heimlich him, the deflection felt like a Hail, Mary. Everyone stared at Ian in anticipation. Finally, he stopped coughing, his face a heart-attack red. "What is *with* you today?" This prompted another round of laughter at my expense, of course.

"Ah, nothing," I mumbled. Okay, isn't it about time for the bell to ring?

I meant to ask Brandon if I could see him after school, but after more awkward lunch conversation, I realized not only had that window of opportunity been shut, it'd been nailed down, glued, and permanently boarded over. I'd just go over to his house and hope for the best.

****

I had a busy afternoon planned, so I called Dad and asked if he could manage a different ride home. I told him I had to study at the library, another fabrication. Actually, my grades and studies had fallen a bit over the past few weeks, as the fates' constant intervention prioritized me to chase down ghosts, both dead and alive. It isn't hard to skate by and maintain a "C" average, but if my future dreams of getting a scholarship are to be realized, I'll have to pull it outta the gutter. Soon…ish. But first things first…

That morning, I'd studied my clothing for an incredibly dumb long time to choose something decidedly unsexy, so as not to stoke the power of the love spell Brandon suffered under. When I realized how ludicrous—and possibly, vain—that sounded, I threw on my usual school clothes, a T-shirt and jeans. Clearly, I'd fallen into procrastinating; I really, really didn't want to have this chat with Brandon.

While parking in front of Brandon's ramshackle one-floor house, I saw his motorcycle standing amidst the overgrown weeds of his yard.

I rang the doorbell. Over the loud thumping of some metal song, the ferocious roar of a dog rang out. Its claws scratched at the other side of the door. Over the din of the music and barking, Brandon yelled, "*Dragon!*" several times. The dog's barking continued unabated, but muffled as if it had been put in another room. Finally, the door opened.

Brandon stood shirtless, his jeans low around his waist, his underwear band showing a good three inches. He held a bowl of cereal and slowly chomped on one side of his mouth as a cow would with its cud. He stared at me, expressionless, through the screen door.

"Ah, hey, Brandon." This time, I kept my over-zealous enthusiasm at bay.

Finally, he pushed the screen door open while swallowing his clump of cereal, the master of lazy multi-tasking. "Hey, Tex." I wondered if I awoke him from a nap, but remembered he constantly sleep-walked through life.

"Um, can I come in?"

Before he answered, he took another bite of cereal. It's going to be a long afternoon if his minimal conversation is delivered around bites of his treasured cereal. He mumbled "mm-hmm" and stood out of the way while I stepped inside.

Dirty and sparsely decorated, the house desperately needed some TLC. Small clumps of dog hair added patchy growth of weeds to the discolored and frayed green carpet. Across the floor lay a variety of dog toys, half torn and shredded. In the living room sat myriad cardboard boxes, the tops open and overflowing, begging to be emptied.

Brandon led me into another room, where yet more boxes surrounded a futon. Not yet mounted but fully operable, a wide-screen television leaned up against the wall, a video game menu sprawled across the screen. Next to the TV sat a stereo with speakers wired across the room. The metal music vibrated out, overpowering the barking dog in the back of the house.

Brandon plopped down onto the futon, miraculously not spilling his cereal. "Want some cereal?" he yelled, nodding toward his bowl of endless wonderment.

"*What*?" I understood what he said but hoped he'd take the hint and turn the music down.

"Want some cereal?"

"No, thanks. Hey, can I turn this down?" I walked toward the stereo, pointing at it.

"Yeah, sure, dude."

I switched the knob down to *two*. My ears still rang

from the window-shaking bass line.

As I sat next to Brandon, I ensured we weren't within kissing distance. And I needed to get over myself maybe. Uncertain how to start the uncomfortable conversation, I bought time as Brandon finished his newest mouthful. Occasionally, we looked at one another, my glances rife with awkwardness, his nothing but casual. His incessant chewing sounded nearly as nerve-wracking as the ear-shredding metal.

Crnch, crnch, crnch, smack, smick, smack…

"Hey, so I need to talk to you."

"Tex, if this is about the other day, don't worry about it. It's already forgotten." Fat chance of that. Potent love spells are not so easily forgotten, at least by me.

"No, no, it's nothing like that. I'm *so* way beyond that." What I thought would be an easy-going laugh, came out as an embarrassing piggish squeal.

"Cool, cool." He wagged his head up and down. "'Cause you and me, we're tight, right?" He continued chewing and staring, the natural two states of Brandon Townsend. I so wanted to yank the bowl out of his hands.

"Yeah, we're tight. Look, I need you to, um, get a message to the Modern Gangstas."

I finally said something that made Brandon relinquish his grip on his golden bowl of culinary treasures. He slowly set the bowl down at his feet and leaned back, stretching his arms behind his head, his chest muscles rippling in waves. I wonder if it'd be too much to ask if he'd put a shirt on?

"Okay."

It floored me he didn't deny knowledge of his

gang. But, he didn't exactly offer anything either. Apparently, the impetus was on me. "You *are* a member of the Modern Gangstas, right?"

He shrugged. "Yeah, I guess so."

How can Brandon remain so laid-back if the Gangstas are as badass as Ian led me to believe they are? "Brandon...do you not *get* how *dangerous* gangs are?" I probably shouldn't have yelled, but I needed to waken him from his slumber.

He shut his eyes for a moment and leaned his head back to rest. Or he'd fallen asleep. Halfway tempted to shake him, he finally woke up and spoke. "Tex, I don't know what you're talking about."

"Well, they're a gang, right?"

He smirked. "That's what they call themselves, anyway."

"Don't you guys get in fights? I hear you have guns and crap."

"I've never seen any of that." He turned sideways to face me. "Sure, we've had a few scuffles before—a few fists were thrown—with another group from Ridge Creek, but that's about it."

"You don't think...*fighting* is dangerous?" Of course, I found this unbelievable. I've spent my entire three years of high school hell trying to avoid fights in the name of self-preservation.

"I guess, maybe a little. Look, I came to this school with no friends. I ran into these guys at the skate park. They said they were a skating gang, and to me, at the time, that sounded like a cool thing. What else could I do? It wasn't like people were lining up to get to know me."

"Now, *that* I get." Even though I didn't want to, I

once again felt a surge of empathy for Brandon. I know what it's like to be an outsider looking to forge his way through a harsh school built entirely on an unjust status system based on looks, wealth, and sports. "Brandon, earlier this week, you said you didn't know James Badger. Why'd you lie?"

Brandon crossed his legs and picked at his toenails. "Well, I didn't *know* him, know him…very much at all, really. I was the newest member of the Gangstas, and they sorta kept me in the dark about what they did a lot of the time. I liked skating with 'em, but if they did anything else, they didn't let me in on it. I kinda' got the feeling they didn't trust me, even though I passed their initiation."

Sorely tempted to ask Brandon about his "initiation," I decided against it since this is the most I've ever heard him say at one time.

"Anyway, Jimmy…He was cool enough. Not very smart." Brandon grinned at me. Huh. Somewhere there's a pot calling a kettle obvious names. "You know he was a second-year freshman, right?" I nodded. "He was the leader of our gang. Usually, he set up times to go to the park and stuff. When I first heard he was dead a couple days ago, it totally blew my mind."

"Yeah, sorry you lost your friend."

"I guess I was more freaked that somebody shot him than losing a friend. I know that sounds harsh, but I just didn't know him…not really." He creased his brow, hinting at a near expression of sorrow. "I didn't tell you guys I knew him because I didn't want you to not hang with me anymore. You guys are chill."

"Brandon, we wouldn't have done that." Truth or lie, I'll probably never know. If we knew he flirted with this kind of danger—to the point we could get caught in the crossfire—it may've been the first time we ostracized someone.

"'S cool." As he continued playing with his toenails, a few flakes floated down over his cereal bowl. I hope he likes it *extra*-crunchy.

"I gotta ask. Do you know anything about James' murder?"

"*No*. Of course not." He paused, for once irritated. "The other guys think…"

"What?"

"Ah, never mind. It's stupid."

"C'mon, Brandon, *tell* me. I have some information that might help things."

He looked at me suspiciously. "Okay, Tex, you tell me yours, and I'll tell you mine." Instantly, he transformed into super-confident, flirty, model-man again, dimple to damned dimple.

"A couple days ago, I was at the park with Ian. And these two jackasses, B-Ryce and Coo-Coo, started talking to us."

Brandon's eyes widened. "I know those guys. They're *dicks*."

"Yeah, well, anyway…Ian told me they belong to a gang at River Creek. The Young Bloods. Last night, they grabbed me from my home and took me on a ride. B-Ryce told me they had nothing to do with James Badger's murder, and he wanted me to pass that on to you guys." I studied Brandon's face carefully, making sure he comprehended everything I told him.

Once again, he narrowed his eyes and stared at me questioningly. "Why would they snag *you*?" The tone of his voice implied "of all people," but putting my fragile male ego in check, I let it go.

"I know, crazy, right? I think it's just because they found out I'm a skater, and I go to Clearwell. Doesn't matter. They're worried about retaliation. They wanted me to let you guys know that. And for what it's worth, I believe them."

Brandon leaned over, sinking his face between his knees. He straightened, shaking his hair back with one brisk toss. "Man, oh, man. The other guys think that those dicks did it." He looked at me with panic in his eyes. "I don't know if they're going after them, but there's been talk."

"Okay, before anything else stupid happens, will you pass this on to them?"

He blew air out his lips, a small human motorboat. "I can *try*, Tex. But…I don't know if they'll believe me."

"Why *not?*"

"They're gonna' wanna' hear it from you. They have a code of honor they live by. You have to earn their trust." What code of honor? Beating up people, kidnapping them, making threats?

Before I had time to regret it, I asked, "What do I have to do?"

"I'll vouch for you. I'll see if I can set up a meet. Oh man, oh man." He continued repeating his newfound mantra.

"Okay, thanks." I guess.

"Hey, Tex? How'd you know I was in the Gangstas anyway?"

"Um, I saw your tat…on your back."

"Oh, yeah, that." I suppose it never occurred to him it's a telltale sign. "They make all of us get one after we pass the initiation."

"Why do you do it, Brandon? I mean, why do you pick fights with these douches from River Creek?"

Brandon stared at me incredulously, his jaw hanging open. "Because they're dicks." He continued gaping at me like he just explained the world is round.

"Because they're…" I give up. There's no sense in arguing with a mind-set like this. When I stood to leave, Brandon bolted off the futon with great speed, making me stumble back slightly in shock. He went over to the stereo and cranked it up again, full blast. He began playing air guitar—slacker's sport of choice—and banging his head, hair flying back and forth.

I turned around and yelled, "*Brandon*."

"*Yeah*?"

I considered telling him not to finish his nail-laden cereal, but he already dumped another cheek-full inside his mouth. "*Never mind*." I waved and left.

I jumped into the car and exhaled deeply. My throat felt parched.

Hello, noose, my omnipresent, unwanted, metaphoric neck adornment. I feel you tightening.

How absurd has my existence become that in order to save a life, I have to meet with a gang to prove myself? Enjoy your latest cosmic prank on me, fates. I know I'm not.

Tex McKenna…Gangsta! It had a certain ring to it I wished had never rung.

****

I drove into the Hasty Shop parking lot, turned off the ignition, and listened to the Bucket cough and sputter its disapproval before finally agreeing it desired a rest. Work crews and customers filed in and out of the convenience store, but no sign of Elizabeth's cement helmet of blonde hair. Fifteen minutes later, an immaculately clean, bright yellow sports car pulled in and parked three cars over. Elizabeth got out of her car, sidestepped the clerk washing the sidewalk, and pulled my passenger door open. She looked around and wrinkled her nose in disapproval.

"*Ew*, can we sit in my car?" She studied my car as if she'd discovered a marble-sized zit that had popped up overnight.

"Um, sure." I got out and crossed behind her car. The license plate read "PRINZESS." Of course it did. I slid into her passenger seat and waited for her to begin explaining. She gripped her leather-covered steering wheel, her knuckles white, and stared into the store's window.

"Why are we meeting out here again?" I asked.

"Because I don't want anyone seeing us together. Duh."

I sighed. "Well, Elizabeth, what *is* the deal with 'Elspeth Chambers'?"

She snapped her head toward me, her hair unmoving and glued into place. Once again her pale blue eyes startled me with their impossibly radiating glow. "You tell me first. What happened?"

Obviously, it's going to have to be her way or no way. "You—or 'Elspeth'—visited me in the library several days ago during lunch. You said I was in trouble, both on the physical and the spiritual plains." I saw no use in holding back. Elizabeth surely harbors secrets of a supernatural bent as well. "You said I'd need help and not even my, um, witchcraft would be enough to protect me."

Her lower lip dropped and quivered like a fish out of water. "Witchcraft," she said quietly. "You're *not* one of those weirdo kids, are you? One of those heavy metal, black magic worshipping *freaks*?"

I winced as if she'd smacked me. "Look, Liz—"

"*Elizabeth*."

"Elizabeth. No, I'm *not* what you said. I inherited witch powers and abilities from my mother. And frankly, I don't believe you're in *any* position to be making judgment calls about anyone different." I bit my tongue, fighting the impulse to lambast her.

Her shoulders slumped, momentarily abandoning her perfect runway model posture. "Yes, you're right. I apologize. So…you're a witch?"

"That's right."

"Huh." I'm not used to how matter-of-factly people responded to my information bombs today. "Does it work? I mean, can you cast spells and things?"

"Yeah, sometimes. It's not an exact science. And I'm learning slowly, but, yeah…"

"Interesting." She placed a long finger against her lips. "Are you a good witch? Or a bad witch?"

I chuckled. She didn't realize she quoted *The Wizard of Oz,* but she may as well be "Good Witch Glenda," the way she floats around school as if being chauffeured inside a magical bubble. "I'd *like* to think I'm good. Okay, I showed you mine, now you show me yours. Who's 'Elspeth Chambers'?"

"All right, all right. Elspeth…is someone I channel."

"You…channel her?"

"Yes. She's a spirit who visits my body. I have it narrowed down to her having either been a woman who'd been burnt at the stake in the Salem trials…or a punk rock girl from the eighties, who died of an overdose." Elizabeth glared at me as if waiting for me to scoff.

"Okay."

Once she realized I had no intention of ridiculing her, a hint of a grin curled up at the corners of her mouth. "It all started in about ninth grade. It began with small blackouts and lapses in memory. I thought I was going crazy!"

"Yeah, I've been there."

"Soon, I was waking up each morning, more tired than I should have been, and noticed weird things around my bedroom." She turned her stereo on, and a boy band sang about how much they wanted the girl next door.

"Like what?" I boldly reached over and turned the volume down.

She wrinkled her nose again. "There was a pack of cigarettes on my dresser. *Cigarettes!* Can you believe that? *Gross*."

"Huh."

"Then, some of my long, gorgeous skirts were cut short…raggedly…into—I don't know—some sort of mini-skirts. And the crazy thing was I had no idea how it'd happened." Defiantly, she turned the volume up again. I resigned myself to the awful soundtrack.

"What did you do?"

"I told my parents. *Duh*." She flapped her hands up into the air, before demurely folding them in her lap as if ashamed of her flippant display of unladylike behavior.

"I'll bet that went over well."

"Daddy poo-pooed it, saying I was just an overly imaginative girl seeking attention. Mother, on the other hand, decided I needed to be seen by the best child psychiatrists in the state." She shut her eyes, fighting back the memories. "I was scared. I didn't know what to do. So...I went along with Mother and saw a psychiatrist. At first, I told the shrink the truth. When I saw the concerned look on her face, I realized this was probably not the best course of action for me to take."

"Why? I mean, if you were truly concerned about your state of mind, wouldn't you want to get help?"

"Okay, look, Richard—"

"Tex," I corrected her. Two can play this game.

"*Richard...*" Obviously, Elizabeth relished the art of combat. "There's one thing you *must* absolutely understand about me. I'm going to go to the Ivy League school of my choice, and nothing is going to stand in my way. Any mention of childhood mental illness in my permanent record would fudge the deal. I will *not* be stalled in my plan." She glared at me like I stood in the way of world domination.

Appropriately verbally spanked, I had no other recourse than to agree and wave the white flag. "Okay, no fudging the deal." I laughed nervously. She didn't join me. Maybe this particular, blonde, robotic automaton missed out on her humor programming.

"Anyway, before I was so rudely interrupted..." She squinted her cold, killer eyes at me. "In the mornings I began finding little messages in my room. They'd say things like 'Elizabeth, tell the shrink you made it up. I won't hurt you. I can help you, Elspeth.' Obviously, it made absolutely no sense to me, but it did supply me with a little bit of comfort. I thought maybe somebody was playing tricks on me. Or something. Either way, it made me feel I wasn't going crazy. So, I told my psychiatrist I made it up to gain my daddy's attention since he was so busy with his work."

"Um, what does your dad do?"

She expelled air in exasperation. "I don't know. Some sort of corporate raider or something." She whipped her head at me again. "That's not important. Stop *interrupting* me." Suddenly she gasped, eyes intently focused on her stereo. "*Wait.* This is my favorite part." She sang the chorus along with the warbling boy. For the first time, she smiled. It shocked me to see a small portion of teenage girl buried deep within this seemingly confident adult with a ninety-year life plan. Uncomfortable as a Satanist at a Baptist fish fry, I fidgeted. The entire scenario felt soooo awkward, and I didn't know what else to do, so I hummed along—even though I *hated* the song.

Mercifully, the song ended, as did Elizabeth's short-lived sojourn into teenage-dom. "So, Daddy was happy he'd been right regarding my motivations, and Mother went back to country club living, content knowing there was nothing wrong with me. Which left me free to figure out what was going on."

"It must've been rough." Blasted again by her icebox stare, I shut up.

"Soon enough, I began to write notes back to Elspeth before I went to bed. I wanted to know who she was and what was going on. She wrote back she was a spirit I was channeling, and we'd be sharing a body for a while. I asked her how she could help me as she initially said she would. Her note said she knew things—things I couldn't possibly know, and ultimately, she could help me get into my choice of school." Elizabeth looked impatiently at me, anticipating another interruption. Once she saw I'd learned my lesson, she continued. "I wanted proof. I wanted to know that this was...*real*...and I *needed* validation I wasn't some sort of schizophrenic maniac. So, I *demanded* proof. The next morning I woke to a message that said 'Sally Beckham's boyfriend is cheating on her.' Of course, Sally is my BFF and her boyfriend, Chip, would never cheat on her. I just knew it. Do you know Sally or Chip?"

I assumed she allowed me to speak. "Um, no, don't think so."

"Of course not." She smirked. "Anyway. I didn't believe it, not for a minute. But the alternative was I was crazy. So, I had to verify it. I walked right up to Chip and said 'I know you're cheating on Sally.' He stuttered and finally said 'How'd you find out?' and 'Please don't tell Sally! I'll stop.' I was so relieved. I wasn't bughouse crazy."

While her methods needed a little finesse—and relief is probably a strange reaction to finding out your best friend is being cheated on—I understood her peace of mind. "What'd you do?"

"I told Sally. *Duh.* Anyway...Elspeth was real, but ground rules needed to be laid out. I told her to leave my clothes alone. She kept fighting me on that and continued to tear my skirts and blouses up. I finally figured out what sort of clothing she was after and told her I'd go shopping for her. I *do* have a fairly unlimited bank account, after all." She smiled at me.

"Oh, yeah. 'After all'..."

"So, I bought her some punk-style clothes in my

size at the retro store. Lots of leather, mini-skirts, boots, leggings, *gag*. I even bought her a couple of black wigs when I saw a box of jet-black hair dye on my dresser one morning. Can *you* imagine? But that kept her out of my clothes. And, *thank* God, my hair." She plumped and patted her hair in a reassuring manner.

"But, Elizabeth," I dared to interrupt, "what— *where*, I guess, does she go? And what does she do?"

"Well, if you'll just wait, I'll tell you! I'm not sure where she goes or what she does. Frankly, I don't want to know as long as she obeys the rules. Does *that* answer your stupid question?"

"Um, yes?" No, not at all. "So, what are the rules?"

"Number one." She extended her index finger, the sharp acrylic paint gleaming in the sun. "*No* smoking. Number two." The second finger shot out. "*No* sex. I mean, really. Can you *imagine*?"

I shook my head appropriately.

"Number three: nothing would be done to my body; nothing would be put into it, and she would not endanger me in any way."

"Um, what about the nose studs?"

"Stick-ons from the beauty store. *Duh*."

"Yeah, duh."

"Finally—and *most* importantly—she's never, *ever* to interfere with my school or my goal to get into my choice of college. *And*, I demanded she aid me in said goal. We came to an agreement." I imagined a contract being drawn up by the family lawyers, Elizabeth signing it in the morning, Elspeth by candlelight at night. In blood.

"So, I keep a set of her stuff in my locker at school. Even though she's *not* supposed to surface at school.

But, whatever, just in case of emergencies. I suppose *this* must qualify as an emergency."

"Yeah, I guess it is an emergency. So, um, how did you narrow Elspeth's identity down to your two selections of who she was in a past life?"

She shrugged and folded her hands again. Good upbringing and all that. "Things she's said in her notes, I suppose. And I did research on her name." Huh. She found more than Daniel could? "Richard...I need to know. It's *my* body you're dragging into this. What kind of trouble are you in?"

"I'm not really sure. But I guess you do have a right to know everything I do." I explained my involvement with the gangs, James Badger's murder, and the ghost of Bob Bellman, keeping everyone's name out of it.

She looked stunned. Finally, I succeeded in shutting her up. "Wow. Just...*wow*. Please tell me you're not crazy."

"I'm not crazy. Well, any more than your typical teenage boy, I guess."

"Wow. And I thought *my* lives were screwed up." She tittered before throwing her hand to her mouth to stifle it.

"Yeah, thanks." For all the amusement I've provided people the last few days, I should seriously consider a stand-up comedy routine.

"I'm sorry," she said, looking nearly human and breaking through the porcelain perfection.

"Okay. What's next?"

"What do you mean?"

"Well, it seems Elspeth offered me her help. She's connected to the spiritual plane, and I need to talk to her again."

"It doesn't *work* that way, *Richard*. She's of her own mind." Well, half a mind, really. "She'll come to you when you need her. I've tried to call on her before, but it didn't work. She's pretty stubborn." Ah, takes one to know one.

"Okay, so...I just wait around?"

She nodded, her hair never breaking stride. "Yes. That's all you can do."

I sighed. "All right. Hey, Elizabeth?"

"Yes?"

"Once this is over—I mean, the part about my being in danger and everything—I know someone who can probably help you."

She frowned. "What do you mean?"

"My, um, mentor, I guess you'd call her. I'm pretty sure she can help you. She might be able to find out more about Elspeth, by talking to her....or even..."

"What?"

"She might be able to send Elspeth on to her rightful place of rest. If that's what you want."

Elizabeth's face transformed from relief to fear and finally, concern. Totally more expression than I'd seen from her, and it all happened within a matter of seconds. "Thank you, but...let me think about it, okay?"

Surprised by her reaction, I agreed with a nod.

"Um, you are going to keep my secret, right?" It didn't take her long to regain the money-taught-and-bought composure I've grown to loathe.

"Yeah, of course. You kinda know a lot of my secrets, too, you know."

"I guess I do. Richard, thank you for believing me

and not treating me like I'm insane." Obviously, humility felt as wrong on her as a pair of overalls.

"No problem. I could say the same thing about you. What I told you is not exactly easy to digest."

"Yes, I suppose you're right." She shot me a quick smile before the sides of her small mouth turned downward. "Now, get out."

"Um, okay." I scooted out of the car. Shutting the door, I bent down to say goodbye, but she'd already shifted into reverse, head swiveled to look out the back windshield. "Guess I'll see you around," I called after her. The store attendant watched me, shaking his head, his cigarette ash falling upon the newly washed sidewalk. "Women," I said, trying desperately to save face. I raised my hands in the universal gesture of male camaraderie. The clerk nodded empathetically.

And now, I wait. But, for what exactly? Trouble on the spiritual and physical planes? I hope Elspeth shows up soon to give me some guidance.

Chapter Eight

With his head buried deep inside his tornado-wracked excuse for a locker, Ian provided an easy target to sneak up on.

"*Ian.*"

Jank! He banged his head on the shelf. "Ow! *Damnit,* Tex." He punched me in the shoulder, hard enough to stop my chuckling.

"Sorry, man, couldn't resist. Hey, have you seen anything…messed up?"

He looked at me, puzzled. "*Oh,* you mean Bellman, right?"

"Well, yeah, that or anything else."

"No, haven't seen him. Thank *God.* How'd your date go with Elizabeth Blackmer?"

"Yeah, well, it wasn't a date. And she's pretty much everything you said she was."

"Told ya. So, she wasn't your hot punk chick?"

"No, she sure wasn't." Elizabeth asked me to keep her second identity quiet, and I meant to uphold my promise, unless Ian needed to know due to a life or death circumstance. But right now, I didn't think anyone would benefit from full disclosure.

"Morning, guys." Allison threw her arms around me, nearly bowling me over.

"Hey, Allison."

Ian smiled as sweetly as he could, a sort of

sideways smirk.

"Hi, Ian." It's funny she didn't offer Ian a hug. I wonder if a discretely withheld hug is her 'tell' she's into someone. They stared at each other while I felt extraneous.

"Um, you ready to draw some apples today, Allison?" I asked.

She laughed. "Yeah, I guess so." Her cheeks turned nearly full apple-red themselves. Good Lord, spring love is in the air, except within my immediate perimeter.

"Me? I'm wondering what I'm doing in that class. My apples look like lumpy bowling balls." Suddenly, someone grabbed my arm. I whirled around to stare into Brandon's eyes, way too into my personal space. I guess spring love has indeed chosen to invade my domain.

I backed up and said, "Brandon, what's goin' on?"

Panicked alertness brightened his eyes more than usual. "I gotta talk to you."

"Ah, okay." I said my goodbyes to Ian and Allison, as Brandon, still gripping my arm, dragged me to the closest bathroom. He pushed open the door and looked around for other students.

"Brandon, you can let go now."

"Huh? Oh, sorry." A sheepish grin crawled over his face. "The guys want to meet you tonight."

"Tonight? What time?"

"Nine. 'Sthat cool?"

"Yeah, I can make that. Where?"

"The skate park." Brandon teetered back and forth on his feet as if he had to go to the bathroom. His fidgeting worried me because nothing ever rocked his world.

"Which skate park?" A sudden cold wave of fear rushed down my spine.

"Clearwell."

"*Clearwell*? What if the Young Bloods are there, too? I do *not* want to get into a gang fight."

"I don't really think we can ask 'em to change it."

"*Damnit*. All right, whatever." I envisioned myself in a hospital bed, tubes running in and out of every imaginable orifice.

"Tex…there's one other thing." Words that are right up there with *we need to talk* in terms of harbingers of doom. "They're not gonna listen to what you have to say until you join us. 'Till you become a Modern Gangsta."

Of course, that's the way it has to be, no problem. I sighed and looked out the non-frosted section of the bathroom window. Tree limbs swayed back and forth, goading me, delivering "Nature's Wave" from the grandstands of the gods. Real funny, guys, *real* funny.

****

The orange sun nearly vanished over the horizon as the moon fought for dominance within the night skies. An eerie, mauve-purplish hue lit the sky as I waited for my visitors. With the humidity high, a breeze swirled the hot air around, cooking me in the simmering, cement bowl of the skate park. I was alone, and thankful for that small favor. Not only did I not want to encounter the Young Bloods, but I didn't want anyone to see me consorting with Clearwell's gang, either.

I sat at the very far end of the park with my back up against one of the tall, stone graffiti-laden ramps. In the past, I've noticed kids sitting back here, and I now recognized it as a safety precaution more than anything. Skate parks are a dangerous place to hang out these days.

The spring wind picked up a few straggling fall leaves and spun them around the park, darting around the ramps and steps. The park's emptiness created an exaggerated sound receptor, magnifying noises made by anything that moved within the adjacent block. An occasional car drove by, sweeping me with its headlights, the sound of its engine reverberating off the walls. Every time I saw a car, I braced myself for the upcoming encounter…until it passed, trailing off into the darkness. My armpits sweated pools as fear mounted. A far-off train whistle called out into the night, mournful and sad, as if wailing for the lost souls still wandering at this time of night. A few minutes before ten o'clock, I heard voices approaching from the entrance of the park.

Three dark silhouettes mounted the top of the wall opposite me, before rolling down the ramp. The sound of their rackety, skateboard wheels set my nerves on edge.

"Tex?" Brandon called out.

I stood up and cleared my throat. "Yeah, hey, I'm here." They rolled toward me, Brandon first.

"Hey, Tex," said Brandon. "Sorry we're late…"

"It's cool."

Behind Brandon, another figure strode forward, moonlight illuminating his face. He suffered from an acute case of acne scarring. Pockmarks produced shadows within shadows. Of course, he wore his long-billed ball cap turned sideways. A too large T-shirt draped over his equally long, baggy black shorts. "This is E-Sizzle," said Brandon. Oh my God, here we go again. But I actually recognized him as a sophomore named Eric Smith, who had been in my gym class last year. We never really spoke, other than an occasional hallway nod.

"Hey, E-Sizzle." The name sounded foolish coming out of my mouth. "I think you were in my gym class last year."

"I think you be right." I never heard him speak like that before. Just what compels these guys to talk this way? Do they go through comprehensive induction courses of watching videos, and listening to training tapes at night? Are they brainwashed? Or do they suddenly wake up one morning and say "by shizzle, yo, this be my new thang"?

"Tex," said the final figure, his hoodie clamped tightly around his head. I immediately recognized the deep, raspy voice. He pulled down his hood, exposing his face.

"Hey, Ken," I said to Daniel's older brother. He swaggered into the moonlight, shoulders hunched over, hands in his pockets. Sweat matted his long hair to his head. He folded his near uni-brow and glared at me. Now I know what Ken's extra-curricular clubs and hobbies are, but then I suspected it all along.

"Call me K-Cross," he said.

"Okay. K-Cross." Man, did I *ever* want to call him "Kenneth."

"Bran says you gots some hot goss for us. I ain't cool on you, 'cause you hang wit' my geeky blood-brotha', but Bran vouches for ya', know what I'm sayin'?"

And me without my *Gangsta To English*

Dictionary. "That's cool," I said. I looked to Brandon for support, but got nothing but an occasional gleam of his white teeth. Of course. Even in the darkness, damn Brandon's a supermodel. "Okay, I have a message for you from—"

"*Hold* up, hold up, hold *up,* holmes. I knows what Bran laid down. But I wanna' know why? Why you messed up wit' those foo's? Why you tryna' pass on intel?"

"Yeah, G, what up?" said E-Sizzle, who obviously fills the mandatory adjunct Coo-Coo role of this gang.

"Look, I really, *really* don't want to even get mixed up in this. The Young Bloods just picked on me randomly to give you the message because they found out I was a Clearwell student."

"Yo, how we know we can trust you, G?" asked Ken. "Alls we know, yo' posse could be waitin' in hidin' for us."

I looked up to the stars for enlightenment on how to deal with this strange species. "I am *not* a member of the Young Bloods, *nor* am I friends with them. This isn't some melodramatic, villainous death-trap I'm setting up." E-Sizzle appeared confused. "I'm telling you guys the *truth.* I'm just trying to prevent another killing." I probably pushed them too far, but my patience with "gangstas" waned.

Ken placed a hand on E-Sizzle's chest, stopping him from confronting me. "Step off, yo," said Ken. "A'ight, here's what we gonna do. I don't trust you, so's you gotta gain our trust. You gotta become with us."

"Okay, whatever. Boom, I'm a Modern Gangsta." Even though Brandon warned me about this, I hoped I could revoke my membership as soon as they listened to me. And I sure didn't want to be charged any dues.

"Ain't that easy, holmes." Ken shook his head.

"Yeah," echoed E-Sizzle. "Ain't easy."

Brandon kept his mouth shut. *Thanks, Brandon.* I wish his witchcraft-induced hots for me would inspire him to leap to my defense, but he chose to hitchhike down the low road.

"What've I got to do?"

"*Initiation,* holmes." I nearly expected E-Sizzle in his excitement to clap his hands and perform a little down-home jig.

"'Sright, G," said Ken. "Now, what we gonna have our boy do? Openin' the floor for sugs."

"Have him whack a *Blood*!" screamed E-Sizzle.

"I'm *not* going to *whack* anyone. In case you forgot, I'm here to *save* a life."

"Boy gotta point." Ken rubbed his hand underneath his fuzz-covered chin. "What you say, B?" He eyeballed the ever-silent Brandon.

"I say…we just lissen to him, G," said Brandon quietly.

An uncomfortable silence filled the air. I couldn't make out the details, but I knew Brandon received the stare-down of his life.

Finally, Ken said, "I know exactly what we gots to have you do." A crooked smile stretched across his face. "You gonna get us a souvenir."

"Uh, what would that be?" I suppose a nice Florida T-shirt wouldn't fit the bill.

"You gots to bring us the bobblehead of Arville Hastings." His voice careened off the cement walls.

"Um, just how am I going to do *that*?"

"Not my *prob,* cuz." He pinched my cheek and shook it like a lecherous, drunken uncle. "But if you wants us to believe y'all, and save a life…" He said the last phrase in a whiny, high-pitched voice. "Then you *best* be findin' a way."

"You're asking me to do the impossible."

"*Look,* holmes…" He jabbed his finger into my chest. Brandon stepped forward then stopped dead. "Those pussies done killed my homie. Until I find out diff, that's just the way it is."

"And that's the kinda thinking that made our country great," I muttered.

"*What* was that, holmes?"

"Nothing."

"'S what I thought." He dropped his board and raced toward the entrance, his two cronies following him.

E-Sizzle turned around and yelled, "Best be bringin' it to us."

As they broached the top of the wall, Brandon turned, board in hand, and shook his head. He hopped down, leaving me alone in the park with my thoughts.

Guess I need to nick the bobblehead of Arville Hastings.

* * * *

Since I had some recon to do, I arrived at school early the next morning. As I walked by the office, I checked out the door, which had an old-fashioned lock on the doorknob. Pushing the door open, I saw two security cameras bolted high on the walls, constantly whizzing and slowly oscillating to cover the entire office. Mrs. Carbody sniffed and went back to her duty of shuffling papers. Through the swinging doors on the office-wide front desk sat Hastings's office. I leaned over the desk to see if I could spy what—if any—sort of lock barred Hastings's door.

"Can I help you?" asked Mrs. Carbody. Great, the one time she doesn't snub me is the one occasion I need her to.

"Ah, no…I'm just looking."

She pressed her lips tightly and smacked the pile of papers on top of the desk. "This is *not* a candy store, Mr. McKenna. I suggest you *look* elsewhere." She scowled, her eyes tiny slits behind her thick glasses.

"No, no. I mean, I was looking for someone. I thought he came in here."

Mrs. Carbody looked around, swiveling her head to and fro exaggeratedly, like a crane, knowing full well we're the only ones in the office. "Well, now. I certainly don't *see* anyone else in here. Do you, Mr. McKenna?"

"No. Guess I was mistaken. Sorry." I lingered, surveying the office for my debut into the world of criminal activity. I noticed an open wooden cabinet attached to the back wall. Within it hung a multitude of keys resting on hooks, small labels above them indicating what they opened.

Mrs. Carbody's bitter smile threatened to eat her face. "Well? Don't you have somewhere else to be, Mr. McKenna?"

"Yes, Mrs. Carbody."

Not only is this next to impossible, it's just plain stupid. Even if I am successful in acquiring Hastings's bobblehead, how in the world does it prove to Ken and company I'm telling the truth? Furthermore, if I'm caught, it could ruin my life, and I could end up in a juvenile home—or worse, should matters take a wrong turn. How in the hell did I get into this mess? I'd been minding my own business, not interfering with matters that didn't concern me. I'm not a thief, nor did I by any means want to be a gangsta. Things grew worse and worse as my life spiraled out of what little control I had to begin with.

Yet, in the back of my mind, I justified the means to get to the end. I'm trying to stop a killing—maybe more than one. This gave me the kick-in-the-pants burst of courage I needed.

Not having slept the night before, I'd chugged gallons of coffee that morning. Now, my bladder begged for relief, so I sought out the nearest bathroom. I passed on the first floor bathroom; too many ghosts. I leaped up the hallway stairs, two steps at a time, hoping not to jiggle anything loose.

Unzipping as soon as I stepped into the bathroom, I ran to the nearest urinal. Something odd challenged the air, almost an electrical charge, like a prelude to a lightning storm. I turned to look at the toilet stalls behind me to make sure all doors stayed shut. Since Bellman liked haunting toilets, I didn't want to get caught with my pants down, so to speak.

"Hi, Tex," whispered a soft voice.

"*Jesus!*" My bladder clamped shut. Elspeth grinned, one leather-clad arm resting casually on the urinal next to me, the other placed sassily on her hip. As she leaned against the urinal, I knew Elizabeth wouldn't approve. I tucked myself into the urinal as far as I could. "Elspeth."

"What ya' doin', Tex?" Her frosty eyes traveled downward. I pushed even further into the urinal. She lifted one eyebrow and brought her gaze back up to meet mine.

"Um…" My face burned in embarrassment, and if I could, I would've risked who knows what sort of germs and crawled deep inside the urinal. I desperately want—need—to talk to Elspeth again, but I really prefer it not to be under these circumstances.

"Tex, when you try to steal the bobblehead, make sure you bring some help. Don't go it alone." Her lips closed to a small circle. "Get it?"

"Uh, yeah."

"Oh, you should wear your black sweater. You look good in black."

My mortification kept me from meeting her eyes. "I'd really like to talk to you, um, somewhere else. *Soon*, Elspeth."

"Cool. But now? Gotta run." She straightened up and bounded out of the bathroom on the tiptoes of her boots. Her leather skirt stayed securely in place, barely covering her bottom. After pulling open the door, she looked in both directions. She turned back and said, "I'll be in touch."

I expelled a great burst of air through my mouth and returned to the business of emptying my bladder when the door cracked open. Once again, a dam wall rose within my body.

"*Richard*!" Bent over and out of breath, Alf Lampbert had his hand over his holstered gun. "I thought I saw your mystery girl leave this bathroom just now, on the cameras."

"Oh, hey, Alf. No, I haven't seen anybody in here." This is ridiculous. I zipped up, jam-packed bladder and all.

Alf rested one hand against the tiled wall. "Are you *sure* about that, Richard?"

"As far as I know, yes. I mean I was doing my duty…" I hitched my thumb back at the urinal. "Maybe I didn't even hear her if she was here. I don't know."

"Well, it just seems a little…*hinky*, if you ask me." He rubbed his face, kneading his rubbery cheeks back and forth. "It's kind of strange this appeared to be the same young lady you'd been inquiring about earlier. And here she is, coming out of the same bathroom you're in."

"Wow, that is strange. But, really, nothing funny went on in here." I felt bad lying to Alf, but I had no choice. I felt even worse for what came next, but I had to take advantage of the opportunity. "Alf…are you not getting enough sleep?"

"What are you talking about?" His eyelids fluttered. Genuine concern painted his face white.

"Well, if you work the night shift here at school, maybe you're not getting enough sleep. Maybe, you're, I dunno, maybe…seeing things?"

"No, no." He waved his hands. "I don't work the night shift."

"Oh, of course. I just sorta' assumed there was a night shift security policeman." I shamelessly added "policeman" because I knew that's what Alf likes to be considered.

"No, you're right." Relief quickly replaced his worry as if I just told him his cancer had gone into remission. "There *is* a night security guard." *Damnit.* This is *not* good news but also not totally unexpected. "Wouldn't call him a 'policeman,' though."

"What do you mean?"

"Well…don't want to be tellin' tales out of school, so to speak…" He burst out laughing at something I must've missed. "But, Seth Calvecchio isn't what I'd call 'good police.'" He winked at me conspiratorially.

"What do you mean?"

"Let's just say, I wouldn't have picked him for my team. Sure, he makes his nightly rounds, I think, but I also suspect…*you* know…" He held his thumb up to his mouth and tilted his head back. He smacked me in the arm, awakening my near-to-bursting bladder from its momentary slumber.

"Oh."

"Anyway. I shouldn't be saying anything."

"Alf, you said you *think* he makes his nightly rounds…"

"Ayup, that's what I said."

"When, ah, when is he *supposed* to make his rounds?"

"Well, a good security police makes them every hour, on the hour, sometimes more often. There's not much resting in security." Alf took great pride in his work, and I felt relief I wouldn't perform my heist on his watch. "Anyway, whether he does that or not is— let's just say—open to interpretation."

"Huh."

"Richard, why're you asking these questions, anyway?" Once again, the suspicious policeman in Alf took over.

"No reason, really. Just curious. Creative writing, remember?" My answer didn't satisfy Alf's probing nature, so I quickly added, "Who knows? Maybe I'm interested in a future in security."

Alf folded his arms and beamed like a proud father.

"Well, if that's the path you feel you should follow, then you come see me. After you finish all your schooling, of course."

"Sure, of course. Hey, Alf?"

"Yes?"

"How's it going with your ex-wife?"

"Great, Richard, just great."

"That's good to hear. I'm happy for you." And even though I'm sick and tired of romance flaunted around me, his joy flowed over.

"Well, it's back to work for me." He straightened his shoulders in what I assumed to be a vigilant security stance. "You keep your chin up there, Richard. Your love life will turn around soon." He stopped at the door. "And, if you're going to meet that 'mystery girl' of yours again, *don't* do it in my bathroom." He winked again, and left.

Okay, there are no flies on Alf. Once again, I turned back toward the urinal, shut my eyes and concentrated. The door swung open, and I prayed for anyone other than another mystery intruder, ghost, or bully.

A hand clapped atop my shoulder and squeezed. Hard. *Good God.*

"Hey," said Brandon. "Dude, sorry about last night."

"Um, hey, Brandon…can we talk about this in a minute?"

"Oh, yeah, sorry." He remained standing behind me. Realizing my hopeless situation, I zipped up and turned to face him.

"What are you going to do, Tex? I mean, about the bobblehead?"

"Not really sure, yet, but I guess I'm going to try and get it, one way or another."

"Yeah." His eyes wandered sleepily off. "Hey, I know Ken and Eric can kinda be douches sometimes, but really, they're all right, for the most part."

My frustration with Brandon grew, further agitated by my neglected bladder. "Brandon, they're more than '*douches.*' They're *thugs.* What the *hell* are you doing with them?"

He shrugged. "I already told you. I didn't have any friends." He brushed his wavy hair out of his eyes.

"Whatever. But now, I'm in the middle of this…*stupid* mess because K-Cross won't believe me. And *now* I've got to do something dangerous. To save the damn life of *another* thug. How is *that* even fair, *Brandon*?"

"I know, I get it. Man, I'm sorry." He placed his hand on my shoulder again, prompting me to jump. Enough inappropriate bathroom touching. But I need to remember, for all his trespasses born of ignorance, I'm equally guilty of tampering with his feelings by causing a love potion to backfire on him.

I sighed and cooled off. "Okay, okay, I know it's not your fault. But is there anything you can do? Can't you *make* these guys believe me?"

"I've been tryin', dude. But they won't listen to me and…never mind…"

"And what?" But I knew, obvious from the previous night's meeting. For whatever reason, these two kids frightened Brandon.

"Forget it. Just let me know if I can do anything to help, all right?"

I didn't know if I trusted Brandon. Not really. Is he

truly the gullible innocent he wants us to believe he is? Or is there something darker behind his dumb-ass façade? I learned last year that monsters sometimes hide in the friendliest of places. "Okay, whatever. Thanks...I guess."

We stared at each other, saying nothing. Finally, he pointed toward the door. "Are...are you gonna go to class?"

"Yeah, but I've got unfinished business."

"Oh, cool. See ya at lunch." He slowly made his way toward the door, looking back at me with uncertainty.

I quickly undid my fly and turned back toward the urinal. The first-hour school bell blasted, giving me the extra push I needed. *Hallelujah*, I nearly screamed as the floodgates finally and mercifully opened.

****

Once again, lunch turned into the usual awkward gathering, worsened by the secrets and repressed feelings reined in by many at the table. The uncomfortable glances and clumsy silences between Brandon and myself couldn't have possibly escaped the attention of Olivia and Ian. I'll have some explaining to do later. But mostly, I watched Daniel, childishly toying with his french fries, unaware of his older brother's extra-curricular activities. Should I tell him about Ken? No. If I'm successful in preventing further violence, I'll spare Danny the heartache. Or at least tell him about it down the road. Right now just doesn't seem like the right time. After all, I don't have anything specific to tell him, other than his brother's in a skate club.

And that's perhaps the most frustrating thing about

this mess. I have absolutely *no* solid information. Thus far, everything I think to be the truth is founded on rumors, whispers, threats, and brags. I'm not even sure what it is I'm seeking. Elspeth, for all her talk and apparent desire to help, is nothing more than an enigma. During lunch, I glanced over at Elizabeth several times, hoping to catch her attention, but she remained ensconced in her world, business as usual, carrying on with her cronies.

Then there's the matter of whether or not to tell Olivia and Ian about how I got mixed up with this gangsta nonsense. Would informing them help in any way? Probably not. They're far enough removed from it all; immediate danger seems unlikely. Do they have a right to know Brandon's a member of the *Modern Gangstas? Maybe.* On the other hand, if I tell them, it'd feel like a betrayal to Brandon, who for the most part just seems to be a dumb, naive guy in over his head. I *think. Gah!* I feel as if I'm struggling to keep my head afloat, gasping for air in an ocean of uncertainty.

Time to prioritize. The most pending matter at hand is my looming heist. Since Elspeth appears to have the inside track in regards to certain unearthly matters, her advice shouldn't be sneezed at. I need backup.

As soon as the lunch bell rang, I chased Ian down to his locker. Once again, he dug through his disheveled mess, looking for God knows what.

"Hey, Ian."

"What's up?"

"Well, I need help. You free tonight?"

He grimaced as if in pain. "Dude, sorry, I'm grounded. I got two Fs on my last two algebra tests. My dad's being a total dick about it until I pull my grades up."

"Damnit."

"Why? What's going on?"

"I'll tell you later…if I'm successful, that is. Either way, you'll find out about it soon enough."

"*Now* what, Tex?" He lowered his voice. "What kinda' crap are you doing now?"

"Just…trust me. I'll tell you everything later, okay?"

"Goddamnit, can't we just have an *ordinary* junior year?"

"Yeah, I wish. Hey, have you got a ski mask?"

His eyes widened as if I'd jabbed him with a pencil. "*Dude*. What are you planning?" I remained silent. "Okay, whatever, of *course* I don't have a ski mask. I live in friggin' Kansas."

"Yeah, I don't have one either."

"Wait a minute. My parents have some. They went skiing last year and bought a truck-load of equipment."

"Could I borrow one?"

"Yeah, I'll see if I can find 'em. Come by after school, before my 'rents get home, and I'll see if I can dig 'em up. You want just one?"

I thought about it for a minute. "Two," I said.

****

I didn't want to involve her, but Olivia is the only other person I absolutely, irrevocably, know would have my back. Even though I knew she'd take fiendish glee in participating in my robbery scheme.

After school, I waited by her car. The old silver sedan looked ready for the junk pile—not unlike my Bucket. When Mrs. Furman bought a new, more eco-friendly car for herself, she bestowed her old gas guzzler on Olivia. I wondered what in the world had possessed Mrs. Furman to do so. I laughed the first time Olivia pulled up in front of my house, a petite girl behind the wheel of a lumbering dinosaur of a death machine. Once she took me out on the roads, though, I soon recanted my sexist notions. She handled it like a pro, always in complete command of the car's size and limitations. I should've known better. Olivia can do anything once she sets her mind to it.

"Hey, Tex." She sauntered up to the car, still struggling with her ginormous backpack. Funny how she can handle a behemoth on four wheels but can't tame her backpack.

"Hi, O'. I need to talk to you."

"Oh, boy, what now? Sure, hop in." She tossed the backpack on top of her car and opened the door. Leaning over, she unlocked my door. I slid in and immediately wanted out. A light vanilla odor permeated the car, her all too familiar scent.

Just get to the point. "Um, do you have plans for tonight?"

"Tex…you *know* we can't go out."

"It's not like that. You always said if I needed your help all I had to do was ask. Well? I'm asking."

Her attitude perked up. "Gotcha. You know I'm always here for you. What's up?" She twisted in her seat to look at me, a frown suddenly crossing her face. "Does this have anything to do with Brandon? I *know* there's something going on between you two."

"No. No, it's a lot bigger than that." I quickly scuttled the topic of Brandon. "I have to do something tonight. Something risky and more than a little stupid. I need your help."

"I'm up for risky. And stupid makes it even better. What're we doing?"

"We're...ah...we're going to steal Hastings' bobblehead." I hunkered down in my seat and waited for the screaming to start.

"What the *hell*, Tex? Why are you going to steal Hastings's bobblehead?" She reached over and punched my shoulder. "What kinda' *dumbass* move is *that*, anyway? You could go to juvie if you're caught. *What*—"

"Olivia. I'm trying to save a life."

"Explain."

"Okay. You know that kid, James Badger? The one who was shot?" She nodded. "Turns out he was in a gang at our school called the Modern Gangstas."

"I've actually heard about them. What does this have to do with you?" Olivia folded her legs underneath her, floating in upholstery.

"They're apparently at war—I guess you'd call it— with a rival gang at Ridge Creek High called the Young Bloods. Ian and I ran into these idiots at the skate park, and they eventually found out who I was and what school I went to. They paid me a visit at home a couple nights ago."

Olivia placed her fingers on her lips. "What happened? Are you all right? I mean, I can see you're all right, but—"

"Yeah, I'm okay. I actually had some help from unexpected quarters, but never mind that now. Anyway, they told me to deliver a message to the Modern Gangstas. To let them know they didn't shoot Badger. And to make sure the Gangstas didn't come gunning for them in retaliation."

"Oh, my *God*, Tex. Have you told them?"

"Well, I tried to last night, but their new leader, who I guess assumed the mantle after Badger's death, won't believe me, until I join them." Hoping for empathy, her unexpected outburst of laughter surprised me. She rocked back and forth on her seat, her knees flapping up and down.

"What*ever*. *You're* gonna be a *gangsta*?" Seeing I didn't share her amusement, she put the brakes on her hilarity. "Sorry. This is just a *lot* to handle out of the blue."

"Anyway, to join them, I have to go through this stupid-ass initiation. They want me to steal Hastings's bobblehead."

Olivia hooted again and immediately clamped her hand over her mouth. "Okay. Okay. This is just damned crazy. But how're we gonna do it?" Suddenly, I felt the overwhelming sense of helplessness lift from my shoulders, as I had company in my mess. Even if we're destined to fail, Olivia stayed true to her word.

"Well, that's the bad news. I haven't exactly got that worked out yet."

"Tex, you've *gotta* have a plan. We can't just break in, waltz in there, and just steal the damn thing."

"I know, I know. I'm working on a few things. I've got a few ideas. Tell you what...if I don't have a good plan by tonight, we'll postpone it. But I'd just rather get it over with and put this craziness behind me." Scared and out of my element, I wouldn't give in to the urge to cry. Ian always says girls hate sensitive guys.

Olivia gnawed at her lips, mulling things over. "Okay, that's reasonable enough. I guess." She let slip a quick, annoying bray. "Who exactly is in the Modern Gangstas? Anyone I know?"

I dared to place my hand on top of hers, barely hiding my joy when she didn't recoil. "I can't really talk about that now. I'm not supposed to. They're a secretive bunch. Just trust me, okay? I've never done anything to not earn your trust, right?"

She wrestled her hand free from mine. She gazed out the window before answering. "That's not exactly true, Tex." Her answer stunned me. "Last year, you didn't trust me enough to tell me everything— everything you were doing or going to do—and you nearly got your damn self killed." Her eyes welled with tears.

She may as well've injected poison into my veins. I never knew she felt this way or so strongly. She'd been harboring these feelings—letting them fester, growing wild, overtaking everything else in the garden of her turmoil—until only weeds of distrust remained.

"Olivia, I never meant… If there was *anything* I didn't tell you last year it was for your own protection—"

"I'm a goddamn big girl, now. You *don't* get to treat me like I'm helpless. Or don't let me have a say in anything. Or don't trust me with the truth…" Whipping her head toward the window, she slipped her sunglasses on. "And now, you don't trust me, again."

"I'm sorry I hurt you. You know I'd never do that on purpose. I just wish you would have told me earlier…about how you felt. Maybe things would be different now."

"Yeah, well, whatever…"

"But, please understand something," I said. "We're

no longer a couple, so I have no obligation…to tell you everything." Ouch. Man, I wish I could suck those words right back in with a vacuum cleaner. Too late. Inner censor, why do you hate me so?

She sniffled once. Gently rubbing her nose, she turned back toward me. "Yes, you're right about that."

"I promise I'll tell you everything—*everything*— once this mess is cleared up, okay?" I offered her a smile. She didn't return it.

"Fair enough." She waved her hands in the air, erasing the mental chalkboard of our discontent. "Okay, enough of this. When do we start?"

"I'll let you know as soon as I find out. And, Olivia, you *don't* have to do this, you know. I'm asking a lot from you…I realize that."

"I know." A small, barely perceptible smile appeared. She touched my hand briefly. "I told you I would. I'm always here for you—in one way or another."

"Thanks." Once again, I struggled with tears. "I really appreciate it."

"No prob. Tex?"

"Yeah?"

"I am proud of you, you know." She scooted across the seat and gave me a warm hug, reminding me of everything I've lost. She released me and took off her glasses, her eyes red and glistening. "I wouldn't expect anything else from you. I mean, about trying to save someone's life. Even if it *is* the stupidest thing I've ever heard." To my amazement, she burst out laughing again, and I joined her.

"Yeah, it is pretty dumb. I'll call you when I have the plan, O'. See ya tonight." I got out of her car and watched her expertly maneuver her clunker out of the parking lot. She rolled down the window when she passed me and said, "Operation Bobblehead is a go."

I have my team. Now I have to go see the mastermind behind the plan. And I dreaded *that* impending encounter.

Chapter Nine

I needed Mickey's help regarding several issues, and there's no other way around it—I have to confess my sins regarding my failed love potion.

As I drove up, I saw her standing on her front stoop, hands on her hips, surveying her miraculous garden. The Battle Bucket chortled and sputtered as I turned it off, a sort of prelude to my impending tongue-lashing.

"You kids get offa' my yard," she screamed.

"Um, hey, Mickey. It's me, Tex." I stopped in my tracks, unsure if I should continue.

She guffawed. "I'm just kiddin'." She doubled over, hacking and gasping for air. "I'm not senile, you know." Her shrill cackle pierced the air, launching nesting birds scurrying for the sky. "I've been expectin' you." She narrowed one of her eyes suspiciously.

"Yeah. Um, Mickey...I've done something really stupid." I walked up the sidewalk to meet her and lowered my head resignedly. "Let's get this over with. Go ahead and thump me." With my head bowed in front of her, I felt like a soldier preparing to be knighted—or beheaded.

Mickey's mouth fell agape. "Why, I ain't gonna thump you."

I raised my head. "Really? Okay, can we sit?" I nodded toward her porch swing.

"Well, I know I can sit, can you?" Apparently, I caught Mickey in a rare, light-hearted mood. I plopped down onto the swing, and she followed suit.

"I'm sorry, soooooo way sorry…but I used the love spell you taught me…and it's backfired miserably." Once again, she burst out laughing.

"You dumb kid. I *knew* you were going to do it. I just *knew* it."

"Yeah…"

"Well, I got news for you, kiddo. That wasn't a *real* spell. Who ever heard of a love spell made with sugar, anyway?" Her amusement gave way to another coughing fit, although her pleasure remained intact. She thwacked me on the back of my head.

"*Ow*! Mickey, you said you weren't going to thump me."

"Well, what fun is it if you expect me to do it?" She finally reined in her giggling. "How dumb do you think I am, kiddo?"

"Um, not dumb at all."

"I just had a feelin' in my bones you were going to try and do a damn fool move like that. So I gave you a—what do you call it?—a placebo."

Nope, Mickey's not the dumb one here. "Huh." I felt slightly betrayed and surprised, but then again, I had lied to her about my intentions. "So, the spell you gave me…it doesn't work?"

"It wasn't even a spell. Just nonsense and crap I made up. *Sugar*! I do swan…" She tittered again, her face turning red. While I watched her "swan"— whatever that means—it hit me that Brandon's amorous intentions toward me weren't supernaturally related. "Now, why don't you tell me what happened between you and your girlfriend?"

"We broke up. I just wanted to put things back together again."

A frown enveloped Mickey's face. "Well, while I'm sorry to hear about you and Olivia, I've told you time and again that you can't use your powers and knowledge for personal gain. Have you not been listening to a thing I've said?" *Thwack!*

"Gah! Sorry, sorry, sorry. I heard you. I just thought I could handle it…and that it was meant to be. I didn't really look at it as harmful. Or for personal gain." Having said that, I realized how lame my arguments were.

She looked at me as if pondering whether she should hit me again. "There are *always* repercussions to spells, Tex. And this was obviously for personal gain. You need to realize love spells might seem innocent enough, but when they go wrong, they go wrong *big*. Besides, would you really want your little girlfriend liking you without any freedom of choice in the matter?"

"No, guess not." She made me realize what I did— or had intended to do—sound fairly vile. I wanted to perform a great injustice on Olivia for my personal happiness, without any concern for her desires.

"There's a history of love spells gone bad that dates back to my ancient ancestors. Any witch worth his grain of salt knows better than to dabble with them."

"Okay, okay. I just thought that—" What *did* I think? "Anyway, someone else ate the spell—not Olivia—and they acted as if they, um, liked me. Well, I never suspected it was a fake spell."

Mickey swung her feet. "Well, maybe this other

girly likes you. Do you have any interest in her, Tex?" She smiled mischievously.

"Ah, no." I'm not sure how Mickey feels about people with alternative lifestyles, but now isn't the time for a debate.

"Okay, then, I hope you're done with this whole love spell foolishness."

"Yeah. Oh, *yeah*, I am." Even if there is a good love spell that works, I realized how wrong it is to force one's feelings. It's akin to emotional rape and made me feel horrible for even contemplating it.

"But I need your help on something more important, though."

"What have you got yourself into this time?" She stopped kicking her feet and held them straight out as if she were doing leg lifts.

"Long story. I need some other spells—one to open locks, and one to turn off electricity."

Mickey appeared not to breathe or blink. "Is this for personal gain, Tex?"

"*No*. Believe me, Mickey, I've learned my lesson about that."

"Fine, then. What's this all about?"

"I'm trying to save someone's life."

"How in the world would turning lights off and opening doors save someone's life?"

I inhaled deeply. The birds Mickey scared away earlier had come back to roost again, once the laughing ogre had quieted. Their constant chirping accompanied the unfolding of my ridiculous tale. On occasion, Mickey shook her head in disbelief and asked for clarification on a few details. When I finished, we both stared out at her stunningly lush green lawn. I stole a few sideways glances at Mickey to see if she'd properly digested everything I told her.

"Tex…" She sighed. "You're in over your head again. It sounds dangerous, and if you're caught stealing this 'boobiehead,' you could go to jail."

I threw my hands up into the air. "I *know* that, but what else can I do? I can't let these idiots go after an innocent kid."

Mickey ran her bony fingers over her chin, drawing the loose skin toward her ears. "Yes, I see your point; but someone's already shot one boy. I don't have a spell to protect you from gunfire."

"Yeah, I kinda guessed that, Mickey. But, again, what else can I do?"

"What about your good lookin' detective friend, Scowlings?"

His name's actually Cowlings, but he may as well be Scowlings, since that's his perpetual look when dealing with me. But correcting Mickey is something I've learned to just let pass unless I want to feel the wrath of her mighty swinging witch-hand again. "I considered calling him, but I can't ask him to help me break and enter into the school. Besides, what would I tell him? I mean, I already told him the Young Bloods claimed they were innocent. He believes me. Now, I've just got to convince these clowns who are forcing me to do it, as well." I stood up and stared down at Mickey, hoping to gain dominance over the situation. "My back's against the wall here. It's the only way out."

Mickey looked up, shading her eyes with her hand. "Fine. Come with me." She propelled her feet back and forth, pumping them into action. Annnnnd…we have lift-off! She sprung out of the swing, a reminder of my innocent youth when the closest I ever came to danger was jumping out of a swing set. She brushed by me, dashing into her house like a hound hunting a fox. I hurried after her. Racing into the kitchen, she pulled open a drawer and riffled through the contents. Metallic items clanked against the sides of the drawer until she found what she needed.

"Aha," she exclaimed. Holding up an antique iron key, she examined it by the curtain-filtered sunlight. A thin rod with one small notch protruded from the oval-shaped handle. "Here's what we need." She pulled open another drawer, grabbed a roll of masking tape and a black magic marker.

"Okay, where did I put that spell? Oh, yes." She rushed by me and planted her hands on a breadbox. Dozens of small pieces of torn paper tumbled out onto the countertop. Humming, she fished through the scraps of paper. "Here we go." She transcribed the Latin words from the paper onto a long piece of masking tape, which she carefully looped over the handle of the key.

"Okay, Tex." She brandished the key over her head like a weapon. "This is what we call, for lack of a better term, a skeleton key." She tossed it to me. After fumbling it back and forth between my hands and securing it against my body, I finally latched onto it. "With the proper spell, this should open almost any lock. Just read it, or whisper it—which is what you'll probably be doing—and *presto*." She clapped her hands, sending a sharp rebound through the kitchen.

"Thanks."

"But, you're *never* to use it for personal gain. I don't have to tell ya that again, do I?"

"No," I said. "No personal gain. I swear."

"All right. Now, as to the other matter…" She searched her breadbox again. "Nope, not in there." She scuttled by me so fast, her sickeningly sweet perfume left a trail behind her. I followed her into the TV room. She ran her hand across the cluttered shelf above her fireplace, disturbing the creepy children figurines from their ever-watchful lookout. She stopped at a plastic pig cookie jar, stretched up on her toes, and pulled the head off. As she struggled to pull out the contents, I ran toward her, assuming I could help, but she quickly fished out a large wad of more bits of paper. As she shuffled through the contents, I once again noticed there were no photos of children or grandchildren adorning her room.

"Hey, Mickey?"

Without looking up from her paperwork, she said, "Yes?"

"Did you ever have any children?"

She shot me a grim look, her shoulders bunched up, not unlike a threatened cat. The silence felt palpable and extremely unsettling.

"Um, I've just never seen any…I'm sorry. Maybe it's too personal?" My voice diminished with every syllable.

Finally, she said, "I had a daughter. Once." With her tone nearly inaudible, she still enunciated each word with extreme precision, as though it pained her. "Maybe, some day, I'll tell you about her." She continued staring at me, hanging somewhere between anger and sadness.

"I'm sorry, I shouldn't have asked."

"No, you shouldn't have." She nodded firmly and

went back to her business. Obviously, I struck a nerve and felt mortified I might've dredged up painful memories. But I really didn't know too much about Mickey's past, other than her husband had died some years before. I thought we'd become close enough to share good and bad reminiscences. Guess not. I wish people were as easy to read as books.

"Here it is," she shouted, giving me quite a start. But I'm glad the no-nonsense witch returned, as opposed to the dark creature that briefly possessed Mickey's body.

Once again she scurried into the kitchen while I strained to keep up. She sat at the kitchen table, duplicating the written spell on a paper napkin. I sat across from her. When she finished, she pushed her handiwork toward me. I looked at it, hoping it to be legible since some of the ink bled through the napkin. "What do I do with it, Mickey?"

"That's the spell to shut down electricity." I wonder if she has a spell for anything and everything. Except for making the spell-wielder impervious to gunfire, of course. "You just read it from within the building where you need the electricity to go out."

"Okay, sounds simple enough. But…is there any way to control what part of the building's electricity I turn off? There's actually a school play going on tonight. I'd rather not mess that up, if possible."

Mickey scowled at me and reached across the table as if to take back her spell. Her short arms couldn't reach that far so she gave up, dropping them to the table with a *thump*. "Kid, if you want precision electrical work, call a damn electrician," she snapped. "Otherwise, it ain't an *exact* science, you know. How many times have I gotta explain that to you?" She whacked her hands down onto the table again.

"No, you've explained it already. Sorry, sorry. Now, this will just affect the school, right? Not any of the surrounding areas, right?"

Mickey chortled and shook her head. "Guess we'll find out tonight, huh? A lot of it depends on the power of the witch." *Uh-oh*. "Should be interesting." She kept chuckling as if pulling a private joke on me. She handed me another napkin with her scrawling covering it.

"What's this?" Once again I checked to make sure I could read it.

"*That's* to turn the lights back on." Frustrated Mickey reappeared. "Don't you dare leave without turning the power back on. You should be able to work this spell outside of the building."

"Okay." Whatever. Stupid, arbitrary spells.

"Now," she continued, "you *are* taking somebody with you in case you get in trouble and need help?"

"Yeah. Yes, I am."

"Who you takin'? Best be someone you trust."

"Um, yeah. Olivia said she'd help me." I looked down at the checkered tablecloth in embarrassment.

Mickey's eyes grew round. "Oh, for God's sakes." She cackled. "That's just *too* much, kid. *Too, too* much. *First*, you break up with her. *Now*, you're trustin' her with your life?" She smacked her knees. I suppose when I'm not around, her knees stand in as a stunt-double for my head.

"Yes, I guess that's the case." Outwardly, I smiled.

"I'd say that things are about to get even more interestin' for you, Tex. *Much* more interestin'. I can't wait to hear what happens next."

Later, I reflected on Mickey's words and realized how prophetic they had been.

****

"What do you want to do for dinner tonight, son?" Dad, his knuckles white, held on for dear, sweet life during our car ride home. I'm not nearly as bad a driver as he thinks I am, but that's just the way he's wired.

"If it's all right with you, I thought we'd just have leftovers. I've got to work on something tonight."

"Oh, a school project?"

"Um, yes." It's a valid lie. It *is* a very challenging school project. "I'm going to see the school play. I have to write a paper about it."

"What's the play?" Dad fell against the window as I careened onto our street.

"*South Pacific.*"

"Hm. Do you have a...date?"

"No, not really. I'm...ah...going with Olivia." His eyebrows lifted. "But just as friends," I quickly added.

"Well... Hope it goes well for you."

"Yeah, me, too." I really didn't want to say anything more about it, but in case things go south, I thought it best to give him some kind of warning. "Dad, you trust me, right?"

"Absolutely." My heart nearly broke when I saw his sincerity. "Of course I do. What's going on, Tex?"

"I just need you to trust me. If you should hear anything later tonight...just please trust me. Things aren't as they appear."

"I don't like the sound of this. Are you in trouble?"

"No, Dad, I'm not in trouble." I should've kept my mouth shut. "But I could be—or *someone* could be—

unless I do what I need to do tonight."

"Tex, you can't just drop these cryptic statements on me and expect me not to worry. Now, what's going on?" We pulled up into the driveway, and I killed the engine like I wished I could kill the conversation.

"Someone's life is in danger. I have to do something tonight which may prove to be a little risky. I just want you to know…it's for a good reason." I really should print that on a T-shirt, since it seems that mantra's been haunting me recently.

"I just want to help. Is *your* life in danger?"

"No, I don't think so. And I *know* you want to help, but this is something I have to do on my own."

"Son, I know I have to let go some time, but it's my job to worry. Especially after what happened to your mother."

"Dad, *my* life's not in danger." At least I don't think it is…*yet*. "I'm not going to die tonight—that I can promise you."

"Does this have anything to do with that Badger boy's death?"

"Maybe a little."

"Then let's call Cowlings."

"I can't do that. It's not that simple. I'm trying to prevent another kid from being shot."

"I don't understand any of this," he said slowly. He pointed a long finger at me. "If it involves guns, it *shouldn't* involve you. That's reason enough to bring Cowlings in."

"I've already talked to Cowlings about this. He knows pretty much everything I do."

"'Pretty much'?"

"Dad, I know I'm asking a lot from you, but you're

just going to have to trust me. Please?" This isn't going well. "And there aren't going to be guns involved."

"Okay, then tell me what you have to do."

"I...can't."

He sighed and looked out the window. "I don't like this. I don't like this *one* bit. You're going to stay in tonight."

"Dad, I can't—"

He lifted his hand. "Yes, you can. If you can't even tell me what you're planning on doing—or why—and you're worried enough to tell me it's dangerous, you're not leaving the house tonight."

I should've known better. There's no arguing with him when he gets like this. I've no choice but to go along with him, then I'll have to sneak out. "Fine, whatever."

He closed his eyes and nodded; the end of the discussion. Relieved, he chuckled at the cats gathered at the doorstep. "Looks like your welcoming committee's waiting for us."

I laughed, probably the last laugh I'll share with him for a while. "Well, let's not keep 'em waiting."

****

When I arrived at Ian's house, I dared to turn on my phone. Four messages, all from Dad. I'm in deep crap with him. I'll probably be grounded until I'm fifty. It didn't take long for him to discover I snuck out. I told him I was going upstairs to do homework, and then I quietly left through the back door. Guess he saw the Bucket missing. I turned the phone off. I didn't know what I feared more—facing Dad's wrath or the daunting task ahead.

Ian seemed a little more jittery than usual when he

answered the door.

"Hey," he whispered. "I got your stuff." He closed the door and disappeared within, leaving me on his doorstep. After several minutes, he pulled the door open just enough to slip a brown paper bag into my hand. "Here ya go. Try and return 'em undamaged, all right?"

"Sure, Ian. Thanks."

"Ian?" A female's voice called out from behind him. "What're you doing?"

Ian sighed and pushed the door open to expose Allison standing behind him.

"Oh, hi, Tex." She clasped her hands together.

"Hey, Allison. Um, Ian, I thought you were grounded."

"I *am*. Allie's here to tutor me—to get my algebra grade up."

"Okay, Ian, whatever." I didn't know how to feel. Did Ian lie to me about being grounded so he could have a date with Allison? I quickly discarded the thought. Who am I to pass judgment on Ian's having a chance at happiness just because I'm denied it? Besides, now I know how Ian must've felt when Olivia and I became a couple, excluding him so often.

"It's true." Allison stepped forward into the fading sunlight. "Ian's parents approved my coming over to help him."

"It's cool, guys. I believe you. No need to apologize for anything." I smacked Ian's shoulder, our totally non-embarrassing display of male bonding. Looking into the sack, I freaked out. "*Really,* Ian?"

"Hey, you didn't say anything about colors."

"What is it?" asked Allison. Even though she was taller than Ian, she strained on her tiptoes to glimpse into the brown bag of mystery.

"Never mind." Ian peered into the street, searching for unwanted onlookers. "It's just a joke."

"I'll *say*," I said.

****

Olivia's mother answered the door, startled to see me. She looked behind her, stepped outside, and closed the door. Apparently, I'm setting a record for most unwanted visitor today.

"Tex," she said quietly, "what *are* you doing here?" She stuck her hands in her jeans pockets and glared at me.

"Um, hi, Mrs. Furman." I felt like a nervous suitor, meeting a girl's threatening father for the first time. "I'm here to pick up Olivia."

"For a *date*?"

"No, no. Nothing like that." I kicked at a few stray pebbles on the sidewalk. "We're going to see a play— as friends."

"Well," she said, relaxing her guard, "remember what I told you?"

"Yeah. And I've tried, but it's really hard not to talk to Olivia...or be her friend. I mean, we have the same friends, the same lunch period, the same school..."

She clicked her lips together, sounding like a match being lit. "You need to try a little harder." She folded her arms, once again playing the defensive line.

"Well, I'll *try*."

"Sorry if I seem intrusive, but it's because I *like* you. And I like you with Olivia. You two were good for one another."

"Well, thanks. I guess. I just wish she liked us

together."

"Don't give up." She smiled sadly at me and pushed the door open. "Olivia," she screamed upstairs. "Tex is here."

Olivia flew down the stairs, her flats slapping against the wooden steps. She yanked the door open and stared curiously at the two of us.

"Mommmm! What are you guys talking about?"

"Nothing," answered Mrs. Furman. She stepped behind Olivia to re-enter the house and turned around. "Seems a little warm for you two to be wearing such dark clothing." Olivia wore a plain black T-shirt and black jeans. I chose my black sweater—the one I presume Elspeth told me to wear—and dark blue jeans. I did feel silly as the sweat rolled down my face. "You look like a couple of mimes. Aren't you hot, Tex?"

Before I could answer, Olivia came to my rescue. "Mom, it's just what the kids are wearing now. Deal, okay?"

Mrs. Furman lifted one side of her mouth, derisively. "Whatever. Olivia, don't be out too late. It's a school night."

"I won't." She rolled her eyes.

Once we got into the Bucket, it didn't take long for Olivia to rant against her mom. "My *mom. God.*"

"She's not so bad. She just cares about you. And you gotta admit, we *do* look kind of ridiculous for eighty-something degree weather."

She looked at me and snorted. "A sweater, Tex? *Really?* That's so, like…*never.*" She burst out with a raucous guffaw.

"Yeah, well, you look like a cat thief. Or a pretentious, Euro-trash art critic."

For one glorious moment, I felt we stepped back in time to last spring when we were in love and couldn't have imagined it being any other way. Then the urgency of tonight's endeavor brought me crashing back to the present, the frisson of panic running through me intensified by the warmth of my sweater.

"Anyway," I said, "I hope we won't stand out *too* much in our dark attire." I hadn't really thought about it, but now realized I may've already made a critical mistake. What if the cameras pick up on my unusual attire? Surely, someone's bound to remember the geek wearing a sweater on an unusually steamy spring night. But could my black sweater possibly have something to do with the outcome of tonight, as Elspeth indicated? Or did she enjoy messing with my head? Thus far, her *help* has been doled out in small, indecipherable squirts.

"Well, it's going to be dark, anyway, right?" asked Olivia.

"That's the plan, at least. Still, I think I might want to ditch my sweater before our plan goes into full effect. I have a white T-shirt on underneath."

"Tex, you *can't* wear white. You'll practically glow in the dark once the electricity goes out."

"Yeah, crap, you're right. Okay, okay, I'll hide the sweater in a safe place—or something—and put it on again once we...achieve darkness."

Olivia laughed again. "I like how you're turning this into a military operation. 'Achieve darkness.' Are we gonna have cool codenames? I want to be phantom girl. No, *wait*. Bad ass *beeyotch*."

"O', you're enjoying this *way* too much. We need to get serious."

"Okay, fine." She slumped down into the car seat.

"Just thought it'd be cool…that's all."

I smiled at her. "You know…"

"What?" She brushed her hair out of her eyes.

"I've missed this. I've missed having fun with you." I looked at her fear-stricken, knowing I took a fun, innocent moment and pushed it too far. "Sorry, sorry, sorry. I can't help myself sometimes."

"It's okay, Tex. I've missed it, too."

The rest of the trip happened in numbing silence. While I saw our exchange as an obvious step toward reconciliation, I wonder how Olivia interpreted it. It drove me crazy. She merely said she missed having fun with me. That probably means nothing to her other than the face value of the words uttered. On the other hand, she said she missed me, right? *Right*? *Argh*! All this double think and triple think isn't what I should be focusing on right now. The mysterious, unfathomable mind of women will have to be explored at a later date. Yet, I couldn't help but wonder if Mickey knows of a mind-reading spell? No. Bad, Tex. Personal gain and all that. Stay focused; keep your eye on the prize. But damn, if she didn't look extra beautiful tonight.

I cleared my head as we entered the school parking lot. People flocked toward the auditorium, students decked out in T-shirts and jeans, the adults wearing suits. Maybe I won't stand out too much after all. Yeah, right.

"So, here's what we know—"

"Operation Bobblehead," shouted Olivia. Since our windows were down, I quickly scanned the lot to see if anyone overheard us. "Call it Operation Bobblehead." She smiled mischievously, toying with her hair.

"Fine, if you promise to keep your voice down.

Okay...Operation Bobblehead." I leaned toward her and raised my eyebrows. "Happy?"

"Ecstatic."

"Okay. *You're* happy...I'm happy. We're going to go see *South Pacific* like everyone else here." I pointed toward the strolling theater-goers.

Olivia wrinkled her nose up. "Wish it was something good."

"We're *not* here to see the show. Anyway, I'm thinking of just bringing my mystery man sweater with me and sitting on it during the show. That way, if we happen to get caught on camera, I'll say I was wearing a white T-shirt and not a dark top. I'll just have to be careful and carry it in a less than obvious manner. Gah." Sweat rolled down my face, so I pulled off my sweater and flung it on the seat between us. Olivia looked at it and made a face.

"Okay, did you bring gloves?" I asked.

Olivia looked puzzled, then disappointed. "No, sorry. I didn't know I was supposed to."

"It's okay. I forgot to tell you. Here..." I reached into the back seat and pulled out two pairs of blue, rubber dishwashing gloves. "I thought ahead. Plenty for everyone."

"Not exactly hi-tech robbery gloves, Tex."

"Yeah, well, they'll have to do." I found the gloves underneath my kitchen sink. I'd never used them before and barely remember Mom wearing them. Since neither one of us had ever been fingerprinted, they were probably unnecessary, but I had to make sure our crime couldn't get traced back to us.

"I'm guessing it happens in about forty-five minutes to an hour, once it's nice and dark outside. One of us will leave and go to the bathroom closest to the front of the main campus. In about ten minutes, the other will follow. We'll text once we're both in the bathrooms."

"You're talking about the bathroom right outside the doors of the auditorium, right?"

"Yeah. We can't get closer to Hastings's office because security puts up that dumb, slotted fence, which blocks the main campus off from events in the auditorium." Olivia nodded. "Now, Alf told me…" Olivia appeared confused. "Come on, O', you know Alf. Alf Landon? Head of Security?" She shook her head. "The guy who supposedly shot himself in the foot several times?"

"*Ah.*" She stared at me disbelievingly. "Tex, you're *not* hanging out with that guy now, are you?" I could tell her thoughts were on my friendship with Red last year. It didn't merit an answer.

"*Anyway,* Alf told me there's a night watchman who's supposed to make rounds at every hour, on the hour. I don't know how long these rounds take, but Alf indicated he's sloppy, doesn't do them all the time, and he may be a drinker—"

"Figures," she said.

"Well, this guy's 'sloppiness' may prove to work in our favor. Either way, we should probably plan on meeting at the johns on the half hour, so if he's going to do his rounds, then maybe he'll be upstairs or somewhere else."

"Gotcha."

"Once we meet at the bathrooms, we'll put these on." I grabbed the paper bag from the back seat. Pulling out the contents, I displayed them on top of the sweater.

"You have *got* to be goddamned kidding me, Tex." She glowered at the pink ski mask like it might bite her. "I am *not* going to wear anything pink."

I sighed, knowing full well I'd hit a roadblock regarding her hatred of everything pink. To Olivia, pink's a sexist color. She despised that such a 'sissy' hue was indelibly linked to females. "Fine, fine. *I'll* wear the pink one. It's gonna' be dark anyway." It didn't exactly thrill me either, but it's better to wear something concealing our identity, than nothing at all. On the other hand, the prospect of getting caught wearing a pink ski mask isn't too enticing, either. There're more important factors at stake here—such as my future and freedom—but for some reason, wearing pink seems more mortifying than simple breaking and entering.

"You're gonna' be the cutest thief ever, with your pink ski mask, black sweater, and blue gloves. Okay, what next?"

"Well, I'm going to put the power out." I checked my pocket to ensure I had the spell safely secured. "Then we're going to open the locks with this..." I meant to quickly fling the key out with dramatic flair, but it got tangled up on a loose thread in my pocket. "Okay, wait. With *this*." I flashed the key for Olivia to appreciate.

"Looks kinda old and clunky."

"Yeah, but it has a spell built into it. We can open up anything." But not your heart, I thought. Jesus, Tex, go cry in a room tomorrow, not now.

"Okay. I'm all in."

"Here we go, O'. Last chance to back out?" I leaned closer, demanding her full attention so she'd realize the seriousness of our situation.

"What part of '*all* in' don't you understand, Tex?" she asked. "I *know* how important this is…"

"Okay, then, in case I don't get to tell you later, thank you."

"We're not going to die or anything." Adrenaline lit her eyes, while fear and dread hovered over me, too close for comfort.

"Then…here's to Operation *Bobblehead*," I exclaimed, hoping to channel some of Olivia's excitement and courage. I held my fist out toward her.

"I am *so* not going to bump that."

I chuckled, knowing she hated fist bumps almost as much as her nemesis, the color pink.

I opened my hand. She grabbed it and yelled, "To Operation Bubblehead."

My nerves were shot as we made our way through the parking lot. Surely, the fates—or whatever it is that decides our lives—would watch over us during Operation Bobblehead? I mean, what we're doing is a good thing—a human life is at stake. The gods wouldn't be so merciless as to not reward our efforts in such a heroic undertaking. Right? I mean, they wouldn't allow anything to go wrong, *right*? I prayed silently to whomever—whatever—may be listening.

Chapter Ten

During the first thirty minutes of the show, Olivia groaned and trumpeted her lips, presumably at what she perceived as Asian and female stereotypes. I finally nudged her so as not to draw unwanted attention. With a nearly packed auditorium, I felt bad for the audience and actors for having to disrupt the performance, but it had to be done.

"Olivia," I whispered, "I'm going now. Come in about ten minutes if everything looks good." She nodded as I excused myself through the row. I walked up the aisle, carefully carrying my wadded-up sweater by my side.

As I exited the auditorium, I looked around the lobby. Other than a young student, bored, sitting at the ticket table, I saw no one else. I zoomed by her quickly, avoiding eye contact, and pushed the door open into the hallway. About 100 feet down were the bathrooms, then the slatted fence. Darkness shrouded the hallways beyond. The video camera bolted up in the corner of the ceiling whirred and twisted, maintaining an electronic focus on my every movement. I ducked into the bathroom.

A shiver fell across me as I entered the farthest toilet stall, the memory of my restroom encounter with Bob Bellman still fresh. I looked underneath the stalls. No signs of feet, but I didn't know if ghosts have feet anyway. I pulled the sweater on and sat down, waiting. The material of the sweater irritated the back of my neck, and I started perspiring again. Checking the time on my phone, I saw Dad called five more times. Great. I switched off the ringer and set it to vibrate.

Several minutes later, the phone jarred in my hand, jolting me.

—*I'm here*— read Olivia's text.

—*Okay, power's going down*—I wrote. —*After that, meet me by the gate.*—

I went over to the bathroom window. As always, the lower window remained sealed shut, but above that a clear window opened slightly but not enough for an AWOL student to escape. I perched on my tiptoes to peer out. Across the football field, I saw houses lining Johnson Drive. With shaking hands, I took the napkin out and unfolded it. I whispered the Latin words and slid it back into my pocket, double-checking I had the make-good spell beside it.

A minute slowly crawled by, the seconds marked by my loud breathing. Nothing. I began to think the spell had lost its potency or something, like an old firecracker that'd lost its fizz. Suddenly, the neon lights flickered and crackled above me. A loud *flumph* exploded, followed by a collective roar from the people in the auditorium. The only light source available came from my phone and the beaming moon.

"*Jesus,*" Olivia yelled from the girl's bathroom. Outside, Johnson Drive was completely immersed in blackness, the street lights out, the houses now shadowy shells.

"Crap." I didn't think I'd shut down the *entire* neighborhood. I grabbed the small penlight out of my pocket. Using the narrow beam of light to illuminate my path, I shuffled toward the door.

I left the bathroom and flashed the light toward the girl's restroom. Olivia stood in front of the doorway, excited and grinning.

"Tex, you knocked out *everything*," she whispered.

"I know." Echoes of laughter and a few screams sounded from the auditorium, bouncing off the lockers like ghosts of students past. "Come on." I scrambled toward the gate, Olivia close behind me, bouncing up and down like a giddy toddler.

"Get your stuff on." Olivia pulled on her ski mask, obviously too large for her small face. She held it in place with one hand so she could see to pull on the gloves. The mask slipped down as she tilted her head back to align with the eyeholes. I put my mask on and forced my left hand into one of the gloves. The rubber material ripped at the end of my fingertips. *"Damnit."* I pulled on the other glove, taking care to not push my fingers all the way to the tips. Not having the full tactile facilities of my fingers, I grabbed the key and nearly fumbled it.

I shined the light onto the padlock holding the gate fastened. The key ineffectively scratched at the keyhole but didn't take.

"Tex," Olivia whispered, "the key's too big for the lock." Her panicked breathing from under her mask made me more nervous. "Mickey needs to get out of the eighteenth century."

Footsteps rapidly approached from down the hallway. I held my breath. A flashlight, bouncing up and down, sprayed a ray of light onto the walls and lockers, growing larger with each rumbling footfall.

"We're going to have to improvise." I snapped off my light and grabbed her by the arm, dragging her back toward the bathroom doors. "Distract the guard."

"Okay." One of her eyes grew wider underneath the mask, the other one lost somewhere within the over-sized fit. "I'm going to have to sneak in behind him once he opens the gate, but you've got to keep him busy." Her head nodded, yet the mask stubbornly stayed in place. I raced toward the corner where the gate latched and plastered myself up against the wall. My palms grasped the tiled wall, fingertips scrabbling as if for a life-saving hold on a cliff wall. The footsteps grew louder, a man's labored breathing trying to keep pace. I glanced over at Olivia braced within the bathroom doorway.

"Olivia," I whispered, "take your stuff off."

She looked at her gloves and uttered, "Oh." She yanked off her mask and pulled off her gloves, stuffing them in her large purse.

"*Help*. Oh, *God*, help me," cried Olivia. Under the minimal moonlight peeking in from the high windows, I saw she positioned herself about thirty feet in front of the gate.

"Hold on, girl," yelled a slightly accented voice. "I'm coming."

I shut my eyes. The guard fumbled with the lock, cursing under his breath, a mere ten feet away from me. I scooted back along the wall another six inches, wishing I had a spell for invisibility. Olivia continued screaming at the top of her lungs, emitting nonsensical phrases. The guard threw the gate open, sounding like tree branches snapping in an ice storm. My only way through is if he doesn't close the gate behind him.

Olivia must've felt the same thing as she upped her hysterics.

The guard's flashlight splashed over Olivia, her arms flapping up and down. He ran toward her. "It's just a power outage, girl, what's the matter?"

"I was in the *bathroom,* and the *lights* went out, and I got scared and lost, and I couldn't see anything and…are there *terrorists*? What's going *on*? I never thought something like this would *happen* to me. I just wanted to see a play and…" She has a great future in improv theater.

"Shhhh, quiet down, girl," said the guard. "I'm here to help you." He led her back toward the auditorium, his arm coddled around her shoulders. I crept toward the gate. The guard had left it open about a foot. I crossed the length of it, glancing toward Olivia and the guard, watching them recede further.

Once through the gate, I broke into high speed, my tennis shoes squeaking across the linoleum. Of all days they had to clean the floor, they picked today. My amplified breathing, contained within the mask, sounded thunderous to my ears. After three hundred or so feet, I nearly skidded to a halt in front of the office doors.

Still holding the key in my hand, I tried it in the office front door. The door appeared to be a stolid leftover from some long-gone era. The key worked like a charm this time. I entered the office.

I burst through the swinging wooden doors to enter the forbidden area so regally ruled over by Mrs. Carbody. The penlight flashed upon Hastings's door. I should have known Hastings would have nothing but the newest, most expensive locking mechanism. Rather than wasting time trying to use Mickey's antiquated key, I remembered the cabinet at the back of the office. I rushed over toward it. My heart leaped into my throat as I saw another small, newer lock embedded on the side of the cabinet door. Out of frustration, I thumped my gloved hand on the panel. For once, luck rode shotgun by me. The cabinet clicked and released the front panel slowly.

I pored over the contents swiftly, looking for Hastings's name. Then I saw *Vice Principal's Office* written on a label above one key. I suspect Hastings doesn't know they don't have his name permanently etched there, or he'd probably rectify it.

From deep within the bowels of the school, a rumbling noise gained in power and volume, rattling the windows in the office. The sound increased, changing into a loud, wheezing tornado siren. A flood light on the wall above me snapped on, the blinding luminescence producing a blinking firefly parade in front of my eyes. Stunned, I dropped my flashlight and scrambled to scoop it up. It must be the back-up generator, which I didn't even consider. One light at a time, the hallway snapped back to life. The camera to the right of me buzzed on and swiveled, a reminder it had its eye on me. I snatched Hastings's key and raced for his door.

With shaking hands, I pushed the key into the lock. The door opened with a reassuring, small *clack*. I swept the flashlight across the room. Hastings's bobblehead smiled grimly at me from his desktop, its dead eyes a terrifying emulation of the real thing. I grabbed the miniature hell-spawn and held it tight. Dropping the office key on the floor, I bolted through the swinging doors and into the front area of the lobby. I peeked out the front door window for any signs of activity and listened carefully. Back down the hallway, voices gathered, some jovial, some exasperated. I stepped out into the now fully lit hallway. The night guard stood in front of the fence, locking himself back into my side of the gate.

"*Wait,* oh, God, *wait.*" I heard Olivia scream. She ran toward him, her purse flapping at her side. "*Please,* mister, you've *got* to help me. I don't like the dark. What if it happens *again*? I'm *so* scared!" The guard quickly undid the lock and jogged back to comfort her. Thank God for Olivia. I know she hates to play the helpless female victim—she's anything but that, as she's once again proven—but her much-needed interference proved invaluable.

Now, I needed a different exit strategy.

On the fly, I thought of the science lab, another several hundred feet down the hallway by the south end of the building. Those classroom windows open in case a horrific lab accident should occur. The problem is they pull inward, slanting up. It may be a problem squeezing through the window, but I think it can be done. I jetted toward the lab, listening to Olivia's non-stop blabbering and the guard's consoling words behind me.

The lab door, too, had an old-fashioned door and lock. I reached for the skeleton key, reassuring myself my two spells were nestled alongside it. But I only found one napkin; the power outage spell. I gave myself a quick pat-down, searching desperately for the spell to put the power back on. I even thumped my chest, knowing full well my stupid sweater has no pockets.

Alarm overtook me. Running quietly back along the lockers, I scanned the floor for the missing napkin while keeping my eye on the gate. Olivia somehow manipulated the guard into once again walking her in the opposite direction, his arm around her shoulder.

The tight ski mask made my skin itch and crawl, and sweat drenched my sweater. I wanted to drop to the floor and roll around on the ground like a dog, looking for relief.

I twisted the doorknob of the office door, pressing inward with my shoulder, only to be met with unmoving force. Quickly, I pulled out the skeleton key and opened the door. My heart fluttered at a dire realization. I'd dropped Hastings's office key on the floor and locked his door behind me. If I dropped the napkin in there, it's over. Not only do I have to get the power back on throughout the neighborhood but Hastings can't find the witch spell in his office. He already suspects me of black magic practice.

I craned my head like the camera above me. The napkin lay on the floor underneath the key cabinet, lightly crumpled but still legible. Grabbing it in one hand, while carrying the bobblehead in the other, I made my way back to the science lab.

Once in front of the science lab door, I put the napkin carefully in my pocket. I double-checked my pocket again, in case there were ill-behaved gremlins at work.

The key turned in the lock. The door swung open.

The lights were off in the lab, and I meant to keep them that way. The moonlight streamed in through the windows, alighting on the assorted beakers and science equipment lining the long tables. The last time I had class here, the room teemed with life—and death, for it'd been pig fetus dissecting day. Groans, shrieks, sounds of revulsion and laughter—mostly supplied by several dumb jocks who tossed around pig parts at the girls—had made the room a loud, vibrant place. Now, it seemed unsettlingly quiet.

Using the moonlight as my guide, I maneuvered around the tables. I heard a small, yet ominous *click*, and swiveled to face the door. It sounded like the door'd snapped shut again. I froze and took in a deep breath, listening for any sort of follow-up. Even though turned off, the overhead fluorescent lights buzzed like bees, before stopping just as suddenly. A flicker of the lights lit up the room for a second and then died. The after-effects of the light flash left a retinal green glowing image of everything I'd briefly absorbed. The images faded, barely still imprinted inside my brain, but one image remained clear. A dark figure stood in the corner of the room.

Static electricity filled the air. My hair rose on end, pushing against my mask, straining to thrust through it. The atmosphere tightened around me, my breath growing shallow. A clammy, cold sensation fell over me, the room filled with moist presence.

Another buzzing sound, this time akin to bacon sizzling on the stove, came from everywhere. Then the low, rumbling, guttural laughter started. In the corner of the room, two narrow orbs of green light materialized out of the blackness. I recognized the spectral eyes immediately. *Bob Bellman.*

Swinging the flashlight toward the doorway, the green eyes snapped shut as soon as I turned the light on. Nothing there. I swept the beam around the room, seeing only distorted shadows lurking within every nook, corner, and table. I ran for the windows and bumped into a table. I dashed the light behind me again, directly into the grotesque visage of Bellman. He grinned at me savagely, his mouth opening impossibly wide. A pale, green hue bathed his entire body. He swung his log-like arms up at me, thus dispelling movie myths that ghosts move slowly to be more creepily effective.

I fell back onto one of the lab tables, dropping my flashlight. The light spun around on the floor, illuminating the room like a strobe light at a wild rave. I continued my momentum and completed a clumsy backward somersault to the floor, positioning the table between myself and Bellman. He reached across the table, his letter jacket crawling back on his arms. I jumped to my feet, struggling to keep my grip on the bobblehead while keeping my eyes focused on Bellman. He emitted a loud, long shriek from someplace very dark within him. The noise reverberated throughout the lab, shaking the beakers on the tables. He easily tossed the table across the room, sending it crashing into the science equipment.

Breathless, I reached the back window. Twisting the window handle, it mercifully pulled open toward me. I needed to get higher to slide through. *A chair...my kingdom for a chair.* Bellman laughed and walked toward me, arms outstretched. A faint, yet visible, stream of green light trailed behind him, exhaust from the devil's vehicle. As I lurched for a chair, he quickly jumped in front of it, countering my move.

"Bellman, *what* do you *want?"* I yelled, not caring how loud I sounded. The security guard seemed like the lesser of two evils.

Bellman feinted my every move. I couldn't reach the chair. I grabbed a large flask holder and threw the flasks at Bellman. He held his hands in front of his face, warding off the blows. I smashed the metal container against the window. It took several blows before the pane shattered, making a nearly shard-free opening through the frame. Bellman, having recovered from my attack, again came toward me, shoving everything out of his path in a display of rage. I hoisted one arm through the window, hoping to pull the rest of my body after it. The remaining glass shards cut through my sweater—which I now appreciated—and into my body. I cried out when one piece jabbed into my shoulder. I dropped the bobblehead back onto the lab floor. I've come this far, I can't lose it now. I pushed my way back inside the lab and dropped to the floor. Hastings's bobbleheaded face wiggled its head derisively at me. I scooped it up.

Bellman's fingers grazed my chest. My free hand grabbed the window frame. With a burst of energy, born out of stark-raving terror, I gave a strong push and propelled myself out the window. Bellman grabbed my right foot, yanking hard on it. Protecting the bobblehead by clamping it to my chest, I readied myself to fall flat into the outside brick wall. I forced my free hand between my chest and the wall to soften the blow. I felt a bone-crunching smack all the way to my teeth as my chin smacked against the bricks. I dropped the bobblehead in front of me, my face six inches from the grass. Bellman twisted my foot, wrenching hard. Placing both hands against the ground for leverage, I kicked as hard as I could. I contacted with something not exactly hard, but not soft either. Bellman groaned, released his grip, and took my right shoe with him.

I scrambled to my feet, grabbed the bobblehead and ran like I've never run before through the grass, around the building, and down to the parking lot. Every few seconds, I looked to see if anything—human or inhuman—chased me. I saw nothing.

I collapsed onto the front seat of the Bucket and quickly texted Olivia.

—*Done, but get to Bucket now*—I wrote.

—*Okay*—she immediately responded.

I stripped off my torn, sweaty and bloody robber gear and kicked it underneath the seat. I checked and double-checked that my doors remained locked. Taking every precaution necessary, I started the car in case we'd need to make a fast getaway. My shaky hands bled from glass cuts. I glowered at the cursed bobblehead next to me and slammed it into my glove box.

My heavy breathing still hadn't subsided, filling the car with what sounded like eardrum-shattering noise. Every outside sound caused me to jump in fear. In front of me sat the row of dead, dark houses I created, their inhabitants now milling about each others' front yards, wondering when their domain's life forces would be restored.

The door handle jiggled. My heart blasted at my rib cage, begging to come out and see what had me in such an uproar.

"Tex," said Olivia, "let me in."

I unlocked the door and slid over. Olivia piled in behind the steering wheel.

"Good God, Tex, you look *terrible*."

"Yeah, thanks." I managed a brief smile. "Let's get the hell out of here. *Now*, okay?"

"What happened?"

"I'll explain...once we're out of here."

"Okay, but I'm driving."

"Ya think?" My trembling hands would steer us into a ditch, no doubt.

"Did you get it?" She backed out of the parking spot.

"Yeah, I got it."

"Good." She looked at me and frowned. "You won't *believe* the crap I had to go through."

"Well, I've got a story for you, too. *Wait!*" On Johnson Drive, she slammed the brakes to a screeching halt.

"Jesus, give a girl a little warning next time, why don't ya?"

With an aching hand, I pulled out the napkin and recited the words as best I could. After a minute, the lights poured into the homes. The reawakened streetlights looked down from on high, almost like rainbows and holding future promise. The people in the yards let out a collective, contagious cheer. Olivia cheered right along with them.

"Okay," I sighed, "*now* let's go."

****

"Tex, are you all right?"

"Dad, I'm fine. I did what I needed to do. Everything's over and done with." Olivia stared at me inquisitively. "Listen, Dad...I'm *really* sorry I went out and—"

"Not as half as sorry as you're gonna be." Oh, boy. "I've been sitting by the phone...waiting...*worrying*!" I

203

could picture him with his eyes shut, rubbing his brow.

"It's okay. It's all over. And the person I was trying to save should be out of danger." Olivia's eyes stayed on me and not the road. I snapped my fingers and pointed to redirect her attention as she swerved out of the lane. She turned her head forward and corrected the car with a jerk, sending me bopping up against the window. "Gah!"

"*Crap*," yelled Olivia.

"What was that?" asked Dad.

"Nothing. Olivia's driving so I could call you. A cat crossed in front of us."

"Hmm." That one little word carried the weight of the world in suspicion.

"Anyway, I'll be home after a while. Um, there's no need for you to wait up." Like *that* wouldn't happen.

"Oh, I'll be waiting all right. Count on it." He paused. "Tex, you asked me to trust you. How in the *world* do you expect me to do that when you go against my orders?"

"I know. I'm sorry."

"We're gonna have a *long* talk." He sighed, a good sign most of the anger storm had passed. "I hope someday you'll trust me enough to tell me the entire story." His words sounded like a thinly veiled accusation of my withholding the truth, eerily echoing what Olivia laid at my feet earlier. I do keep requesting my loved ones' trust but am seemingly unable to reciprocate. I used to blame it on forces outside my control, but I have to wonder if it's a character flaw of mine. Is it fair of me to ask such things of those closest to me? Or am I trying to justify my actions because I'm really a self-centered, narcissistic jackass?

"I *will* tell you, Dad, just not tonight, okay?"

"I'll see you when you get home." He hung up.

"Tex," said Olivia, "did you really tell your dad what we did tonight?"

"No. No way. I just sort of gave him a vague...warning, I guess, that he could get a bad phone call from the police if we screwed up and got caught."

Olivia's mouth dropped. "Really? And he didn't ask for any deets?"

"No. Well, I sorta snuck out when he told me not to go."

"*Damn*, I wish my mom was that cool." I guess my dad's being "cool" sorta trumped my being in trouble with him, at least in Olivia's eyes. I can only imagine how "cool" he's going to be tonight. But, what's done is done.

"Your mom's all right, O'."

"Oh, whatever." She wagged a hand in front of her face. "Okay, *okay*. Let me tell you what happened to me." She scooted up farther in her seat. "So, did you hear my fit?"

"Which time?"

"*Exactly*. So, this Seth Calvechhio, the night watchman, is all trying to comfort me and can't keep his hands off me while I'm screaming and cryin' about being afraid of the dark, and he's all 'there, there, little lady, let Seth take care of you,' and it took everything I had not to knee him in his *junk*."

My laughter made the cuts on my chest jab a little deeper.

"You know how *hard* that was for me?"

"I can probably guess." I applied pressure toward the pain on my chest, the warm moisture of blood slowly seeping through my T-shirt.

"So, Sethie takes me back to the auditorium where there's a bunch of people hangin' out and flickin' their lighters in the lobby like they're at a rock concert or something. He tells me to stay with the crowd and everything'll be okay. So he takes off and *blammo*. The lights come back on. Well, I freaked, so I immediately ran back out to the gate. There he was, getting ready to lock and close it. And I saw you down the hallway, looking like a pink-faced deer caught in the headlights."

I curbed my amusement for fear of more pain. Olivia thought she'd endured pure, unadulterated torture while I fought for my life against a ghost. But, I've come to understand that pretending to be a helpless little girl *is* akin to hell for Olivia.

"So, I had to turn into a blubbering mess all over again." When the streetlight beams crawled over her face, I saw her smile beat through her indignation.

"Olivia, thanks. You saved me."

"*God,* don't make me do that *again*. Everyone thought I was a freak show. If anyone gives me *crap* about it tomorrow…" She balled up a fist and pumped it in the air, grunting a few times. "Anyway, I was totally freaked out about you and nearly passed out until you texted me. So, where's our booty?"

"In the glovebox."

She snorted. "I can't wait to see how Hastings is gonna handle that."

"Yeah, we need to talk about that." I winced in pain again, this time mentally. Everything had gone to hell so fast, I couldn't be sure if I left behind any incriminating evidence.

"Okay, but now, tell me your story."

I told her the entire saga of the clumsy heist, how I had trouble with the keys, how I'd lost the spell, and finally, my near-death escape from the ghost of Bob Bellman.

"*Day-um,* Tex," she said, before settling into a thoughtful silence.

I took advantage of the quiet and studied her. The moonlight bounced in and out of the car, alighting on her face sporadically. Shadows slowly peeled away as if alive—an animated death shroud pulled back, exposing her pale appearance in the low nightlights. She appeared at once beautiful, yet scary in a way—a potent reminder when you play dangerous games, you're one step closer to becoming a young corpse. Perhaps a visual warning that despite our youthful feelings of invulnerability, we're fragile creatures, prone to the follies of the fates that control when it's time to die? I hoped—prayed—this isn't a portentous omen of some sort.

I shook myself out of my morbid reverie. "I don't understand why Bellman's back." I shivered. And not from the Bucket's air-conditioning, which hasn't worked as long as I've been its proud owner.

"What're you gonna do?" The shadows crawled back and forth over her face, until I forced myself to stare at the mundane homes of suburbia.

"I guess I'll go talk to Mickey again. I wish I'd talked to her about it earlier today when I was over there, but with everything else going on—and the fact I thought Bellman's first appearance was maybe a one-off fluke of some sort—I put it on the back burner."

Olivia bit her lower lip, possibly the only time *ever* at a loss for words.

"But," I continued, "you need to be careful, too, okay?" She nodded. "He's...not like what I thought a ghost is supposed to be."

"What do you mean?"

"He can actually *hurt* you. He's...I guess, corporeal."

"Huh. Crap."

"Yeah. When I fought him, he could throw stuff around. And he grabbed my foot and tried to break it. When I kicked him back, I think I made contact with his head...and it was *weird*."

"'Weird' how?"

"It felt both soft *and* hard. *Weird*."

"Yeah, that *is* weird."

"And he took my shoe."

So involved with telling my tale, I only now realized she pulled up in front of her house. She turned off the Bucket that, for once, didn't sputter or backtalk. I guess it only has mad rage for me and not any other driver.

"What are we doing here at your place?"

"Tex, I need to get you cleaned up. You're a mess."

"I'm okay," I said, although I really, *really* did want to go inside.

"No, come on," she demanded. "My mom's at work. Let's go." She scooted out and ran over to my side of the car. She pulled open the door, bowed, and waved her hand. "Will Madam be needing my driving skills any further tonight?" she asked, in a lousy British accent.

She grabbed the pile of thief garb from under the seat and ushered me inside, pushing me down onto her brown leather sofa. Olivia's home is an interesting one. More care had been spent on decorating with eye-catching colors and painted accents than the actual furnishing of the house. While the walls were ablaze with reds and contrasting gray trim, and adorned with many three-dimensional hangings, the actual furniture remained sparse. I assumed this to be due to financial constraints, but the overall appearance came off as a modern art work-in-progress.

"I'm going to toss this crap into the wash." She frowned at the sweater and the ski masks. "Except for the gloves." She held the plastic blue gloves up for inspection. Mine were completely torn and shredded by the lab window's glass. "Let's throw these out and call it pretty." She smiled and scuttled off.

I stared at the fireplace in a semi-daze. On the shelf above it sat literally dozens of small, framed photographs of Olivia through the years. I spotted a very young Olivia, red hair pulled back in pigtails. She appeared very different, but still unmistakably her, the same mischievous glint in her eyes proclaiming, *Look out, world, I'm coming on strong*. Watching her grow in the chronologically positioned photos just made me miss our relationship more. Even when she appeared angry in the photo array, an obvious zeal for life and a stubborn refusal to settle for anything rang out loud and clear: her way or the highway, *damnit*.

Humming from the washer drifted out from the kitchen, and seconds later, Olivia appeared. She brandished a first-aid kit, a box of adhesive bandages, and a roll of medical bandage. "Stop looking at my mom's embarrassing shrine."

"Oh, sorry. It just looks like your mom's really

proud of you."

"Yeah, whatever." She sat down next to me. "Take off your T-shirt," she ordered.

Dutifully, I began to whip my shirt off, somewhat embarrassed by my mostly muscle-free, scrawny and pale appearance. Oh, to be able to swap bodies with Brandon. "Ouch!" Blood from one of the cuts had matted to the T-shirt. When I finally got the shirt off, the bleeding started again.

"Damn, you cut yourself pretty good." She rubbed alcohol or some other evil, burning liquid on my wounds. I wanted to scream, but realized that's not what the wondrous Brandon would do in such a situation.

"Come on, Tex," she chided. "You wanna piece of leather to bite down on?" She continued tending to my wounds, both on my chest and right hand. The cut underneath my chin had mercifully stopped bleeding. Olivia examined it closely, the clean smell of her skin wafting into my nose. I'm sure I smelled like a football player's support cup.

"I don't think you're going to need stitches," she said, sitting back.

"Good. Hey, we need to get our stories right for tomorrow."

"I know." She smiled. "Seems like old times." The old times weren't always good, as we had to deal with bullies and serial killers, but we obviously both thought of when we had to concoct matching stories about our takedown of Bob Bellman last year.

"Yes, it does." Before I let myself get carried away in the moment, I decided to forge on—Mr. All-Business, that's me. "Okay, your story is already set, and it's a good one. You went to the bathroom, the lights went out, and you freaked. You were afraid of the dark." She frowned and crossed her arms. "When the lights came back on, you panicked—worried it could happen again. No one'll even suspect you had anything to do with it."

"Whatever. I just *hate* it." Her frown looked nearly comical in its severity. "People are going to think I'm afraid of the dark. Stupid. What next? Wetting the bed?"

"I know it's a lot to ask of you. And I wouldn't do it, if it weren't necessary. But you can handle this. You're the bravest kid at our school. I've always thought so..."

"That's not true."

"No. No, I think it *is*. Not once were you afraid tonight. And you risked everything for a friend. Besides, I think your reputation's gonna survive this." And it's true, too. Through our ordeals from last year up until now, she *is* braver than I am. She shows remarkable courage in the most terrifying situations and never backs down from an adversary.

"It better had," she said defiantly. She flexed a muscle and bellowed, "Hoo-*Hah*."

"Anyway," I continued, "my story's a little trickier. The cameras were on us. I'm going to tell them I wasn't feeling well, sick to my stomach, so I hung out in the bathroom, waiting for relief, I guess."

Olivia's mouth turned down in disgust. "Tex, your story sucks even more than mine."

"That's okay," I laughed. "I don't really care if anyone makes fun of me for having irritable bowel syndrome, to tell you the truth." Olivia giggled. "So, I was hunkerin' down in the toilet when the lights went out. I think we'll need to tell whoever—if we're even questioned—we came to the play together, because they probably saw us on one of the cameras. And it might look kinda funny that we were in the johns at the same time, but…" I shrugged my shoulders. "I don't think they can prove anything. At least, I *hope* they can't." I began mentally retracing our steps from tonight.

"Wait… What's wrong?"

"Well, when the lights came back on, they caught me on camera. I was wearing my mask—"

"*Pink* mask," Olivia interrupted.

"Um, yeah, pink mask. I don't think I was identifiable, but I am concerned. Also, I lost my flashlight in the lab and my shoe as well."

"Tex, I really, *really* doubt they can trace those back to you."

I wondered. Then I wondered what shoes I'm going to wear tomorrow.

"Maybe. Maybe not. But there is that risk. And then I probably left some of my blood and bits of my sweater on the broken window." Olivia wrinkled her nose at the thought of the dreaded black sweater. "And my left glove's fingertips gave out. Now I know they can't take our fingerprints unless they can directly tie us to the scene of the crime, but there is a possibility—"

"Tex, you're borrowing trouble."

"Um, what does that exactly mean?"

"I'm not really sure. It's something my mom says. Doesn't matter." She waved her hands in the air. "Just relax."

"I'm trying to, but you know I'm always…tightly wrapped, I guess."

She placed a hand alongside my cheek. "I know, right? Sometimes I think I know you better than you know yourself." She let her hand drop. I wanted to grab it and put it back where it belongs.

"And then there's the issue of the damage in the lab. What started out as what could've been described as a 'harmless prank'—and I don't think there's *any* way they can possibly blame the power outage on us—has now turned into what they'll consider vandalism."

"Yeah, there is that." We sat quietly pondering our potential future as jailbirds. "So, do you think we accomplished what we needed to do?"

"That's what I'm hoping. We should be good to go."

"Cool."

"Anyway…" I turned to meet her eyes full on. "Olivia, I really want to thank you for everything. I couldn't have done it without you."

She placed both her hands on my cheeks this time. "You're welcome." To my ecstatic surprise, she leaned in and pressed her lips on mine. I wrapped my hands gently behind her neck. The interplay started soft and sweet, before bursting into heavy breathing and longer, more passionate kisses.

Her scent flooded my nose with a wondrous sensation, both of sweet memories and of hopeful futures. Our hands caressed each other's backs; mine taking care not to be too aggressive, hers, cautious to not disturb my wounds. The moment seemed to last forever, yet not nearly long enough when the infernal buzzer from the washing machine blared off in the kitchen. Lips still interlocked, Olivia giggled, sending a pleasant vibration throughout my lips. I laughed, too.

She pulled away slowly, eyes still shut. "Wait here," she said softly. Her hand grazed my cheek again, before she ran into the kitchen.

Grinning like the town idiot, I attempted to regain my composure. She came back into the room, my torn black sweater stretched between her arms, dripping water on the floor.

"Tex, um, I think we're going to have to give your lovely sweater a funeral."

I stared at the sweater and nodded. Then realization swept over me, snapping me back to other, less desirable concerns. "Wait, let me see that."

She came closer and held it in front of me for inspection, in much worse shape than I thought. Large, gaping holes lined the sweater's front, looking like it'd been worn by the victim of a bear attack. Had I not worn that tonight, the cuts on my chest would've been much more extensive.

"Maybe…maybe that's why Elspeth told me to wear that," I said, under my breath. But not quiet enough.

"What?" She dropped the sweater to her side. "*What*? Who, or *what*, is *Elspeth*?"

I opened and shut my mouth several times, no words feeling right. I knew what my answer would be, and she wouldn't like it. But it's the only answer I have. "I'm sorry, O', but I can't tell you about it. Not now."

A much worse sadness replaced her earlier fury. "Tex, this is what I was talking about earlier. You're still the same." Tears brimmed her eyes. My heart shattered. I'd rather she be angry at me than feel betrayed. "I trusted you with my future tonight, yet, you're *still* keeping secrets from me. You don't trust

214

me..." Her voice cracked.

"No! Olivia, it's not *like* that." I stood and put my hand on her arm, attempting to embrace her with a hug. She pulled away.

"Don't *do* that. You *don't* get to do *that*."

"Sorry, I'm sorry..." My voice wavered as well. "I do trust you. I...*love* you. It's just I made a promise to someone else not to say anything."

She ran to the kitchen, and I heard the dryer door open. She came back and threw the two masks at me. "Take them and get out. *Now*." She pointed toward the door.

"Olivia, please, I *will* tell you everything. I just *can't* right now. But I promise, *I swear* I will as soon as I can."

"How do you expect me to be in a relationship with someone who won't tell me the truth?" Tears rolled down her cheeks. "Just leave me alone. Get out..."

"I'm *so* sorry."

"*Now*."

I walked toward the front door. Her sobs filled the house with sorrow, wracking my soul with guilt and remorse. I turned to try and salvage the damage I'd caused one last time, but when I saw her squatting on the floor, her small body shaking, her face buried in her arms, I thought I'd only make matters worse.

Somehow I made it to the Bucket and fell in. I stared at her front door, hoping against all impossible odds she'd come running out, but I knew futile wishes were fiction, born of bad movies. One more time, the fates decided to be supremely cruel toward me. For one fantastic moment, they granted my fondest desire, only to snatch it away from me seconds later because my misery affords them great amusement.

I fell against my steering wheel and sobbed. "*Goddamnit.*"

Chapter Eleven

"Hey, Brandon." While leaning up against the soft drink dispenser, he munched out of a bag of potato chips. "I got what I was supposed to." Ian lurked behind me, straining to hear what we said.

Brandon's sleepy eyes widened. "I *know.* Everyone's talking about it. How'd you do it?"

"It wasn't easy."

"Ken wants to meet tonight. Can you be at my house at eight?"

"Yeah, I'll be there."

At least I *think* I can make it. Last night when I got home, Dad pretty much ignored me out of anger. He glared at me, shook his head, stuttered, and said, "This isn't over." I think his relief lightened the blow of his gavel. Doesn't mean my punishment's not still forthcoming. "And when I pass off the bobblehead, then it's all over. Right?"

Brandon winced as if stung by a bee. "I don't know, Tex."

"What do you mean?"

"Ken's kinda…I think he still doesn't believe you or your story about the Young Bloods."

"I did what he asked me to do. He *has* to believe me."

Brandon shrugged and said, "Okay." He looked toward Olivia, sitting at our table, and sauntered off in her direction.

"What was that all about?" asked Ian.

"I'll tell you later."

"Tex." Ian nudged me. "There's Rebecca Hogan, Jim Badger's girlfriend. I think it's her first day back." Ian pointed toward a girl with scraggly blonde hair packed into black tights and a low cut shirt with her bra straps sassily on display.

Before I could stop myself, I approached her. She walked slowly as if in a dream state, barely keeping her lunch tray level. "Um, excuse me," I said.

"What do you want?" She avoided eye contact, focusing on the cafeteria tables.

"Hi, I'm Tex. I just wanted to tell you how sorry I am for your loss."

She snapped her head around, her eyes narrow slits of anger. "Did you even *know* Jim?" Other students stopped talking to watch the commotion.

"Um, no, but—"

"Then what the *hell* are you doing talking to *me*?"

"I just…sorry. Sorry to bother you." I turned around quickly, hoping to end my newest embarrassment.

"Yeah, you better run," she shouted. "They're gonna *get* the bastards who did it. I *know* who did it. You *don't* want to get on my bad side."

I stopped in my tracks. Part of me felt compelled to ask her who she thought killed James Badger, but with everyone staring at me, I just wanted to crawl under a table. Across the room, Olivia smirked at my latest bad decision. There's to be no respite for me today at lunch. I stalled, thinking I'd kill the rest of the lunch period by the condiment station. As soon as I spun around, I bumped into Elizabeth Blackmer. The milk carton on her tray wobbled before finally giving into gravity and spilled down the front of her navy blue sweater.

She dropped her tray with a *clang*, held her hands out in outrage and yelled, "*What* did you *do* to me?"

"Ah, sorry. Here…" She stroked her tie tenderly as if nursing a wounded kitten back to health. I grabbed a napkin and shook it in the air impotently, sort of a white flag of surrender.

"You've *ruined* my outfit. " She knocked the napkin away and shrieked. Two for two now, a stellar day.

"Sorry, sorry, sorry…" I felt the blood rush to my face as students laughed at my newest folly. "What can I do?"

"You've done *enough*. Just get *away* from me."

"I'm *really* sorry, Elizabeth. Um, I know now's not a great time, but could you let Elspeth know that I'd like to talk to her?"

Her eyes flew open, her lower lip trembled, on the verge of boiling over. She pointed in the direction she wanted me to leave. I hung my head, muttered apologies a few more times, and slunk toward our lunch table.

Ian and Daniel giggled, Olivia shook her head in disbelief, and Brandon chewed his chips, obliviously happy to be in processed food nirvana.

"Jesus, Tex," said Ian. "Is there a single girl here who you're *not* going to harass?" Daniel burst out laughing, spraying bits of bread across the table.

"Um, yeah, whatever." I glanced at Olivia. "Hey."

"Hi." She stared down at her untouched meal. Brandon continued his incessant chewing motion, his gaze wandering around the room. While Ian and Daniel obviously sensed the tension, apparently Brandon's foremost concern lay in what's gonna happen when he finally runs out of chips.

"Tex, what *are* you doing?" Olivia raised her eyes. "Is this some kind of stupid attempt to make me jealous?"

"Oh, boy." Ian scrunched down in his chair, trying to vanish, apparently having had more than his fair share of drama by proxy for one lunch period. And Brandon fought the good fight, not leaving one chip unchewed at least fifteen times.

"No, that's *not* what I'm doing. I'm just—" And there it is again, my inability to tell Olivia the truth. "Never mind," I muttered.

"Whatever." Olivia dismissed me with a wave of her hand. "Anyway..." She turned toward Brandon, flashing her pearly-white smile. "What's up with you, Bran?"

Brandon blinked, stymied by the question. Finally, he said, "Nothing" and re-commenced eating. Olivia guffawed.

"Hey," said Daniel. "Did you guys hear someone broke into school last night and trashed the lab?" Olivia's laughter slipped away. I looked at my hands, kept my eyes locked down tight. We even found a topic that forced Brandon to stop eating. Finally, Daniel added, "Well, that's what I heard."

"*You.* And, *you,*" croaked the hoarse voice of Arville Hastings. Hovering over us, he pointed at Olivia and me. His upper lip pulled back in a sneer. "In my office. *Now.*"

Olivia feigned surprise. "Me? I haven't finished

lunch, yet."

Hastings swept his ham hock arm in front of her and grabbed her tray. "You're finished now."

"Hey," shouted Olivia. I cast an urgent glance her way, hoping she'd dampen her indignation. Obviously angry, I didn't want any more fuel added to Hastings's fire.

"What's this about, Mr. Hastings?" I asked, my voice uneven.

He whipped his square head toward me, sharing none of the fluidity of his bobblehead. "I think you know." He stormed out of the cafeteria, Olivia and I straining to keep up with him. Following Hastings down the hallway, I noticed Olivia giving me sideways nervous glances.

Hastings pushed open his office door, letting it slam shut in our faces. I opened the door, and we stepped in. Already behind his desk, Hastings stared at an empty spot on the wall, his fingers placed contemplatively alongside his jowls. We sat down in the two chairs opposite him. For the longest time, Hastings's accelerated breathing through his distended nostrils supplied the only sound.

Olivia cleared her throat, and Hastings turned his unwavering death stare toward her. "You have something to say, Ms. Furman?"

"Um, yeah. Why are we here?"

I swallowed hard, the audible gulp clicking loudly in my throat.

"I think you know the answer to that."

"No, not really." Olivia shrugged.

"Well, as you no doubt *know*,"—he slammed his hand on the desk—"last night, someone shut the power down and vandalized the science lab." Swiveling back and forth in his chair, he rested his head on the back. He wrenched to a stop and glared at us. "And—*someone*—stole my *bobblehead*." *Whack*. His hand came down again on the desk. He stared forlornly at the spot formerly occupied by his beloved bobblehead.

Olivia snorted ever so slightly and said, "Well, I heard something about that, but what does it have to do with us?"

Hastings's jaw dropped. "Our security cameras have shown us some *very* interesting events from last night." His infamous two-fingered salute pinpointed us. "So, the two of you went to see the play last night?"

"Yeah," I said, clearing my throat. "Yes, we did."

"Well, why is it the two of you went to the bathroom, and we *never* saw either one of you exit again?" He leaned forward and entwined his fingers.

Olivia scrunched her nose up. "I didn't know it was a crime to go to the bathroom. But if you *must* know, I left the show because it was making me sick."

"*Sick?*" Hastings once again swiveled. I suppose it's his daily workout.

"Yes, sick," repeated Olivia. "The show was full of racist and female stereotypes. Not exactly the kind of politically correct show I'd expect a forward-thinking school like Clearwell to be associated with." Hastings resembled an enraged German Shepherd, ready to take a bite out of crime. "I took it for as long as I could, then I told Tex I'd meet him after the play. While I was in the bathroom, the power went out."

"You were in there for twenty minutes!"

Olivia rolled her eyes. "Do you *really* want a play-by-play detailed account of what I did in there?"

Hastings ignored her and turned toward me. "And what about *you*?"

"Well, I was actually literally sick." I placed my hands over my stomach. "I think I had food poisoning or something."

Hastings processed this, again staring at the ceiling. "So…you mean to tell me *you* were sick, and *you* were offended by the play?" he asked the ceiling.

"That's right."

"I think—that's all a load of *crap*." He pounded his desk again for emphasis. "I think the two of you destroyed the lab and stole my *bobblehead*." Every time he mentioned his beloved bobblehead, his voice raised as if mourning the loss of a son.

"No, sir. We had nothing to do with it. I mean we were both in the bathrooms when the power went out. Honestly."

"Uh huh. And *you*, Ms. Furman? Why all the histrionics?"

"What histrionics?"

A wry smile stretched across Hastings's face. "All your blubbering about being afraid of the dark?"

"Well, it's true. I am afraid of the dark." She shot me a pained look. "Always have been."

"Is that right?" Hastings now had his chair completely turned around, conducting his interrogation out the window.

"So, we went to the bathroom, and I'm afraid of the dark." Olivia's tone sped directly into the danger zone. "Those are crimes? We had *nothing* to do with your dumb bobblehead." Olivia mockingly shook her head like Hastings's vanished artifact.

"Tell me something, Richard." He twisted his chair

back around and gestured toward my bandaged hand. "What happened to your hand?"

"Oh, that." I waved my hand about, trying to think of something—*anything*—to say. "I had an accident doing yard work."

"That's funny. I don't recall seeing those bandages on your hand in the security footage."

"Oh, well, I did yard work when I got home last night."

"What kind of yard work do you do late at night?"

"Um, I needed to bundle up some sticks…the next day was trash day."

"Uh huh."

"You can ask my dad if you don't believe me."

"Oh, I will. Count on it. What about your footwear, Richard?" He pointed toward my shoes. This morning, out of necessity I threw on my hideously green-stained yard shoes. At least five years old, only grass stains held them together. "That's an interesting choice of shoe for school."

I self-consciously rubbed my hand over the green stains. "Well…I wear 'em quite a bit."

"I really doubt that. I don't think they'd pass the school dress code. Did you, perhaps…lose a shoe last night, Richard?"

"No. How could I lose a shoe?"

"Uh-huh. What size shoe do you wear?"

"Um, ten and one-half."

"Isn't *that* quite the coincidence? That's the size of the shoe we found in the lab last night."

What a liar. I actually wear size eleven. But hey, if Hastings can lie to me, then I can lie to him. "It's not my shoe, Mr. Hastings."

"You know, it's funny…" Hastings swung around again to stare out at the grassy commons beyond his window.

"What's that?" I smiled, hoping Hastings discounted me as a suspect and suddenly cared to share an amusing anecdote with me. No such luck. "The security camera caught someone wearing a pink ski mask. Odd choice for a vandal, wouldn't you say?"

"Guess so." Olivia's mouth puckered up into a grin.

"The perp seemed to be about your height, Richard." He paused expectantly.

"I don't know what you want me to say, Mr. Hastings. I was in the bathroom the entire time until the lights came back on."

"I don't know how you did it. I don't know how you turned the power off…" He spun around, nearly leaping onto his desk. "But I know it was you." He pointed his fingers from his eyes to mine. "I'm watching you. This isn't over. Not by a *long* shot."

I shook my head. "Mr. Hastings, I'm sorry about your bobblehead." Olivia chuckled, prompting Hastings to whip toward her. "But, really, we didn't do this. I don't know the first thing about turning electricity off, and why would I want to destroy the science lab? I *like* science."

"Sure, you do. Too bad I don't believe you."

"No, it's true. I really like science. Don't I, O'?"

"Oh, yeah, Tex just *loves* science. The other day, he told me he couldn't wait to get to science and slice open another pig—"

"*Enough.* This is going to be an ongoing investigation. You two—excuse me, I mean the *perps*—" He raised an eyebrow. "The perps were pretty sloppy last night. They left behind a lot of clues as to their identity."

"Huh." I needed to swallow again, but Hastings carefully scrutinized my every movement. Olivia sat in silence, either out of boredom or fear.

"And I want my damn *bobblehead* back." Out of the corner of my eye, I saw Olivia struggling to withhold her laughter. Hastings fell back into his chair, obviously spent by his investigation and the tragedy of losing his firstborn bobblehead. "Get out." Probably not the best time to ask him for a late pass.

We didn't say a word until we reached the safety of the hallway. "Tex, *what* did you leave behind? What does he have that can connect us to last night?"

"I lost a flashlight and bits of my sweater. And a shoe. But that's it. At least, I think so."

"You *think* so?"

"Yep, pretty sure."

"*Pretty* sure isn't good enough, Tex."

"I know. Okay, I'm almost positive I didn't leave anything else."

"How is 'almost positive' better than 'pretty sure'? Gah." Her fists pounded her hips.

"O', I think he's bluffing." At least that's what I hope. But no need to tell Olivia this. "I think he's just trying to trip us up...to gauge our reaction. He's probably hoping for one of us to break down and give him a vice-principal's-chambers' confession."

"Too many cop shows," said Olivia, smiling.

"Yeah. Hey, about last night…"

Her smile faded, and she held a hand up to ward me off. "It's done, Tex. I don't want to talk about it."

"But I feel that I need to apologize."

"Just forget about it. It was a mistake letting things get so carried away. And you're right, you know…you don't owe me anything." I felt my heart stomped on all over again. "I've got to get to class." She walked down the hallway slowly, her head down.

"It wasn't a mistake. It felt *right*." She continued walking, her shoulders shuddering. "Olivia."

She stopped and turned halfway around. "Goodbye, Tex." I watched her vanish down the hallway, hoping her farewell wouldn't be as final as it sounded.

****

Once again, I disturbed Brandon's epic conquering of his cereal bowl when I arrived at his house. Hooray for small favors, though; at least this time he wore a T-shirt

"Hey, Tex." He opened the door, a repeat of last time, complete with the metal music blasting out from the TV room.

"Hey, Brandon." I held my hands over my ears and yelled, "*Do you mind?*"

He stared at me, chewing his cereal until his synapses finally snapped into working gear. "Oh." He walked toward the stereo and turned it down.

"Where are the others?"

"Not here yet. My mom's at work, so we won't have to deal with her."

I sat down on the futon, while Brandon finished his cereal. As Brandon stared at me like a fascinating scientific anomaly, I watched the clock's hands on the mantle slowly tick away.

"I hope it goes down okay," he finally said.

"Yeah, me, too." At eight-thirty, they still hadn't shown up. "Hey, Brandon, you mind if I ask you something?"

"Yeah, I mean, no."

"How come you don't talk like those guys? You know? Like K-Cross and the rest of 'em with their gangsta slang?"

Brandon hefted his shoulders and dropped them quickly. "I don't know. Seems really kinda stupid."

"Yeah. It really, really is."

"I'm just interested in skating, not making a...I don't know...a lifestyle out of it or anything like that." Every time I write Brandon off as a moron, he displays the shocking capacity to surprise me with common sense.

The doorbell rang at eight-thirty-five. Brandon jumped to his feet and went to the door as I stood and prepared myself.

Ken and E-Sizzle strutted into the room, both decked out in tripp pants, their chains jangling as they approached me. "*Yo.* What up?" asked Ken. He threw back his head, knocking the hoodie off. "You get the goods?"

"Yeah." I handed my paper sack to him.

Ken opened the sack and looked in. He pulled out the bobblehead and held it up for E-Sizzle to examine. "How you jack this, yo?"

"Luck and a lot of hassle."

"Why you take down the lab, holmes?"

"That was an accident—more or less. I was just trying to escape, and I got sloppy." That reminded me of something. "Hey, Ken...um, K-Cross. Was...Bob Bellman a member of the Modern Gangstas?"

Ken delivered a double-take like I insulted him. "*Hellz* no. We don't run wit' no jocks, yo." *Not even psychotic jocks?* I wanted to ask. "Why you axin'?"

"Yeah, holmes. Why you axin'?" parroted E-Sizzle.

"No reason. Anyway, the bobblehead's yours now. I held my end of the bargain. All is peaches and cream in the land of warring gangs. Now…will you let up on the Young Bloods?"

Brandon quietly watched, scooping up every last flake of corn as Ken set the bobblehead down on the futon. He crossed the room toward me.

"Yo, you ain't one of us, *yet.*" A sneer replaced his earlier delight. E-Sizzle stepped behind me, boxing me in.

"What…what do you mean?" Ken stood so close I smelled his rancid breath. I heard E-Sizzle shuffling behind me, ready to pounce like a tiger if his master snaps his whip.

"You wants us to lissen to ya, but you gots to become one of us, cuz."

"I thought that's what my initiation was all about."

"You done good, there, holmes. But, now you gots to get ink done to prove your loyalty." E-Sizzle let out a whooping roar of laughter.

"We had a *deal*. I risked my life getting the damn bobblehead, and all I'm asking from you is to leave the Young Bloods alone. They did *not* kill Badger."

Ken's nostrils flared. "You best step off, son, and respect." He thumped his chest three times.

"Yeah, respect, homes." E-Sizzle shoved me in the back.

I sighed and gestured my hands up in the air. "Fine.

If I get a tattoo, then we're square, right?"

"Maybe, holmes, maybe not." Ken looked at me sideways and grinned. "But it's def a way to gain our respect, yo." He took out his car keys and shook them. "Let's go get ink."

"Wait," I said. "Um, I'll get a tattoo…but I want to use my own, ah, tattoo artist."

"You gots your own inker?"

"Yeah," I lied.

"Show me your tats, holmes."

I panicked. "Um, you don't *really* want to see them. They're on places…that only women get to see." I mustered up some ludicrous macho swagger.

E-Sizzled screeched again. "Yo, home-boy's got ink all up on his junk."

"A'ight, holmes," Ken finally said. "You get yo' ink done, then we sit down." He pulled his wallet out and yanked out a piece of paper. On it was a sloppy drawing of the skull with wings that Brandon has on his back.

"Fine, I'll get it done. Then we're straight, right?"

"We'll see."

"'At's right, holmes, we'll see," offered E-Sizzle. I bet he's fun at parties.

"Gots to beat feet." Ken grabbed the bobblehead, E-Sizzle scampering behind him, and nodded toward Brandon on the way out. I guess K-Cross is too cool for 'goodbyes.' After the front door slammed shut, I heard tires squealing, fading into the distance.

I fell back onto the futon, groaning. Brandon sat down next to me.

"You really gonna get a tattoo, Tex?"

"I don't know *what* I'm going to do," I shouted to

the rafters. "Brandon…are these guys just dicking with me? Are they ever going to listen to me?"

Brandon paused before answering. "I don't know. Ken's kinda hard to read sometimes."

"Ya think?"

Brandon nodded, missing the point of my sarcasm. "And he can be kinda scary, too."

"Yeah, I get that." I rubbed the back of my neck. Now I have to figure out a way to get a tattoo…yet *not* get one.

****

Allison cheerfully answered her phone with a "Hi, Tex."

"Hey, Allie."

"What's up?"

I drummed my fingertips on my desktop, wondering how much I should tell her. "Well, I need a good artist, and since you're the best artist I know…"

She giggled, and I imagined her blushing. "Well, I don't know about that…but why do you need an artist? Sounds kinda…strange."

"Yeah, well, that's sorta how my life's been lately. Strange, I mean."

"Huh."

"Anyway, I need to ask you a *huge* favor."

"Sure, Tex, anything."

"I need you to draw a tattoo on my back."

The silence on her end made me wonder if our call dropped. "What?" she finally said.

"I know it sounds weird, but I need you to draw a tattoo—in permanent ink or something—on my back." I waited for the questions to start.

"Okay," she said, drawing the word out. "Why? I

mean, if you really want a tattoo, why don't you go get one?"

"I don't really want a tattoo, Allie. I have to make it look like I got a real one, though."

"What's going on, Tex?" This is, without a doubt, my most-asked question this week.

"Okay, look, have you heard of the Modern Gangstas?" Another extended silence prompted me to call her name out again. "Allie?"

"Yeah, I'm here. Why are you messing around with those guys? They're dangerous." Apparently, I'm the only one in the student body unaware of the Gangstas's shroud of terror and tyranny over Clearwell. "You're really dumb if you hook up with them."

"I know, I know. I'm trying to get a message to them from the Young Bloods—a rival gang from Ridge Creek—that they didn't kill James Badger. But they won't listen to me unless I get a tattoo." Still more silence from her end. "I know, right?"

Allison expelled a long breath. "God, really?"

"Yeah...*really*."

"And these idiots won't even listen to you until you get a tattoo?"

"Yeah, I know, right? It doesn't make a lot of sense to me either."

"Well, okay, I guess...let's make you a tattoo," she said with all the weight of planning a trip to the grocery store.

"Cool, thanks."

"Can you come over to my place after school tomorrow?" she asked.

"Yeah, I think so. I'll bring some pens and stuff. I have a drawing of what it's supposed to look like. I'm sure yours will be better, though…"

"We'll see."

"Thanks again, Allison."

I had to make another call. It wouldn't be easy but I couldn't put it off any longer. One of these days once—if—my life straightens out, I need to focus more on homework instead of, you know, survival and murder and other such typical high school concerns.

"Hi, Tex," whispered Daniel. I looked at the time. Surely at nine-thirty, his parents hadn't already sent him to bed.

"Hey. Did I wake you from your beauty sleep?"

He chuckled, a sorta whispery and quiet scratching sound. "No. What's happening?"

"You wanna go skating tomorrow? About four or so?"

Danny didn't really like skating all that much, but he barely contained his excitement nonetheless. *"Hell,* yeah. Can you swing by my place and pick me up?"

"No problem."

"Tex?"

"Yeah?"

"What's really happening? I mean, there was your *total* weirdness today in the cafeteria, and then when I mentioned the lab being vandalized, I thought you were going to have a heart attack. Then Hastings talked to you. What's going on?"

I sighed. "Dan…Danny, I need to talk to you. I'll tell you all about it tomorrow, okay?" I really need to quit telling people that and actually follow up on it for a change.

"Okay." Suspicion rose in his voice. "Does this have anything to do with the lab being vandalized?"

"Yes, but I'll tell you about it tomorrow."

"Oh my *God*, did you do it? I knew it. I just *knew* it." Danny covered the phone's mouthpiece as he yelled at his mother through the bedroom door. "*Nothing, Mom. No, I'm not on the phone.*" Rustling bumps sounded through the phone before he returned. "Sorry. My mother...*God*. Anyway, I can't believe you did it."

"It's not something I'm proud of, and you can't tell anyone, okay?" Danny sounded in awe of my crime. While maybe not exactly ashamed of my actions, I thought it certainly nothing to be admired.

"Okay. Later, Tex."

I'm not sure how Danny will take the news, but it's time to let him know his brother's a member of the Modern Gangstas. Ken's dabbling with danger, possibly coming close to committing a murder. Danny has a right to know in case things take a turn for the worse. Yet, I also hoped against hope maybe Danny can talk sense into his brother if all my efforts fail. Regardless, one thing I've learned—secrets, even those born of good intentions, usually turn out harmful to someone.

Chapter Twelve

Allison's grandmother opened the door a crack. She lurked behind the door, her gray-haired head peering out from within the safety of the house.

"Yes?" she said.

"Um, hi, Mrs. Brubaker."

"Oh, you must be Parker, Allison's friend from church." She flashed a warm smile, her eyes swimming in rippling wrinkles.

"Ah, no, I'm Tex, Allison's friend from school. I was here earlier this year for her birthday party?" She continued to stare at me, still smiling. "We met then." I soldiered on, hoping to jog her memory.

She turned to yell up the stairs. "*Allie*, your little friend Parker is here."

"No, ma'am, I'm Tex McKenna."

She opened the door for me to enter. "Come in, Parker, come in."

Startling me, Allie's little brother skittered up the stairs quietly like a lizard, using all four of his limbs.

Allison trotted down the stairs, ignoring her brother in passing. "Oh, hi." I couldn't tell if I heard disappointment register in her voice, but she appeared surprised. Mrs. Brubaker maintained her frozen smile like a creepy waxwork. "You go relax now, Grandma."

Mrs. Brubaker wandered toward her rocking chair. "You and Parker have fun now, okay?"

Allie mouthed "Sorry" and motioned for me to come upstairs. Once we reached the top, she said, "Sorry about Grandma, Tex. She's getting worse and worse these days. Some days she can't even remember where she is."

"It's cool. It's gotta be kinda tough taking care of your grandma…and everything else."

"No, it's fine. It's what I'm supposed to do." She smiled at me warmly. I should take a cue from her and learn a little something about this strange thing called "optimism."

"I take care of my dad sometimes. It's not the same thing, but I can relate."

"I know."

I cleared my throat, desiring to leave behind any sort of maudlin path we found ourselves treading down. I've suffered enough emotional traumas this week. "I have all sorts of markers, pens, you name it. I got sort of a darkish green, because that's what tattoos look like."

Allie examined the plastic bag's contents and steered me into her bedroom. "I think we can make this look pretty good." A small bed anchored the center of the room, an array of plush, stuffed animals residing on top of the homemade-looking quilt covering it. The walls were fairly barren, except for a drawing I recognized from art class. A still life Allie prided herself on depicting a bowl of fruit.

"Oh, I'm glad you hung that one, Allie. I always thought it was great."

She dismissed me with a flourish of her hand. "It's nothing, really." She beamed before changing her expression to one of concern. "Tex, I was worried about you today. I didn't see you all day, and Ian said you weren't at lunch."

"Yeah, well, I've been uncomfortable around Olivia. I just thought it best to keep my distance for a little while." Today, I'd sought refuge in the library, but I know I can't hide from Olivia forever. Also, after I made two different girls scream at me yesterday, the idea of showing my face in the cafeteria didn't sound all that appealing.

"Oh, that's too bad." She held her fingers to her mouth, reminding me of how shy she used to be when I first met her.

"I guess you know we broke up, right?" I grimaced at how painful the words sounded out loud. Now that it's a matter of spoken record, it seems so *final*.

"Yeah, I heard that."

"So, anyway, what's going on between you and Ian?" Nosy, sure, but I wanted to deflect the blistering spotlight off me.

"Oh, nothing, really." She averted her eyes, staring down at her bed's menagerie of animals. "Can you keep a secret?"

Keeping secrets had worn out its welcome with me, but I said, "Of course."

"I think I kinda' like Ian." Finally, she mustered the courage to meet my eyes. Looking as if she'd laid her entire life bare, she braced herself for my derision and laughter. She leaped forward with a bold, big step, and I couldn't have been prouder of her.

"Well, I have two things to say about that, Allie. Number one, I think it's great. Number two...*duh*." My second point appeared to shock her momentarily until we both broke out laughing.

"Oh, is it that obvious?"

"Yeah, kinda. But if it makes you feel any better, I think Ian likes you, too." Although Ian hasn't told me any such thing, the signs are definitely there. And here I am, a loser in love, playing matchmaker at high school romance.

Allie swayed back and forth, grinning demurely. "Anyway…" she said brightly. She swooped all the stuffed animals off her bed with one quick brush of her arm. "Let's get going. Get on the bed."

"Okay."

"Take off your shirt," she ordered. "I assume you want it on your back?"

"Um, yeah, I guess so." I tugged off my T-shirt, feeling embarrassed at my bony build. I crawled onto the bed, lying on my stomach.

"Tex, you don't have to be shy around me."

"I know. I just don't look like Brandon. Anyway, the drawing's in the bag underneath the pens."

The plastic sack crinkled as she dug through the contents. "Are you *sure* you know what you're doing?"

"No, no, I'm not. I'm practically never sure about anything I do. But I'm gonna do it anyway. It's for a good cause—crazy as that sounds."

"Okay, as long as it's for a good cause." She went to work, the cold tip of the pen prompting me to jolt. After many stern orders of "relax" and a seeming eternity, Allie sighed with satisfaction.

"I think that'll do it." She led me to a standing mirror in the corner. "Take a look."

Allie had indeed improved upon Ken's crude drawing. The skull angrily bared its teeth, but her artwork took the edge off the implied menace and danger. The detail looked impeccable, with added hints of shading and depth. "Man, it looks great."

She tilted her head and smirked. "Whatever. I hope it's what you need."

"It should do. How long do you think it'll stay?"

"Oh, you're gonna' be with that tattoo for several weeks at least, by my guess."

"Huh. Okay. Anyway, thanks again."

"No problem. Oh, and Tex?"

"Yeah?"

"Two things," she said, mimicking me from earlier. "First of all…" She ticked off one finger. "Please don't tell Ian what I said."

"You got it."

"Second, be careful, okay?"

"I will." I threw my shirt on, turned to leave, but changed my mind and sat back down on her bed. "Hey, Allie?"

"Yeah?" She plopped down beside me, once again nervous.

"Do you mind if I ask you a personal question?"

She struggled for her reply. "Depends on what it is."

"Okay. And you don't have to answer, if you don't want to. I know how it is to—"

"Just ask your *damn* question."

"Um, 'kay…What happened to your parents?"

She took in a deep breath, her large shoulders heaving up and down. "Maybe…some other time I'll tell you, Tex. Not now."

"You know I lost my mother. It's okay to—"

"*Not now.*" Her lips quivered as she struggled to gain control of whatever dark demon I inadvertently unleashed. Finally, her lips cooperated and formed a weak smile.

"Sorry, Allie." I reached out and gently patted her shoulder.

"It's okay." She shook her head and instantly transformed into a shining ray of sunshine again. "Well. You'd better go get doing—whatever it is you need to be doing." It seemed as if the prior conversation never happened.

"Yeah. I'll let myself out. Thanks again."

"De nada," she sang as I pulled her door shut behind me. Way to go, Tex. The fourth girl I made yell at me this week. If this were an Olympics competition, I'd obviously be going for the gold.

As I walked down the stairwell, I heard a hissing sound. Peeking through the slats in the upstairs railing sat Allie's creepy, little brother, chortling at me. I hurried through the front door, wondering just what secrets Allie's family carried.

****

Dan barreled out his front door, his skateboard tucked underneath his arm. He dropped it, cursed, and picked it up. "Let's go," he shouted.

I put the Bucket into drive and pulled out slowly. Mrs. Cross stood in the doorway, wringing a hand towel. I recognized her worried appearance as one I know intimately from my father. "Where the hell's the fire, Danny?"

"Ah, my mom's just getting on my nerves." I suppose it's the natural order of things; teenagers are hard-wired to despise their parents. That's why Allison's attitude toward her grandmother seems so refreshing. I have no idea what Brandon thinks of his mother—in his infinite sleepy wisdom, I imagine he wonders who the woman is with whom he shares a house.

"You're not going to get into trouble for hangin' today, are you?"

"No. Whatever. I don't know. She never lets me do anything."

"She's probably just worried. That's what parents do. Maybe she doesn't want you hanging out with the wrong crowd."

Danny grinned. "Yeah, if she only *knew* what you did to the science lab."

"Yeah, not one of my proudest moments."

"You gotta tell me everything."

"I will."

"*Hey*, where were you at lunch today? Everyone wanted to know if you got busted or something."

"No, nothing like that. Girl problems."

"Ah, yeah. Chicks." Sadly, I don't think Danny's experienced any girl problems *or* pleasures. He nodded and rubbed his chin, signifying his understanding of the "fairer sex" and the hassles and mysteries they pose.

Relief filled me fully when I saw the skate park empty. The Young Bloods must be steering clear of this park until everything blows over.

We passed by the creepy bronze statues flanking the entrance. One statue consists of a head resting upon a skateboard. The other is a foot, cut off at the ankle, riding a board. They look like victims from a bad horror film. I don't know who the city of Clearwell commissioned for the sculptures, but surely someone lost their job over it. Either that, or somewhere an artist is laughing all the way to the bank.

I sat down on top of a wall and motioned for Danny to join me.

"Okay, Tex, let's hear it."

I inhaled deeply. "I don't really know where to start. So, here we go…"

Danny stared at me, his eyebrows raised behind his glasses.

"Have you heard of the Young Bloods? From Ridge View?" He nodded. "Well, they paid me a visit one night and took me for a ride."

"That's messed up. What'd they do to you?"

"Nothing, really. They dropped me in the middle of nowhere, but they didn't hurt me or anything. Anyway, they wanted me to give a message to the Modern Gangstas."

The color drained from his face. "They're…Clearwell's gang."

"Yeah. Anyway, they wanted me to tell them they had nothing to do with killing James Badger."

"But, that's what everyone thinks. I think they *did* do it, Tex."

"That's just it, Danny. I don't think they did it. So, I tried to get a message to the Modern Gangstas."

"Wait. How'd you do that?"

If I'm going to tell him about his brother, I thought it best to tell him how I infiltrated the Gangstas. There's no other way. "Brandon. I found out Brandon's a member."

Danny's board slipped out of his hands and swirled down the curved cement wall. *Brandon?* Wow…Brandon."

"Yeah. I'd appreciate it if you keep that quiet. At least for the time being, okay?"

"Sure."

"So, turns out the Modern Gangstas wouldn't listen to me until I joined them and went through an initiation."

"The science lab. That was your initiation?"

"Yeah. They wanted me to steal Hastings's bobblehead."

Danny looked puzzled. I assume he's never had the pleasure of visiting Hastings's office. "Hastings had a bobblehead made to look like him. The Gangstas wanted me to steal it."

"Ohhhh," he said, again nodding his head in understanding. "Figures."

"Yeah, anyway, I got the bobblehead, but they still won't believe me."

"Well, that sucks."

"Yeah, it does. Dan...Danny...I need your help."

Danny shook his head, the sunlight dancing off his polished lenses. "What can I do to help?" I really didn't want to drag Daniel into this—sitting on the cement wall, he looked fragile and small, like one of Mickey's delicate big-eyed figurines—but, he's already involved by proxy through his brother. Even though he has no knowledge of it.

"Here's the thing..." I pinched his elbow, ensuring his full attention. "Your brother, Ken...is now the leader of the Modern Gangstas."

Danny shot to his feet and ran down the curvature of the stone wall. He jumped on his board and slowly, carefully skated toward the back wall of the park. Hunkering down against the wall, he covered his head with his hands and buried it between his knees. I skated after him, popping my board up as I neared him. His arms muffled his sobbing.

"Danny? I'm sorry. Sorry, man. I didn't want to have to tell you. But I thought you had a right to know. Your brother could be in danger…or might try to harm one of the Young Bloods. I'm sorry. He's one of them."

He raised his head, took off his glasses, and rubbed his eyes. "You don't *understand*."

I sat down next to him. "Tell me. What don't I get?"

He stared at me, eyes glassy and swollen. "My brother *hates* me. And, I love him…but he hates me." Hardly the reaction I expected.

"He doesn't hate you," I said, realizing my words probably sounded hollow.

"Yeah, he does."

"I'm sorry you feel that way, but—"

"But nothing!" Quietly, we sat on the wall until Danny's sobs vanished with a long, stuttering, cleansing gasp. "Sorry," he finally said. "Sorry."

"There's nothing to be sorry about. You—"

"I actually suspected it, Tex…"

"Suspected what?"

"That Ken was in the Gangstas."

"Oh."

"His late nights…the people he hangs out with. Things he says. How he dresses. But I wanted to give him the benefit of a doubt."

"Yeah, we, um, never want to think the worst of our…loved ones." I knew I sounded like a greeting card, but it's all I had.

"And now…*now*, he's gone and done something really stupid. I don't want to see him get hurt…or anything. Or whatever."

"I know, Dan. And he wouldn't want anything to happen to you either, I'm sure."

"He doesn't care what happens to me. He doesn't give a damn about me. I don't think he even cares about himself."

"Huh." I ran out of reassuring platitudes. Plus, I couldn't help but agree with his last statement. Ken Cross doesn't give a damn about himself or the people who cross his path.

"But...Ken wouldn't kill anyone. I know that." He put his glasses back on.

"I'd like to believe that. I just want to make sure he doesn't. That's why I wish you'd talk to him for me."

Danny let out a whoop of laughter. "You *really* think he'd listen to me, Tex? He doesn't even talk to me."

"Could you try, Danny? Please?" I spread my hands. "I'm out of ideas. I even had to get a fake tattoo."

"Let me see your tattoo."

I'm totally against showing my body off in public, but once I saw Danny easing up, I obliged happily. I whipped my shirt off and turned away, exposing my back.

He chuckled. "Nice tat."

I pulled my shirt back on and grinned. "Yeah, whatever, thanks. I guess."

"Fine, I'll try and talk to him. I doubt it'll do any good. No promises...but I can *try*."

"Thanks." I clapped him on his back.

"But, you know, I told you I love him...I'm also sort of afraid of him."

"Well, you're not the only one." I thought of

Brandon's earlier proclamation, and yes, I'm also a member of the "Ken Cross Fear Society."

"Tex, you really, *really* should leave these guys alone. From what I hear, they're dangerous. You could get into trouble, too." He seemed genuinely concerned, and if it wouldn't have seemed too unmanly, I would've hugged him. Careful so as not to break him, I timidly patted his shoulder again.

"I promise I'll be careful. And believe me, I'm trying to put all of this goofy-ass gangsta nonsense behind me as soon as I can." That drew another chuckle out of him. "I'll let you know anything else that happens, and I *will* be careful."

"Okay."

"Now, come on. You wanna' skate or what?"

Danny looked down at the park. "Not really," he said, wincing. "Can we go to Sonic instead?"

I smiled. "My treat."

****

Daniel trudged up the sidewalk to his front stoop in less than a straight path, obviously killing time. He'd also stalled in the Bucket, clearly not looking forward to going home.

I hope I'm not putting him in danger by asking him to talk to his brother. He's been through enough emotional turmoil as it is. But if anyone can talk sense into his thug of a brother, Danny might have the best shot. Before he entered his home, he shot me one last, sad look.

As I turned over the Bucket's engine, I saw a figure in my rear-view mirror staggering down the sidewalk as if drunk. No, not drunk. Just Ken with his affected, sloppy shuffling. His feet scraped along the pavement, kicking out in every direction, his cuffs dragging the ground. His ambulatory choice gave him the appearance of a street person as opposed to a street-wise gangsta. I braved myself and got out of the car.

"K-Cross." He stopped and shook off his hood, his hands still tucked in his pockets.

"Yo, what you doin' at my crib?"

"Um, I was hangin' with your brother."

He closed the distance between us in seconds.

"If you gonna' run wit' us, you don' be hangin' wit' my pussy lil' bro." He displayed his teeth, his nostrils stretched to their limit. His cold gray eyes seethed.

"Look, K', I'll hang out with whomever I choose to. And speaking of your brother, maybe you should go a little easier on him." He came closer, the tip of his nose nearly touching mine. I held my ground.

"I can't believe you, holmes." He twisted in both directions, scanning for onlookers. "You come to *my* crib and start preachin' to me about my own brother." He jabbed a finger into my chest. "You don't do that. You owe allegiance to me. You *needs* to show some—"

"Respect, yeah, yeah, I know. Why don't you show your brother some respect?"

"*You* don't get to *talk* about my brother." I noticed he dropped the gangsta talk.

"Your brother loves you, you know." Dumb to harass the gorilla, but I felt emboldened by the certainty he wouldn't attack me in front of his parents' home.

He glared at me, backing off an inch. "Don't talk pussy." He spat on the ground. "You be mindin' yo' own bizness, yo." And the lovable 'gangsta speak' came back like an unwanted boomerang. "What I gets up to ain't no concern of your'n, holmes."

"I'm just saying Danny's a good guy. He's a good friend, and I bet if you give him a chance, he'll be a great brother—"

"Enough!" We stared at each other as his breathing slowed to something resembling a human. "You get yo' ink done?"

"Yeah."

"Show me." This time I scoured for spectators, uncomfortable as always in the skinny sack that's my body. I inched my shirt up. Ken grabbed the shirt and yanked it up hard. With a strong grip, he pinned one of my arms behind my back and threw me onto the trunk of my car. He pulled the shirt up to my neck, nearly tearing the fabric. Still holding my arm, he stared at the faux tattoo. He spit into his hand and rubbed Allie's drawing. His calloused palm bit deep into my skin, creating a burning sensation.

I closed my eyes, hoping the ink held as permanently as the markers' packaging promised. Finally, he pushed himself away from me.

I straightened, pulled my shirt back on, and glared at him. "Satisfied?" I reached around to massage my back but couldn't quite touch the sore area.

He wiped his hands together and laughed. "Yeah, holmes, look like you done good."

"That's it, then. We're done here. Call off your crew or whatever. Let the cops sort it out."

"Sheeit. Five-O don't know jack."

"*What* are you talking about, Ken?" I called him by his real name, but frankly, after he attacked me, how worse can it get?

"I be sayin', I gots to meet with my homies to

discuss it. I gots to order a council."

"I did *everything* you asked. You want to talk about 'respect'? What *respect* do you deserve by not keeping your word?"

"Lissen up, punk-ass beeyotch." Once again, he orbited into my face, making him appear like a Neanderthal Cyclops. "My word is *good*. You be ' spectin' me to take your word. Who are *you*? I don't know you. You come to my crib, talkin' smack. Somethin' ' bout you don't track right, ' s'what I'm sayin'." He lowered his voice. "For all I knows, you be workin' wit' the Young Bloods."

He made it painfully obvious he wouldn't listen to reason; soooo way beyond unreasonable, and maybe even hoarding an assortment of mental issues. But it didn't stop my big mouth. "What about you? Huh? Ken? Who are you? You ask for respect, but what have you done to deserve any? You want to be this big supah suburban gangsta." I rolled my eyes and waved my hands. I knew I'd regret it, but I fully embraced my rollercoaster roll. With the week I'm having, I needed to vent. And I'm way over this gangsta idiocy.

"You want to be known as big bad K-Cross and have people drop respect in your path. But you show no respect toward your family, your brother, even your so-called homies." He balled his fists up menacingly. "Let me tell you something. You *don't* live on the 'mean streets.' You're *not* an urban kid born into poverty. This...ludicrous gangsta lifestyle you've chosen? It's a laugh. A *joke*." I forced a lifeless laugh. "Your stupid gangsta talk. Look at the way you dress. Sloppy, baggy pants hanging down off your ass doesn't earn you respect. You're *not* living this way to survive. You're living out some stupid, idealized lifestyle you saw on a TV show. You're nothing but a spoiled, suburban bully."

"You best shut your *goddamned mouth*." He pulled an arm back, ready to take action.

But I couldn't stop, just couldn't do it. "I'll bet you even get paid a weekly allowance. What do you think, Ken? Sound about right?"

He swung his fist into my stomach. I doubled over, the air socked from my body.

"You've just made a *big* mistake," he said.

I straightened up as well as I could, holding my stomach.

Suddenly, the front door of the Cross house opened. Oblivious as to what transpired in her front yard, Mrs. Cross called out, "Ken, supper's ready. Will you be joining us?"

He looked back at me, his eyes full of fury. He leaned toward me and whispered, "Watch your back, holmes. You just made some fierce enemies."

I swallowed hard and pushed out another laugh. "You'd best be getting in for supper, 'K-Cross.' Even 'gangstas' need to be eatin', yo. Don't keep your mama waiting."

He kicked the back fender of my car and repeated, "Watch your back," under his breath. He pulled his hoodie up and strode determinedly, angrily, toward the front door.

I crawled into the Bucket and with shaking hands, put the keys into the ignition. *Wow,* really, *really* stupid. Not only did I blow the chance at the Gangstas listening to me, but did I really upset Ken so much, they might come gunning for me? It's a possibility. So the current tally reads: two gangs, one irate vice principal, and a ghost are all out to get me. And somewhere in the mix is a killer.

I needed protection.

Chapter Thirteen

As soon as I got home I texted Danny from my car. *Danny, forget it, don't talk to your brother*. It now seemed like a terrible idea for Danny to try and barrel through his simian brother's defenses in light of what happened. I didn't want Danny catching his ire, and I certainly didn't want to fan Ken's flames of anger even higher. Seconds later, Danny called.

"Tex, what the hell happened?" He again spoke in a hushed tone.

"Um, I had an altercation with your brother after you went inside."

"Oh, *man*. He's super-pissed, even more so than usual."

"Yeah, I can imagine." I explained our throw-down.

Danny responded with silence. "Well, what now?" he finally asked.

"I don't know. I mean I tried. I've done everything I can. I think I'm going to just wash my hands of everything."

"So, you don't think I should even talk to him?"

"No. I'm pretty sure it'll just make things worse."

"Tex?"

"Yeah?"

"I think maybe it's better for both of us this way." He sounded greatly relieved.

"Yeah, you're right, but I really wanted to tell you thanks, anyway."

"I didn't do anything."

"But you were ready to. It means a lot to me. You're a good friend."

"Whatever," he said nonchalantly. But I sensed his pride. "Talk to you later."

I hung up and went inside. Dad poked his head through the kitchen doorway. "Tex?"

"Yeah, hi, Dad." Not only have my grades fallen off lately, but I've also been putting more pressure on Dad to get rides home from work. Unfortunately, it doesn't look like it's going to let up anytime soon.

"Ruth's here."

"Hi, Ruth," I yelled back into the kitchen.

"Hellooooo, Tex," she sang out. For once, I welcomed Ruth's presence. It meant my impending punishment for disobeying Dad would wait another night. Maybe he'd just forget about it. Yeah, right. "How was school?" she shouted.

Realizing how unproductive it is to have a conversation with three rooms separating us, I went into the kitchen. Dad sat at the table, his hands resting on his chair wheels. Ruth, busy as ever, stirred up something rather odd-smelling on the stove.

"Fine. Um, what smells so...ah...interesting?"

"Ruth found a new recipe for an Indian dish she's been dying to try out on us," said Dad. *Uh-oh*. The way he said "try out on us" sounds like code-speak for torture, with Ruth as the Grand Inquisitor of the kitchen, punishing us with her newest sadistic meals. Dad flashed a smile, but when Ruth turned away, he raised his eyebrows, frowned, and shook his head once.

Erasing my grin, I said, "Oh, should be good." Dad rolled his eyes. I know Dad loves Ruth, but since Mom died, we became food snobs. We knew what we liked—what tasted good—and this decidedly did not smell even remotely good or even fit for human consumption.

"Straight out of my women's magazine," said Ruth, merrily humming away at her culinary atrocity.

"How long 'til dinner?" Or how long until death by dinner, more like.

Dad checked his watch. "Well, we've been holding up for you for a while, but it should be any time soon."

"Okay. I've got to make a call first."

"Is everything okay, Tex?" This is our new routine. Dad asks his vague questions, I evade them as best I can. I know he wants the truth from me, but sometimes, I almost get the feeling he's relieved I don't tell him everything. As they say—out of sight, out of mind.

I went upstairs and called Cowlings.

"Cowlings," he answered, no time for pleasantries.

"Hi, Detective Cowlings. It's Tex." Quiet. Heart attack quiet. "Um, Tex McKenna?"

"Yes. You're the only Tex I know. What can I do for you?" His question seemed loaded with a bit of wariness and a whole lot of suspicion.

"Well, I tried to get word to the Modern Gangstas about what the Young Bloods told me. They're not listening."

"Go on." Bred on crime TV shows, my dramatic pause for effect didn't evoke the kind of response I desired. What exactly I expected, I'm not sure, but the precise, yet bland "go on" hardly fulfilled my melodramatic quota.

I told him about my encounters with the Gangstas,

leaving out my excursion into breaking and entering. I also left out the names of the Gangstas.

"You're not giving me much to work with here, Tex. What exactly is it you want me to do? I can't post a guard at your door."

I smiled, thinking that would actually be quite nice. "No, I just wanted you to know that I'm finished with everything. I'm done trying to deal with these guys. They won't listen. Maybe, they're even crazy."

"Uh huh."

"I was wondering…if you might talk to the Gangstas's leader. Tell him you don't believe the Young Bloods killed James Badger either." I held my breath and blew it out. There's no going back now. "The leader's name is Ken Cross."

I heard Cowlings's frantic scribbling through the phone. "'Ken Cross.'" He sighed. "Listen, Tex, you say you're done with this affair, which I agree is a very wise decision, but you realize, by giving me this information, you may've stepped into it yet even further."

I guess I hadn't considered the ramifications of my action. "Uh, what exactly do you mean?"

"*Even* if I don't tell this…Ken Cross…you gave me his name, he's probably going to figure it out. He doesn't sound like a brain surgeon, but somehow, these guys have kept their identity fairly quiet all this time. I've talked to students—and even some parents—who are too frightened—too intimidated—to name names. He's going to put two and two together and come up with 'Tex.'" He paused, waiting for my response. I had nothing. "Are you sure you want to do this? I mean…you've already given me the information, and

I'm duty-bound to go forward with my investigation, but I suppose I'm saying be *careful*. From where I'm sitting, your hands aren't quite scrubbed clean, yet."

"Yeah, I guess I get it." I deflated, my shoulders sinking low. "Um, is there anything new you can tell me about your investigation? I mean, about Badger's murder?"

"Things are pretty much at a standstill."

It could mean anything. "Hmmm."

"Do *you* have anything else you'd like to...ah...inform me about?"

"No, no. No!"

How come Detective Cowlings has mastered the pregnant, dramatic pause so much better than I have? "Interesting reaction. By the way, I did receive a call from our friend, Vice Principal Arville Hastings, several days ago."

"Oh?"

"Yes. It seems he's more than a little upset about someone stealing his...bobblehead. He dropped your name. You wouldn't happen to have anything to do with that, now, would you, Tex?" I heard the springs of his chair squeak and papers shuffled about.

"No. I didn't take his bobblehead...and I wouldn't ever vandalize anything either." I attempted to swallow, without Cowlings hearing the nervous lump being choked down.

"I never said anything about vandalism."

"Um, I know that, but Hastings already grilled me and Olivia about it and told us what had happened—"

"Oh. Olivia, as well?"

"Yeah. We, um, went to the play together that night."

"Interesting." I imagined Cowlings taking great, sadistic pleasure in his latest dramatic display of silence.

"Uh, anyway, what did you tell Hastings?"

"I told him I was busy with a murder investigation, but I'd send down a couple of uniforms."

"Yeah, how'd he take that?" I asked, grinning.

"Not very well. He huffed and puffed for a while—said he was paying my salary—the usual nonsense I endure more often than I should." I heard a *thwack* presuming he tossed his notebook onto his desk. "Tex, I'll talk to this boy, but now more than ever, stay in contact with me. All right?"

"Yeah, okay," I said, staring at his business card. "You'll be proud to know I'm still carrying your card."

"Good. Just be careful and let me know what you hear…and for God's sake, stay out of trouble."

"Okay."

"One final thing."

"Yeah?"

"In all of your dealings with these two gangs, have you ever seen *any* evidence of a gun?"

Whoa. For all the fear and rumors of firearms, I realized I haven't seen anything remotely resembling a firearm.

"No, I guess I haven't. I've been kidnapped, threatened, punched, pushed, given a very rough back massage—"

"A rough back massage?"

"Um, yeah, that's not important. I've also had more fingers jabbed into my chest than I ever care to have again, but no, I've not seen any guns."

"Isn't *that* interesting?"

I have no idea what Cowlings is getting at. Could he possibly be hinting that James Badger's murder has nothing to do with gangsta warfare? Am I overlooking something? "Yeah, that is kinda interesting. I know you can't tell me, but what about Badger's girlfriend? Could this have been nothing more than a, ah, romantic tiff getting out-of-hand?"

"I'm looking at everyone. Her mother vouches for her whereabouts that night." He chuckled. "She was a particularly volatile woman."

"Yeah, I can imagine." I recalled my earlier encounter with Rebecca Hogan. Apparently, the apple truly doesn't fall far from the tree.

"Stay in touch, Tex."

"I will." I severed the connection. It seems every time I go to Cowlings for aid, I come away experiencing guilt, feeling the walls closing in on me, threatening to smother my freedom. I need to keep in mind how sharp a cop he is. He's not as easy to buffalo as…well, the buffalo that's our vice principal.

****

As expected, dinner was a total gastronomic disaster.

"It's called Paya Nahari." Ruth glowed with satisfaction. "I added chicken to it. I made it with trotters."

I'm not sure what a trotter is, nor do I particularly care to find out, because I suspect it might be so-named because it sends you trotting to the bathroom.

"It's really…good, Ruth." Dad aimed a quick, stern glance in my direction to ensure I was on board with the kitchen table subterfuge.

"Oh, yeah. It's really…" I pushed a mysterious

round item around on my plate. "How'd you make the chicken into round balls, Ruth?"

"That's not chicken, silly." I gulped and waited for her to fill me in on her secret recipe. She laughed, and I realized my answer wouldn't be forthcoming. Perhaps mercifully so. Dad coughed into a napkin, hiding his smile. "Are you okay, honey?" asked Ruth.

"Yep, fine and dandy." Sweat formed on Dad's forehead from the overwhelming spices.

"Anyway, I'm really glad you boys like it. I went extra crazy with the cloves." Apparently, Ruth's barometer of deliciousness is measured by how much she makes the McKenna men's eyes water. "If you'd like, I can make it *every* week." She grinned so hard, her cheeks bunched up underneath her eyes, nearly closing them.

"Oh, well..." stuttered Dad, "don't know if I can afford the calories." He patted his stomach.

"Hmmm," I said, and continued pushing food around my plate, hoping it'd drop into a black hole, when the doorbell rang. Saved by the bell. "I'll get it." I threw the napkin onto the plate, more or less throwing in the towel, so to speak.

"Hold on a minute," said Dad. "You remember what happened last time. Grab the bat." Dad started keeping the baseball bat by the front door in case of any other unwanted visitors.

"Got it." I picked the bat up and swung it through the air. Pulling the curtains back an inch, I peered out. B-Ryce and Coo-Coo stood at the front door, shifting anxiously back and forth in their high-tops as if cold. "Um, I'll take care of this, Dad. Just some kids." Even though I hadn't yet finished my home protection spell, I still felt a little more prepared this time. I took in a deep breath and pulled the door open, brandishing the bat in front of me.

"Lookee here, Coo-Coo," said E-Bryce. "Look like Richie think he gangsta as shit." Assorted Band-aids dotted their faces from the earlier cat attack.

"Yeah, what choo gon' do wit' dat wood, holmes?" asked Coo-Coo.

"You be ridin' wit' us again, yo," said B-Ryce.

I flipped on the outside light and swung the bat. They backed away. "Whoa, whoa," said B-Ryce. "Ain't like dat, yo. Just wanna' speak at choo, s'all I'm sayin'."

"If you have something to say, you can say it here." I forced them further into the yard. Once again their car sat with one tire in the yard, engine running, with Diddy-Bang manning the wheel. "I am *not* going with you anywhere."

B-Ryce inclined his head toward Coo-Coo, who let out a whoop and lurched at me, attempting to grab ahold of my shirt. I swung the bat down toward his knee, contacting with a painful-sounding *crack*.

"Ah! Jesus!"

I continued swinging the bat, corralling them toward the street.

"I said I'm not going with you. If you have something to say to me, say it." I snapped my fingers merely for show and called out, "*Cats!*" Eight or nine cats scurried out from the bushes, flanking B-Ryce and Coo-Coo on both sides. One particularly scruffy-looking black cat hissed, its back arched high into the air. "Now, unless you guys want a repeat attack from my pets, I suggest you start talking and do it quickly." I pointed a finger at one of the cats, who spat as if on demand. "They're getting antsy."

"Yo, it's chill, Richie." B-Ryce pulled his hood tighter around his face as if for protection. "A'ight. Step off, Coo-Coo."

Coo-Coo hobbled back toward B-Ryce and turned around, scowling.

"Are you going to be cool, Harold?" I knew it'd piss Coo-Coo off hearing his actual name, but my patience with everything gangsta long ago evaporated.

"Don'choo *call* me dat."

"It's your name, isn't it? Harold?"

"Richard?" called out a familiar voice. "Richard? Is everything okay?" Mr. Cavanaugh stood, hands firmly gripping the railing, on his shadow-covered front porch.

"Everything's fine, Mr. Cavanaugh," I said, holding my gaze upon my two visitors. "Go back inside, please. It's just a few kids blowing off steam."

"Well," he huffed. He pretended to leave but backed into the porch's darkness.

B-Ryce laughed and placed his hand on Coo-Coo's chest. "Simma' down now, young blood. Richie be doin' his homework, 'pears to me." Coo-Coo scowled. "We all friends here, ain't that right, Richie?"

I didn't answer him. "What do you want?"

"We just be checkin' in on our Clearwell boy. You talk to them punk-ass beeyotches yet?"

"Yes, I did. I delivered your message."

"You tell 'em we didn't cap their boy?"

"Yes."

"How they take it?"

I paused for a moment, unsure as to what to tell

them. Even though they're morons, it's probably best for them to be armed with a little bit of knowledge and a whole lot of truth. "I don't think they believed me."

"What?" shouted Coo-Coo. I gestured toward another cat to keep Coo-Coo in line. The cat grumbled, its eyes two glowing golden rings in the moonlight.

"I tried. I really did. And maybe they believed me, but they acted like they didn't."

B-Ryce sighed and pulled back his hood. For the first time, I saw fear in his eyes. "Damnit," he muttered under his breath. "Well, can you try again?"

"They're not going to listen to me. Sorry. I *did* try."

B-Ryce rolled his shoulders several times as if cranking up his courage. "Well, yo. Dem punk-ass bitches best not be messin' wit' us. We tried to counsel wit' em. If they wants to go to war, we'll show 'em who's gangsta."

"Okay, fine. But keep me out of it." I slapped the bat into my hand. "My best advice to you, B-Ryce?"

"What dat?"

"Go to the police. Tell them your side of the story before it's too late."

"Can't do dat, holmes."

"Why in *God's* name not?"

"Ain't da' gangsta way, yo," he said, matter-of-factly. Yes, of course, how utterly, mundanely un-street of me.

"Okay, I'm done with you guys," I said. "Reason obviously doesn't work. If you need to talk to me again, you stay away from my house. You contact me with a text, online, or whatever." I wasn't really looking forward to adding someone like Coo-Coo as a social online cyber-friend, but it certainly felt like a nicer option than a front-yard brawl.

Coo-Coo spat on the ground. "Yo, social media's for *pussies*!" Hearing their name evoked, several cats hissed and strolled closer to Coo-Coo.

"Uh-oh, Harold. Looks like you might've stirred them up."

Coo-Coo stumbled several steps back, his hands instinctively covering his face. "Not da face, not da face!"

"Hold, cats," I said. They dutifully stopped.

"Let's bounce," said B-Ryce. "Come on, Coo-Coo." They turned to leave, Coo-Coo expressing another look of anger.

"Hey, B-Ryce," I called after him.

"Yo?"

"Just watch your back. 'S'all I'm sayin'." And I couldn't believe my own ears, as it sounded a *lot* like gangsta talk. I'll need to wash my mouth out with soap and water.

B-Ryce nodded and hopped in the car, his little toady following him. The car tore off down the street, whipping wildly around the corner until out of sight.

I waved toward Mr. Cavanaugh's front porch. "Good *night,* Mr. Cavanaugh." I knew he still lurked in the shadows, eavesdropping. "Do you like my new friends?"

Finally, I heard Mr. Cavanaugh mumble, "Good night…"

Well, this visit certainly went better than the last one by the Young Bloods. I didn't get kidnapped and maybe—hopefully—I'm done with all this lunacy.

It felt like a minor victory.

"Milk all around," I yelled to the surrounding cats, as they purred and rubbed up against my legs.

****

After Ruth left, I reassured Dad things were okay. I told him the same kids who took me on the joyride earlier rang the doorbell, but now they're going to leave me alone. He demanded to call Detective Cowlings, but I told him he didn't need to and that I'd called him earlier. Finally, he resigned to the fact he couldn't get anywhere with me tonight and went to bed.

I crawled up the stairs and opened the window. The night breeze washed over me. Jeans still on, I fell into bed. The drapes flapped in the wind, like a ghost flitting about the room. Exhausted by the emotion and confrontations of the day, I fell into a fitful sleep.

Around two in the morning, a noise awakened me. I sat up in bed, attempting to adjust my sight to the night's blackness. The drapes whipped back and forth, stronger than before. A light skittering sound raced across the floor. I leapt out of bed, ran toward the window, and slammed it. Any unwanted visitors, dead or alive, needed to stay out in the night.

Back to the safety of my bed, I hurried, like a child frightened by the imaginary monster in his closet. Although in my case, there just might be a monster in my closet. I reached for my bedside lamp and pulled the chain. Like a sudden burst of lightning, the room filled with brilliant light.

"Boo!"

I shrieked. Elspeth sat on my desk, her leather-clad legs crossed. She laughed, a low steady sound, not unlike the purring of a cat. "Nice scream, Tex."

"Why do you *do* that to me?" I lowered my voice

264

so as not to wake Dad. "God, do you have to always sneak up on me?"

"Yes." Her pale blue eyes pierced me. "So, you wanted to talk. Let's talk." Her small mouth set in an amused smile, the dark lipstick a black halo.

I didn't know where or how to start. "Well, can't you just…like, you know…come up and talk to me like a normal person?"

She tilted her head, shaking it like Hastings's bobblehead. "Do I *look* like a normal person to you?"

"I suppose not."

"It's not like I can come up to you at school and say, 'Hi, Tex, I don't go here, but I need to talk to you about your safety.' Besides," she sneered, "Elizabeth doesn't let me come out and play at the best times."

"Yeah, that might be a problem." Still groggy, my powers of conversation lacked.

"She's not very pleased with you, you know."

"Yeah, I kinda' got that." I sighed. "It was just milk. It'll wash out."

She shrugged her shoulders, making her leather jacket crack. "Welcome to my world."

"What *is* your world, exactly?" I attempted to rub the sleep out of my eyes. "I mean, who are you?"

"I told you. I'm Elspeth Chambers."

"Well, that we've pretty much established. But, where are you from? Why are you doing this? Helping me, I mean?"

"I have my reasons." Her gaze fell to the floor, and she squinted as if studying a strange species of bug.

I changed the topic since any straightforward answers appeared not to be her style. "How'd you get in?"

She nodded toward the window.

"You climbed up the side of the house?"

"Yep." She stood and leisurely strolled across the room, kicking her legs high, arms folded behind her as if a punk version of a cheerleader. The leather of her pants creaked, the floorboards beneath her squeaking competitively. She drew a finger across the top of my framed copy of *Giant Sized X-Men* #1 as if inspecting for dust, and smiled sardonically at me. She continued her exploration around the room, looking like a cocky, black rooster lording over the barnyard, her rigid, black mane displaying proud dominance. She stopped in front of my Star Wars figurines. Picking up Darth Vader, she turned and said, "You really are a geek, aren't you?"

How do you answer that? "Um, yeah. Guess so."

She walked toward my bed, hopped up in the air, and landed on her back next to me. "Okay, without getting too personal, what do you want to know?" She sat up, crossed her ankles, and rested her chin on top of folded hands.

Everything I wanted to know seemed personal. "You can see things, right?"

"Yes."

"Can you see who killed James Badger?"

"Doesn't work like that, Tex," she answered solemnly. "Sometimes I get visions—hints of future events, sometimes past. I can't control it, and whoever's allowing me these visions, certainly seems to be choosy about it. But no, I can't see who killed James Badger. For some reason, that whole area seems...foggy."

"Foggy?"

"Yep. Believe me, if I could see who killed him,

I'd probably save you a lot of future trouble."

"Yeah, well. *That* doesn't sound too encouraging." She laughed and lay down on her side, her head resting on one outstretched palm. "So, if it's not getting too personal, you're like a spirit…or something?"

"Or something."

"And you chose Elizabeth to channel through."

"Sort of." A small twinge of sadness drew across her face like a dark shadow. "I'd like to think it's a bit more than channeling. I mean, I'm really here. *Really* here."

"Yeah, I can see that."

"And, I didn't really get much choice in the matter about who I get to share a body with."

"Well, who chose for you?" While I fished for an answer to one of life's most prominent big queries, I realized my extreme naivety.

She smiled. "Not that I can tell you, Tex, but even if I could, I wouldn't. There're certain things you're not supposed to know yet." I scooted up further against the headboard. "But, truthfully, I don't really get it yet, either. I think because I'm of two worlds, they don't show me everything yet."

"'They'?"

She shrugged. "Whatever you want to call it. *Anyway*, before you interrupted me…" So, there is *some* Elizabeth Blackmer in her. "I think they chose Elizabeth because she's the right age when I…well…" When she fell silent, I reached out a hand to comfort her. She snapped her head back at me as if in warning. I quickly recoiled. "Secondly, I believe they chose her because she comes from money…and would be able to help finance my work."

"What is your 'work' exactly?"

"Sometimes, I think it's to help people. Sometimes, I think I've been given a second chance at life—a small one at that—to *live* a life. But, really, I'm full of about as many questions as you are, Tex."

"Okay, well, I know you've been helping me. In your own round-about way. So, thank you. Did you *really* know my sweater would keep me from getting cut?"

She smiled and nodded.

"Huh." I hesitated before asking my next question, but I couldn't help myself. "Have you...seen or talked to my mother?"

"I've seen her once. She shares your aura, you know."

"My aura?"

"Yep, and it's a big, bright one, at that."

"Well...what did she say? Is she all right?" It's a tough topic for me. But I've been curious about it long before Elspeth came into my life.

"She's fine. She wants me to help take care of you."

"What else did she say?" I asked, my voice tinny. "*Please*, Elspeth, tell me."

"You certainly have a curious nature. I'll bet if there were a corpse in your house, your curiosity would get the better of you, and you'd end up getting your DNA all over it." She waited for a response, but I didn't have one to her strange analogy. "Anyway, that's all she said. Really. Sometimes, you just need to let sleeping dogs lie."

Fighting back tears, I sunk back into bed.

Elspeth quickly added, "But, she's fine. She misses

you, and she loves you."

"Okay." I cleared my throat. "Tell her...I miss and love her, too, would you?"

"I will if I see her. Okay?"

I sucked in a deep breath and moved on. "Now, let me ask you about Bob Bellman."

Fear flooded into her eyes like murky water from a well. The corners of her mouth drooped down. "I don't know much. I know he's a mean, scary son-of-a-bitch—who for *whatever* reason—has escaped from, um, where he was, and he's hell-bent on getting you. Pun obviously intended."

"Have you encountered him?"

She tightened her lips into a thin, black line. "No, not really. I've felt his presence nearby at times, closer than I'm comfortable with. It's like he's lurking around corners, waiting for the right moment to pounce. It's a *strong* presence, and sometimes, it almost hurts my being here." She shuddered and rubbed her arms as if caught in a cold draft. "When I'm in—elsewhere—I can feel him. Sometimes I hear him roaring your name, chanting it over and over. I know he's coming for you, and he's coming on *strong*."

"Great."

"One thing I *can* tell you, and I don't know this for a fact, but I have a feeling—a *strong* feeling—that in some weird way, he wants you to expose the killer of James Badger."

"But I have no idea who killed him. I don't even know if I know the killer."

She shrugged, her favored form of communication. "Plus, well, there is the whole thing where he sort of blames you for his death and wants to kill you. I mean, even in Hell, he's a bully."

"Nice to know I'm popular somewhere. I really, really hoped I was done with all of this stupid gangsta crap. Now, even Bellman's ghost is trying to drag me into it. Gah."

"Sorry, Tex. You've still got some work to do."

"Crap."

"Yeah, 'crap,'" she mimicked me. "I'll try and help you as much as I can." She suddenly jumped off the bed. "Gotta' roll. Little Miss Perfect needs her beauty sleep." She rolled her eyes, prompting me to laugh.

"You don't like Elizabeth much, do you?"

She opened her eyes wide. "Do *you*?"

I didn't answer, but our shared laughter said it all. "Wait, Elspeth. I've got about a hundred more questions for you." I stalled for more than one reason. I actually *liked* Elspeth.

She wagged her head back and forth, smiling. "I'll be in touch." She expertly straddled the windowsill like a gymnast. "Oh, Tex, I almost forgot."

I ran to the window and bent down. "You're kinda' cute." She grabbed my hair and pulled me toward her, pressing her lips onto my mouth. Using my ears as handles, she manipulated my head into a better kissing position, her tongue flitting in and out of my mouth like a kitten lapping up milk. Warm breath from her nose expelled onto my face. She released my ears and pushed me back onto the hardwood floor. Out-of-breath, shock—and other, warmer feelings—rattled my body. She looked down at me and laughed. "I don't care *what* Elizabeth thinks about you…"

She dipped out of sight, leaving me with the unforgettable vision of a wicked-hot punk goddess framed in my window, like a mysterious Goth Mona Lisa.

By the time I caught my breath, her face popped back into my window.

"*Jesus, damn!*" I fell onto my back again.

She snickered. "You really scream like a girl, Tex."

"Um, thanks?"

"One last thing. You're going to need a date for the upcoming Spring Fling. Later." She vanished again. I scrambled to my feet. By the time I reached the window, I saw her skipping and leaping through the front yard like a graceful leopard until she vanished into the dark foliage.

"Huh."

I couldn't sleep at all the rest of the night.

Chapter Fourteen

Right as I finally drifted back to sleep that morning, my phone rang. As I swept my hand across the bed stand to retrieve it, the alarm clock clonked to the floor.

"Crap," I answered. Not a very fitting salutation, but the best I could muster in my half-asleep state.

"Hey," said Brandon.

"Hey, Brandon." I cleared my throat and sat up in bed.

"It's Brandon."

There was a long silence. "Hey," I said again. *Come on, Brandon, you called me. The impetus is on you.*

"Yeah, hey."

I sighed. "What do you want, Brandon?" I picked up the alarm clock to make sure it still worked. It read eight-thirty.

"Dude, *what* did you do to Ken?"

I blinked several times, recalling the front yard foray from yesterday. "What do you mean?"

"He's s*uper* pissed at you. He says you're dead to us, and you're an enemy of the Gangstas now."

"Oh, well, yeah." I told Brandon what happened.

"Wow. I mean…wow."

"Yeah, it wasn't one of my smarter moments.

Listen, Brandon…"

"Yeah?"

"Do you think there's any way Ken will listen to the message I gave him from the Young Bloods?"

Another eternal silence on Brandon's end. I could practically hear the cogs of his brain crank, slowly trying to disseminate the information. Finally, he said, "I doubt it, dude. He's really hatin' on you."

"Yeah, I kinda got that. Do you think he's going to act out against the Bloods?"

"I don't know. Last night, all he talked about was you. He didn't say much about the Bloods."

"Well, what do *you* think?"

"I think…he might go up against them, yeah. He's so ultra-pissed at you, he might go after them, just to— what do you call it—spite you."

What a cool way to start my morning. I didn't want a murder on my conscience. Immediately following my hissy fit with Ken, I knew I'd made a colossal mistake, but at the time I didn't even consider I might be responsible for accelerating a gang war. "Brandon, please do what you can to stop him, if you see he's headed that way, okay?"

"I'll do what I can. But I don't know how much good I can do."

"Just keep me posted if you hear anything, all right?"

"Cool."

"And Brandon?"

"Yeah?"

"Maybe it'd be a good idea for you to stop hanging with me. For your own safety."

Another long, Brandon-patented hush. "I'm not

gonna do that, Tex. I'm gonna hang with whoever I want."

"It could be dangerous for you. I mean, now that I'm Public Enemy Number One to the Gangstas. Won't that seem like you're in bed with the enemy?"

"It is what it is." And there's the *Zen Life According To Brandon Townsend*. Someday, he'll probably make a bundle on a self-help book, fully illustrated with photos of him shirtless, eating cereal, staring into the camera with his big, brown, soulful, searing eyes. I can't figure out if he's a stand-up guy, a good friend, or just too stupid to be afraid. Probably the latter.

"Just be careful."

"Um, Tex, there's something else I want to ask you…"

"What's that?"

"Ah, never mind. I'll talk to you about it later. Gotta go."

While showering, I wondered what Brandon wanted to mention, but quickly filed it into my mental trash bin. My brain already overflowed with items of more import. I guess I need to get a date for the upcoming Spring Fling. I've never been to a school dance—the thought kinda filled me with anxiety—mostly because I've never danced before. I'm fairly certain I can't dance, since the McKenna men are the most clumsy, lumbering beings on earth. Besides, these sorts of events are the kinds of things my friends and I railed against in the past. We always saw them as parties thrown to celebrate the popular and the pretty. The organizers never cared about the rest of us. I imagined we'd be nothing but mere ornaments, resigned to wallflower status, as the Chosen Ones' party played out in front of our eyes. We'd be expected to applaud the Pretty People as royalty and we're but their lowly servants. And just like in England, the constituents would have no say as to whom the school leaders are, as they're born into it through perfect genes and money.

Putting my prejudices aside, the daunting task of finding a date seemed kinda impossible. In the past, I would've taken Olivia, but that seems unlikely now. Then again, Olivia *did* say she'd always help me if I needed her. And I suppose I *do* need a date—for whatever reason. Why would Elspeth tell me I need a date, anyway?

I caught myself smiling like a lunatic at the thought of Elspeth, and, distracted, I dropped the soap. Bending over to pick it up, I bonked my head on the wall and let out a howl, thus confirming my earlier observation about my innate clumsiness. Didn't matter. I couldn't get over the wild kiss last night. Completely different from the soft, gentle kisses I'd shared with Olivia for a year and a half. It played out rough, almost animal-like, and totally blown up with unbridled passion. Once I became accustomed to Elspeth's rhythm—ready to plow ahead, so to speak—she quickly broke it off, dismissing me. Apparently, Elspeth deemed herself the only one who had any say in the matter. Despite that, I grinned at the fond remembrance.

Regarding the women in my life, it definitely has been a roller-coaster week. I've been chastised—no, publically humiliated—by three girls, yet, as a seeming cosmic balance, I also kissed two girls this week. The two girls couldn't be more different—sugar and spice, maybe. At the same time, they both share fierce independence. That's a bit daunting, but also extremely sexy and attractive. Perhaps there's a softer, gentler God or Fate toying with my love life now, the mean ones on holiday.

Once out of the shower, I shook my hair and tried to shake all thoughts of romance away. I don't need teenage hormones clouding my mind while ghosts and a killer are on the rampage. Rather, I need to up my arsenal of tricks for protection. So I called my very own weapons master.

"Hi, Mickey, it's Tex."

Mickey coughed a few times as a matter of greeting me. "Pretty early, kid," she grumbled.

"I know, and I'm sorry, but you told me you're an early riser."

"I am. Ten o'clock is early, not now."

I checked the time on my phone, a little after nine. "Oh, sorry, but I need your help—badly."

I've never seen her in the morning before. Hope she's a morning person. "All right, kid. Well, hurry up then. I ain't got all day."

Well, yes she does. As far as I know, she rarely, if ever, leaves her house.

"I'll be right over—" Before I could say "thanks," she hung up. Nope, not a morning person.

****

Mickey answered the door, cackling like a proto-typical witch. "Hee," she screamed, sending the morning birds fleeing for cover. "You sure did turn off the lights the other night, didn't you, kid?"

"Yeah." I stepped inside. "A bit more than I bargained for."

"You musta' turned out several blocks, at least. They interrupted my stories to report it." She bounced back and forth, dancing a little jig, displaying more energy than I'm accustomed to.

"Yeah, well..."

She smacked her lips. "You're a lot more powerful witch than I gave you credit for. Mmm... The things you're gonna be able to do." She strolled toward her sofa, shaking her head.

"Oh, by the way, here's your key back." I fished the key out of my jeans pocket. "Um, you might want to think about updating the model."

She plopped down onto the sofa and frowned. "What do you mean?"

"Well, it wouldn't open all the locks I needed it to. It was, um, too big." I sat down next to her. "Maybe...too old-fashioned."

She snatched it out of my hand. "Never had no problems with it before. 'Update the model,' the very idea. You kids today want everything handed to you on a silver platter."

"Yeah, um speaking of which, Mickey...I need protection."

She gasped and sat straight up. "*Oh.* Oh my." She placed her small fingers to her lips. "Tex, if you think I'm going to give you... Oh, my." She smacked the back of my head.

"Ow!"

"Don't they teach you about *protection* in that school of yours? What do you think I am, the local drugstore?"

Mortified when it finally dawned on me what she inferred, I waved my hands to ward off any further head smacks. "No, no, *no*. That's, um, not the kind of protection I'm talking about." Her eyes narrowed at me in disgust. I chuckled and quickly diverted it into a cough. "I need protection—witchcraft protection—from both the living and the dead, I guess."

She fell back against the sofa cushion, relaxing her guard. "Well, then, why didn't you say so?"

"Uh, I was trying."

"Looks like we got a lot to talk about." She utilized a nine-point turn until she faced me on the sofa. "So, start talkin'."

"Okay, I told you a little bit about the gang stuff going on at school."

"Yes."

"Well, I've been threatened more than a few times. And I think they might come after me. I was wondering if there's something I could get for protection." She stared at me, her face expressionless. "Maybe?"

"What do you want, kid? I can't exactly conjure you up a suit of armor."

"No, that's not what I meant. What about a spell of some sort?"

"You're using the house protection spell, right?"

"Yeah," I said, although I still hadn't finished it. When have I had time? It's a tedious method requiring seven nights of a full moon and painstaking digging.

"Well, then, what is it you're looking for?"

"I don't know, but…say someone comes at me, threatening to beat me up, or shoot me. Is there anything I can do? I mean I'm a witch. There's gotta be *something*."

"I see." She drummed her fingers against her chin. Her eyes lit up, sparks of enlightenment blazing through her glasses. "Wait here." She climbed off the couch and made a beeline for the kitchen. I heard drawers opening and shutting, her step stool scraping across the linoleum, what sounded like a near tumble, and finally, her voice humming. The eyes of her creepy figurines watched me empathetically, as if saying, "You poor, pitiful child, you." One of them looked just like Ruth in her sickly empathetic mode.

Then she came back in, scuttling across the rug like a demented wind-up toy. She waved another one of her napkins in front of me.

"Here's the deal…you don't need protection, kid," she said, beaming triumphantly. "What you need is to take the offensive."

"What do you mean?"

"I mean, if you get a chance to read this spell—The Spell of Sleep—to your attacker, before he gets to you, he'll instantly go to sleep for a few minutes."

"Oh, man, thanks. Sounds *exactly* what I need." Kinda wish I knew about it earlier.

"Now, there're a couple of problems involved here."

"Like what?"

"First, you need to touch your attacker's forehead after you recite the incantation."

"How am I going to do that if he's holding a gun on me?"

Mickey sighed. "I don't make up the rules, kid."

"Okay." Maybe it's not such a great spell after all.

"It'd probably be best if you memorized it," she continued. "*And* if you use it, the person's gonna wake and remember you said something that put them to sleep." She fell back exhausted onto the sofa.

"Hmm."

"You *can't* let your attacker know you're a witch."

"Huh." What good's the spell if I can't use it?

Mickey must've seen the defeat in my face. "Then again, Tex," she said, beaming like a sweet, kindly grandmother, "if your life's in danger…well, I wouldn't blame you for using it."

"Yeah, but how will I explain it later?"

She looked at me nonplussed. "You lie your way out. I swear, *where* is your common sense?" She went off on another tirade, mumbling to herself. "Maybe I need to go to that school of yours and teach them a thing or two about how to prepare you kids for the outside world."

"Yeah, I don't think that's necessary, Mickey." I took the risk, said it, but it effectively stopped her rant. And the horrific notion of her speaking to my classmates about the pros of lying.

"Now, what's this about the dead coming after you?"

"Yeah, *that*. All right, you remember my telling you about Bob Bellman last year?"

She squinted one eye. "Isn't he the dead bully?"

"Yeah…that's one way to describe him. He's back, Mickey."

"'Back,' you say. 'Back' how?"

I told her about my two ghostly encounters with him. She remained rigidly still throughout my story, except for her blinking eyes. When I finished, she clucked and straightened her skirt.

"Now, this is the same boy you tried to call from beyond, last year, right?"

"Um, yeah." Sighing, I smacked the back of my

head myself, hoping to beat her to the punch. Besides, I already paid for this mistake once last year.

"Heh." She smiled and coughed into her fist. "Anyway, you *do* realize how stupid that was?"

I nodded dutifully.

"Well," she continued, "could be—*could* be—when you tried to vanquish him last year, you didn't quite get the job fully done."

"Huh."

"But I don't think that's the case. I don't reckon it would've taken him this long to come after you." She looked lost, deep in thought, her head sinking into the back of the sofa. "Tell me something. Did you happen to evoke his name recently?"

"No," I answered immediately. "Wait, what? What do you mean by *evoke* exactly?" I mentally retraced my steps prior to his first visitation.

"Oh for…did you speak his name? Maybe in conversation and in some sort of spiteful or disrespectful way?"

A cold, harsh realization struck me like one of Mickey's dope-slaps. "Um, yeah, I think maybe I did." I recalled my first encounter at the skate park with the Young Bloods. "When I first met one of the gangs, my friend told me to lie to them about my name. Bob Bellman's name was the first one I thought of—" *Whack*! Mickey's hand bit my head, striking like a hidden snake on a floral-covered tree limb.

"You *dumb* kid. You know what you've *done*?"

"Uh, yeah, I can kinda guess."

"Well, guess *again*." She shook her fists at me. "You opened up the gates. You practically *offered* him a written invitation that says, 'Hey, would you mind coming back to our world so you can kill me? I'll be waiting, yours truly, Tex.'"

"Oh, man... I guess I need to be more careful. I have a lot to learn yet."

"You're *damn* skippy you do." She took several deep breaths, her chest heaving in and out. A rattle wheezed from deep in her throat, sounding like angry bursts from an air rifle.

"Come with me, kid." She jumped up and hustled through her front door. I followed her onto the porch. She leaned against the railing and lit a cigarette. She inhaled, held it, and blew it up into the air. Brushing by me, she sat down on her swing. I cautiously sat next to her. This is gonna be bad, if she needs an emergency smoke.

"What worries me most about this," she finally said, "is when you kicked him at your school, he was part corporeal and part...not."

"Yeah. What does it mean?"

"It means he's nearly physically formed again." She puffed again and again. "We can *deal* with ghostly hauntings—spirits from the otherworld—whatever you want to call them. But when they get strong enough—when their mass starts to become completely physical—it's another thing entirely." She blew several smoke rings into the air above her. "Once he crosses completely over—back into our world—not only is he gonna be a booger to get rid of, but he could upset the entire balance between the physical and the spiritual planes."

"I don't understand..."

"Of *course* you don't," she snapped back. "He's not supposed to be here, but when you invited him back, his existence upset the natural order of both realms. Once he becomes physically complete, it opens a door between the worlds that will be nearly impossible to shut again. Other evil entities could piggyback on the free ride you gave him."

"Oh, wow." I—a humble witch boy—opened a gateway to Hell merely because I lied about my name. Witchcraft kinda sucks. "What can we do, Mickey? I mean, can't we just go in your house now, call forth his spirit, and vanquish him?"

She stubbed her cigarette into the filthy ashtray next to her. "He's strong enough we won't be able to summon him. He's been choosing when to come to you, and that's when you'll see him next—when *he* chooses to come again."

"There has to be something…"

Mickey swung her short legs underneath her, rocking both of us. "We have to be proactive."

"Okay."

"You're gonna have to call him out."

"But, you said we couldn't do that."

"Sure, but we need to trick him into thinking it's his own decision," she said. "You're going to have to choose a place of his liking. You say he appeared to you in the bathroom and the lab?"

"That's right."

She tightened her lips. "What do those two places have in common?"

"Um, they're both at school."

"Okay, that's a start. He only visits you at school."

"Yeah. I guess that makes sense, since that's where we had all of our encounters last year."

"So, he likes the school." Absolutely true as he

reveled in being the King of Terror at Clearwell, while both alive and dead. I guess even ghosts need hobbies. "Anything else in common with the two visitations?"

I thought long and hard, something niggling at the back of my mind. "Wait. There aren't security cameras in the crappers...um, sorry, Mickey...I mean, restrooms." She rolled her eyes. "And there's not a camera in the science classroom. Maybe... he doesn't want to be seen? I mean, by anyone else?"

"Hmmm. That might be. Even though he's attempting to break through to this realm, as long as he's part spirit, he's still bound by the rules of his...leader." I shuddered at the implications. "I'll bet he can't let anyone from the physical plane see him—except for you. So you've got to lure him to you."

"How?"

"What does he want most?"

"Well, he wants *me* for starters—for revenge, I guess. And I think he wants the killer of James Badger caught."

Mickey looked at me suspiciously. "How do you know this?"

I sighed. Telling Mickey about Elspeth is probably acceptable, particularly under these circumstances. I explained everything, including the fact Badger was Bellman's cousin.

To my surprise, Mickey laughed. "Oh, boy, kid." She coughed, sounding like she might expel part of a lung. "You're just full of surprises today, ain't you?"

"Yeah, that's one way of looking at it."

Her lower lip enveloped her upper one. "I'd really like to meet this girl sometime. I might be able to learn a few things myself."

"Well, I can ask, but I have a feeling pigs might fly before she comes here for a, um, visit."

Mickey looked disappointed. "Well, we'll talk about that later. Okay, so you need to find a place...a place with some sort of connection between you and this Bellman and lure him there. It's gotta be a place without a security camera and anyone else there. And it'd be best if it was at night 'cause that's when he's more corporeal. *That's* where you'll be able to do to him what you're gonna have to do to him." A fleeting sadness passed over her face like a portentous shadow. "You gotta' place like that in mind?"

Inspiration gob-smacked me. "Yeah. Yeah, Mickey, I think I do." I knew *exactly* where and when this encounter would have to happen.

"Good. Then you'll call Bellman forth and offer him the name of the killer. That oughta' draw him out for sure. In the meantime—and this is gonna' be very dangerous—you'll need to open up a portal to his plane and vanquish him through it."

I gulped, the lump in my throat taking the long way down. "I understand." I felt very small and weak and really, *really* wanted my mother.

"I wish I could be there to help you, Tex, but he ain't gonna show up if I'm there." She placed her hand on my knee. "I *can* give you the vanquishing spell and the spell to open up the portal, but you have to remember—stay as far away from the portal as you possibly can. If you get too close, well...*poof*." She raised her hands, waving her fingers like the smoke that drifted off the porch earlier. "You might go through with him."

"All right." I held my head in my hands, imagining

the terror of what lay ahead.

"Tex, I *think* you can do this." She gave my knee an iron-grip squeeze, waking me out of my fear-induced torpor. "You're a helluva' powerful witch, and I believe in you. But you've got to believe in yourself. You can do this."

"Okay…thanks." The pep talk didn't amount to much, but it's all I had.

She stared at me for a moment before gymnastically launching herself off the swing. "Now, let me go get those two spells for you." She bolted toward the kitchen. After a few moments of trying to gain my courage, I followed her. The bald soles of my "lawn shoes" shuffled and squeaked against the kitchen floor. Note to self: buy new shoes before the impending demon invasion.

She sat at her kitchen table, a black, monstrous, tattered book splayed open in front of her. I have no idea from where she produced this heretofore unseen book, or how she even carried it to the table by herself. She scrawled away madly, this time forgoing napkins and reproducing the spells onto what appeared to be ancient parchment paper.

"Mickey?"

"Mm-hmm?" she said, without turning a hair.

"Remember last year when we did that mirror scrying spell? To find the killer?"

She looked up from her writing. "Yeah, kid. What about it?"

"Do you think we could do it again? I mean…to find out who the killer of James Badger is?"

"Well, now, that depends on you. Did you have any emotional connection to this Badger boy?"

I shook my head. "I didn't even know him…"

"Then there's your answer. Wouldn't work. You've got to have that connection for the spirits to be able to help."

"Okay." Stupid, dumb, hard-to-work-with spirits.

Mickey slammed the big book shut. Dust swirled up, momentarily highlighted by the sunlight streaming in through the window. "Here's what you need…" She handed me the two pieces of parchment. "Just remember to follow my instructions and be *very* careful." She stood.

"Thanks, Mickey. For everything. *Really*, thanks." It felt like a final farewell to Mickey.

To my shock, she threw her arms around my back, her head resting low on my chest. I hugged her back. "No problem, kiddo," she said. "I'm beginnin' to think you're my 'lot in life.'"

I forced a weak laugh in return. "Well, I don't want to be *anyone's* lot." Mickey wouldn't break the hug, worrying me that she considered it final as well. "But if I have to be someone's lot, I'm glad it's you."

She finally pushed me away and clapped her hands. "Okay, now, go, kiddo. You got work to do. Any idea when you're going to do this?"

"Yes. In six days. Next Friday night."

She frowned. "I hope that's not gonna be too late."

"Mickey, given all the requirements I need, it's the only time I can do it—without breaking back into the school. And I'm *not* going to do that again. The security guard will be watching more carefully. If I get caught, I can't stop the demons from coming through the portal from a jail cell." I managed a frail smile.

"I suppose so. Okay, now, scoot."

"Bye, Mickey." With slumped shoulders, I plodded toward the front door.

"Tex," she called after me. "*Please,* be careful."

"I will, promise." I looked back one last time. With her hands entwined beneath her chin and her head lowered, she appeared vulnerable enough to become lost within the multiple gloomy rugs and impossibly soft furniture of her now-ominous house. Larger than life Mickey had vanished. Now she appeared so tiny, weak and scared, she frightened me. I ran to the Bucket before I lost my courage. If my one motivational supporter doesn't believe I can pull this off, what chance do I possibly have?

****

After finding out I unleashed an evil spirit, with possibly more on the way, the thought of finding a date for some stupid high school dance I didn't want to go to seemed like a cakewalk in comparison. Or so I kept telling myself. I didn't know which scenario filled me more with terror. Maybe I should've gone date shopping before I visited Mickey, as I couldn't get too excited about the Spring Fling. Not with the world potentially ending. But the dance seemed like the perfect opportunity to vanquish Bellman. Or *try* to. Elspeth said I need to take a date, so perhaps the two events are intertwined on some weird mystical plane.

I parked in front of Olivia's house and steeled myself. Another dreaded encounter, I knew she wouldn't embrace the idea of being my date, but I need her help, now more than ever. I also decided to come clean about Elspeth and tell Olivia everything she wants to know. If I swear her to secrecy, I'm confident she'll take the information to her grave.

At least her mother didn't appear to be home. Yet another old car I didn't recognize sat behind Olivia's in the driveway.

Olivia answered the door, eyes wide in shock. Fear, maybe? "Tex, what are you doing here?"

"Hey. Sorry I didn't call, but I need to ask you a favor."

She stepped outside, pulling the door shut behind her. I tried to peer inside to see who the car belonged to. "Um, I know this sounds crazy, but would you please go with me to the Spring Fling?"

"Tex, what—"

"I really need your help."

She shook her head. "It's *not* a good idea—not at all."

"Please, Olivia—"

"Tex, I can't. Besides, Brandon already asked me." She nudged open the door. Brandon stood inside, earnestly devouring a bowl of cereal. *Olivia's* cereal. Cereal she'd never offered me before. It felt like a great big, crunchy bowl of betrayal drowning in milky deceit.

"Hey." If possible, Brandon looked more sheepish than usual, his eyes everywhere but on mine. "I, um, was gonna ask you if it was cool, but I figured you guys were broken up and..." He shrugged and continued munching.

"No. No, it's *definitely* not 'cool.' In what *world* could this be considered '*cool*?' There's not a '*cool*' thing about it. In fact, if you looked up 'uncool' in the dictionary, there'd be a picture of *you* eating cereal! And a tattoo, saying '*backstabber*' across your..stupid, perfect, toned, bronzed back!" I stomped my feet like a temperamental child. For some reason, watching him eat Olivia's cereal seemed *much* worse than catching them kissing. It felt personal, private, very intimate. I've seen how Brandon nearly makes love with the food he oh-so-sensuously eats. And now he's invading her personal, private stock of cold cereal. The ultimate symbol of cuckoldry poured into a porcelain breakfast bowl.

"Sorry, dude." Brandon's spoon froze in mid-air. As if in slow motion, I watched drops of milk slowly splash down into the bowl. *Kerplop. Plip. Plep...* Sorta a symbol for what my lack of love life had been reduced to: my drowning in a whirlpool of milky-white tears, while the secret lovers laughed at me from on high, nudging me aside with their spoons of love to spelunk for crunchy nuggets of lust.

Olivia turned toward Brandon. "Brandon, give me a few minutes, okay?" He nodded and disappeared into the house. "Tex, let's talk about this. Have a seat." She sat down on the front stoop. I circled like an airplane that couldn't land, before crash and burning next to her with a fiery thud. "I'm sorry you had to find out this way." As an afterthought, she added, "It's just a date to some stupid dance." She attempted a winky, knowing smile. Added insult to injury.

I raised my hands toward the sky and roared, "I can't *believe* this." A momentary urge of pettiness washed over me. Unfettered, I spat out, "You *know* he's bi, right?"

Olivia gasped. "What?" Her small lips formed a circle as she contemplated the news.

I felt a small tinge of sadistic satisfaction. "Yeah, he's bi."

"Oh. I thought...I thought he was gay." Uh-oh.

"My 'gaydar' must not be working right." As she stared dreamily into the sky, I saw her entire perception of Brandon and possibly, what their future could be together, change. Her initial shock transformed into hopeful—even, lustful?—desire. And I had no one to blame but myself. Crap. "How long have you known?"

"Some time. He, ah, tried to kiss me."

Olivia snorted. "Bet that went over well."

"Yeah, well...*whatever*." Trying to appear nonchalant, I felt only lost.

"And you didn't think this was important enough to tell me?" Annnndddd, this just got way worse, hard to believe. Somehow, the tables had turned on me. Olivia seethed with unspoken fury.

"I just thought it should've been him to tell you. It wasn't like I was *actively* trying to keep secrets from you." My acidic argument sounded lamer than scathing to my ears.

"More secrets." She stood up, huffed, and crossed her arms. "You come over here, ask me on a date, and you're *still* keeping secrets from me."

"It's not like that."

"Whatever." She held up her hand as if placing a banishing spell on me. "Gah! You *never* change, do you, Tex? *That's* why it'll *never* work out between us."

"Olivia, I came over here to tell you everything. I was going to tell you about Elspeth, and I really need—"

"Forget it! Just...forget it."

"Olivia—"

"*No*. I've given you *plenty* of chances." She paced up and down the sidewalk. Finally, she said, "I still would like to be friends." Even though she didn't sound like it.

I looked up at her, shading my eyes from the cruel sunlight. I had nothing else to say that would change her mind. But at least I'd leave giving her a piece of my mind. "I can't believe you let him eat your cereal."

"*What?*"

"I said, 'I can't *believe* you let him eat your *cereal.*'"

Olivia belted out a quick peal of incredulous laughter. "Whatever." She walked toward her front door. "Goodbye, Tex."

"Wait… I'm sorry!"

"Goodbye, see ya, talk to you later." With that, she walked inside and closed the door on us and everything we'd meant to one another.

I faced the door, wondering what atrocities are going on behind it. My rage returned. I pounded on the door and yelled, "Thanks a *lot*, Brandon! You're a *real* stand-up guy. This is definitely not '*cool.*' You're the '*anti-cool.*' It's so not '*cool,*' it became 'cool,' and bounced back to being '*uncool*' *again.*" I hurried down the sidewalk, my body quaking with pent-up fury. I turned around, ran back to the door and hit it once more. "I hope you *choke* on her *cereal.*"

That's telling them.

****

I drove into the large circular driveway in front of Elizabeth Blackmer's huge mansion. Maybe it's not a "mansion," but it could eat three houses the size of mine and still have room for the front yard within its bowels. The lawn itself must require at least three to four professional gardeners and displayed the most dazzling green I've seen besides Mickey's garden of

292

witchy wondrousness. Professionally trained vines covered the ivy-league-inspired brick and stone exterior. Large, double-bay windows glared at me disapprovingly, wanting to know why a mere pauper had dared come to visit. The wooden front doors spanned nearly as much space as my bedroom. A castle wedged into the middle of suburbia. I parked the Bucket behind Elizabeth's car and killed the ignition. The Bucket sputtered its disappointment. It must've felt as out of place as I did, the poor boy and his trusty steed, stuck in the middle of all of this opulent, capitalistic decadence.

I grabbed what I needed from the car, walked up the twisting sidewalk, and spent a few minutes futilely searching for the doorbell. Finally surrendering, I gave up, lifted the heavy brass knocker, and let it fall, several times.

A wiry old man, dressed in a green polo shirt tucked into khaki shorts with white athletic socks pulled up past his knees, answered the door. Although silver-gray, his hair remained full and buoyant, the elderly male version of Elizabeth's unflappable mane. He squinted, eyeing me distrustfully. "Yes?"

"Um, hi, sir. Is Elizabeth at home?" I gulped and felt stupid, especially since I held six yellow roses in one hand. He sized me up and down, his eyes traveling along my body. The visual tour ended with him glowering at my grass-stained tennis shoes.

"What do you want with my daughter?" He looked past me, sizing up the Bucket.

"I'm, ah, Richard McKenna, sir." I tucked the contents in my other hand under my arm and offered him a handshake. He left me hanging. "I'm a friend of hers…from school?"

He sighed and turned, yelling out Elizabeth's name.

"Who is it, Daddy?" Elizabeth called out from seemingly miles and miles away.

"You have a…'friend' here to see you." Elizabeth stepped into view, wearing a sweater vest over a white blouse and an immaculately ironed, long, plaid skirt. Her cutting blue eyes grew when she saw me, but not in a good way. Her mouth fell into an awful grimace as if she'd just received a B+ on her report card.

Elizabeth placed a hand on her father's shoulder. "I'll take care of this, Daddy." Noticing her father's obvious disapproval, she quickly added, "He's just a boy in my science class…my lab partner. Nothing to worry about."

Finally, he said, "Okay, fine, then," and wandered off into the palatial halls of his kingdom.

"Um…hey."

"*What* are you *doing* here, *Richard*?" She tucked a strand of her long, blonde hair behind her ear, preparing for battle.

"I, ah, well, first of all…here." I handed her the box of detergent. "This is for your sweater. The one I spilled milk on the other day?"

She looked at it in amazement. Tough crowd, these Blackmers. "It has to be *dry* cleaned."

"Oh, sorry. Can I pay the bill?" Self-consciously, I lowered the flowers, hoping we'd both somehow forget their existence. How could I've possibly thought flowers sounded like a good idea?

"*No*." After a miserably long pause, she finally said, "What else do you want?"

"Okay. This…may sound kind of crazy, but I was wondering if…maybe you would go to the Spring Fling with me?" I swallowed, waiting for the aftermath.

I thought her scary, blue eyes were going to explode. "You. Have. *Got*. To. Be. *Kidding*. Me." I'm really not a fan of how she draws her sentences out, one agonizing word at a time. It's kinda moot anyway, as I understand her sentiment long before she's finished. But the laws of courting demand I stand there and suffer. "Why would I want to go to the dance with *you*?"

I heaved a sigh, almost a groan. "Well, because Elspeth said I need a date and—"

"I don't care *what* Elspeth told you." She lowered her voice. "She's probably just messing with me. It wouldn't be the first time. But this is *my* life. I am *not* going to be made a laughing stock out of at the Spring Fling. There's no *way* I'm going to go with you. *Gag*!"

Okay, now more than a little pissed off, I worked hard not to lose it like I did earlier with Olivia. Easier said than done. But I decided to try a different tact, one of Brandon-styled ignorance. "So…I guess you're excited about our date?" I winked, as awkward as it is for me.

"*No*. I am *not* going with you." She shook her fingers in the air as if drying her freshly painted nails.

"What time should I pick you up?"

"*Oooooh*."

"So that's a hard yes, right?"

"Get out of here now!"

"Oh, hey, here." I waved the flowers in front of her face. "These are for you."

"I'm *soooo* not taking those!"

"Does this mean we're going steady?"

"Oh. My. *Gawd*!" Although she slammed the door, I—and the rest of the fabulously filthy-rich neighborhood—heard her continue ranting behind the heavy doors.

Well, *that* went well. Yessir, all in all, a really good day.

I didn't even get a chance to tell Olivia I need her help because of—you know—an open gateway to Hell. And, now, my pride won't allow me to tell her. Not now, at least. And Elizabeth, of course, provided absolutely no help. Why can't she be Elspeth most of the time, instead of the dreadful Elizabeth?

I'm absolutely terrified and alone. With *no* idea what I'm going to do.

Chapter Fifteen

Mercifully, the rest of my weekend passed quietly for a change, the indisputable highlight being Ruth's surprised look at receiving a half-dozen yellow roses from me. She swooned over them, repeatedly moving them from the hearth to the kitchen table and back again. Dad, on the other hand, looked more than a little suspicious about the entire undertaking.

Once Ruth left, Dad asked, "Okay, son, what's the story behind the flowers?"

I told him of my romantic woes, holding nothing back, the idea to keep running interference to avoid my inevitable punishment, which *still* hasn't surfaced. "Well, hang in there, Tex. I'm sure things will turn around for you soon."

I nodded, although I didn't believe it for a moment.

Throughout Saturday, Brandon texted me, and I ignored him.

—*Sorry, dude, I thought it'd be cool with you, I thought you were over Olivia*—and many variations thereof were the more lucid messages. Yeah, right. I'm over Olivia. It's been like, practically almost an entire week since we broke up, after all. In Brandon's world, that's more than enough time to mend a broken heart. I blocked his number.

Both Ian and Danny texted me, looking to hang

out, but I told them I couldn't. I needed the weekend to think things through, to further embellish my plan to vanquish Bellman once and for all. But, mostly, I needed to catch up on some much-needed sleep. And wallow alone in my self-pity.

I spent a lot of time in bed, but constant nightmares haunted my sleep. As in the worst fever dreams, an endless cycle of events played across my mind's screen, dominated by green-eyed demon bullies, threatening gangstas, and possibly worst of all, angry, screaming, teenage girls.

****

I arrived as late as I could to school on Monday, hoping to avoid my new fan club. While face-deep in my locker, someone grabbed my hair and yanked me out. Ken hovered over me, his chest heaving in and out.

"Yo, punkass." His quiet tone oozed with malice. "You called five-o on me, didn't you?"

I avoided eye contact, having learned that trick with gorillas in the zoo. "I don't know what you're talking about." I shuffled books and papers around in my locker before Ken slammed it shut. "Look, Ken, I didn't call the police—"

"You lyin' to me, holmes. Saturday night, I got done visited by the po-po. They be lookin' to know if payback be in store fo' the Young Bloods. How they know dat? Unless you snitched?"

"I didn't *call* them, okay?" This time, I left my locker open. I'd rather sacrifice the textbook for my first class than risk losing a limb. "Look, I *am* sorry about the things I said to you the other day." I figured it's worth a shot.

"I *know* you called 'em, holmes. And the Gangstas

don't look kindly on bein' shown no respec', you hear I'm sayin'?"

"I...I know what I said was harsh, and I'm trying to apologize for it. I was out of line." I gulped and prayed the bell would ring soon to usher the animals back into their cages. "So...I'm really sorry."

"Too late for dat, yo. You done made an enemy out of the Gangstas. You know what dey say about dat, yo?"

"What?" I didn't really want to know, but proper etiquette and all.

"Payback's a 'mo-fo'. If I was you, holmes, I be watchin' my back." He stepped away, his jeans sweeping the floor. "We be comin' at you." He slumped off down the hallway, bumping into every male smaller than him, snapping his head to see if they dared to challenge him.

I raced down the hallway, past the office, toward my first class. The door to the security office popped open. Alf peered out.

"Hi, Richard. Mind if I talk to you?"

By the wall clock, I had a couple of minutes to spare. "Sure, Alf, what's up?" We squeezed into his cramped quarters, and he assumed his position behind his desk. I stood facing him.

"Richard, I want you to tell me the truth." His bottom lip dropped as if he bit into something sour.

"Sure."

"Tell me you had nothing to do with the vandalism that went on in the science lab earlier this week."

"Come on, Alf." I mustered a false chuckle. "I didn't do it. I *wouldn't* do it." I truly hated lying to Alf, as he seems to be the one person in authority who *wants* to believe in my innocence.

"Well, I didn't think so…" He kicked his feet up on the one bare spot on his desk. I couldn't help but check out his legs for telltale signs of past gunshots. "But, Mr. Hastings—he thinks you're the one."

"I know. He's always out to pin something on me. He just doesn't like me—for whatever reason." I spread my hands as I imagined a lawyer would, displaying my humility.

He sighed. "I don't think Mr. Hastings is going to rest until he gets his bobblehead back."

"Huh."

"He's constantly on me to find out who did this. I just wanted to talk to you…make sure I'm not going to find out it was you."

"It wasn't me."

"I hope not, for your sake. I don't want you to throw your future away."

"Um, I don't want that either."

"I mean, you'd *tell* me, Richard, right?" Even though it's great having someone on my team, I hope Alf isn't going to take too much of an interest in cracking the case of the missing bobblehead.

"Of course I would."

He stared at one of his computer monitors, the light gleaming off his glasses. "So, tell me…what's going on with you and your…little mystery girl?" He smiled.

"Not much to tell on that front. I really, truly know nothing about her. I've only seen her twice. She just bounces in occasionally. I'm not even sure of her name, her real name, at least."

"I see. I hope you don't let her lead you down the path to…doing bad things."

"No, no, no."

"Okay. Well, do me a favor and let me know if you *do* hear anything about this act of vandalism, will you?" He winked at me conspiratorially. "You'll be my man on the inside."

"Yeah, sure, Alf." Great, I've been deputized to find the culprit to a crime I committed.

"I don't think Mr. Hastings is going to back off on this one." His eyes appeared sad again. "Let's *not* give him what he wants, if you know what I mean."

I didn't understand exactly what he meant, but the implications unsettled me. "Ah, okay."

"All righty, Richard, come and visit whenever you can."

"Will do. But I've got to get to class now. Bye, Alf."

I darted into the hallway, hastening my escape from Alf's sly interrogation. I'm not sure what to make of him, but I know he's not the doddering, foot-shooting, incompetent rent-a-cop I first thought him to be. I need to be careful. Especially with my upcoming Friday night excursion into secret high school derring-do.

I had exactly one minute to get to class. Of course, I bumped right into Johnny Malinowski. Par for the course.

"Hey, *faggot*. I haven't forgotten what you did to me in the bathroom." He rolled back his shoulders and clenched his fists.

I didn't have time for his bullying nonsense, so I doubled over, holding my stomach. I made fake gagging and retching sounds, straightened up, and cupped my hand over my mouth.

"*Don't* you do it *again*," he said, backing away. A few lingering kids in the hallway watched with curiosity.

I repeated a mock heave. He fell back against the locker, letting slip a high-pitched shriek. I laughed as I ran to class. *Much* better and safer than a witchcraft spell.

****

At the picnic table outside, the sun cooked me with its heat, but I planned to avoid Olivia and Brandon at lunchtime, at all costs. My altruistic side reasoned I did it to protect Brandon from hanging out with me to avoid a conflict with Ken, but really, I just can't bear to see them together. It still hurt massively—and in retrospect, I felt more than a little embarrassed about my puerile tantrum on Saturday.

Out of a sense of male camaraderie, Ian and Danny joined me. "Tex, it's hotter than crap out here." Ian, clearly uncomfortable in his black T-shirt and jeans, never could take the heat. Unseasonably hot, it hadn't rained in nearly three weeks, unusual for this time of year in Kansas. The resulting temperatures rose daily. "You've *got* to get over this thing with Olivia."

Dan nodded while chewing on a peanut butter and jelly sandwich, the crusts cut off as per usual.

"Look, I appreciate you guys eating out here with me. I really do, but don't blame the weather on me." Danny swatted at a fly buzzing near his sandwich. "You don't have to be out here."

"Well, we're here for you, man," said Ian. Danny nodded again, too involved with his sandwich to communicate audibly.

"Besides, I just can't get over it. I need some time.

That…jerk, Brandon."

"I don't think he's a jerk, not really," offered Ian, the traitor. "I think he's just too dumb to realize he broke the Bro Code."

Danny laughed, spraying out breadcrumbs. "Yeah, he's not the brightest guy around."

"Anyway, he's okay," said Ian. Danny shrugged his small shoulders.

"Whatever. Besides, he ate her cereal," I said.

"Yeah," said Ian with a chuckle. "What's up with *that*? Olivia said you went off about her cereal."

Why did I even bring it up? "Ah, it's just something dumb. When I went over to her house to ask her to the dance, he was there eating her cereal." I looked around for corroboration, but only vacant stares met me. "I don't think she ever offered me cereal, not in the two years I've known her."

Ian shook his head. "Jesus, how would you've reacted if she offered him a sandwich?"

Danny held out his sandwich as a visual aid. Both of them burst into a laughing jag.

"Yeah, well, I guess you two have fallen under the magical, powerful thrall of the ever-so-wonderful—and who could forget, stunningly handsome—Brandon Townsend."

"Hey," Ian said, "Olivia's not mad at you. She's…concerned about you, and maybe, a little, I don't know, sad, I guess."

I don't know how I feel about that. On the one hand, it might mean the doors to communication could be reopened, but hearing she's sad makes it seem as if she's concluded it's over between us. She's mourning the finality. That we're a lost cause. I almost prefer her anger. At least then, I'd know she felt *something* for me.

"Whatever. Ian, are you going to the Spring Fling?"

Ian stopped fidgeting and stared at me. "Um, yeah, I guess I am."

"Are you bringing a date?" asked Danny.

Ian nodded and looked down at his mostly untouched lunch. "I'm going with Allison." He grimaced as if embarrassed.

I reached across the table and clapped him on the shoulder. "That's awesome. I'm happy for you guys."

"It's *not* like we're getting married or whatever."

"Ian, Allie's a cool girl. Why do you look like you're going to a funeral?"

"It's not *that*." He lowered his voice. "It's…going to this stupid Spring Fling. I never thought I'd be going to one of these stupid school sponsored dance things. We used to make fun of them." I understood where his emotional turmoil came from—his inner anarchist fought his desire to do something a "regular teenager" might enjoy.

"Ian, I think your rep will survive this."

"Whatever. What about you, Dan? You goin'?"

Danny squirmed on the bench. "I couldn't get a date in time. Um, everyone I asked had already been asked."

Feeling uncomfortable for him, I chimed in. "That's cool, you can hang with me. I struck out, too."

"Yeah," said Ian. "We can all hang out together." Ian smiled impishly at me. "Even Olivia and Brandon."

I chose to ignore Ian's horrific comment. "No, really, Danny, you should totally go. We'll have fun, even if we have to bring it ourselves."

Danny smiled, entertaining the notion. "Okay, cool, maybe I will come."

"Tex, why are you so hell-bent on going, anyway?" asked Ian. "Wasn't it just last year all of us more or less made a pact we'd never go to one of these deals?"

"Yeah, well. I guess since we're teenagers, we can change our mind?" Totally lame reasoning, but I can't tell Danny my real reasons, since he doesn't know I'm a witch. Maybe it's time to let Danny into the inner circle of witch associates.

"What*ever*," said Ian. "And, hey, is it true you actually asked out Elizabeth Chambers? And she totally shot you down?" Ian bounced up and down on the bench, excited and full of morbid curiosity.

"Um, yeah."

"Dude, you so gotta tell us about it," shrieked Ian.

"All right...*fine*. First of all, she's one of the richest people I've ever seen. Her home is a mansion. Wait. Not only is she one of the richest, she's also one of the *meanest, most* stuck-up..." Finally, I let my roll snowball into an avalanche. "*Most* insensitive—"

"Tex," Ian whispered.

"...*most* selfish, stubborn—"

"Tex!" Danny looked paler than usual.

"...*most* self-centered—"

Ian kicked me under the table. "What?" I yelled, ending my tirade. He raised his eyes several times over my head, not a subtle look at all.

Ian stood up from the table. "Gotta skate," he said, brushing the crumbs off his shirt. "Come on, Danny." They shuffled away as fast as their legs would carry them.

"What's going on?" I called out after my retreating friends. I turned around to meet the freezing cold eyes of Elizabeth.

One hand perched on her hip while the other hung lazily at her side. Given the incredible heat, she looked totally comfortable in her pink sweater. I bet she's physically unable to sweat. "I hope you enjoyed that, Richard," she said, ice freezing every clipped syllable.

"Um, hi…what exactly did you hear?"

"Let's see…" She counted off her fingers. "Selfish, stubborn, self-centered. I assume you were telling your little friends all about me?"

"No, no, no. Yeah, okay, whatever, sorry."

She shrugged as if those were traits to be proud of. She sat down across from me. "I wouldn't deny any of those things. I believe I've *more* than earned the right to act that way." Self-centered? *Ding*. She flashed me a very fast, full-toothed smile before re-establishing her rigid demeanor. Obviously, she believes smiling promotes wrinkles.

"Well, Elizabeth…after last Saturday, you're the *last* person I thought I'd be having lunch with." Suddenly, it seemed very cold outside.

"Does it *look* like I have *food* in front of me? We are sooo *not* having lunch together."

"Okay, we're not having lunch. What do you want?"

She exhaled slowly, dug out some sunglasses, and put them on. Going for incognito, no doubt. "Fine. Elspeth left me a note and said it's very important I go with you to this dumb dance." She sneered.

"Good… Um, I guess." I said the last two words under my breath.

"But you need to tell me what this is all about. *What* are you getting me involved in? What's so *important*?" She wiped away the crumbs Ian had left behind with the arm of her sweater, carefully avoiding any contact with her precious skin.

"Fair enough. All right, where to begin?"

"How about the beginning? *Duh!*" Her mouth dropped open.

"I need to vanquish an evil spirit—and I need to do it Friday night—during the dance." I waited for her sure-to-be outraged response.

She merely snorted like she'd heard it all before. "Well? Go on."

"I don't know if you remember Bob Bellman?"

"Yes, I know who he was." Her upper lip curled in disgust.

"Well, he's back. Apparently, if I don't get rid of him, other spirits might sneak into our world as well. Things could get, ah, much worse."

"Why does it have to happen during the dance?" If someone dropped this craziness on me, that probably wouldn't be the first question I'd ask.

"It's a long story, but—" I paused for dramatic emphasis. Elizabeth didn't go for it—no time for the common man—so I sped things up. "I need to vanquish Bellman in the boy's locker room—where I had my first encounter with him—where I can draw him out to end this. It's isolated, so no one else will witness it, and there aren't any video cameras. Friday night's the only time I'll be able to get in there with nobody else around."

"You're *not* asking me to go to the boy's locker room." Definitely more of a demand than a question.

"No, Elizabeth." I sighed. "It's something I have to do by myself."

"Well, good." She wrinkled her nose at the thought of the locker room. "What, exactly, am I supposed to do?"

"I really don't know. Maybe nothing. You might be better off asking Elspeth that. All I know is she told me I need a date to the dance. She hasn't been wrong yet. There's also something else I should probably tell you as long as we're doing the full disclosure thing…"

"Oh, God…I'm listening."

"You know about that James Badger kid who was shot, right?" She nodded. "I don't know if this has anything to do with Friday night, or if it's related to what Elspeth knows, but…I'm also kinda trying to find out who killed him."

This seemed more shocking to her than the fact there's an evil spirit running amok through her high school. She shook her head, her hair defiantly unwilling to budge. "*Why*?"

"Okay, well, basically, I guess I need to do it because I'm trying to prevent another possible murder."

"*God,* I just can't *believe* you."

"And because it's the right thing to do." I hoped to reach whatever humanity remained buried deep within her but realized it's probably a lost cause.

"Okay, fine, *but*…there are going to be some ground rules."

Oh boy, here we go.

"Number one," she said, extending her first finger, royal highness of countdown lists. "This is *not* a date. You will *not* pick me up. I'll meet you in the parking lot." Her second finger flipped up. "I will buy my own ticket." Well, *good.* "Third, if anyone—and by *anyone,* I mean my friends—asks, I'm doing this merely because I feel sorry for you." Frankly, the thought of her having friends seemed kinda crazy. "Fourth, there will *absolutely* be no hand holding, dancing, and especially, *no* kissing." I wonder what she'd think if she knew Elspeth kissed me? "Do I make myself *clear?"*

And there's insensitivity, selfishness, and stubbornness all wrapped up in her little rant. *Ding.* Triple points. Thanks for playing along with the studio audience, Elizabeth, and proving my point about what an awful person you are.

"Do. I. Make. Myself. *Clear?*" she said in that agonizingly long and condescending manner.

I nodded. This is going to be a fun date.

"I need you to say it. Do *you* understand me?" She leaned in to make sure she had my attention. Thankfully, she wore sunglasses; otherwise, it'd be hard to hold up under the scrutiny of her killer's eyes.

"Yes. I understand." As a stupid afterthought, I mumbled, "What about French kissing? Is that okay?"

Whack. Her hand slapped the table. "Don't you ever, *ever* even say that to me again! I'm *not* messing around here, Richard!"

"Wish I was going with Elspeth instead," I mumbled.

"What? What did you *say?"*

"Ah, um…nothing."

She drummed her fingertips on the table. When she realized how vulgar her actions were, she quickly withdrew them as if afraid of germs. "Richard," she said quietly.

"Yeah?"

"Maybe…maybe, I was a little tough on you Saturday."

"Ya' think?"

She released a small laugh, then ended it abruptly. "What*ever*." She hesitated and then said, "I don't hate you, you know. My daddy hates you, but I don't."

"Um, well, thanks for that, I guess. Tell your dad I'm *awfully* fond of him."

"You know, this is just the way I was brought up. Daddy taught me to get everything I want out of life. I have to be tough and demand it. Otherwise, well…" She shrugged her shoulders as if this made perfect sense.

"Huh," I managed.

"And you need to realize that nothing—*nothing*—is more important to me than—"

"I know, I know. Getting into the fabulous Ivy League college of your choice."

"Exactly, and I'll stop at nothing to get what I want. So don't screw that up for me, okay?" She took off her glasses, exposing her eyes, a hint of trepidation about them. "Okay?"

"Well, I'll *try* not to. Thanks for doing this, Elizabeth. I know it's not easy for you."

She stood up, dismissing me with a regal flourish. "Yeah, yeah, yeah, whatever. I'll meet you Friday night in the parking lot, by my car, at seven."

"Okay." She sashayed off, never breaking stride in her perfect runway glide.

Okay, I guess I have a date for the Spring Fling. But I'd *still* rather be going with Elspeth.

****

For once, I had minutes to spare before my psych

class began.

"Dude," said Dan. "What *happened* back there? Did she bust you for what you said about her?" So vividly excited to hear about my trauma, his eyes practically bulged.

"Well, yeah."

"Oh, man." I tried to hush him by lowering my hand several times. "So, what'd she do?"

"I guess I have a date with her for the Spring Fling."

"What? Oh..." His shoulders slumped as he slid down in his chair, defeated.

"Just as friends," I quickly added. I don't want to start breaking her Royal Highness's rules right off the bat. She's liable to have her personal executioner take my head off; plus, I saw how the news totally deflated Danny's good mood.

"That's cool," he said. "I guess I won't go to the dance, after all."

"No, no, Danny. Dude, you *gotta* go. Look, my so-called 'date' doesn't even *like* me. I promise. We'll hang and have a good time, okay?"

"I don't know. I don't want to be the only one there without a date."

"Oh, come on. There'll be others there. Besides, we're gonna hang in a group."

Danny smiled weakly. "Okay...maybe, I guess."

Mr. Jensen stormed into the room. *Uh-oh.* It's always easy to spot when he's in one of his moods. He surveyed us, said nothing, and paced across the floor. The students wisely shut up, their whispers and laughter dying like a toy with depleted batteries. The bell rang, and Mr. Jensen stood, silent, occasionally shaking his head. He went to the chalkboard and with his back to us, bellowed out, "Does anyone have anything important they'd like to discuss today?" The students knew better than to interrupt his outraged reverie.

"Well, if you don't mind…" He smiled sourly. "I'd like to start today's topic." He scratched the word "diversity" across the board, in jagged, sharp lines, then underlined it, three angry times.

"Say it, people," he ordered.

"*Diversity*," we repeated.

"What does it mean to you?" He lifted his eyebrows and swept his gaze across us, looking for that one brave—or dumb—soul who might give him the answer he sought.

Suzie, the vapid yet pretty cheerleader, offered, "It means living in a world full of people of diverse races, religions, and other stuff, Mr. Jensen, and tolerating them." I lifted one eyebrow at Daniel, who grinned. She actually gave an answer better than I thought her capable of.

"That's very good, thank you, Suzie. But…the one word you used that I wouldn't necessarily use myself, I'd like to expand upon— tolerance." He smiled at Suzie, who beamed back. She didn't understand Jensen called her out as a "what not to say" example. "To me, the word 'tolerance' suggests 'putting up with.' Sometimes, when you 'tolerate' someone, you're merely acknowledging their difference, not necessarily welcoming them with open arms. I think a better word might be 'acceptance.' This connotes not only 'putting up with' but *also* accepting one's peers' differences gladly. Does everyone understand my distinction between 'acceptance' and the more commonly used 'tolerance'?"

The class nodded in unison, half out of fear, the other half wanting to get the lecture over with.

"Now…I know we're a—how do I say this—upper middle class, predominantly white, suburban high school in Kansas," he continued. "There aren't a lot of minority students who go here, due to regional and economic issues." One kid in the back of the room snickered. Mr. Jensen's frightening glower just as quickly ended it.

"But, there is *still* a lot of diversity at this school," he said.

"What…how do you mean, Mr. Jensen?" Susie never knows when to quit.

"Thanks for asking, Susie." She's his straight man today, the wing man with all the right questions and answers. "Look around you…" He paused. "I said, *'look.'*" Heads swiveled. "We have jocks, cheerleaders, straight and gay people, non-binary gendered students, theatre kids, music folk, emo people, hipsters, computer whizzes, geniuses…"

Daniel smiled and straightened up in his seat.

"art kids…probably, I'm willing to guess, a few stoners…"

A few people laughed, and Mr. Jensen actually smiled. *Smiled*!

"There are even some of you who stubbornly refuse to belong to any group but who are comfortable with their own identity." He glanced at me. I immediately scrunched down into my seat. I'm not comfortable with…well, *anything*. "Looks like a pretty diverse bunch to me. So, Suzie, as you can see, 'diversity' doesn't only deal with matters of race and religion and, ah, 'other stuff.'" The classroom giggled. "And I'm proud of everyone who's strong enough— *brave* enough—to forge their own identity."

A jock called out, "Are you proud of the stoners, too, Mr. Jensen?" The classroom broke out into laughter.

Mr. Jensen squinted, one side of his mouth hitched up. "Well, Deke, I don't know if I can say I'm actually *proud* of them, but if they're comfortable in their own skin, who am I to judge?" He gestured large hands into the air. "I do know it can be hard sometimes, particularly in high school, where there's so much emphasis to be 'popular.'" His air quotes hooked high. "But, people, I would *implore* you...be true to your own selves...your own *identities*." He went back to the board and wrote *identity* underneath *diversity*.

He sat down and exhaled, enfolding his hands behind his head. "Now, the worst possible thing anyone can do is to forge a false 'identity.' It's come to my attention that there's been a lot of talk lately amongst both the students and the faculty...about gangstas." *Uh-oh*. Daniel twitched uncomfortably in his seat.

"Apparently, there are certain kids—in *this* school and other schools—who have decided to adopt a false identity, if you will, of something they know *nothing* about, of living the lives of *gangstas*. I don't know if they've seen it on TV or whatever, but they're glorifying a lifestyle based on threats, violence, and totally unacceptable behavior. There's a certain...darkness that has fallen over the school. People are afraid. I've even seen teachers and parents who are scared to death of the stories that are being perpetuated about these...punks.

"In lower-income areas, being gangsta is forced upon poor kids due to harsh economic realities. They don't have a chance, people, not like *you* do. And for me to see someone, here, in our nice upper class, little suburban school, adopting these patterns—*glorifying* this behavior because they think it's romantic in some preposterous fashion—makes me sick. And now...they're affecting everyone around them. One boy's already died because of it. It needs to *stop now*." He slammed his fist on the desk, jolting several students alert.

Suzie unrelentingly thrust her hand in the air and said, "But, Mr. Jensen, what's the difference between someone wanting to be a gangsta and say...a goth kid or something?"

"Good question, Suzie. But there's one *major* difference. I don't see any of the goth kids wielding knives, making threats, or shooting kids. Listen up, people, your sense of identity...your right to freely express yourself through clothing, lifestyle choices— whatever—*ends* when it infringes upon the freedom and rights of others. These *gangstas*..." He sneered when he said the word. "These *gangstas*...their entire so-called identity is based upon something completely fabricated...and it's based on threatening the welfare, the rights, of everyone else in this school. Does that make sense, Suzie?"

Suzie nodded, turning a shade redder than her usual fake orange tint.

"I would ask—*implore,* even—that if any of you— *any* of you—know anything about these gangstas, to come forward and tell someone what you know. It needs to *stop*." He looked at me. I shook my head, possibly too quickly.

He took a deep breath and regained his composure. "As I said, I know it can be hard, people, but just be *who* you are. Don't be someone just to fit in, or for some even more ludicrous reason. I guarantee you, people, if you find out who you are—and let that identity come through naturally—you'll gain friends, acceptance, maybe even a boyfriend or girlfriend." Deke, the jock, let loose a quick catcall. "I know it sounds like a cliché, but follow your own path…listen to your inner self." He stood and went over to the blinds. He stared out onto the football field for several long, quiet moments. He looked at the class again and sat down. "Okay, before I start sounding like some late-night self-help infomercial, open your textbooks to page one hundred fifty-six."

And that's why Mr. Jensen is still my favorite teacher. I don't even hold it against him that he's the football coach.

Chapter Sixteen

To my great dismay, Ruth got it in her head to teach me how to dance.

"Come on, Tex," she sang. "I was known to cut quite a rug in my day." She giddily circled the room, humming to the Tony Bennett CD she put into the stereo. Arms in the air, she embraced her invisible dance partner while she swooped, bent, twirled, twittered, and skated across the floor. Dad sat silently in the corner, a sadistically amused look on his face. I think he finally found my proper punishment. Well played, Dad, well played.

"No, Ruth, I appreciate the offer," I said, "but I don't think that's the kind of music they'll be playing at the Spring Fling tonight."

"Silly boy," she said. "Dancing is dancing. It transcends *any* style of music." She bounced about, counting "one, two and three" repeatedly. As she made her way toward me, I looked for a fast exit. "Come on." She grabbed one of my hands, held it in the air, and slipped her other arm around my waist. She pulled me to the center of the room. "Now, just follow my lead."

Finally, Dad came to his senses. "Oh, hey, look at the time. Tex, aren't you supposed to meet your date soon?"

"Oh, wow, you're right."

Ruth released her death grip on me, her look of disappointment heartbreaking. "Oh, well, maybe next time."

"Yeah, sure." It didn't take me long to bolt from this hell on earth. I snagged my car keys by the door and said, "Good night, guys."

"Wait, Tex…wait." Ruth scrambled toward me, her camera obscuring her face. "We've got to get some pictures."

I sighed. "Okay, maybe one quick photo, then I've really got to get going."

"You look so handsome in your suit," she said. I had put on my blue suit, black shirt, and a matching blue tie. It's the first time I've worn it since I tried it on at the store. But Dad always insisted I need to have a suit ready for any occasion. Due to my continuing height gain, we had to buy a new suit each year. The cool blue color didn't thrill Dad, but I thought it better than the standard "banker suits" we've purchased in the past.

"This won't take but a minute. Your little date can wait for you, for pity's sake." Ruth snapped the picture the moment I rolled my eyes. That'll be one for the ol' scrapbook.

"Okay, Ruth, let the boy go." Dad wheeled toward me. "Have a good time, son." While I hardly expected to have a good time for more reasons than one, I didn't want to saddle Dad with that information.

"Thanks, Dad. Love you."

"Love you, too." He frowned. He knows when I profess my love it's usually because something dire awaits. "Is, ah, everything okay, Tex?"

"Yeah. I'm just a little nervous about my date, I

guess."

"You have nothing to be nervous about."

Beg to differ, Dad. "Okay, thanks. Gotta go." I ran toward the Bucket before Ruth started dancing again.

A strange, purplish tint overcast the sky. The air itself felt quiet, thick, almost palpable like soup du dread. The spring breeze that cooled us off for the last several weeks had gone south. Clouds gathered overhead, merging like giant mushroom caps. Our three-week-long dry spell ended tonight.

Several minutes later, I arrived at Danny's house. My giving him a ride to the dance finally cinched the deal for him. No way had he wanted his mom dropping him off in front of everyone. While he knew I had a "pseudo-date," he also understood I'd attend stag. I really didn't think I'd enjoy the dance at all—even if I didn't have to face my demons, so to speak—but I would have felt terrible if Dan didn't go.

Once again, Dan dashed toward my car as if the devil had a pitchfork poised at his butt. Which suited me just fine as I didn't savor another encounter with his brother.

Danny wore an ill-fitting black suit, the pants legs much too short. The dress shoes looked about two sizes too large, and he nearly tripped as he stumbled to my car. His black tie came up short as well, and I made a mental note to re-knot it once we arrived. Take off the jacket and tie, and his outfit looked pretty much like his regular school attire.

Dan's mother stood in the doorway, flour dusting one side of her face, still wearing her apron—did she sleep in it?—and waved.

"Let's go, Tex." He appeared torn between extreme

anxiety and anticipation about what mysteries the upcoming dance might hold for him.

"Well, hey to you, too, Danny," I said, pulling the Bucket out into the street.

"Sorry. My mom was driving me crazy, saying stupid things like 'Oh, you're so handsome,' and 'Oh, you'll knock the ladies off their feet.' It's just so dumb."

"Yeah, I got some of the same treatment."

"Stupid, right?"

"Yeah." I chuckled. "It's stupid."

We pulled into the parking lot, and I took a cursory glance around, looking for Elizabeth's yellow sports car. I should've known better than to expect her early. I think it's part of her so-called tough upbringing and training to make everyone wait on her.

"Hey, I've got to wait for Elizabeth, but first, let's fix your tie." I pulled at the knot on his tie.

"Thanks, Tex. My mom tied it. I didn't think it looked good, but whatever."

"Hold still…"

"Why *are* you going with Elizabeth to this dumb dance, anyway? I mean, I thought you still liked Olivia. And Elizabeth kinda sucks."

"Yeah, I agree."

Dan squirmed like a little kid getting a haircut, making it next to impossible to get a good length on his tie.

"Then, why?"

I'd been thinking of telling Danny about my being a witch. He's earned the right. But is now the appropriate time? Oh, what the hell, I might not get another chance.

"Okay, here we go. Dan, what I'm about to tell you stays between us, okay? You can't tell anyone. Promise me?"

"Yeah, sure, it's cool." He looked so visibly excited, I wondered if anyone's ever confided secrets to him before.

"I'm a witch."

Dan stared at me before exploding with nearly hysterical laughter. "Come on, Tex!" I let the disbelief work its way through his system. When he saw I didn't share his amusement, he finally fell silent. "What do you mean?"

"Last year, I found out my mother was a witch. I inherited her witch powers." Danny's eyes widened. "I know, right? It's been weird for me, too. But ever since I found out about it, I've sorta been a supernatural magnet for bad things."

"Wait. So...you're a witch?" For a genius, he had the hardest time grasping what the rest of my friends so readily accepted. I guess it doesn't fit into his highly logical world paradigm. "Are you into like, black magic and all that? Satanism?" I couldn't tell if he's nervous to be in my company or thrilled about hanging out with a witch. I finally gave up working on his tie. He definitely wouldn't hold still now. At least I managed to put a little more length on it.

"No, nothing like that. I'm a good witch." I realized how silly that sounded, and we both shared a laugh. "I try to do good things...and tonight, there's a spirit loose, and I'm going to attempt to vanquish him. For *whatever* reason, I'm supposed to bring a date to the dance. Outside of Olivia and Allie, Elizabeth's the only one I could think of."

Danny shook his head. "None of this makes any sense."

"I know. Sometimes—*most* times—I wonder just what in the hell is going on."

"What does Elizabeth have to do with your spirit vanquishing?"

"Hell if I know. Maybe nothing. But I was sent a message to bring a date."

"A message? What kind of message?"

"Let's just say it came to me in my sleep." Not a bad half-lie, if I say so myself.

"I don't know, Tex. This sounds kinda screwed up, if you ask me." He cast a shy glance at me to see if I might be punking him. When he saw my solemnity, he said, "Okay. Man! Okay…so you're a witch?"

"Yes," I sighed. "Thought we'd already established that."

"I know, I know. It's just a *lot* to take in. Who else knows?"

"Just you, Olivia, and Ian."

He smiled warmly as though honored to be privy to our inner circle. "Well, you can count on me to be silent. Do you need any help tonight?"

"I appreciate it, Dan. But it could get dangerous, and the spirit won't show up to anyone but me." He nodded. I think he finally found a way to make this information coexist with his logic.

"Can…can I see you do some stuff some time?"

"Well, I don't really go around doing 'stuff'…but I can tell you about things I learn, how's that?"

"Sick." He grinned ear to ear. "Where do you learn it? Does your mom talk to you from beyond?"

"No. I have a…well, I guess you'd call her a

'mentor.'"

"*Bad-ass*."

"Okay. I'll tell you more later. Right now, you'd better go in. I've got to wait for Elizabeth." Danny suddenly looked like he'd rather be anywhere than here. Probably afraid to walk in by himself, and quite frankly, I didn't blame him. I wouldn't want to either. "Hey, don't worry. I bet Ian and Allie are already inside." My words did nothing to soothe his fear. "Okay, forget it. You can come in with us." I wonder how Elizabeth will take this news. Just fine, I'm sure. Not only will she be escorted by one geek, but she'll now have the pleasure of matching bookends. But once I saw the look of relief on Danny's face, Elizabeth's hell-brought ire will be worth it.

And just *where* is she anyway? It's ten after seven, and still no sign of her. What's the point of even waiting for her, since she's made it apparent she's not even going to pretend to be my date? I mean, she has her own ticket anyway.

"Whatever. Let's go on in. I don't see her anywhere." I jumped out of the car and let Danny out. A low, deep sound rumbled above us. The clouds rolled, swirled, and gathered at an angry speed. The gods appeared to have indigestion, upset that release is still beyond their capacity. But when they finally let loose, it's going to be a torrential downfall of long-awaited relief.

Just then, the familiar yellow vehicle zoomed into the spot next to ours. Elizabeth briefly glanced over at us and went back to the more important work of applying her make-up. Danny and I stood by her car, waiting, hands in our pockets. I felt like a well-dressed carwash employee waiting for a tip.

Finally, she left her car.

"Elizabeth," I said, "it's twenty minutes after seven. You're late."

She stared at the two of us. "If you *needed* a date so badly, you should've let me know you already *had* a date." Annnnnd we're off to a rip-roaring start.

I sighed. "Elizabeth, this is my friend, Daniel Cross."

"I *know* who he is." She bared her teeth at Dan as if to bite him. For his part, Dan looked thrilled she knew who he is. "*Why* is he here?"

"Because I *said* he could come, Elizabeth. Remember, it's *not* a date." As pissed as I felt at her rudeness, my anger subsided once I saw her full get-up. She looked stunning. I halfway expected her to dress down for my benefit, but I should've known better. She wants to be seen, whether I'm a factor or not. Packed tightly into a formfitting dress, it inched up higher than I imagined her tastes running. She wore black tights and high heels, something more out of Elspeth's playbook. Her blonde hair appeared less rigid than usual, tousled, teased, and curled up, fluid waves dropping down across her forehead. All heat on the outside while icy cold on the inside.

Then I noticed the color of her dress matched the exact deep blue of my suit. Apparently the same time she did. "You. Have. Got. To. Be. *Kidding.* Me! Is this some sort of *joke*? Did you dress like me on *purpose*? When people see us, they'll think we're a *couple.* *Gawd!*"

"Elizabeth, calm down." Some dance-goers stared at us, looking to see which girl I pissed off this time, I suppose. "I can assure you, I had *no* idea what you were wearing. How could I?" Danny sensibly remained quiet but smirked nonetheless.

"Whatever." For the first time ever, when she shook her head, her hair actually moved.

"In fact, I thought about calling you to find out what you were wearing, so I would know what color…well, here…" I handed her the white corsage I bought earlier.

She stared at the box in my hand, but didn't budge. "I said this *isn't* a date. I am *not* going to wear that." She shoved the box back toward me. "*You* wear it."

Cursing under my breath, I put the box back in the Bucket. At the time, I wondered if the corsage might've been a bad idea, but I also envisioned it as a peace offering of sorts. I thought some of the ice had melted between us on Monday. Apparently, I thought wrong. The ice remained so thick that not even a sledgehammer could chip through it.

"Okay, let's go to the dance." I attempted a smile, but my cheek muscles twitched, betraying me.

The gods chose that moment to relay a loud, ominous thunderclap, followed by a flash of lightning. "Come *on*, already. Let's get this over with before my hair gets rained on," said Elizabeth.

Our little circus of unhappy dance-goers marched through the parking lot, led, of course, by Elizabeth, the ringmaster, chin held arrogantly high, followed by her two scampering clowns. Even though she wore high heels, Danny and I had a hard time keeping up with her. By the time we reached the front door to the commons area, sweat ran down my temples and dampened my back.

While I searched for my ticket, Elizabeth hurried ahead and vanished through the line. Finding it in my jacket pocket, I showed it to the teacher to gain passage. Danny made it through the opposite line when someone called out, "*Stop.*"

Mrs. Learned, the elderly librarian, said, "Every fourth couple who comes through the line must go see Mr. Lampbert. You're the lucky fourth couple this time. Now, which one is your date?"

I scanned the crowd and saw Elizabeth, mouth wide with horror. I pointed at her and said, "Um, her, Mrs. Learned. Elizabeth."

"*Oh*," said Mrs. Learned. "Oh, my. Well, yes, of course I know Elizabeth." I hoped the revelation of my date wouldn't cause her a heart attack. "Okay, would you both follow me, please?"

She toddled down the hall, motioning for us to follow her. I turned toward Elizabeth and mouthed, "What's going on?"

She rolled her eyes and said loudly, "We've been chosen to be breathalyzed. *Duh*! Don't tell me you've *never* been to a dance before?"

"Um, no, guess I haven't."

She expelled a deep breath as if that was the most pitiful thing she'd ever heard.

Mrs. Learned led us to Alf's small den of security. She pushed the door open and waved us in. Alf stood in front of his desk, holding a small device in his hand. His eyes widened when he saw me. "Hello, Richard. It's nice to see you here. If you would, please blow into this." He held the device up to my mouth.

"Is this your date, Richard?" He jutted his jaw toward Elizabeth. Unable to speak due to the contraption in my mouth, I nodded. "Huh. I thought you might bring the little gal with the black rooster hair." Elizabeth blasted me with her potent death-ray glare.

"Okay, you're fine. Your turn, little lady."

Alf changed something on the breathalyzer and pushed it toward Elizabeth's mouth. "Sorry if I put my foot in my mouth there, you two," he chuckled. "Say, you look familiar, miss. Do I know you from somewhere?" *Crap.* Elizabeth's and Elspeth's distinctive eyes are hard to forget.

Elizabeth spat out the breathalyzer and said, "Well, I *am* a student here."

Alf looked slightly taken aback and issued an apology. "Of course you are. Okay, you're both good to go. Have fun, you two."

"Yeah, *right*," said Elizabeth, already bolting out the door.

Alf turned to me and said, "Richard, maybe you *should* have brought that other girl."

I gave Alf a knowing nod, then ran out the door to catch up with Miss Runaway, already halfway down the hallway.

"Elizabeth, wait up."

"*What*?" She stopped in her tracks. "What was *that* about?"

"Um, he saw Elspeth a couple of times on the security camera when she came to visit me."

"*Ohhhh.* This just gets *worse* and *worse*."

Yeah, for me. "I think it's fine. He didn't get a good look at you. I mean, Elspeth."

She swiveled and made her quick trek toward The Dance From Hell. We entered the commons area. Students, dressed in an array of clothing from casual to extremely formal milled about the hallway between the cafeteria and the gym. Tables spread everywhere, decorated in a blue and white motif, with confetti and streamers strewn sloppily across them. Bags of candy were attached to helium-filled balloons floating overhead. Four candles in plastic holders nestled in the middle of the overly crowded tables—two blue, two white.

Calypso music penetrated my ears from the intercom speakers, obnoxiously and jauntily plinking along like torture in some exotic tourist trap.

"Elizabeth, what's with the music?"

She sighed and said, "*Really?* You're so clueless. It's the theme of this year's Spring Fling, duh—'Under The Sea!'" She stated this so empathically she assumed it should make sense to everyone. Because who could possibly think of anything more appropriate to celebrate high school life than Under The Sea?

"Huh, of course." I spotted the large plastic punch bowl on the long table in front of the cafeteria. Behind it stood two vigilant teachers, handing out cups—but more than likely on the lookout for students looking to add a more potent additive. Even though the mysterious, blue punch didn't look very appealing—it resembled glass cleaner—I forged ahead anyway. "Elizabeth, would you like some punch?"

Looking like she was ready to punch me, she snapped, "*No.*"

"Okay, whatever, fine. Do you want to get a table?" I peered into the cafeteria and saw more ghastly decorated tables filling up fast.

"Look, just because I said I'd go with you—for *whatever* reason—do *not* expect me to hang out with you the entire time."

"Fine, fine. *Whatever*. I'll see you around." I left, hoping to find a friendly face. I entered the cafeteria, the repetitious Calypso music accompanying my steps with a cartoonish soundtrack. I attempted to step out of rhythm so as not to be held hostage to the merciless music.

Suddenly, I felt so deeply humiliated at being cast aside by my "date," I needed a safe haven. Scanning the crowd, I saw Ian, Allie, and Danny sitting at a table near the back. I excused myself through the throng of students, trying not to catch anyone's eye.

"Hey, guys," I said.

"Tex!" Ian's attire looked pretty much the same as always, everything in black. At least he adorned his outfit with a tie this time. Allie stood and approached me, arms open wide. She wore a long, daring, strapless pink gown, which I'm sure she agonized over for some time. Her hair had been carefully styled and pinned up over her head, two long curls perfectly framing her face. Wearing makeup more apparent than usual, she still looked tastefully understated. Contact lenses obviously replaced her glasses. She looked absolutely unrecognizable and very pretty.

"Hey, Allie. You really look great." I hugged her.

"Thanks." The blush of her cheeks burned through her lightly rouged makeup. "You don't look so bad yourself."

Ian rushed toward Allie's side. "*Hey*! Hands off my date." Quite the mismatched couple, the short, pseudo goth boy in black standing next to the tall, pretty in pink Amazon. But they both appeared happier than I've seen them in some time. Ian and Allie sat down. "Where's your date, Tex?" asked Allie.

I hitched my thumb behind me. "Um, somewhere out there, I guess, whatever." I sat down at the table quickly, to take the fallout like a man.

Ian and Danny busted up. Allie shot them a glare I didn't know she had in her.

"Anyway, what's up with the theme of the dance?" I asked.

"Yeah, I know, right?" said Ian. "*Totally* lame."

"Lame," Danny repeated. "Who comes up with this crap?"

Allison said, "I think it's the student council. I've heard most of the council don't even really care about the themes to the dances, but for some reason, they always feel compelled to make one up."

"I guess they have to have something to do," I said, "other than make hollow promises that usually go nowhere."

"Maybe I'll run for student council next year." Ian's jaw dropped down as if struck by divine inspiration. "*Yeah*. I'll make the senior prom theme 'Total Anarchy.' We'll have fires on every table, people won't be allowed in unless they're wearing nothing but underwear…the chaperones will be all gangstas instead of teachers."

A hush fell across the table. Ian noticed and stopped. "I'm just joking. Jesus." Danny stared down at his folded hands, his cuffs pulled high on his arms, exposing nearly three inches of shirt.

To lighten the mood, Allie tapped Ian playfully on the arm. "Oh, you." We exchanged a round of uncomfortable smiles.

"Hey," said Danny, "did you guys like Principal

What's His Name's speech today before school ended?" We called our principal that nickname because we rarely ever saw him—couldn't pick him out of a police line-up—and frankly, we could never remember his name, a rather nondescript one. He'd poke his head out of his office every now and then, only to swiftly retreat like the groundhog afraid of his own shadow. Most students wondered about the identity of the small, suited man who wandered the halls on occasion. Every time before a dance, he ended the school day with a small speech on the intercom system, delivering the same message every time.

"Yeah. Awesome," chimed in Ian. He set his face solemnly, pitched his voice higher, and dragged out his poor, yet undeniably funny, imitation of our Mystery Principal. "'Now, there will be plenty of chaperones tonight, students, so, this means there will be *no* shenanigans, *no* grinding…and absolutely *no* booty-jacking.'"

Allison covered her mouth tentatively with pink-colored fingertips. "What does 'booty-jacking' even mean?"

"No one really knows. One of life's great mysteries," I said. "Only the principal knows."

"What kind of porn does he watch, anyway?" shouted Ian as the rest of us continued laughing so hard the surrounding tables stared at our ruckus.

"*Ian.*" Once again, Allie's cheeks blossomed into an apple red.

"Hey, guys." *Olivia.* Blue and white paisley trimmed her long denim skirt and vest. Over it, she wore a faded blue jean jacket, a few of her retro-band buttons supplying the bling. Toes peeked out from underneath the skirt through white sandals. Her hair didn't deviate from the usual manner, except for a matching streak of blue flopping over one eye. Never have I ever seen her in a skirt before. She, at once, looked formal, yet stubbornly maintained her unique sense of style and independence. Needless to say, she looked beautiful. My heart sank. I'm blatantly, overwhelmingly still in love with her and always will be. Cue the violins.

"Hey, O'." My casual, laid-back approach ended up squeaking like a cartoon mouse. "You look pretty damn…good." I avoided meeting her eyes.

"Hey, you look nice, too." She turned to Allison. "*Allie*, look at *you*. You look *fab*. I tried to get you to go there before, girl, but you wouldn't listen. Now, look at you."

Allison's blushing cheeks worked overtime tonight. "Thanks. Maybe we can go shopping sometime soon?" With a little encouragement, Allie felt ready to run the marathon.

"Sounds great." Olivia gave Ian and Danny an appreciative once-over. "Boys, you don't look too shabby either."

"Whatever." Despite his nonchalant response, Danny seemed genuinely thrilled at the compliment.

"Hey, where's Brandon?" asked Ian.

Maybe a bus t-boned his motorcycle? My malicious thought made me wonder how in the world Olivia *did* get to the dance in that skirt on Brandon's motorcycle.

"He's getting us a drink," said Olivia. "Did you see that blue…*crap* they expect us to drink?" Everyone laughed, and I forced myself to join in.

And when you speak the devil's name, he appears. Brandon, sleepy-looking as ever, carried two cups of blue toxin. Unbelievably, he wore a T-shirt, emblazoned with a print of a tuxedo over it, and black jeans. I wanted to guffaw, but bit the inside of my cheeks. I couldn't *believe* Olivia wouldn't ridicule his sense—or lack thereof—of style. She would've been mortified if I wore something like that and let me know about it. Just recently, she gave me hell about my black sweater.

Worst of all, I noticed a ton of girls at nearby tables, staring at Brandon. Not the kind of bemused glances one would expect because of his T-shirt, either. No, these were dreamy, glazed-over glances of romantic longing and lust for the ever-delectable charms of Captain Handsome himself, Brandon Townsend. I caught the eye of a guy at the next table, apparently another victim, as his girlfriend visibly swooned over Brandon. For an instant, we formed a Bro camaraderie forged in the fires left behind in Brandon's wake. I gave him a wary, knowing nod.

"What's up, guys?" Brandon's lazy gaze swooped over all of us, finally landing on me. "What's goin' on?"

"*Nice* shirt, dude," yelled Ian, grinning like a lunatic. I couldn't tell if Ian truly admired the inherent anarchy of Brandon's apparel, or if he scoffed at the ridiculous shirt. Either way, it prompted Danny to giggle.

"Thanks, dude." Brandon smiled, totally oblivious to his sartorial choice.

I thought I caught Olivia smirking. Just a bit. She snagged two chairs from an adjacent empty table and placed them next to me. As she sat in the chair further away, she glanced at me, then scooted over. Her choice made me imminently thankful, as I really didn't want to sit next to Brandon. Olivia fiddled with the hair over her eye and suddenly turned toward me, smiling. I snapped my eyes away, feeling foolish she busted me staring at her. Fleeing the table seemed like both the best and worst possible option.

While I pretended to look out over the crowd in the cafeteria, Brandon leaned behind Olivia and said softly, "Hey, Tex."

"Uh, hey," I said. Time to run interference and be cool. "So, Danny, did you get your psych homework done yet?"

Danny looked like a deer caught in the headlights. "*What* homework? I didn't think we had any. Besides, it's Friday night."

"Oh, yeah. Whatever." Man, am I cool or what?

"*Ohhhh,* no," said Olivia. "You guys are *not* going to talk about homework here. There's gotta be better things to talk about. Aren't we going to, you know, make fun of Under The Sea?"

"Already been done," I mumbled.

"Yeah, Olivia," said Ian. "It's so cool you dressed up in the color scheme for Under The Sea." Olivia froze the sarcastic grin right off his face.

"Yeah, *right*," she said. "Whatever. I didn't even *know* about this…this *stupid* Under The Sea theme."

"You guys wanna see something *really* stupid?" asked Ian, wide-eyed and hyper. "You gotta check out the gym. You *won't* believe it."

We agreed to change the venue, me more vocal than any of us. "Yeah, I need to go find my date, anyway." I meant to sound casually off-hand, but even to my ears, it sounded like bragging.

"You…have a date?" asked Olivia.

"Oh, yeah," replied Danny. "Some date. And wait 'til you see who it is."

Wanting to leave before Olivia uncovered the truth, I jumped to my feet. "Okay, let's go, guys." I pushed back my chair and glanced over at Olivia, who seemed disoriented. She swiveled her head back and forth, presumably looking for her purse. Naturally, Brandon saved the day and handed it to her.

I led everyone through the crowded cafeteria, across the even louder commons entryway, and into the gym, mercifully leaving the jaunty Calypso music behind. The gym, once the domain of nightmares, had been transformed into a gaudily-colored playground for teenagers. The wooden bleachers were pushed back against the walls, leaving the floor bare except for the basketball court markings. Large cutout drawings of waves hung across the walls, presumably created by the theatre kids' props department. Blue and white flashing lights pummeled us from above, circled, rose, dipped, and splashed over us again. I adjusted my eyes to the visual chaos and looked up. Several mirror disco balls rotated madly. An army of strobe lights flanked them, designed to give an epileptic nightmares for months.

Bombastic sounds of Top 40 music bombarded our ears, the bass turned up so high our chests thumped. I nearly longed for the gentle monotony of the Calypso music, but not really. The sounds emanated from a small, elevated booth next to the gym's stage. Some foolish-looking hip-hop DJ, wearing a sideways ball cap with an unfortunately long bill, gyrated wildly to the sounds of a boy band. I wondered if Principal Who Are You Again? might bust him for booty-jacking. Ginormous speakers lined the stage, blasting staccato audio bullets like not-so-friendly fire. Between dodge ball and bad music, the gym will forever be a place for teenagers to come to get pummeled.

A multitude of students danced in front of the stage and the DJ's stall. Several teachers patrolled between the dancers, obviously stuck with booty-jacking patrol. Arville Hastings leaned against the bleachers, watching over the constituents of his cathedral of agony like a sullen gargoyle.

Ian yelled into my ear, *"That's where the avid dancers dance."*

I screamed back, *"Yeah, I kinda figured that out."* In the other half of the gym, another throng of students stood about. They drew up their wagons of friends into circles, an implied warning that no outsiders better cross their lines. Many of them appeared to be gossiping, having fun, and laughing. Others looked miserable, frowning, speaking with visible condescension on their faces. I suppose this is where the avid complainers complain.

Not forgetting my ultimate mission, I looked over toward the boys' locker-room doors. Chained and padlocked, not a big surprise, probably to keep out booty-jackers. I didn't think to ask Mickey for another skeleton key, as I thought I wouldn't need one again. Or at least one that, you know, might actually work. But I prepared for this. I planned to enter from the hallway down by the music room, hoping that section of the school wouldn't be locked off for the night.

The music stopped abruptly, our ears ringing from

the aftershock. The DJ hollered, *"Okay. I'm gonna slow it down now for y'all for just a lil' bit. I see some of you need some...lovinnnnnnn'."* He dragged out the last word ruthlessly long, but at least I could now speak below a screaming level.

"Have you guys seen any booty-jackin, yet?" asked Ian.

"Only from the DJ," said Olivia.

A hand snagged my arm, prompting me to jolt. Brandon's eyes held a sense of unusual urgency. "Hey."

I shook free of his grasp. "Brandon..." I vowed to myself I would try and be civil toward him tonight. After all, I couldn't continue to eat outside in the sweltering heat every day at school to avoid him. But every time I looked at Brandon, I considered that outside lunches aren't so bad after all.

"Hey, man." Brandon glanced at Olivia, deep into a conversation with Allison. "I really want to apologize for my dick move."

I smiled so sourly, I thought my face might split. "Yeah, it *really* was a 'dick move.'"

"I really didn't do it on purpose. I just went over to her place to kinda, you know, hang...and then, we just sorta decided to go. Well, I kinda had been thinking about asking her, but you know..." He shrugged.

"Whatever, Brandon. It's done."

"Look, man, if you don't want me going out with her again, I won't."

I thought about jumping at his offer but realized it'd probably just piss Olivia off even more. But I also didn't want to give my blessings toward a future relationship between them. "Brandon, you do whatever *you* feel is the right thing to do." Spoken like my dad.

He tilted his head slightly, as a dog would upon hearing a strange sound. "Okay. And, hey, I promise you I'll never eat her cereal again."

I studied his perfect Greek god-like face for any slight hint of sarcasm. He stared at me, eyebrows arched, unaware of the total stupidity of this beyond stupid conversation. And I saw true sincerity in his seeking my forgiveness for eating Olivia's cereal.

"Brandon, I'll tell you what. Let's just forget about the stupid cereal, okay? Please. I'm still bummed out about the whole Olivia thing…but no more talk about cereal. *Please*."

"Cool," he said, smiling. "Are we cool?"

No, not really. Not even close, but his damned puppy dog routine wore down even my defenses. Damnit. This guy is truly blessed by the gods. I'd love to remain mad at him for a while longer, at least. So I thought I might mess with him a bit. Petty, sure, but when you're battling a Greek God, you have to use whatever mortal weapons you have in your arsenal. "You know what, Brandon? You can eat Olivia's cereal. But…*not* the Shredded Wheat. Stay far, far away from the Shredded Wheat."

Without missing a dull beat, he nodded. "Got it. No Shredded Wheat. So we're cool?"

"We'll see, Brandon." I turned away because I thought we were finished.

"Hey, Tex," he called after me. I kept walking, pretending I didn't hear him. "I need to talk to you about something else. Something important…" His voice faded away as I hurried out of the gym.

I entered the hellish hallway of Calypso music. The same damn melody repetitively popped along as I made my way to the bathroom. I peered down the long corridor to see if the passage to the front entryway of the boys' locker-room had been locked off. Hey, something in my favor for a change: open! Unfortunately, I also remembered the teacher's lounge is located in that corridor. What with all their chaperoning and patrolling tonight, they'd need their place of respite. So, I had to make it past their hideaway.

As I entered the bathroom, I bumped into a slew of jocks drinking out of hipflasks. Ordinarily, I'd be accosted by at least a few of them, but now, they seemed perfectly content to lose themselves in their alcoholic excursion. I quickly brushed by them, head down, took care of business, and left.

When I re-entered the gym, Ian, Allie, and Danny hovered at the edge of the complainers' club. Ian jerked his chin toward the dance floor. On the dance floor, Olivia and Brandon swayed together slowly, his hands around her waist. I cringed and took a deep breath. I have to stay focused and not let my romantic problems interfere with my mission, yet it's difficult. Ever since I got here, my mind's been wandering in too many directions, rendering me weak and vulnerable. I'm also guilty of postponing the inevitable.

In the corner of the gym, I saw Elizabeth in a heated argument with Hastings. He waved his hands about, pointing toward me several times. She responded with her typically chilly body language, arms crossed, and rolled her eyes. After he stalked off, I approached her.

"Hey," I said.

She sighed. "What do you want?"

"Um, just checking in with you, I guess. What did Hastings want?"

Her lips formed a tight, grim line. "He wanted to know why I came to the dance with you. Mrs. Learned told him we came together. He told me you're one of the worst attitudes at Clearwell."

"Yeah, he's my number one fan. What'd you say to him?"

"I told him I would go to the dance with whomever I wanted. *Nobody* tells me what I can or can't do." I was shocked and pleasantly surprised she defended me. "I told him to chill out and you were nothing but a pity date." And, she had to ruin it.

I threw my hands in the air and left, glancing at Olivia still on the dance floor with Brandon, laughing merrily away. Back in the commons, I sat at an empty table, trying to gain the courage I needed for my impending appointment with an evil spirit.

Ian, Allie, and Danny soon joined me. "Having a good time, Tex?" Ian nudged me with his elbow.

"Oh, yeah, I'm really rocking it. Let's see...my date hates me, my ex-girlfriend is hanging all over some guy, and I have this...*damn* calypso music on an endless loop in my brain."

"What are we doing here?" asked Ian warily. "I mean, *really?* We used to make fun of crap like this." Allie averted her eyes, possibly a little hurt.

"I don't know. You know, maybe it's because we vowed not to turn friends away. Maybe we need to be open to experiences...without shutting them out just because we think they might be lame." I shrugged my shoulders. "I guess I wanted to experience a school dance before I..." I caught myself before saying "die."

"Before what?" asked Danny.

"Hey, guys." *Gah.* Brandon again. But at least he saved me from saying something stupid. He straddled a chair across from me.

Olivia, flushed and grinning, plopped down next to him. "You guys having a good time?"

"Oh yeah. Livin' the dream," said Ian.

"I know, right?" said Olivia. Although it looked like she'd been in dreamland on the dance floor a few minutes ago. Her eyebrows rose. "Tex, are you okay? You don't look too well."

"Just Calypso overdose." Sudden heat roasted me. I ran my finger around my collar, attempting to loosen it, only to notice my trembling hands.

Elizabeth quietly slid into the chair next to me, startling me. She smiled wryly, the corners of her mouth slightly upturned. Her cold, Elizabethan eyes stared at me hard, but something looked different about them, perhaps slightly warmer.

I quietly mouthed her name, "Elspeth?" She nodded once and leaned against me, her shoulder resting on mine. My tablemates stared in shocked silence. Brandon indifferently munched mints, while Olivia's mouth gaped wide.

"Um, guys, this is my date, Elizabeth." A goofy grin grew across my face at my friends' reactions. Especially Olivia's.

Elspeth nodded around the table, her gaze lingering on Olivia. "So...this must be Olivia." She scanned Olivia from head to toe. She turned to me and said, "She's...cute." She didn't say that last word very "cutely."

Olivia expelled a huff of air. "You know,

Elizabeth, we *have* met before."

"Have we? I don't remember you."

"What*ever*." Olivia slashed her hand through the air.

"Elizabeth, this is Ian, Allison, and Danny." I pointed them out, then stopped at Brandon. "Oh, yeah, that's Brandon," I added quietly. I didn't want Elspeth falling sway to the magical enchantment powers of Brandon Townsend.

She smirked at Brandon. "I haven't seen a shirt like that since the 80s."

Brandon nodded dopily. Elspeth turned toward me and placed her hand on my chest. "Come on, Tex. Dance with me."

"Um, I don't really know how to dance."

"I'll show you," she whispered into my ear. The warmth from her breath raised goosebumps on my neck and arms. Before I could respond, she jumped up, tugging me out of my seat. "Let's go."

The idea of dancing seemed nearly as terrifying as my impending showdown with Bob Bellman. Hands entwined, I followed along behind Elspeth. She merrily bounced through the crowds with a much lighter step than Elizabeth's carefully calculated gait. At first, it confused me seeing Elspeth with Elizabeth's hair and wardrobe, but the differences in their personalities were totally distinct and easy to differentiate. I glanced back and saw my friends tagging along, out of curiosity. Olivia looked flustered, maybe even a little angry, which absolutely made this worth it. *Almost.*

Elspeth dragged me in front of the stage. The bathroom drinkers now cavorted merrily across the stage, breaking up at their own perceived hilarity. Mr.

Hastings watched them with great amusement and parental pride since football players can do no harm in his eagle eyes.

Holding onto Elspeth's hand like a lifeline, we upstaged the merry, drunken antics above us. Everyone watched us. Whispers traveled through the crowd. The music slowed down. Elspeth grinned. She pulled my arms around her waist and wrapped her hands around my neck. She rocked back and forth slowly, pulling me along with her. We moved in a circular pattern while she rested her head on my chest. Suddenly, she pushed me away. Her hips swayed back and forth, her skirt inching up higher, exposing her shapely thighs. She waved her arms in the air, turning in a circle, eyes shut, head tilted upward as if performing a rain dance. She'd given herself completely over to the music, seemingly a million miles away from here. Every set of male eyes was focused on her, the drunken jocks even stopping their shenanigans to watch her. I now know the true meaning of "booty-jacking."

Mr. Hastings's mouth hung agape as he stared at Elspeth in utter horror. Elizabeth's not going to be too happy about this.

The music stopped, and Elspeth once again cradled her hands around my neck. She looked up into my eyes. "Tex," she whispered, "it's time. You need to go take care of your business."

I nodded grimly because I knew I couldn't postpone the inevitable any longer. "Okay. Um, thanks for, ah…my first dance."

She smiled and kissed me on the cheek. "Good luck," she said. Before I could reply, she pranced across the dance floor and ran out the door.

I joined my friends at the back of the gym. Olivia avoided eye contact and looked elsewhere. With his face buried in his phone, texting, Brandon appeared concerned.

"*Damn*, Tex," said Danny. "I thought she was gonna strip there for a minute."

Olivia snorted.

"Um, guys...I'm not feeling so well. I'm gonna hit the john."

"Thanks for sharing," said Olivia. "Gah!" She acted a lot more peeved at me than my bathroom comment merited.

"Hey, O'," I said into her ear. "I'm...sorry for how I behaved last Saturday. And I'm sorry for having kept secrets from you."

She looked startled and met my eyes. "I know."

"I just wanted you to know that."

"Tex, what're you up to?" She grabbed my arm.

"Nothing. I just need to do something...by myself." And I knew I had at once told her too much, yet still kept secrets from her. But my impending literal date with death came first. "I promise I'll tell you everything later tonight, okay?"

"Tex..." She squeezed my arm even tighter.

"I've gotta go. I just..." My mouth dried up.

"I know," she said. "Me, too."

And upon hearing those words, I left. I don't know what they meant, but for now, they're enough to bolster my courage.

Chapter Seventeen

The calypso music receded into the background like a Jamaican music box sinking into the ocean. A small sliver of light escaped from underneath the closed door of the teacher's lounge. Merry laughter rang out, and I could only imagine what debauchery happened within. I stopped, listened, and quickly scuttled past the door. Reaching the end of the hallway, I edged the stairwell door open and walked down. Random lightning flashes from outside provided patchy illumination. Thunder rattled the windowpanes.

Once in the basement, I crept along the shadow-laden corridor. I pushed open the stairwell door next to the band room and climbed the steps back up. With the hallway empty, I crossed the hall to the boys' locker room. A sudden lightning flash eerily lit the hallway, showering it with a blue, electric light.

I entered. My hands shook when I pulled out the parchment paper. Making out the Latin words in the dark could be problematic, but the small, red EXIT sign light supplied just enough visibility. For the first time in a year, I walked past the lockers, noting the creepy silence without the noise of clanking locker doors, rowdy students, and loud-mouthed bullies. My footsteps sounded faint and hollow, swallowed up within the cement, metal, and tiles of the cold, cold room.

I navigated toward the shower stalls, where I had my first real-life encounter with Bob Bellman. It seemed like such a long time ago, when he'd held Josh down underneath the scalding water. And it's here where I finally hope to be rid of Bob Bellman.

I stood in the middle of the shower stall and quietly read, "*The power is within me to bring forces from beyond. I call upon this power to beckon forth the spirit of Bob Bellman.*" After reading the last part in Latin, I folded the paper and put it back in my pocket, with the portal opening spell firmly gripped in my other hand. I waited for what seemed like an eternity. Behind me, a dripping faucet plopped down drops of water onto the tiled floor.

"Come on, Bob," I said. "I know who killed your cousin. So let's get this show on the road." Goading him with false information is probably not the wisest thing to do, but I had no other choice.

The shower stall slowly lit up with a neon green tint, growing brighter and stronger. The surrounding air hummed and sizzled. Hair on the nape of my neck tingled. A murmuring sound, almost a gurgle, filled the stall. In the entryway to the showers, a green, glowing mass of energy formed, wavering in and out. Body parts briefly materialized before vanishing again. Finally, they congealed until Bob Bellman stood before me, dead eyes glowering. His mouth opened, exposing green and yellow teeth swirling about, trying to gain an anchor-hold within his ghostly gums. The faucet at my back suddenly twisted on, hissing down boiling hot water. The other faucets likewise turned on, forming a mist of steam. He walked—*floated*—toward me as if in slow motion.

Paper rattling in hand, I read the portal spell. A burning smell flooded my nostrils, followed by a loud, thunderous *crack*. I whipped around. A circular hole hung in the air, full of lava-like red and oranges and fiery yellow, a kaleidoscope of unearthly colors twizzling around one another. Darkly curious to study it further, I also realized that therein might lead the road to insanity.

Bellman stopped when he saw the demonic portal behind me. His jaw dropped inhumanly far, and he bellowed in diabolic rage. The lockers trembled. Now I had to get him through the portal. He rushed toward me. Startled, I fell back against the wall, slipped on the wet tile, and crashed to the floor. Hot water burned the back of my hand as I scrabbled on all fours to evade the boiling jets. Crawling like a crab on the bottom of some hideous green ocean depths, I maneuvered myself again in front of Bellman and the portal. He kicked my back hard, cracking my chin onto the tile. Then, in a sickening, nearly loving manner, he stroked the back of my neck before encircling his hands around my throat. I gasped for air within his vice-like grip. My vision blurred, a blanket of stars obscuring everything. Except for the green visage of Bellman. The last thing I'm ever going to see is the leering spirit of Bob Bellman.

"Hey, *bee-yotch,*" rang out a voice. "Why don't you pick on someone from your *own* realm?"

A dark beacon of hope, Elspeth stood in her resplendent, black-leathered glory, her black faux-hawk towering above her, legs straddled for action. In her hands, she wielded a vaulting pole. Bellman released his grip, leaving me gulping like a land-locked fish. Elspeth ran at him, the pole pointed toward his stomach, a distaff Don Quixote tilting at windmills. She plunged the end of the pole into Bellman's gut. The shock of the impact sent her flying back to the ground. Bellman screamed, pulling at the pole wedged deeply inside him.

"Come on, Tex," shouted Elspeth. "*Vanquish* this son-of-a-bitch already."

On my feet now, I ran toward Bellman, grabbed the pole, and shoved it in further. I corralled him with the pole, angling him in front of the portal. A strong, sudden intake of wind pulled from the gaping hole, dragging me toward it. An otherworldly moan groaned from beyond it. Through the orange and yellow miasma, a set of three beastly eyes peered out at me, wet and full of hunger. Still holding onto the pole for leverage, I rammed my body against Bellman, and shoved him into the hole. Suction pulled at him, his back completely enveloped by the portal, while his arms, legs, and head stuck out, waving about madly. With one massive last blast of energy, I threw my weight onto the pole and watched as Bellman flew into the crimson void. I stumbled back, the portal still sucking me toward it like a mini-tornado. My feet lifted off the ground as my body inched closer.

Elspeth jumped on top of me, attempting to weigh me down. "Close it, Tex," she screamed.

As my feet drew upward, I recited the spell. A loud, wheezing, whistling sound careened off the walls and then stopped. My feet dropped to the ground. The portal vanished.

I leaned my head back onto the tile. Elspeth, still lying on top of me, collapsed across my body like a living blanket. She lifted her head and laughed.

"Well…that was interesting," she said.

"You *think*?" We lay still, listening to each other's ragged breathing as steam wafted around us.

"Come on," she finally said. She sat up on top of me and reached for my hand. "There's still more to do tonight."

I rolled my eyes. "We just saved the world, Elspeth. What *more* can we possibly do?"

She frowned. "We've got to hurry. You need to go say goodbye to your friends. I'll meet you by your car." Before I could protest further, she jumped to her feet and raced out of the locker room. I *hate* when she does that.

****

"Tex, *why* are you wet?" By the look of Ian's agitated state, I knew his dance days were coming to an end. Allie and Danny sat next to him, clearly bored or just tired of dealing with Ian's crazy mood swings.

I looked down at my soaking wet suit. "Um, I stepped outside to get a breath of fresh air. I got rained on."

Ian looked out the window. "I didn't think it rained yet."

When all else fails, toss out a shrug. "Where, um, where's Olivia and Brandon? Are they dancing again?"

"No," said Danny. "It was weird. Brandon got a text message. He turned white as a ghost and said he had to get out of here. Olivia said she was going with him. So they bolted."

I had a bad feeling about this. "Crap. I think Olivia might be in trouble. Ian, can you give Danny a ride home?"

"Sure. Where ya going? You want us to come?"

"No, that's cool," I said. "You guys enjoy the rest of the dance, such as it is. But I've gotta go." I have no idea *where* I'm going, but apparently, it's urgent.

"Goddamnit, *wait,* Tex," Ian shouted behind me, but I was already out the front doors.

****

Elspeth sat idly on the hood of the Bucket, her legs dangling over the side. I scrambled for my keys and opened the door for her.

"So, what's going on, Elspeth? Where are we going?" I started the car and pulled out.

She looked worried. When Elspeth looks worried, it's time for *everyone* to worry. "There's a gang meeting going on between the Modern Gangstas and the Young Bloods. We need to get there before anything happens."

"Oh, my God. *Where?*"

"Same place where the Badger kid got shot."

"Elmleaf Elementary school? Why there?"

She raised her shoulders. "I don't know, Tex. You now know everything I saw."

"When did you *see* this?"

She thought for a moment. "While I was on my way to the locker room to help you. It just flashed on me."

"Did that idiot Brandon take Olivia there?" I asked, fearing the answer.

She nodded. "We gotta hurry." For the next five minutes, we rode in silence. Elspeth took out the corsage meant for her alter ego and slipped it around her wrist. She smiled coyly at me. "I never…went to a high school dance, Tex."

"Well, now you have. And you were the greatest

350

date a guy could have."

"You're sweet."

"Elspeth?"

"Yes?"

"Thanks for helping me. I mean, with Bellman and well, pretty much everything…"

"You're welcome," she said quietly. "It *really* stank in the locker room."

"Yeah, well, it is the boy's locker room."

She stared out the window, playing with the corsage on her wrist. The wind had picked up, blowing tree limbs back and forth with alarming ferocity. Angry lightning torched the sky. Yet, the rain still hadn't arrived.

"Tex?" she finally said. "I really hate gangs."

"Yeah, I'm not a big fan either."

"That's how I died, you know." She turned toward me.

"What? *How*?"

"In the eighties, I was a wild, punk rocker kid," she said. "I skipped school all the time and went to all of the punk bars in New York City. I either snuck in or used my fake ID. One night, I hooked up with this gang. Buncha' leather-wearing punks. I didn't know any better. Stupid me, I thought they were cool." She splayed her hands. "They took me out to a back alley…beat me…and… Whatever. I died a slow death in an alley in New York City… Alone." A tear rolled down her face.

"Elspeth, I'm *so* sorry. That's…really terrible…"

She shrugged again and set her mouth to one side. "It is what it is, I suppose. I never got to go to any school dances, never even learned how to drive. But now? Now, I've been given a second chance…sort of…"

I reached over and squeezed her hand. "I'm glad you have."

Seconds after we reached Elmleaf Elementary School, the skies finally opened up and unleashed a huge outpouring of rain. I pulled up beside Olivia's parked car. A volley of thunder blasted over us, followed by a jagged shot of lightning. I jumped out of the car, Elspeth following close behind. I ran around the fence and over to the playground. By the jungle gym, Brandon stood over a body lying on the ground. His palms were held up toward the sky, as if calling upon the spirits for guidance. Blood covered him.

"*Tex*," shouted Olivia. She ran toward us, her phone out and ready to be used. "*Help*."

"What happened?" I asked Brandon.

"I…I don't know," he said. I knelt to look at the body. B-Ryce had been shot twice in the chest. "I…just got here. I saw him on the ground. I tried to stop the bleeding…"

"Olivia," I said, "Call 9-1-1!"

"I already did." She appeared stunned, yet fully in control.

"Is he alive?" I asked.

Brandon shook his head. "I don't think so."

"Quick… Tell me what happened from the beginning…"

"At the dance…I got a text from Eric—E-Sizzle—saying there was going to be a meet-up between the Gangstas and the Young Bloods. Ken was trying to keep it secret from me, I guess. Eric said he thought it was gonna be here…" Brandon shook his head in disbelief.

"So, you came out here to be a *part* of it? And you brought Olivia?"

Olivia watched our transaction with a puzzled look.

"No. It's not *like* that. I was going to try and *stop* their fight. Olivia was my ride…I told her to stay in the car."

"Like *that*'s ever gonna happen," she said. "Now why don't you boys tell me what the hell you're talking about?" She glared at both of us. Seemingly bored with our conversation, Elspeth casually kicked through puddles of water.

I shot Brandon a harsh look. "Brandon, maybe it's time you tell Olivia about the Modern Gangstas." Brandon touched Olivia's arm, and they stepped away. I reached for my phone and dialed Detective Cowlings. While the phone rang, Olivia shouted, "You have *got* to be kidding me."

"Cowlings," he answered upon the fourth ring.

"Yeah, uh, hi, Detective Cowlings," I said, rushing my words together. "It's Tex."

"What's going on?"

"Um…I'm at Elmleaf Elementary School. There's another body on the playground."

After an eternal silence, Cowlings finally said, "I'll be there in a few moments. Call 9-1-1…and do *not* touch anything." I looked at Brandon, covered in B-Ryce's blood and thought his boat had already sailed. He hung up without saying goodbye.

"Tex," said Elspeth quietly. "I've got to go. I can't be here."

"Yeah, okay. I get it."

"Good luck." She jogged down the sidewalk

leading to the street, playfully jumping in pooled puddles from the rain.

The ongoing heated debate between Olivia and Brandon burned hotter and louder. Between the ordeal of finding the body and the torrential rain, I don't think either one of them even saw Elspeth. Good. One detail I wouldn't have to explain.

Cowlings arrived shortly after the ambulance did. The paramedics checked out B-Ryce's body, barked a few questions at us, and proclaimed him dead. Cowlings stood over the now-covered body, shaking his head.

"What are you doing here, Tex?" His goodwill toward me had crashed into the wall of bad tidings.

"I, ah, heard there was going to be a meeting between the Modern Gangstas and the Young Bloods. I was going to try and stop it."

"And how did you hear about this information?"

"From Brandon." I nodded in his direction. "Eric Smith texted him it was going to happen…so he came here. I followed him."

"Eric Smith," repeated Cowlings, writing it down in his notebook. "So, when you got here, you found the body? Nobody else around?"

"Not exactly. When I got here, I saw Brandon standing over the body…and Olivia was here but not at the scene of the crime."

"Don't you think you should have called me first?" he said. "Maybe before you decided to come out here?" He pressed his lips together into a thin slice of anger.

"I really didn't even know if the information was good. I didn't want to call you out on a false call…or something. Whatever." I shuffled my feet nervously.

"And *now* we have another dead body." He sighed and called out to one of the policemen, "Hey, Gardner, you find the weapon yet?"

The policemen looked glumly at Cowlings and shook his head. "Haven't found anything yet."

"Of course," Cowlings said, under his breath. "Okay, you can go, but I'm keeping your friend."

"Who? Brandon?"

"Tell me about Brandon. What do your...*instincts* tell you about him?"

I looked over at Brandon, trembling from the rain or possibly out of fear. "I really don't think he did it if that's what you're asking."

"He's covered in the victim's blood. So, he's either a viable candidate for the killer—the only one I have at this point—or he's the stupidest kid in the world."

"I really gotta go with the latter option."

"We'll see. I'm taking in him for further questioning; then I'll decide to arrest him or not. But, Tex...I'm really beginning to wonder why I keep finding you around corpses."

"Um, just unlucky I guess." I attempted a small smile, which Detective Cowlings did not return.

"Uh-huh. One of these days, you and I are going to have a nice, long talk."

"Sure, um, that'll be nice." Cowlings walked over to Brandon to speak with him.

"Tex," said Olivia from behind me. "You've got to do something. *We've* got to do something. I think they're going to arrest Brandon. He didn't do this..." She looked very white in the dark night. "*Please.*"

"Yeah, I don't think he did it either. But I have no idea who did...and that may be the only way we can save Brandon. Find the real killer."

"Can't you perform a spell or something?"

"I don't think so. I have to be emotionally connected to the victims for a spell to work, at least that's my understanding of it. I'll go see Mickey tomorrow and find out if there's *something* we can do. Otherwise…"

Disappointment covered her face before withdrawing into rage. "I can't *believe* he's one of those stupid Modern Gangstas. And you guys—neither *one* of you—thought to *tell* me about it? Don't you think I had a right to know? I had a *date* with the guy."

"O', it really wasn't my…secret to tell you."

She punched my chest. "I could've been *shot*." Those words attracted the attention of several policemen. "And you didn't think you should *tell* me?"

"Sorry, Olivia…"

She shook her hands in the air and settled down. "Okay, whatever. The first thing we're going to do is you're going to tell me everything—*everything*—about this stupid gangster business. Got it?"

"Got it."

"Then we're going to find out who did these two shootings."

"Okay."

Detective Cowlings escorted Brandon into the back of his car. Olivia called out, "Brandon, don't worry. We'll find out who did this."

Cowlings shot us an angry glare over the roof of his car. "I really wish you wouldn't," he said. "Why don't you leave the policing to the professionals?"

He got in his car and slowly drove off. Brandon peered at us from the back window, like a doomed pet taken away to the pound, dumb puppy-dog eyes working overtime.

Chapter Eighteen

For once, she answered on the first ring. "Hi, Mickey, it's Tex."

"Kid, I've been worried sick about you. How'd it go last night? Did you vanquish that Bellman boy?"

"Yeah. There aren't any spirits running wild around here."

She laughed. "Good job, kiddo. Even if it was your fault in the first place. Now, what can I do for you?"

"Well, it's this gang stuff again. There was another murder last night. I *need* to put a stop to it."

"We've been through this—"

"I know, Mickey, but it's got to stop. Everything else I've tried hasn't worked out. I couldn't stop this kid from getting shot last night...maybe, if I tried harder then—"

"Stop it! You didn't put a gun in none of those kids' hands. It ain't your fault." I had nothing to say, so Mickey picked up the torch. "Well, all I can say is we can try. No promises, no guarantees. Especially since you're not emotionally connected to any of the dead boys."

"That's all I ask." While it's true I have no emotional link with the dead gang members, I feel I've been through the emotional wringer.

"Hurry up, then. I'm hungry." I'm not quite sure what Mickey meant by being hungry, but there's usually a method to her madness.

I didn't want to keep Mickey starving, so I hurried to pick up Olivia.

Last night, after we left the scene of the crime, I told Olivia everything (well, not about the love spell), from my involvement with the Modern Gangstas, to Brandon's membership, and my vanquishing of Bob Bellman. She alternated between anger about kept secrets to mortified she couldn't aid me. And she's more hell-bent than ever on finding out who the killer is. I couldn't tell if her reason is to get Brandon out of trouble, or if she just wants to put an end to the killings, but I know there's no stopping her when she's like this.

For every tender gesture Olivia displayed the night before, she bounced back with a thorough tongue-lashing. Every time the conversation swayed toward Brandon, I looked for a sign of how she felt about him, but I took away nothing, one way or the other. It *did* seem like we were a team again, and for that, I'm cautiously hopeful.

Along with my newfound optimism, a new day began. The sun went back to work after taking the previous day off. Raindrop remnants slithered off tree leaves, sinking with relief into the ground. A thick clamminess hung in the air, a portent of future humidity.

When I arrived at Olivia's house, she startled me by suddenly knocking on the passenger window.

"Morning," she said as she slid into the passenger seat.

"Hey."

"Okay, what first?" She pulled back the purple-colored strand of hair covering one eye.

"Well, I guess we'll see if Mickey has any ideas. I don't really know what else to do."

"All right then, Bucket, full speed ahead." She pointed through the windshield. Her attitude had changed quite a bit since the night before. Maybe my optimism had rubbed off on her. "I heard from Brandon this morning. They didn't arrest him, but Cowlings questioned him most of the night."

"Huh."

"You don't think Brandon did it, right?"

"I don't think so." Although, it certainly would make my love life simpler if he had.

"Yeah, I know he didn't."

My balding tires hydroplaned across the rain-soaked streets all the way to Mickey's house.

Mickey stood on her front porch, surveying what the rain had done to her garden overnight. When she saw Olivia walking up the sidewalk, she scowled. "Oh, I see you brought your little friend."

"Yeah, hello to you, too, Mickey," said Olivia.

Mickey bounced her lips back and forth as if preparing to spit. "Well, come on in, then," she finally said.

We went inside the house. "I guess I'm a little surprised to see you two together. I thought you broke up…and then there was all that love spell nonsense." Mickey chuckled as my heart galloped into my throat.

"Wait…*What*?" said Olivia.

Mickey cackled. "Ooooooh, you didn't know about that?" She grinned, tongue lolling about, having a grand old time.

Olivia shot me visual bullets. I stared at my feet, wondering if now might not be a good time for them to whisk me away. "Tex, tell me you did *not* try and put a *love* spell on me."

"No, no, I *didn't*. Well, I *thought* about it…but I didn't, not really. I mean…not successfully…" My voice rode away into a tiny whisper. I lifted my eyes to meet Olivia's cold glare. Mickey, thoroughly enjoying the show, laughed raucously. If she only had a bag of popcorn, I'm sure this would rival her "stories" for sheer entertainment value.

Olivia stomped her foot on the floor, sending a cat scurrying for cover. "You've got some explaining to do. *Later.*" She snorted loudly and crossed her arms. Goodbye my fleeting, barely met friend, Optimism. Hello to habitation Back In the Doghouse.

"You kids. I swan. Anyway…you didn't come over here about that." She walked into the kitchen, and we followed her, ensuring I kept a safe distance between myself and Olivia.

"Sit, sit." Mickey pointed at the well-worn chairs surrounding the table. "First of all, tell me everything about last night, Tex." She fell down into one of the chairs while I began my story.

"My, my." She leaned back, lost in thought. "I've *never* seen one of those portals myself, you know. Haven't had need to."

While Mickey seemed envious, I hope I'll never see one of those portals again. "Well, it was something, all right. Mickey, I really need to find out who the killer is. I don't want any more deaths."

"Let's see what we can do." Mickey went to the sink, poured a glass of water, and grabbed an egg out of the refrigerator. She carefully cracked the egg over the glass rim and dropped the contents into the water. She placed the eggshells into her sink and sat at the table, shoving the glass in front of me. "We're going to try some Oomancy."

"What's that?"

"It's a form of divination where you read the difference in the outer and inner shapes of eggs. You want to pay particular attention to the white portion of the egg." I ignored Olivia's sneer.

"Um, okay." It didn't seem like the *best* method of divination, but she's the experienced witch. "Do I need to say anything?"

"Go on. Ask your question." She gestured toward the glass.

I cleared my throat. "Um…Spirit World…can you help guide me through Oomancy to find the killer of James Badger and, ah, B-Ryce?" I forgot B-Ryce's real name. Olivia stifled a snort. Mickey raised a scornful eyebrow toward her.

The yellow yolk of the egg remained still, floating in the center of the glass. The white part swirled and circled like smoke from one of Mickey's cigarettes. It bounced around as if alive, gathered, and, to my surprise, enveloped the top part of the yellow yolk. I gasped. It formed an obvious hood.

"What? What is it?" asked Olivia.

"Look," I said, pointing at the glass, "what do you see?"

"An egg."

"I see a hoodie."

Olivia hunkered down, staring intently at the glass. Mickey said, "What does that mean to you, Tex?"

"I think our killer wears a hoodie. And I think I know who it is." Of course, all the gangstas wear hoodies, but there's someone who wears his constantly. "Thanks, Mickey. It's something to work with. We really gotta go."

"Well, you be careful, kid. Girly, you watch out after him, you hear me?"

"I'll do my best," said Olivia.

"He's a good kid. You'd be lucky to take up with him again, you know."

I sighed and turned many shades of red. "All right. Gotta go." I gave Mickey a small hug.

"Wait," called Mickey. "You want breakfast?" She dumped the egg and water into a frying pan on the stove. Olivia wrinkled her nose and turned away.

"Um, no thanks, Mickey. We really need to go." There's something about eating one's own spells that seems somewhat cannibalistic.

Mickey shrugged. "Suit yourself, then—waste not, want not, I always say. But you kids, be careful. And call the cops, for once."

"We will," I called back from the front door. But I wouldn't. Not until I know for sure.

****

I nearly hit another curb when Olivia punched my shoulder. "Ow!"

"I can't *believe* you were gonna put a goddamn *love spell* on me. *Idiot.*"

"I'm sorry…but I didn't do it." Although I *tried*, I thought about adding, but that wouldn't help my case in the least. "I was heartbroken and—"

"And you were a jackass. Doesn't what *I* want count for anything?"

I didn't know what else to say, so I said it anyway. "I love you, Olivia."

She shook her fists in the air and screamed. We rode in silence until she finally said, "*Whatever. Where are we going?*"

"We're going to Danny's house."

"Why?"

"I need to search his brother's room."

"Ken? Why?"

"I have a feeling we're going to find the gun in his room." Chills ran down my back even though the bucket felt like an oven. "Ken wears a hoodie all the time. And knowing what I do about him, it's really not too big a stretch. I think he shot Badger and B-Ryce."

"Oh my God… Should we call Cowlings?"

"Right now, I'm just going on a hunch—with a little help from an egg. I can't tell Cowlings that an egg told me so until we know for sure…"

"Okay, then, what's the plan?"

"Are you sure you want to go along with this, O'? It could be dangerous."

Olivia cocked her head and smiled. "Since when have you known me to shy away from danger?"

"Good point. Well, first of all, I'm hoping Ken isn't home. If he keeps to his usual patterns, that shouldn't be an issue."

"Right."

"And I'm assuming Danny will be home—that's how we'll gain entrance. But, you're going to have to keep Dan occupied while I make an excuse to use the bathroom or something."

Olivia grinned. "You've been having an awful lot of bathroom issues lately, Tex."

"Yeah, well." I tried to return her smile, but I knew the outcome of our search expedition would be nothing less than grim.

I rang the bell. Mrs. Cross answered, *still* wearing her apron. "Oh, good morning, kids. Danny's upstairs in his room. I'm sure it'd be fine if you went up to see him." She walked off humming, and I couldn't help but feel heartbroken for her. If my theory proves correct, soon she won't be humming.

"Hey, Danny," I called through the door. "Yo, you gotcher pants on?"

Danny pulled the door open. "Hey, guys. What's up?" He attempted to tame his hair, looking like he just rolled out of bed. "Come on in."

"Just in the 'hood. Thought you might want to hang."

Olivia admired the drawings on Danny's wall. "These are pretty good, Dan."

Danny beamed. "Thanks. Hey, what happened last night, anyway? The cops came here and talked to my brother about where he was all night. Of course, he wouldn't tell me what it was about." His shoulders slumped.

"Yeah, well, a Young Bloods gangsta kid was found shot last night. At the same place that Badger was killed." I sat down on the end of Dan's bed. "Brandon found the body."

"Oh my God. Did he *do* it? Did they *arrest* Brandon?" He fell down next to me, obviously in shock.

"No, they talked to him for a while, but they released him. They don't know who did it."

"You don't think...Ken..." His voice fell away. I put my arm around his shoulders.

"I really don't know anything. Hey...your

brother's not here now, is he?"

"No. He never is. Why?"

"Ah, no reason, except he's not too happy with me now." I empathized with Danny's concern for his brother. I guess even sociopathic jackasses can be loved.

Sensing our awkwardness, Olivia changed the subject. "Hey, did anything good happen after we left the dance?"

Danny shook his head. "No, not really. Totally lame. I mean…Under the Sea, right?"

"Yeah, that *was* ridiculous," said Olivia.

I wanted to get this over with. "Um…hey, can I use your john? Something I had last night's really getting to me…"

"Probably that blue punch, right?"

"Could be…"

"Sure, just go down the hallway and to the right."

"Thanks." I left, pulling the door shut behind me until I heard the click. Olivia plunged in, shooting non-stop questions to Dan about his drawings.

I closed the bathroom door so as to make it appear occupied. To the left sat Ken's room, the door with the KEEP OUT sign. I entered.

Monstrous piles of clothing lay scattered across the floor, predominantly hoodies, T-shirts, and baggy jeans. Posters of various death metal bands and rappers decorated the walls. A variety of chains hung on the back of the closet door. Fast food wrappers lined the floor. Whereas Danny's room and bed are usually immaculate—thanks to his live-in maid-mother—Ken apparently opted out of this service. I didn't know where to start. I looked under the rumpled bed and saw a guitar case. Pulling it out, I peeked inside, a beaten-up electric guitar its only occupant. Wadded up clothes and undergarments over-stuffed the dresser. I found a bag of weed and a pipe but nothing resembling a weapon.

When I opened the closet door, a mass of clothing tumbled about my feet. On tiptoes, I felt along the top of the shelf, discovering three boxes. Carefully, I stacked them on top of one another and pulled them down. With shaking hands, I carried them to the bed and opened the first one. More drug paraphernalia. The second box contained newspaper clippings, most of them dealing with gang violence on both coasts and rappers shooting one another. A couple of articles detailed the shooting of James Badger, and a quick scan showed a mention of the Modern Gangstas.

I opened the third box. A gun, bullets rattling around next to it. I knew better than to touch it, but I sniffed it to see if it had been recently fired: a burning, metallic odor. I took in a deep breath. Should I take the gun and give it to Cowlings? Or should I put it back in place and tell him about it?

Behind me, the door exploded open.

"What the *hell* are you doin' in here?" Ken hurled toward me with wicked speed and force, knocking me backward while he landed on the bed. "I'll *kill* you."

While I sat stunned on the floor, Ken lay on the bed above me, shrieking, a nightmarish slumber party. I cleared my head, trying to remember Mickey's protection spell. I jumped to my feet at the same time he scrabbled off the bed. Facing me, his forehead and cheeks burned red. He stared at the open boxes on his bed, the realization of what I found dawning on him. He leapt for the gun in the box. I blocked him, attempting to claw him away from the gun. Suddenly, the Latin words of the spell came to me. He pulled the gun out of the box and pointed it at me, the barrel wavering wildly about the room. I recited the spell and slapped him on the forehead. His eyes rolled up as he crumpled to the floor. The gun bounced out of his hands, landing with a clack in the center of the room.

I plopped on the bed, hyperventilating, staring at Ken's sleeping body.

"What are you *doing*, Tex?" Danny stood in the doorway, swiveling his head between his brother and me. His gaze fell upon the gun on the floor. Before I could get up, he lunged for the gun, grabbing it in one quick motion. "What...have you *done*? What did you do to my *brother*?"

He waved the gun in the air and paced the floor. Where's Olivia? For that matter, where's Danny's mother?

"Danny...Danny, I'm sorry...but I think Ken killed Badger and B-Ryce."

"No," he screamed. "No, he *didn't*." Tears rolled down his cheeks.

"Danny...Really...I know it's hard, but I think that's the murder weapon."

Danny stared at me, an unexpected coldness seething from his eyes. "You're *wrong*, Tex. He *didn't* do it. Why couldn't you have left this alone? *Why*? What have you *done*?"

"Come on, Danny. I know—"

"*No*. You don't know *shit*. *I* killed Badger!"

"What?"

"You heard me," he said, his voice calming. "I shot James Badger." Danny lowered the gun but continued walking back and forth across the floor. Behind him, Olivia stood in the doorway, looking on in horror.

"You...you don't mean that. You're just saying that...to protect Ken—"

"*No. Goddamnit,* Tex...*I did* shoot Badger..."

"But...Why?" I felt like I'd been smacked upside the head with a wooden plank. I couldn't believe it. I didn't *want* to believe it. I *couldn't* believe it.

"Because...they wouldn't let me join the Modern Gangstas." Gulps strangled his voice. "I asked my brother..." He pointed toward Ken's sleeping body with the pistol. "He just laughed at me. Said I was a pussy. Said I wasn't man enough—didn't have the balls. So...I was gonna show them. I knew Ken had a gun. One night I took it. I called Badger and told him I had news for him...to meet me at the grade school." Danny took off his glasses, dropped them to the floor, and dabbed at his eyes with the back of his gun-wielding hand.

"Danny...it's okay. It was an accident."

"*No.* No, it wasn't. I shot him *four* times in the chest. I didn't...go there to kill him. I just wanted to show him I had the balls to carry a gun. When he showed up, I asked him to let me join. He *laughed* at me. I pulled the gun out and pointed it at him. He called me a *pussy*. He...walked toward me and reached for the gun. So I *shot* him. He kept holding onto the gun. I shot him *again*...and *again*...until he fell."

"But why, Danny...*why*?"

"Because I wanted *respect*. I wanted to be admired. I wanted girls. I wanted my brother's...love and respect." Danny's legs buckled, and he slid to the floor. "All the things I've never had before..."

"But…why did you shoot B-Ryce?"

"He didn't…" said Ken groggily. "I did…I knew Dan shot Badger. I ain't stupid. I can count bullets. But I needed it to look like a gang retaliation shooting—to protect Dan. He's got a future in front of him. I ain't got shit. I didn't care if I went away for it…"

The three of us sat silently in the room staring at one another as if in a lazy man's Spaghetti Western; everyone too afraid, too stunned, to make the next move. Olivia hovered in the doorway, unsure of what to do.

Suddenly, Danny moaned, loudly and agonizingly so. "Oh…God. It's all over. What have you done, Tex?" He whipped the gun toward his head, his finger on the trigger.

I jumped to my feet. "Oh, God, *no, Danny, please!* God*, no, don't do it, Danny. Please!*"

"Why, Tex…why not?" he said quietly. The gun shook next to his temple. Ken, fighting off the sleep spell, struggled to get to his feet.

"Because we *love* you, Danny. Please, God*,* just *put* the gun down. You have us. You'll *always* have us." My words ran together into one litany of plea bargaining. Olivia joined me, and to my surprise, Ken even urged Dan to put the gun down.

Danny shook his head. "My life is over…"

Ken walked toward him and forcefully grabbed the gun out of his hand. "It's not over, Dan. I believe in you…you *will* have a future." Danny looked up at his brother. Ken reached out a hand to help him up. Danny accepted it and got to his feet. Ken clapped a hand on his shoulder and pulled him toward him, embracing him. Ken tossed the gun on the bed next to me. I sat back down, trembling from head to toe, staring at the gun, all the death and destruction it had caused. I couldn't control my sobbing. The entire bed shook from my moans. I leaned over and threw up. Olivia hugged Danny, then came toward me and draped an arm around my shoulder.

Mrs. Cross showed up at the door. "My goodness, what's all the commotion about?" Her eyes widened when she studied the room and the people within.

I sobbed until my tears ran dry.

****

I left the house to go sit outside on the curb, dry heaving for several more minutes. Olivia, level-headed as ever, remained inside to watch over matters and, I presume, to remove the gun out of the path of temptation. Several police cars arrived, followed by an ambulance. Shortly afterward, the medics left the house with Mrs. Cross on a stretcher babbling incoherently.

"Hi, Tex," said a voice above me. I shaded my eyes with my hand and saw Detective Cowlings. He hitched up his trouser legs and planted himself next to me on the curb. He sighed and pulled out his notebook. "Rough day, huh?"

"You could say that…" Crying had ravaged my voice. I breathed in heavily several times.

"Olivia called me…told me a little bit about what happened." He enveloped a knee with his arm and surveyed the neighborhood. "If you're up to it, I'd like to hear your story."

I told him everything that had occurred from the moment I arrived at the Cross household. He shook his head and said, "Damn pity."

I nodded in silent agreement.

"The older boy…Ken…says you put him to sleep. How'd you manage that?"

"I don't know what he's talking about." I didn't have the energy left to even concoct a decent lie.

"Uh huh. Tex, what you did was damned dangerous and stupid. You could just as easily have been shot, like the other two boys. You need to learn to trust me—and *call* me."

I thought for a minute before responding. "It's not that I don't trust you, Detective. I…don't know if I trust myself. Not anymore. I was just going on a hunch. I wanted to make sure that—"

"I know, I know," he cut me off. "Before you called me out on a false call." He looked exasperated.

"How's…Mrs. Cross?"

"She's pretty hysterical. The medics gave her something to calm her down; then they're going to watch her for twenty-four hours." He rubbed his leg as if trying to knead out a painful cramp. "Your vice-principal is going to be ecstatic; we found his bobblehead in Ken's room."

"Oh?"

He grinned. "However, he's not going to be thrilled. Someone drew a Hitler mustache on it."

I managed a chuckle. "What's…what's going to happen to Danny?" For the first time, I met Cowlings' eyes.

He stretched his legs out into the street. "I'm just spitballin' here, but given his good record—his outstanding academic achievements—if he gets good and lawyered up? Maybe five years, maybe less. And, I would imagine, time off for good behavior."

"Go easy on him. He's…one of the good guys."

Cowlings glared at me. "Okay," he finally said. "You know…it's a helluva thing. Two boys shot— *murdered*—all for nothing. All because these kids got it in their head they want to live a…'dangerous gangsta life.' Well, looks like they got their wish." He smiled at me sardonically. He stood up, straightened his pant legs, and brushed off his backside.

"Yeah…"

"Tex, I don't want to see you mixed up in anything again," he said slowly. "I know you're not guilty of any crime, but you have a way of turning up like a bad penny."

I stared up at him, a halo forming behind his head from my blurred vision. "What makes a penny bad?"

"Goodbye, Tex."

Soon, Olivia sidled up and sat down. She nudged me with her knee. "How you doin'?"

"Oh, just great. Just great."

"You know…this *isn't* your fault." She placed a hand on my knee. "*You* didn't cause any of this."

I looked at her, my eyes brimming over with tears again. "Look at what I did to their family. If it weren't for my interference, the Cross family would still be one happy, sit-com-like, perfect family. Now…" I waved my hand at their house. Just when I thought I'd finished, the tears came again.

"Tex…shhhh…Tex…" She cradled my head to her chest. "If it weren't for you, maybe more people would've been shot. Danny and Ken made their *own* decisions."

"Sometimes….sometimes, I think maybe…the world would be better off without me."

"*Don't* you say a stupid thing like *that*." She

swatted my head. "Don't even *think* that." She began to sniffle along with me.

I collected myself and asked, "How's Danny doing?"

"Not great. He's been sitting in the back of a cop car for the last half hour. He needs us, Tex. *Go* to him..." She pointed toward a parked police car in front of the house. "Go talk to him. Tell him...he doesn't need to be alone."

I gritted my teeth and stood up. She's right. As usual. I need to put my emotional self-pity behind and think about my friend in trouble. I slowly approached the police car, my vision uneven from my endless torrent of tears.

A police officer placed his hand on my chest, halting my progress. He looked toward Detective Cowlings who stood in the open doorway. Cowlings nodded and yelled, "It's okay. Let him talk to his friend." The officer reluctantly opened the car door for me. I slid in and sat next to Danny.

"Hey, Tex," Danny said quietly, his hands cuffed behind him.

"Nice ride," I said, and to my amazement, we both laughed. "Look, Danny, I want you to know that we'll be here for you. We'll come and visit you, and we're still going to be your friends when you get out. Always."

Danny glanced up at me. His eyes looked as red as mine felt. He attempted a smile, but the tears clamped it down. "I'm scared..."

"We all are." I placed my hand on his shoulder much to the obvious dismay of an on-looking officer.

"I...wish I could take it back...all of it. Oh God,

what have I done?"

"Danny...you made a mistake...a pretty bad one, but it's *not* the end of your life."

"I don't know..."

"And I want you to know something else. Earlier you said you'd never had respect. I respect you. I *always* have and always will. In my eyes, you're one of the bravest guys I know."

Danny rubbed his eyes on his shoulder. "How am I brave?"

"Every day you show up at school, that's how. You're never afraid to be yourself...to be different. Each day you showed up, showing true courage...and a willingness to never give in to defeat. I know it's hard at school. It is for all of us...but you keep going. I just want to make sure you keep going now."

"You mean that?"

"Yes...and I'll tell you something else..."

"What's that?"

"Your brother's love. Look what he did for you. I mean, it was crazily misguided, but there's no denying he did it for you."

"I guess...whatever."

"Just promise me you'll keep your head up, okay?"

He nodded.

"I love you, man." I attempted an awkward hug, not easy to do with someone in handcuffs. "We all do..." Once again, the floodgates opened up, and I had to get out of the car before the two of us started blubbering like knee-skinned grade-schoolers. I knocked on the window for the policeman to open the door.

"Goodbye, Danny," I said in a choked voice.

****

Olivia drove me home. Ensuring I felt okay—at least as good as I possibly could—she told me she'd bring my car back tomorrow. I don't know how she did it, but she acted as sturdy as Elizabeth's hair.

I shooed the cats out of my path and entered our house.

"Hi, guys." Dad and Ruth sat planted in front of the TV.

"Son?" said Dad. "You don't look so well. Are you okay?"

I paused, standing in the doorway. My shoulders shook as I started crying again. "No…not really," I muttered. "I'm going to bed." I ran up the stairs, while Dad called after me.

Several minutes later, a soft knocking pestered my door. I really didn't want to face anyone, but I thought it best to get it over with before they bugged me all night long.

I cleared my throat. "Come in."

Ruth poked her head into my room. "Tex? Are you decent?" She averted her eyes so as not to catch me in my underwear, I suppose.

"I guess so."

She timidly entered and sat down on the edge of my bed. "Your father and I are worried about you. What happened today?"

My mouth wavered open and shut until I found the strength to speak. "I found out…today…one of my best friends killed James Badger."

"Oh. Oh, my…" She placed her fingertips over her bottom lip. "Are you okay?"

I shook my head back and forth.

"Come here, honey." She extended her arms toward me.

I crawled into her embrace and cried into her shoulder. "It's not fair…"

"I know…I know."

I howled like a baying hound.

"Let it out, honey," she said.

"I miss my…mother…"

"I know, Tex. It's only natural. I'm so, so sorry for you. I know…I can't ever replace her, but if you ever need me, I want you to know I'll be here for you. Both your father and I…well, we both love you."

She rocked me back and forth for a long time, repeating words of comfort. Finally, I fell asleep in her warm, motherly arms.

****

A rapping sound pulled me out of a dull slumber. Half asleep, I flipped on my lamp and noted it was a little after midnight. I had slept for seven hours. Realizing the consistent rapping couldn't be written off as part of a mad dream, I looked at the window. Elspeth waved at me. I crossed the room and pulled the window open. Without saying a word, I stumbled back and fell into my bed.

"Hey, Tex." She walked toward me and dove onto the bed. She hitched herself up on one elbow and asked, "How you doin'?"

"Okay, I guess."

She smiled slyly. "I understand you caught the gangsta killers. Sorry it turned out to be one of your friends." She pursed her lips. "I really, *really* didn't see that coming."

"Tell me about it."

She placed her hand along my cheek. "Poor Tex..." More females lent me support and comfort today than I had experienced in...well, ever. "I'm truly sorry for you. It's gotta suck."

I nodded.

"I just wanted to tell you...you did a good thing," she said. "A *good* thing. Olivia's right about that, you know. It's not your fault."

"I guess." While the sleep helped to settle me, today's events still seemed extremely surreal. Just the night before, I joked and laughed with Danny at the stupid school dance.

"Things will get better for you," she said. "You'll see." She grinned, yet her eyes filled with sorrow. "I think...things are going to work out for you and Olivia."

"Did you see that?" I asked, possibly too enthusiastically.

"Let's just call it women's intuition."

A sudden thought hit me. "Hey, Elspeth, I've been trying to think of a way I could repay you for your help." She raised her black eyebrows inquisitively. "You said you never learned how to drive. How about if I teach you?"

She looked stunned, meeting my eyes with her gloriously scary, beautiful, pale blue gaze. "That's sweet. How about if I get back to you on that?"

"Come on, Elspeth. It's the *least* I can do."

She hesitated. "I don't know, Tex. I'll have to talk it over with Elizabeth...and I might be going away for a while."

"Wait...*what*?"

"I might be taking a little vacation for a while."

"You're not…moving on…or anything, are you?" I realized how much I've truly come to like Elspeth and didn't want to lose her, too.

"Something like that." She touched my face again. She pulled me toward her and kissed me, this time gently, as if I might fold like a wet tissue underneath her touch. Softly she caressed my face, and I did the same to hers. The moment lasted an eternity—sweet, soulful, slow kissing. Then it ended just as suddenly when she pulled back. "My work's done here for now. Gotta run," she said as if the moment didn't happen at all.

"*Wait. Don't* go. I'll miss you…"

She stood up and twirled around. "You'll see me again. Just not for a while. You're going to need my help again in the future. You have important things to do with your life." She whirled and cavorted merrily toward the window. "Ta ta for now, Tex." She blew me another kiss and hopped out the window.

I raced to the window and saw her vanish down the street, dancing and skipping into the dark screen of the night. How is it her last words filled me with both longing—the excitement at the prospect of seeing her again—and fear as to why I might need her help in the future?

****

Things settled down at Clearwell High as the school year rapidly approached its much-anticipated end. Arville Hastings glowered at me in the hallway on occasion, but for the most part, he kept his distance. Surely, with only a few weeks remaining, I could avoid the bulldog's path.

Brandon swore to me his days with the Modern

Gangstas had finished. Without James or Ken to lead them, they pretty much disbanded, anyway, and he wanted to distance himself from Eric Smith, aka E-Sizzle. I saw Eric several times in the hallways. One time I attempted to say hello to him, but he just sneered at me. He still talked in the same idiotic manner and wore ridiculous clothing, but from what I heard, no one took him seriously—considered pretty much a joke. Whatever fear the words *Modern Gangstas* once evoked in the student body had now dissipated like a wisp of inconsequential smoke. I haven't heard what happened to the Young Bloods, but I highly doubt anyone would accept leadership from Coo-Coo or Diddy-Bang.

I made my peace with Brandon—more or less—so I rejoined my lunch table instead of sweating it out in the pre-summer heat outdoors. Exactly one week after the Spring Fling, Elizabeth approached our lunch table and said brightly, "Hi, Richard."

"Uh, hi, Elizabeth. How are you?" I looked at Olivia, who bit her lip in trying to be tolerant. To no-one's great surprise, potato chips stole all of Brandon's attention. Ian took it all in with his usual, anxious curiosity.

"Can I, um, talk to you for a minute?" She tilted her rigid hair away from the cafeteria.

"Sure, I guess so." I followed her outside, where we sat down at the closest picnic table. "What's up?"

"I guess...I *feel* Elspeth has left." To my surprise, she looked almost sad. "Do you know anything about that?"

I nodded. "She visited me a week ago and said she's finished her work for now. But she said she'd be

380

back…in the future."

Elizabeth brightened. "Wow…just, wow." She toyed with her hair and stared into the sunny sky. "I don't know whether to be relieved…or sad. In a weird way, I think I'm going to miss her."

"Yeah, I think I already miss her."

"Anyway, I am *told* she made a guest appearance at the Spring Fling." She eyed me suspiciously. "Anything you'd like to tell me?"

"Um, no, not really. We managed to do what we set out to do. I couldn't have done it without Elspeth's—and, I guess, your—help. So…thank you." She smiled, more graciously than I thought she possibly could. "Oh, and we danced," I said in a hurried jumble.

She lifted one blonde eyebrow and waited a beat before speaking. I swear I thought I saw steam rise off her. "Yes, so I *understand.* Anyway, for *whatever* reason, it's obvious Elspeth really likes you." She rolled her eyes but forced herself to stop with what looked like quite a great internal struggle. "So, I guess you can't be all *that* bad." She stood and extended her hand for a very prim and proper handshake. I grasped her hand, and she squeezed hard, shaking it up and down, approximately three times. "Goodbye, Richard," she said.

"*Please* call me Tex."

"Okay, fine. *Whatever.* Goodbye, Tex. Have a nice summer."

"See ya, Elizabeth. I hope you have a good summer, too." But before I could complete my words, she had already soared away. It appears the one thing Elspeth and Elizabeth *do* have in common is their predilection toward making fast getaways.

****

The following Saturday, we visited Danny at the Juvenile Center in downtown, Olathe, Kansas. It took some coaxing for Ian to come along—he felt somewhat betrayed by Danny's actions—but he finally relented. Even Brandon attended. I thought the more support Danny had, the better he'd feel.

The guard ushered us into a smaller version of our school cafeteria, with wire netting covering the windows. Nine small, round, laminate-topped tables sat in front of several vending machines, most of them empty. I noticed a heavy-set woman sitting with a young, long-haired kid. She openly sobbed, while he outstretched his feet indifferently. The five of us crowded around a table until Danny came in, dressed in an orange coverall.

"Hey, guys," said Danny as he joined us.

"There's the hardened convict," said Ian. Olivia shot him a potent glare. Ian appeared chastised, cleared his throat, and asked, "How you doin'?"

Danny shrugged. "Not bad, I guess. They've got me working in the library—with my computer skills and everything—so I guess that's kinda cool." He stared out the window as if engrossed by the weather. "And Ken's looking out for me," he added.

I'm not sure if that's a good or bad thing. On the one hand, a small kid like Danny probably needs some extra protection, and for that, I'm grateful for his larger, menacing brother. Then again, I can't help but think Danny might have a better chance at a future if he can distance himself from his brother. But he finally has what he wanted more than anything—bonding time with his brother. It's too bad it took two murders and a stint in Juvenile for it to happen.

"Is there anything we can do for you?" asked Allison. "Can we bring you anything? Cookies?"

Danny's eyes lit up, looking like the young, naïve kid I knew in what now seemed like a different lifetime. "I won't turn down cookies." A sudden darkness fell across his face. "If they'd let me have them…"

"How's Ken doing?" asked Brandon, whose attention vacillated between the vending machines and Danny.

"He's okay."

"Tell him I said hey," said Brandon.

"Danny, what has your lawyer told you?" I asked.

Danny tapped the tabletop with his fingernails. "He says if we get the right judge, I'm looking at best…five years, maybe. They're trying to plead it down."

I swallowed hard as everyone else squirmed uncomfortably. I never thought I'd be discussing such matters with one of my best friends. "Well, good luck."

"Thanks," he said quietly. He almost acted medicated, his focus constantly drifting.

"How're your parents?" asked Olivia, leaning in. "Is your mom doing okay? After…you know, last week?"

"They're keeping her pretty drugged up. The couple times she's visited, she was pretty loopy and wouldn't stop crying." I looked at the crying woman at the other table. Something tells me that mothers act like that a *lot* in this place. "My dad won't visit me…"

Allison's hand flew to her mouth. Danny shrugged, his foot repeatedly tapping against the floor.

I couldn't believe how much he's changed in little over a week. The boisterous, life-loving, goofy, nerdy kid I'd treasured had vanished. I hardly recognized this troubled soul, full of apathy, indifference, and moodiness.

"I guess the Badger family and some other families…have banded together and started picketing my house," he said. "My mom's freaking out about it. Their signs say 'send the killer to prison' and other…more aggressive things."

"Sorry, Dan." I reached across the table to tap his hand. He recoiled and placed both his hands underneath the table. "Um, that's gotta suck for your parents."

"Yeah, well…" He shrugged again.

"Danny, man," I continued, "just remember to keep your head up. Things *will* get better for you. You've got a bright future in computers—"

"Or anime," chimed in Olivia. "Your drawings are awesome." Allison and Ian agreed.

We waited for Danny's response. He stood up and looked at us. "You know…I just really don't care about those things anymore. Listen, I've got to get back to the library."

I stood up, and the others followed me with a mumbled chorus of, "Oh, yeah" and "sure." I approached Danny and extended my arms for a hug. He backed off and said, "Thanks for coming." He quickly walked out of the visiting area, leaving us there, staring at him, my arms still foolishly extended and hugging nothing.

****

On the ride home, I reflected on our cold, unsettling visit. I truly hope Danny hasn't given up or had the life crushed out of him. I know what he did was wrong, *horribly* wrong. But I kept telling myself he made a poor decision—a lapse in judgment—that he didn't act with his full mental capacity. What teenager *hasn't* done that? But it usually doesn't end in murder. And after his behavior today, I wonder if I'm making excuses for my friend's actions. Is he a troubled kid in need of help and guidance? Or is he a cold, calculating murderer? Goosebumps prickled my skin. What if Danny *planned* everything—maybe he even played us. I don't want to see Danny in that light, but the unsettling thoughts burrowed into my mind.

I dropped everyone off except for Olivia. "Thinkin' about Danny?" she asked me.

"Yes." We pulled in front of her house, and I switched the Bucket off.

"That was…not how I thought it'd go," she said.

"Yeah, I hear that."

"Do you think he's given up hope, Tex? Of living a life again?" She looked at me pensively.

I threw my hands up and let them fall into my lap. "I have no idea. I guess all we can do is keep visiting him and giving him hope."

"Yeah, but he didn't look exactly thrilled to see us either."

"Let's just give him some time."

"You wanna come in?" she asked. "My mom's not home."

"Sure." I scooted out and opened the door for her. Once inside her house, she went into the kitchen and asked, "Do you want something to drink?"

"Soda?" My faulty internal censor must be on the blink again because I quickly added, "And how about a bowl of cereal?"

She slammed the soda can down on the kitchen

table in front of me and glared.

"Sorry, couldn't resist." We both sat at the table, emotionally drained. "Are you…ah…seeing Brandon?" I didn't know what they meant to each other after the horrendous Spring Fling. From all indications at school, even their mutual flirtation appears to have dried up. But it could be a possible cover-up.

She shook her head and smiled. "No."

"But I thought…you think he's hot."

"Oh, he is," she said dreamily. "But, he's not my type. What would we talk about? Video games? Cereal?" She grinned at me.

"Ouch, okay, touché. I totally deserved that, I guess."

"Yeah, you so *totally* did."

"Can we finally put the cereal story behind us?"

Olivia let spill her familiar loud laughter I've grown to love. "Whatever, *you* brought it up. But not only can't I have a real conversation with Brandon—he's not you, Tex."

I straightened in my chair, as if it'd been wired. Or I'd misheard her. "Well, yes, thank God, for that…I guess."

"When I found out you were thinking of giving me a love spell, I was so pissed. Then part of me—*just* a very little, teeny-tiny, small part—thought it was pretty damned romantic. I know, right? It sounds lame, and I'm probably setting back female empowerment by several decades, but I can't help it."

My guilt got the better of me. "Um, as long as we're going all 'full disclosure' here, I have to confess something…" She stared at me, bracing herself for terrible news. "I did try to give you a love spell; at least

I *thought* it was a love spell, but Mickey lied to me. And Brandon ended up eating it, and then tried to kiss me, and I thought it was working on him and—" My words ran together like an out-of-control freight train.

"*What?* Dumbass! Thank *God* for Mickey." I waited for her trouncing. To my amazement, she laughed again. "That's the funniest thing you've done yet."

"Uh, yeah, I'm a real comedian. Look, O', I'm really sorry I did that to you. And I swear—*swear*—I won't try anything like that ever again…no matter what happens between us."

She settled down. "Tex, you don't need a love spell with me. It's *always* been you. I just needed some time to realize it."

"Well, there was Brandon…"

"He was a momentary diversion, nothing more." She waved her hand. "I wanted to see what else was out there. None of them were you." She leaned in and kissed me. The familiar taste, smells, and sensations rode back in like a stampede, like the warm embrace of a long-unseen friend. I felt like circling the table, waving lit sparklers and yelling *Hallelujah!* Before things got too heated, she pushed me away.

"Several things…" She held my face between her hands. I opened my eyes to gaze into hers. "What about Elspeth?" She wrinkled her nose in distaste.

"Well, she's gone. At least, for now."

"Oh, isn't that too bad?" Unable to suppress a smirk, the color of jealousy looked great on her.

"Yeah, actually, it is." Obviously, I said the wrong thing, so I diverted the crap out of the situation. "What else?"

"No more withholding the truth from me," she demanded. "I'm tired of that. We share *everything* from now on. Got it?" She still held me captive with her hands.

"Yes. I *swear* you'll know everything I do. No more secrets."

"Finally," she continued, "we're starting over from scratch. That means you need to woo me—to date me. It's all gonna be fresh."

"Wait, what exactly does 'woo' entail?"

"Oh, shut up. Go look it up."

I smiled. The first natural smile I've felt in weeks. "You've always been there for me. So I promise I'll be there for you—emotionally, physically, *fully*. I agree to your demands, Olivia." I kissed her for a long time, enjoying the fresh, yet wonderfully familiar sensation of it all. And so began our Summer of Love.

AFTERWORD

The Modern Gangstas and the Young Bloods may appear completely ludicrous, but they're actually based on suburban gangs and a tragic shooting that occurred at my high school several years ago.

The local media reported that the gangs had parents and even some teachers terrified to come forward with information because they were fearful of retaliation.

Violence—particularly school violence—has become sadly more commonplace in our increasingly scary world. It's up to us to prevent it. Whether at school, the workplace, or elsewhere, we need to be wary of our surroundings and respect the people coexisting alongside us.

A word about the author...

Stuart R. West is a lifelong resident of Kansas, which he considers both a curse and a blessing. It's a curse because…well, it's Kansas. But it's great because…well, it's Kansas. Lots of cool, strange and creepy things happen in the Midwest, and Stuart takes advantage of them in his books. Call it "Kansas Noir." Stuart writes thrillers, horror and mysteries usually tinged with humor, both for adult and young adult audiences.

Stuart spent 25 years in the corporate sector and had to bail, splitting his time between writing and real estate. He's married to a professor of pharmacy (who greatly appreciates the fact he cooks dinner for her every night) and has a 29 year old daughter who's dabbling in the nefarious world of banking.

If you're still reading this, you may as well head on over to Stuart's blog at: http://stuartrwest.blogspot.com/ It's what all the cool kids are doing.

Thank you for purchasing
this publication of The Wild Rose Press, Inc.

For questions or more information
contact us at
info@thewildrosepress.com.

The Wild Rose Press, Inc.
www.thewildrosepress.com